The Missing Pieces of Sophie McCarthy

B. M. CARROLL

PENGUIN BOOKS

PENGUIN BOOKS

UK | USA | Canada | Ireland | Australia
India | New Zealand | South Africa

Penguin Books is part of the Penguin Random House group of companies
whose addresses can be found at global.penguinrandomhouse.com.

First published 2018
002

Copyright B. M. Carroll, 2018

The moral right of the author has been asserted

Set in 12.5/14.75 pt Garamond MT Std
Typeset by Jouve (UK), Milton Keynes
Printed and bound in Great Britain by Clays Ltd, Elcograf S.p.A.

A CIP catalogue record for this book is available from the British Library

ISBN: 978-0-718-18671-5

www.greenpenguin.co.uk

For Brian

I

Sophie

I know instantly. At the first tug of consciousness, long before I open my eyes. Before I tune into the sound of traffic on the road outside, or register the cool air that's wafting through the open window on to my face, I know that it's going to be a bad day. The pain circles my half-asleep body, its menace penetrating the warm duvet and the last shreds of sleepiness.

'Sophie?'

Of course Aidan is already awake. Rising early has been drilled into him. Courage, initiative, respect, teamwork: the official army values. Rising early is intrinsic, as is routine. They're like robots, programmed to execute the same tasks at the same times each and every day: rise by the crack of dawn; arrive at the barracks clean-shaven and wearing general duty dress ironed free of wrinkles; eat breakfast, lunch and dinner at the required times; undertake boot polishing, hair combing, nail clipping and other fastidious grooming routines; aim for maximum physical activity, minimum alcohol consumption and going to sleep at a sensible hour.

Aidan once told me that there are even stipulations about underwear. Apparently it must be plain and of a

I

similar colour to the uniform. Seriously! I remember laughing at the idea, and asking to inspect his briefs to make sure they fitted the guidelines. Now, having had more exposure to the army way of life, I don't know how he can stand it. The rules, the rigidity, the stark lack of individualism and flexibility. Don't get me wrong, I'm not opposed to a certain amount of rigour. Methodical, logical, systematic: that's me to a tee. I'm just saying that the army takes things too far.

'Sophie?' Aidan tries again, before deciding that I'm still asleep and swinging his legs over the side of the bed.

It's only when I hear the sound of the shower that I open my eyes. The pain immediately becomes real. It settles into my chest, my neck, my back. It's not intense, not yet, but it holds the threat of becoming so. From experience, I know I'll get nothing more than a couple of functional hours. Then I'll have to give in to it. Lie down. Take more painkillers. This is why I ignore Aidan when he calls my name. I need to be alone when I wake up. So I can gauge the pain, have the chance to rally myself for the day ahead. Aidan peering at me anxiously doesn't help. If only it did.

He's singing in the shower. The hiss of the water mingles with his baritone and I can't decipher the tune. Probably some song that's popular now but will soon be forgotten. Aidan has a strangely unsophisticated taste in music. This surprised me when I first got to know him: his taste in music seemed out of sync with the rest of him. A pop-loving army captain . . . seriously? I used to find this anomaly in his personality rather cute. No, I *still* find it cute. I'm erring on the side of irritable this morning, that's all.

My eyes veer to his side of the bed, to the digital clock, angled so we can both see it: 6.05 a.m., 22°C, Tuesday, 27 February.

Two hundred and eighty-five days. Nine months. *Three quarters of a year.* How can it still hurt so much? Will it ever stop? I'm beginning to think it won't. That the pain will go on and on and on. That this is it, my life, and I'll simply have to get used to waking up feeling as though someone is sitting astride my chest, pinning me down while stabbing needles into my neck. That I'll eventually forget what it felt like *not* to be this way.

The shower turns off. Aidan is economical with water; it's a valuable resource, and resources must not be wasted. He'll be drying himself now, briskly rubbing a towel over his lean body, not a single gram of extra fat on him. Physical training is part of his job, and he's extremely controlled about what he eats. Balanced, nutritional meals. No snacking. Definitely no binge-eating. In the meantime, my own weight has been creeping up. Another thing that's just not fair. Going for a jog, working out at the gym, swimming – most forms of exercise are out of the question. Food is one of the few things in life that gives me pure pleasure. I was never like that before.

I should get up. Go to the kitchen and make him a cup of tea. Have a chat with him before he leaves for work.

The en suite door whips open before I can motivate myself to move.

'Hey, you're awake,' he states. He's naked, and totally at

3

ease with the fact. I still feel a jolt of surprise when I see him like this, that he's *here* in my house, that we're together, despite what everyone's said about us.

'Yes,' I answer, averting my eyes only because I feel so awful.

'How did you sleep?'

'Not great.'

The wardrobe door squeaks as he slides it open, the metal hangers clanging as he selects his clothes. Through slitted eyes, I watch him. Camouflage trousers, brown vest, his shirt, which takes a few moments to button up. He looks good in uniform. His hair and skin are dark enough to carry all the browns and greens. Men with paler skin or hair tend to look washed out in it.

He stands beside me, kisses my forehead. 'I'll get your tea, madam.'

'Thanks.'

Once he's gone, I move myself up in the bed. Slowly, slowly. That's it. Careful movements. I'm so very gentle with myself. No whipping around, or kicking out, or bounding up stairs, or suddenness of any description. The gentleness seems to combat the violence of what has been done to me. Maybe, one day, when the gentleness outweighs the violence, my body will finally recover.

'Tea service.'

Aidan is back, holding a steaming mug of tea. He puts it down on the bedside table next to me.

He imparts another kiss, this time on my lips. He tastes of sugar – his one dietary weakness – and toast.

'You're leaving already?'

'Yeah,' he answers, halfway out of the room. 'The bus was early yesterday. I nearly missed it.'

My tea is exactly how I like it: strong, dash of milk, no sugar. Funny how I crave sugar in everything but my tea and Aidan is the opposite. I can hear him moving about, getting his boots from where he keeps them at the back door. A few moments' silence while he laces them up. Then the jangle of his house keys.

'See ya,' he calls, before the front door opens and bangs shut again.

Alone. A whole day to fill. *Again*. Despair weighs me down in the bed.

Get up. *Come on*. For fuck's sake, Sophie. Move yourself.

Bathroom first, the mirror still steamed up after Aidan's shower. I shuffle like an old lady, using the towel rail to steady myself.

Then clothes. Old jeans, tank top, light cardigan: aeons away from the crisp business suits that still hang in my wardrobe.

Breakfast. Eggs and toast, the assembling and cooking of which can be broken down into hundreds of tiny movements. Even the way I eat has changed. Each bite slow and considered, chewed to death.

Time for my faithful laptop. Quick scan through my emails, mostly junk. A flick through Facebook, glimpses of other people's full and pain-free lives. Now, the spreadsheet: at last, a flash of something other than despair.

I wish I had thought of tracking everything while I was in hospital, but in the first few months I trusted in the doctors and in my recovery; I *assumed* I would get better.

Four times a day (morning, noon, afternoon and last thing at night), I input data, a rating on a scale of one to ten. One means I'm feeling good, strong. Ten means I've had to call the doctor or go to hospital. Complex formulas convert the raw data into averages and means, and spit out professional-looking graphs in bright primary colours. This morning is an overall eight. No, I'm being too negative. Seven point five. That's fairer. Now, a more detailed rating for my chest, my back and my neck. There. That's about right. Refresh.

The screen blanks for a second, and for a few moments I have that faint sense of anticipation. That today will be the day I'll crack the pattern, the underlying logic, the day that I'll pinpoint a slight but definitive long-term improvement in my mornings, or my nights, or my afternoons, or – a miracle – my whole day. That my chest is still stuffed but, look, there is statistical evidence that proves my back has been giving me a little less trouble.

The screen fills with the updated graphs and I lean closer to study them. It doesn't matter how hard I stare, there is no pattern to be found, no improvement at all; categorically, no end in sight.

Use your superior mathematical ability to solve real problems. I can still remember the catchphrase from that brochure, the one I happened across at careers week at school. *Solve real problems. Become an actuary.* I've always liked solving things, ever since I was a little girl. There was a stage when I was obsessed with jigsaw puzzles, content for hours with my latest thousand-piece endeavour. Later on, I channelled those skills into black-belt sudoku, cryptic crosswords and accelerated maths. Standing in the school hall with the actuarial-studies brochure in my hand, I knew I had found the right career for me.

Now, you could say I have a 'real problem' of my own. A problem I didn't see coming. A problem that is not my fault. A problem that impacts on me in every way imaginable. I have measured this problem, analysed it, written mathematical equations and thrown all my intelligence at it. And the fact that I am no closer to solving it is almost as debilitating as the pain itself.

Don't, I tell myself. Don't start feeling like this. It only brings on the pain. Don't start feeling sorry for yourself. Don't start feeling depressed at the thought of today, and tomorrow, and every other day that will start like this. Don't start getting angry with Aidan for being the cause of all this.

Just don't.

2

Richard

You don't really know what love is until you have children of your own. In my opinion, anyway. The love lodges itself deep in your gut, like a parasite, and hijacks your body, your mind, your whole life. I wasn't one of those men who are born to be fathers. You know the ones: bouncing nieces and nephews on their knees, kicking and throwing balls in the garden with the children of their friends, distributing tickles and hair ruffles wherever possible. It was Dee who wanted kids – I just went along with it. That's why the love took me so much by surprise. How selfless it was. How primal. How a mild-mannered man like me could contemplate killing someone with my bare hands if they harmed Jacob or Sophie.

Jacob was our firstborn. A fat, cheerful baby, my heart used to freefall at the very sight of him: his thick legs and gummy smile, the way he would hold out his arms to be lifted up, how he used to explore my face with his pointed finger. You could say that Jacob primed me for Sophie, who came eighteen months later. I would never admit this, not then or now, but I was worried I wouldn't love her as much. Ridiculous, I know. I must have thought there was a quota on how much love a father could have for his children and that I had used it all up on Jacob. So I was taken completely by surprise, again. Even more astonishing was that I loved Sophie in a whole different way. She didn't make me feel gooey and affectionate, like Jacob did; she made me feel proud. Right from the moment she was born, six weeks before her due date.

'Such a big rush to be born,' the nurse cooed. 'She's a fighter, this one.'

My newborn daughter, a fighter. Those words stirred me, evoking a fierceness the like of which I'd never experienced before. If my daughter was a fighter, I would be too. I'd protect her, provide for her, make sure she had the best opportunities in life, and that she was treated right. These promises I made standing in the Special Care Unit, looking down on Sophie in her see-through plastic crib. Various wires and tubes connected her little body to drips, monitors and other machines. Her lungs were underdeveloped, the paediatrician had explained, and she needed some help with her breathing. She had a white woollen hat on her head – all the premature babies wore these knitted hats, to keep them warm – and a pink ID band around her tiny wrist. Sophie Elizabeth McCarthy. Fighter. Well, they were right about that.

Dee strolls into the kitchen, bringing a halt to my contemplations on fatherly love and the day that Sophie was born. My wife of thirty-five years: hair blow-dried into smooth waves, lightly applied make-up, neatly yet casually dressed. I'm lucky. With my children and my wife.

'What time is it?' Dee's one of those people who's always asking the time.

'Half past ten.' And I am one of those people who always know the answer, often without having to check my watch. 'Are you ready to go?'

This is our routine now. She goes out to work; I stay at home. Funny how time can turn everything on its head.

'I'll just have a quick cuppa,' she says, flicking on the switch of the kettle.

'You'll be late,' I warn with a degree of resignation.

She doesn't reply. Being late doesn't bother her. Strangely, it doesn't seem to bother her boss either. She works a few hours a day in a small boutique in Coogee. I get the impression that business is slow and being ten minutes early or late doesn't have much of an impact. Nevertheless, tardiness is a bad habit, no matter what the circumstances. That's my opinion, for what it's worth.

'What's on the agenda for today?' Dee asks, sitting down next to me with her cup of tea.

'The garden. Some painting. Get a start on dinner.'

'It looks like it might rain.'

'Hopefully not before I mow the lawn.'

'Are you going to drop in on Sophie?'

This question is slightly guarded, as is my response.

'I might . . . I'll see how I go for time.'

Dee thinks we're too involved with Sophie. In her view, we should back off a little, give Sophie the chance to rely more on her own resources. Dee loves Sophie as much as I do, of course she does, but I don't think she understands the full intensity or indeed the ceaselessness of the pain she's in. And what else would I be doing if not supporting my daughter in every way I can? I have time on my hands. Far too much of it, to be honest. Too late to change my mind now, though. I can't exactly 'un-retire'. Unfortunately.

'Come on, Dee.' I stand up and snatch the car keys from where they're lying on the counter. 'I can't stand it when you're late.'

Traffic is surprisingly light and we get a satisfying run of green lights. It's bang on eleven when we pull up outside the boutique.

'I can walk home if you like,' she offers before getting out.

'No, I'll come and get you.' Any excuse to get out of the house.

'Richard?' she stalls.

'What?' She's squandering the time we made up with the traffic. If she just got out now, and hurried slightly, she would still be on time.

'Nothing,' she says, after a considerable pause.

'Are you going to sit here until you're actually late?'

'You're such an old woman,' she snaps. 'I'm going! I'm going!'

The car door slams shut and she walks towards the shop. It pleases me to see her hurrying. I love Dee dearly but, when you've been married as long as we have, some things can begin to grate. The timekeeping thing, for instance. And tidiness, or lack thereof (Dee is always leaving jackets and shoes strewn around the house; it drives me mad.) And, more than anything, the children. You'd think we'd be past disagreeing about the kids; they're adults, for God's sake. This time last year it seemed like we'd finally struck the right balance between our independence and being involved in the lives of our offspring. Then Sophie's accident happened, after which boundaries of any description became senseless.

Dee turns to give me a wave before opening the door of the boutique and disappearing inside, our spat already forgotten. She's not one to hold grudges.

Ten minutes later, and I'm home again. It's an indulgence, dropping Dee off and – usually four or five hours later – picking her up again, but it gives some structure to my day. Right. Straight to work. The lawn. The mowing takes only half an hour. The small square at the front of the house, the puny strip of grass at the side and the more generous space at the rear. In my mind, it always seems a bigger task than it actually is. I'm stowing the mower back in the shed when my mobile vibrates.

'Hi, Dad.'

She often calls at this time, just before lunch. Trying to fill in time, I imagine.

'Sweetheart! How are you today?'

'Not so good, Dad.'

I don't like hearing that response. No father would. 'Should I come over?'

'I'll be all right.'

'You don't sound all right.'

'You're probably busy –'

'Busy? Don't make me bloody laugh. I'll see you in an hour or so. I'll stop at the shops and pick up some lunch.'

There goes the painting I was planning to do. No big deal. It'll still be waiting for me tomorrow, or the day after, or the day after that.

Now, I'm all business. House keys, car keys, short drive to the deli, fresh ham, bread and salad.

Sophie's house is in Randwick, the next-door suburb. A redbrick three-bed bungalow, common to the area. I helped her find it (we house-hunted for months), and I was there – proudly standing next to her – at the auction when she outbid a family who had their heart set on it too. The lock on the front door can be tricky at times. Neither Aidan nor Dee knows that I have my own key.

Sophie's sitting on the sofa, watching daytime TV, a cotton blanket over her legs, despite the fact that it's a relatively warm day outside. It's a depressing sight. No way for a thirty-one-year-old woman to be spending her life.

'There you are, sweetheart. I have food!'

She looks up and smiles. It's her mother's smile, but it's my face: oval, pale skin, long nose. Even the thick, dark hair that she wears down past her shoulders is from my side of the family. Sophie's a little on the short side, but that never stopped her. She's smart; Sophie is so smart it makes my heart want to burst with pride. I could tell from early on that she noticed things. I loved to see her work things out – how to roll and sit and crawl and walk. She leapfrogged all the usual developmental milestones, almost overtaking her older brother. At school, she was unstoppable. Curious, motivated and breathtakingly quick to pick things up.

'Here, let me help you over to the table,' I say now.

I hold out my arm, and she exerts pressure on it as she stands up. My heart breaks just a little bit further. This is the same girl who used to demand to walk everywhere.

She wouldn't stay in her pram for us. She would kick and scream until one of us would relent and let her out. Jacob, on the other hand, was happy to be wheeled everywhere. I used to shake my head and marvel at how different they were.

'Will I butter your bread?' I ask when she's seated at the table.

'Please.'

She wouldn't let us feed her either. What a mess she would make – food all over her face, her hair, the floor. She would insist on doing it herself.

I can't bear to see her like this – so dependent, so frail.

Once Sophie is sorted, I fill my own plate and sit down opposite her. To be honest, it's hard to enjoy eating when I'm so consumed by her pain.

My thoughts revert to what I was thinking about this morning. Before Dee came into the kitchen. The love I have for my children. How surprising it is. How powerful. How potentially brutal. How I would kill for them, if it came down to it. How desperately I want to punch Aidan Ryan, knock him to the ground, kick at him with all my strength, with everything I have in me, over and over again, until *his* chest caves in on itself, until he fully appreciates the pain that my daughter is in. *Because of him.*

Sophie would be horrified if she knew I had thoughts like these. So would Dee.

I don't understand it, I just don't. How can she love him? How can she live under the same bloody roof as him? How? I ask you.

After what he's done to her?

3

Chloe

Dr Wheatley gives me a probing look from behind his glasses. 'So what exactly is the problem, Mrs Ryan? Is it that Jasmin won't *go* to bed? Or is it more that she won't *stay* in bed?'

Mrs Ryan. That hurts. So much so I momentarily lose concentration. The thing is, I *was* Mrs Ryan when I booked this appointment, ten weeks ago. I even complained to Aidan about having to wait so long. He was living with us then, he was ours.

I glance over at my daughter, who's kicking her heel against the leg of the chair she's sitting on. 'Jasmin goes to bed without any trouble. We have a routine – dinner, shower, read for about twenty minutes, lights out. It's usually about 9 p.m. She's tired, often yawning, when I kiss her goodnight. Everything's good for the first half-hour or so.'

'And then?'

'Then she gets up. Comes downstairs. Says she's not tired any more. We – I mean, I – put her straight back to bed. Ten minutes later, she gets up again. And every five to ten minutes after that, until she gets to the point where she refuses to go back to her room. It's late by then. She's extremely agitated, I'm at the end of my tether, both of us are too wound up to feel the slightest bit sleepy. I've tried lying down next to her. I've tried warm baths, yoga, bribery. I've tried everything under the sun. Nothing works. *Nothing*. Last night it was 2 a.m. before she finally fell asleep. That's five hours' sleep before I had to wake her for school . . . She's only nine years old – all the experts say she should be having at least ten hours a night. She's exhausted. *I'm* exhausted . . .'

My voice breaks. Don't cry. Oh, for pity's sake, don't cry in front of this man, this stranger. He'll think you're the one who needs the psychologist, and he'd be right, because I barely recognize myself these days. This tense, erratic, slightly hysterical woman – is she really *me*?

'It's all right,' he says, his gaze becoming kind.

'Sorry, I'm tired, emotional. You must think –'

'I don't think anything at all, Mrs Ryan. I'm just here to listen, ask questions, and help you.'

But I'm not Mrs Ryan any more – at least not in the true meaning of the term. 'My husband and I . . .' Jasmin stops fidgeting and turns her head to stare at me. 'Just call me Chloe.'

'Thanks, Chloe. And I prefer to be called Matthew.' He looks at Jasmin and smiles. He has a nice smile. It's slow, and it stays on his face for what seems to be a long time. 'It's better to be informal, I think. Makes it easier to chat about things . . . When did sleeping start to become an issue?'

'More than a year ago. It was a gradual thing; she started to take longer and longer to settle down at night. We tried to solve it ourselves. Relaxation techniques, reward charts, consequences . . .'

'Does Jasmin have siblings?'

'No.' Now I want to cry again. Because I always imagined myself with a brood of brown-eyed children. 'We had difficulties . . .'

Dr Wheatley – Matthew – nods, as though no further explanation is needed, and then angles his body so he's facing more towards Jasmin.

'Now, Jasmin, you're in Year Three, right?'

Jasmin sits up straight in her seat, ready to talk. 'No, I'm in Year Four. I'm the youngest in my year. But I'm not the smallest.'

Matthew hides a smile. 'Who's the smallest?'

'Jessica Zang. And Daniel Morgan is the smallest boy.'

'Right . . . And do you like school?'

Jasmin frowns, as though the answer should be obvious. '*Yeees.*'

It's such a blessing that she loves school. She's happy to go every morning and is full of talk when she comes home. Homework isn't a problem, or class speeches or other projects. 'An enthusiastic student', her end-of-year report said. I'm lucky. I know from talking to other mums that not all children enjoy school life the way Jasmin does. They have trouble learning, or paying attention, or behaving themselves. Then again, at least those children go to sleep at night. 'Your teacher? Do you like him?'

'She's a lady, not a man. I *really* like Mrs Stanley. She's my favourite teacher so far. Except for Mrs Burns, who I had in Year One.'

Matthew pauses to make some notes before taking a slightly different direction. 'Is there anything worrying you when you go to bed?'

Jasmin looks surprised at the thought. 'No.'

'Nothing about school, or your teacher, or some other kids who might not be nice?'

'You mean Nathan Finnerty?'

'Yes, Nathan Finnerty, for example. Does he pick on you?'

'No, I keep out of his way.'

'And who are your best friends, Jasmin?'

'Amelia, Jessica, Lilianna, Eva, Stephanie . . .'

Jasmin has accumulated a nice group of friends, which is reassuring. New names pop up on a regular basis, such as Amelia. I should call the mother, organize a play date.

Matthew makes a few more notes before dropping his pen and leaning back in his seat. 'What are you thinking of when you're lying there in bed? Before you get up the first time?'

'Stuff.'

'Like?'

Jasmin shrugs, then fiddles with her hair. It's the first time she's struggled to answer. 'I don't know. My thoughts move around. They're *eclectic*.'

Jasmin collects words in the way other children collect stamps or toys or shells. She picks them up, examines them, stores them away, and enjoys showing them off, especially to strangers.

'And later, when you're upset, what are you thinking?'

'That I want to be like other kids. To fall asleep as soon as I go to bed, and not always be really, really tired.'

Sleep is such a simple thing. A simple, everyday thing that we all take for granted. But when it's a problem, lives begin to unravel, personalities begin to change . . . for the worse. Children who are usually bright and obliging turn into little horrors. And parents become cross and mean and nothing like their true selves.

'And how's school the next day? Do you find it hard to concentrate? Are you sleepy?'

'Some of the time . . .' Jasmin concedes with an embarrassed glance in my direction. 'But I can usually make myself snap out of it.'

'How do you do that?'

'By asking to go to the toilet. Or the water bubblers. The fresh air wakes me up. Sometimes I splash water on my face.'

These are the lengths my daughter has to go to in order to remain focused in class.

I clear a lump from my throat. 'From what we've told you, do you have any idea what could be causing this . . . this . . . inability to fall asleep?'

Matthew takes a few moments to collect his thoughts. 'There could be any number of issues causing this problem. The best way to approach it is methodically – ruling out possibilities one by one.'

'But you must have some idea.' Desperation whooshes through me. I need a name for this, some way of labelling it, so I can begin to understand it, deal with it, stop it from consuming our lives. 'With your experience, I imagine that you have seen many similar cases . . .'

He remains infuriatingly firm. 'I don't like to put names on things, Chloe. Not until I gather enough evidence. Try to be patient while I go through the process. To start with, I have some questionnaires. There's one for Jasmin herself, and for you and your husband, and for Jasmin's teacher.' Matthew swings his chair around to face the shelves behind his desk and extracts a lever-arch folder from a line of similar folders. 'Please ask the teacher to return the completed form directly to me. Also, it's best that you and your husband complete your questionnaires independently. Any kind of conferring detracts from the results and that won't help Jasmin.'

No more excuses, Chloe. You must tell him. You should have brought it up at the start. Now, don't start crying. Strong voice. And don't look at Jasmin. 'We don't live together . . . Aidan and I have recently separated.'

He pauses, and looks up from under his glasses. 'Did the sleeping problem become worse after the separation?'

'No, not really.' My cheeks ache from the effort of holding back tears.

'Will Jasmin's father be willing to fill out the questionnaire?'

'Yes, he's very thorough like that.' A giveaway wobble in my voice. Oh, for pity's sake! Now, he knows. He can tell that the separation was not my idea, that it goes against all that I am, and that it hurts so badly it's all I can do to contain a howl of pure agony.

'Well, that's enough for today, I think . . .'

What? The session is over? It can't be. Pull yourself together, Chloe. This is about Jasmin. That's why we're here. And it's not 'enough for today', thank you very much. What about six hours from now, when the bedtime battle starts all over again?

'Is there any kind of medication we can give her?'

He adjusts his glasses. 'Sleeping pills are highly addictive . . . They're a last resort, Chloe, especially with children.'

'But what should I do tonight, when we get home?'

'There should be no major change in routine,' he tells me. 'It's best to keep things as they are while we gather the information we need. But do keep a diary – what time Jasmin gets up in the morning, what activities she does, what she eats, what time she goes to bed, etcetera.'

A diary? Is that all? Why does it feel like we're at the start of something, rather than the end? How many more sessions until the end? Until we find the answer?

'Hang in there, Chloe. I'll do my very best to help you. You just have to hang in there.'

The knowing and kindness in his voice are my undoing. The tears are finally unleashed and gush down my face. *Hang in there.* What if I can't? What if I'm not strong enough? The logical part of me understands that there's a process we must work through to help us solve the problem. And I believe him when he says that he'll do all that he can to help me. But I feel as if I'm on the precipice of a nervous breakdown, and that Jasmin could collapse at any moment from severe exhaustion.

I find an old tissue in my handbag and quickly dab my face with it. 'When do we see you again?'

Please, not another ten-week wait.

'Tell Sarah at the desk to squeeze you in sometime next week.'

Sarah is probably used to the nutcase mothers getting priority.

I scramble to my feet, trying to shield my blotchy face from both Matthew and Jasmin. 'Time to go, Jazzie. Say thank you.'

'Thanks, Matthew.'

She didn't need to be prompted. Jasmin has good manners. Everyone says so.

A teenage girl with purple hair and numerous piercings on her pallid face sits on a chair in the otherwise empty waiting room. Her arms are wrapped around herself, and she's rocking back and forth. Matthew's next client? Jasmin stares at the girl while I settle the bill.

We emerge into late afternoon in the city. The sun has dropped behind the skyscrapers and everything's in shade.

'Fancy some McDonald's?' I ask on impulse. My next thought is how Aidan would disapprove.

Jasmin's face lights up, and for a moment she looks heartbreakingly like her father: the smile, the dimples, the shine in her dark eyes. 'Really, Mum?'

'I think you've earned a treat . . . I was proud of you in there. You sounded very grown up. You answered everything very clearly. Well done, darling.'

She's a marvellous child, she really is. Sweet, honest, eager to please, a joy. Just not at bedtime.

As we're sitting munching our way through two Happy Meals, Aidan sends a text.

How did it go?

Rage balloons inside me. He has no right – *no right at all* – to expect up-to-the-minute status reports. Who does he think he is?

Her father, that's who.

The rage goes just as quickly as it comes. Despite the decisions he's made, and the fact that he's broken her heart as well as mine, I can't deny that he loves her fiercely and is just as desperate as we are to solve this sleeping problem. *We're in this together, the three of us.* Besides, I don't have it in me to hold out on him, to keep him waiting, worrying. I'm not hard enough. I care too much.

I have to concentrate in order to find the right words to reply to his text, words that don't betray my confusion, my hurt, my come-and-go anger and – more than anything – my profound sadness.

No fast answers. We'll need more sessions.

There. A cool, businesslike tone ... How have we come to this? Aidan living with another woman; communicating about our beloved daughter by text; anger and despair and what seems like a thousand other complex emotions tainting every transaction between us. All this from a family that was once so close and loving and blissfully happy that people used to envy us.

It's because of Sophie McCarthy, that's why.

It's awful of me to think this. A dreadful, dreadful sin. It only comes into my head when I'm at my absolute lowest – like now – but a small, despicable part of me wishes that he had killed her outright that day, and that she was completely, irrevocably, out of our lives.

4

Aidan

I miss Jasmin. I miss hauling her out of bed in the mornings, helping her with her homework, all the time we spent together in the car – going to friends' houses, birthday parties, soccer matches, swimming lessons – talking, laughing, our eyes meeting in the rear-view mirror. I miss the times when her developing sense of humour took me by surprise and made me roar with laughter; the satisfied feeling when I taught her something new – a fact, a technique, an interesting word – and I could practically see the cogs turning in her brain; the times when she used to look to me for advice on school, sport and friends; the times when she thought her dad could do no wrong. At weekends, when I go to make myself a sandwich, it feels strange not to ask, 'What do you want for lunch, Jazz?' Damn it, I thought I'd never say this, but I even miss the theatrics at bedtime. The tears, tantrums and lost tempers, and dragging myself into work the next day, not having had enough sleep.

That's what I feel the most regret about: the nights, not being there, leaving Chloe on her own to deal with it. I deserve to miss out on the good parts of being Jasmin's dad – you could say that's my punishment for screwing up so badly – but it's not fair that I should automatically miss out on the bad parts too. Poor Chloe. I know she's struggling. I've seen her snap, cry until she's red in the face, completely lose perspective. It was my job to calm her down, to step in and restore order and peace. Between the two of us, we would get through the night. Now, she has to deal with it all on her own.

Leaving my family, moving out of my home, becoming distant from the good parts and the bad parts, has been the hardest thing I've ever done. Harder than the most gruelling military exercise. Harder than the pieces of shrapnel that had to be dug out of my left arm in Iraq. Harder than my mother dying when I was fifteen years old, when I still really needed her (even though I thought I didn't).

The only thing that I can say in my defence is that it was the only honourable thing to do in the circumstances. Once I faced up to the fact that I was in love with Sophie, I felt I had no option but to be honest with everyone involved, including myself. Being deceitful would have been an even bigger betrayal. At least that's how I felt . . . feel. Guilt has a funny way of bringing things into focus, of making the hardest decision of your life more clear-cut. Not only did I love Sophie, I had this driving need to make good to her, to right my wrong, to do everything in my power to help get her back on her feet. It's what they teach us in the army: *never leave a man behind*.

The phone on my desk rings. It's the chaplain.

'Good morning, Aidan . . .'

'Hey, Jack.'

I get calls like this at least once a week and, as a result, the chaplain and I are on first-name terms.

'I wondered if you might have time to see me today. It's about one of your men . . . He's having some . . . ah . . . issues . . .'

Jack starts with the phone call, then he comes along to see me and we discuss the soldier involved. 'Some issues' is usually an understatement of the situation. More often than not, the men don't go to see the chaplain until things are bad . . . very bad. Their first instinct is to try to battle through the problem on their own. They are proud and resilient: these are great attributes for soldiers, but not when it comes to asking for help. Jack and I are trying to change this culture, to make them see that talking to us is not defeat but actually the opposite: it's fighting back.

'No problem . . . I can see you at three,' I say, doing a mental reorganization of my day in order to fit in the appointment. 'That's unless it's urgent enough for you to come here right away. Just say if it is.'

I've learned – the hard way – always to check the level of urgency. A few years ago, during a particularly busy period, I put off the chaplain until the following day. The soldier in question attempted suicide that same night. Luckily it was a call for help rather than a serious attempt, but it was a lesson I won't ever forget.

'Three is good, Aidan,' Jack says. 'See you then.'

Every day is different, even in 'peace time'. The only constants are the 'O group' meetings in the mornings – where I go through the orders for the day with the junior officers – and the paperwork that I tend to do last thing.

In between can be anything. Today it's a weapons inspection and organizing transport and equipment for Panther, the code name for a major training operation that's happening in a few months' time. Panther will involve a twenty-kilometre hike and 'enemy attack' in the mountains at the dead of night, and anything to do with its planning sucks up hours and hours of time.

All too soon it's 3 p.m. and Jack knocks on my door, ready to discuss the marital situation of one of my sergeants, Bradley Lynch. It's not the first time Jack and I have sat across from each other and dissected other people's marriages, and it won't be the last. The army is tough on relationships: wives, husbands, girlfriends, boyfriends, children . . . especially the children.

'Bradley says it's largely his fault,' Jack sighs. 'He dislikes peace time, he's bored with army life, and he admits he's not easy to live with.'

Boredom: we've all experienced it. The disappointment of everyday training, kitchen parade and weapons inspection after the intense life-and-death experience of Iraq or Afghanistan. It's the reason so many soldiers end up leaving. They don't know how to readjust to real life, where the only action happening is in their dreams: frame-by-frame raids and attacks that replay in their heads while they're asleep. When I go to bed at night I see faces, the dead, the people I failed to keep safe, their blank expressions playing in a reel. The sons, brothers, fathers, daughters, sisters, mothers. The innocent civilians and children, the baby-faced soldiers. They resurrect at night, come alive, bleating, 'Save me, save me . . .' Peace time is a myth. Once you've experienced war, you'll never be at peace again.

'Bradley's wife has had enough of his moods and wants to separate . . .'

I've met Mrs Lynch a few times. She seems like a nice woman, warm and chatty, supportive of her husband, but I guess we all have limits.

'What does Bradley want to do?' I ask.

'He wants to take a few months' leave, see if he can work things out with his wife, establish where his future lies, if it's in the army or elsewhere . . .'

I approve three months' leave of absence, the chaplain goes on his way, and it's four thirty before I can start on my paperwork: DVA (Department of Veteran Affairs) forms that must be filled out, emails that need to be forwarded on and/or responded to, a few minor staff-related disciplinary issues. At 6 p.m. I shut down my computer, do a quick tidy of my desk and lock the filing drawers, before donning the distinctive green beret that marks me as Special Forces.

My exit from the barracks is punctuated by the salutes I receive from all the soldiers I encounter on the way.

'Good evening, sir.'

'Bye, sir.'

'See you tomorrow, sir.'

I'm greeted by a strong breeze as I come out from behind the shelter of the gymnasium; all the flags in sight are flapping strongly. There's a game of soccer happening on the parade ground. A social match against the navy. Physical, by the looks of it. Shouldering, and some shoving – out of the referee's sight, of course – and the usual high degree of competitiveness, despite the 'social' tag. This time last year I would've stopped and watched – I might even have put my name down to play – but that was in another lifetime.

I stride past the officers' quarters, where Chloe point-blank refused to reside.

'I'm sick of army accommodation – all those houses look and feel the same. They have no soul.'

I'm not sure if she knew what she was turning down in this instance: charming historical sandstone terraces with original slate roofs. Still, I have to say that having our own – non-army – house made her happy. She bought statement pieces of furniture and bright cushions, hung our own curtains and covered the walls with family photos. It really did feel like a proper home. Until I fucked it all up.

'Goodnight, sir,' says the soldier at the gatehouse.

'Goodnight.'

Then I'm through the archway and into the outside world. The bus stop is directly across the road, and it's more or less the same crowd waiting there every day. The banter fizzles out as soon as I arrive – I'm too many ranks above these soldiers for them to feel comfortable around me.

The bus arrives, I hold my opal card against the machine and take a seat near the front (the soldiers seem to prefer the rear of the bus). A faint smell of vomit emanates from the old man sitting next to me. The bus has barely taken off when it stops again. It drives me crazy, this stop–start, stop–start. I usually end up walking the last few blocks.

A young girl and her mother get on at one of the stops. The girl is around Jasmin's age. I miss my daughter so much it's like missing a limb. It's been a couple of months now. Time enough to broach the subject of custody, of Jasmin staying some nights with Sophie and me? I expect resistance on all fronts: Jasmin, Chloe and even Sophie, who is perfectly nice to Jasmin but is one of those people who just doesn't know what to do around kids.

I'll teach Sophie what to do. She's smart, she'll learn. Jasmin is not negotiable. I need her to feel whole. I need to be her dad. My hands curl into fists on my lap. I have the sudden urge to hit something hard, really hard. To feel my knuckles crunch. To fight someone, anyone. The bus stops yet again and, unable to bear it, I jump up and bound towards the doors, just making it through before they close.

5

Richard

Sophie is lucky to be alive, no doubt about it. When I first saw her at the hospital, she was in a bad state: fractured sternum, extensive soft tissue and nerve damage, broken ribs, punctured lung, broken cheekbone, fractured eye socket, concerns about her spinal cord and even her heart. The first few days were touch and go. Dee and I were distraught, although our shock manifested itself in quite different ways. I went into overdrive, peppering the doctors with questions, demanding explanations and recovery statistics, ultimately seeking reassurance that my daughter was going to make it. Dee was dazed and almost mute.

'Shock can have very different effects on people,' explained one of the nurses, who was thoughtful enough to bring Dee a sugary cup of tea. 'I've seen demure women morph into screaming banshees, and stoic men smash their fists through plasterboard walls.' She grimaced. 'Once we had a man take out a pane of glass . . . in the end, he needed more stitches than his son!'

By some miracle, Sophie made it through those first few critical days. They had to operate to put her sternum back in place and to try to repair some of the nerve damage. Dr White, the specialist, explained that the sternum would take a few months to heal, but a full recovery was expected. The nerve damage was more complex, though. Apparently brachial plexus injuries are categorized according to the type of trauma experienced by the nerve. In Sophie's case, the axons (equivalents of the copper filaments in an electric cable, Dr White explained) had been severed.

'The prognosis is moderate, Mr McCarthy,' he said. 'Nerves are very delicate and hard to repair, much more difficult than bones.'

I realize now that he was trying to tell me that a full recovery was unlikely but at the time I wouldn't hear of it.

'Sophie will overcome this. She's a fighter . . . She never gives up, does she, Dee?'

Dee nodded in a confused manner. She was so upset that all the medical nitty-gritty was going right over her head.

Once out of ICU, Sophie spent another two months in hospital. Dr White has continued to see her on a regular basis since she was discharged. She also sees a back specialist, a physiotherapist and, of course, her GP. I drive her to all the appointments and usually sit in while she's being treated. In my opinion, it's better to have two of us across the medical jargon, not to talk about keeping tabs on all the different drugs she's on.

Today we're back with Dr White, for Sophie's monthly check-up. Parking is difficult; it's often that way in the hospital car park. The lifts also prove difficult, one of them being taken out of service by maintenance staff. We're a few minutes late for our appointment, something that has never happened before.

'Hello, Sophie,' Dr White says as we come through the door. 'Good morning, Mr McCarthy.'

For some reason I feel the doctor is less pleased to see me.

'How have you been, Sophie?' he asks, once she has sat down.

'Some good days, some bad days.' Her face scrunches in frustration. 'Overall, no real change.'

'You're looking well today.'

Sophie does look well. She's wearing a white shirt and dark, fitted pants. She often dresses in some combination of the colours black and white, and the effect is crisp and professional. Her hair is swept into a loose ponytail that rests on one shoulder.

'Today has been good . . . so far.'

'I have your most recent CT scans in front of me. As expected, the sternum has healed nicely . . . Hop up on the bed and we'll check things out.'

Sophie unbuttons her shirt and I can't help noticing that even this carefully executed task seems to cause her some degree of discomfort.

Checking things out means the doctor pressing and massaging areas of her chest, her ribs and her clavicle.

'Does this hurt?'

'Yes.'

'On a range of one to ten?'

'Eight. No, seven.'

Then he tests her range of movement by gently manoeuvring her arms, her shoulders and her back.

'Turn your head to the right. As far as you can go.'

Her lips tighten, holding in a wince. 'That's an eight. Definitely an eight.'

'OK. Gently does it. Turn to the left now. I can see that hurts. Is that an eight too? . . . Thanks, Sophie, we're done now. You can get dressed.'

Back at his desk, he types up some notes on the computer. The printer spits out a script: for more pain-relief medication, no doubt.

She's white in the face when she sits down again. I reach across and squeeze her hand. It's all I can do: offer my support. I wish I could take the pain away, I really do. I don't envy the doctor his job, seeing people in terrible pain, how it must change their personality over time, drag them down.

Sophie bends over carefully, picks her bag up from the ground and extracts an envelope which she slides across the desk. 'My spreadsheet . . .'

She gives the doctor an updated copy of the spreadsheet every time she sees him. I think he admires her thoroughness and mathematical ability as well as her proactive attitude to her recovery.

He puts the spreadsheet aside after only a brief glance.

'I thought you might see some pattern,' she says, flicking her hair from her shoulder. 'Even though I can't.'

His smile is sympathetic. 'Nerve damage is not something that can be graphed and extrapolated . . . It's just not that easily pinned down. Unfortunately, for everyone involved.'

There's an awkward pause. Then he says the worst thing imaginable.

'I think we've reached a plateau, Sophie. Progress from now on will be in small degrees, almost indiscernible, one might say.'

She looks stricken at this news. *I* am stricken at the news. This can't be as good as it gets. It can't.

'As a matter of fact, I don't need to see you quite as regularly. We'll ask Mary to book your next appointment for August.'

'August?' Her eyes bounce from me to the doctor and then back to me again. 'But that's *six months* away.'

I can't help getting angry then. 'My daughter is in pain. You can't just *dump* her like this. Can't you see she needs all the bloody help she can get?'

'Mr McCarthy, I assure you that I am not dumping your daughter. I'll continue to monitor her condition, but there won't be as much change from now on and we really don't need appointments every four weeks.' He turns his attention back to Sophie. 'Pain medication and physiotherapy are the main focus now. And one other thing – a very, very important thing – mental attitude. You must fight the pain, not give in to it. Deny its existence as much as you possibly can.'

'Are you saying the pain is in my head?' she whispers, looking deeply affronted.

'Of course it's in your head ... That's how the brain works. If it anticipates pain, then it will feel pain, even if the pain's not really there.'

'The pain is *real*, Dr White!' she cries. 'I'm not imagining it, I'm *not*.'

'I know it's real, Sophie. I was the person who operated

35

on you, remember? I saw the damage first-hand. The point I'm trying to make is that how we think is often an underrated part of the treatment. We can allow the pain to consume our lives, or we can try to keep it in its place.'

Her frown has traces of anger, hurt and desperation. And the only thing I can do is squeeze her hand again. I feel so bloody useless.

'Forget the spreadsheet, Sophie. It's having the opposite effect to what we want here – it's making you *fixate* on the pain. And I recommend quite strongly that you go back to work –'

'But I've already *tried* to go back to work!' she exclaims, looking to me for support.

'She went back last October,' I interject, a little too forcefully. I don't seem to be able to hold myself in check today. 'Don't you remember? She didn't last a bloody week!'

'Try again,' he says, with unnerving calmness. 'Some things in life take a few attempts before they're successful. You'll benefit greatly from the routine of work, Sophie. It will be something to focus on. Yes, it will be hard to begin with, but you'll adapt, I know you will.'

'But on my bad days I can hardly get out of bed.'

'You have bad days how often? Two, three times a week?'

'Yes, about that.'

'So, more good days than bad days . . . Days when you could be out of the house, with colleagues and work responsibilities to take your mind off things . . .'

I can see from Sophie's face that she is beginning to

consider the idea. To be honest, I'm coming around too. Sophie loved her job; it would be a new lease of life if she returns. I just can't help worrying after what happened last time, that's all.

'Maybe you could ask about working part-time,' I suggest. She nods, and suddenly I don't feel so useless any more.

'Three days would be ideal.' The doctor stands up from behind his desk. He leans across and holds Sophie's hand in his. It's obvious that he likes her a lot. 'You know, I've had other patients like you, young men and women who've survived terrible injuries and whose lives will never be the same again. Some of them spiral into a lifetime of chronic pain and depression. Some learn to cope, adapting and getting on with their lives as best they can. A small percentage thrive, using their pain or disability as a motivator, a daily reminder to make the most of things and celebrate life.'

It's like Dr White is issuing a challenge, and Sophie being Sophie, she's already squaring her shoulders. The fighter in her is mentally pulling up her sleeves, drawing on the grit and determination she will need to be in that 'small percentage'.

'I'll look forward to seeing how you are in August, Sophie. Good luck.'

Luck. Now that's something I've thought a lot about over the last nine months. Yes, there's no doubt at all that Sophie is lucky to be alive, and luckier again to be able to walk in and out of the doctor's office unassisted. The nerves could have been pulled clean from the spinal cord, or they could have been severed completely.

But luck is a matter of perspective. As her father, as some-one who saw all her infinite potential shattered into pieces, as someone who witnesses her daily grapple with pain and her personality shift as a result, as someone who knows that returning to work on even a part-time basis will push her to the very limits of her endurance, *unlucky* is the word that comes most to mind, even though I try hard – bloody hard – to make myself think differently.

6

Sophie

It's even harder than I expected. Getting up at the first trill of the alarm clock. Showering, straightening my hair, putting on make-up. Dressing, having breakfast, being ready by a nominated time. It's 8 a.m. when Dad pulls up outside the house, and I already feel as if I've done a full day's work.

Dad reaches across and swings open the passenger door. 'Morning, sweetheart. Hop in. The traffic's bloody terrible.'

His car is like him: vintage. When he retired, he splurged some of his lump sum on a fat 1980s Mercedes, and it swallows more of his lump sum every day, guzzling fuel and constantly needing expensive repairs. As I turn – perhaps a margin too quickly – to put on my seatbelt, I feel a burning sensation across my chest. I should be more careful.

Dad's right about the traffic.

'The round trip is going to take you for ever,' I say when we come to yet another halt. 'Sorry. I didn't mean to take up your whole morning.'

'Ah, what else would I be doing?' he asks, shooting me a wry smile.

Other, more important things, my mother would reply if she were here. Mum makes it clear that she doesn't approve of Dad being my chauffeur. She thinks his time would be better spent on other tasks, and that I should be more independent.

'She's not a princess, Richard.'

'Darling, Sophie can't rely on you for everything. She's a grown woman.'

'Richard, you're spoiling her . . .'

She makes these protestations right in front of me. Dad and I roll our eyes, before proceeding to do our own thing anyway. My friends have always found it odd that I'm closer to Dad than Mum. It's not that I don't love Mum, it's just that our personalities are polar opposites. Mum potters through life. She's had no career to speak of, and she finds my ambition and self-discipline quite confounding. Jacob's just as lacking in focus as she is. He's been stuck in the same job for years, renting the same dreary three-bedroom house, happily lining someone else's pockets when he should have got on the property ladder ages ago. I don't have much in common with my brother. But Dad's like me, or I'm like Dad – whatever way you want to look at it. We're both career-focused (Dad was chief financial officer in a pharmaceuticals company before he was offered an early-retirement package last year), and we share a lot of the same values: attention to detail; doggedness; always striving for our personal best. Dad and I have always got along. Mum and Jacob sometimes act like it's a bad thing to have get-up-and-go.

Neither Dad nor I is a great morning conversationalist

so we let the talk show on the radio fill the car with chatter and laughter. Despite the excruciating stop–start nature of the journey, I feel my mood begin to lift. Maybe it's the hubbub of rush hour rubbing off on me, the thought of all these cars, all these people converging on the city. Or maybe it's the somehow exhilarating sight of the high-rise buildings that form Sydney's skyline. This morning, I'm part of it: the rush hour, the city, the excitement, the promise. It's been so long since I've been part of anything.

My old confidence struggles to the surface – groggy, tentative, but there.

You can do this, Sophie. You can do this.

It takes fifty minutes to get within the vicinity of Real Cover Insurance, where I have worked for the last six years (although I am not sure I can legitimately count the last nine months).

'I'll have to leave you out here.' Dad's a bit flustered by the traffic now. It's clear to both of us that I'll be getting public transport from here on in. 'I think you'll walk the last few blocks faster than I can bloody drive them. Will you be OK?'

'I'll be fine.' I lean over, kiss his cheek.

'Good luck, sweetheart.' His voice cracks. He's the only one who really understands. 'Don't push yourself too hard.'

'I won't. Thanks again, Dad.'

Getting out of cars isn't easy. Don't rush: that's the main thing I've learned. All those years when I scrambled out in an inelegant flurry of arms and legs.

'Good luck,' Dad says again, before I shut the door.

The car behind him hoots and he hastily pulls away, only to stop again a few metres up the street. For a while I stand still on the footpath, the city surging around me. The traffic, the people, the colours, the noise, the smell of petrol fumes and coffee beans – I breathe it all deep into my lungs. I've missed it. Even more than I realized.

Real Cover Insurance is spread across three floors in one of the many office towers on Kent Street. Our slogan is blazed across the wall behind the reception desk: *Keep it real with real cover.* I don't recognize the receptionist. She must be new. Where has Sandy gone? Sandy's like a permanent fixture in the company, one of the longest-standing employees, and I'm thrown by her absence. Should I stop and introduce myself to this receptionist, or proceed through to the offices behind? The fact that she's clearly busy on the phone decides me. I'll make a point of introducing myself later. My access card still works, and I pause for the slightest moment before I push open the security door and step back into my old life.

I pass the call centre, a babble of voices coming from heads framed with oversized earphones. I nod at a few familiar faces in the Home Insurance department, smiling vaguely at the surprised 'good morning's thrown in my direction. Then it's Travel and Income Protection, before my own department: Motor. Disappointingly, the first person I come across is Jane. She's standing outside the kitchen, a mug in her hand, deep in discussion with another woman whom I don't recognize. They seem relaxed, enjoying their conversation, and in no evident rush to start their working day. Some things never change.

Jane finally notices me.

'Oh, hi, Sophie. Welcome back.' She sounds resoundingly insincere.

'Thank you,' I reply stiffly.

'This is Hannah,' Jane continues, glancing at her companion. 'Hannah's new. She's going to be your admin assistant, but you have to share her with Peter.' Jane laughs lightly. 'No fighting now.'

Alyssa, the HR person, had already called me to explain the new reporting lines. I'm not crazy about sharing my admin assistant but I guess that, if I'm part-time, my assistant must be too.

'Hello, Sophie,' Hannah says quietly.

Now that I'm looking closer, Hannah seems vaguely familiar. Maybe she's transferred from another department. With over three hundred people and a relatively high staff turnover rate, it's hard to keep track of everyone.

'You look good, Sophie,' Jane says, her eyes sweeping over me. 'Healthy.'

What can I say, except that looks can be deceiving? That's one of the most frustrating parts of all this: I don't *look* as if there's anything wrong with me. Everything's internal, invisible, so it's harder for people to believe – sometimes I even doubt myself. Yes, perfect on the outside. No one can tell – least of all Jane, who is not known for her perceptiveness – that everything inside me is perpetually tensed up, waiting for the next trigger: pushing open a door, standing up, turning my head too quickly, that seatbelt this morning. I'm forever bracing myself for the pain that's sure to follow.

'Are you free, Jane?' My tone is brusque; small talk has always made me feel impatient. 'I'd like to catch up as soon as possible.'

She looks taken aback. 'I have a meeting in ten minutes.'

'When will you be done?' God, it feels *so good* to be back in charge, to be my old self again.

'I should be out by ten thirty.'

'I'll see you then. Bring the files you're working on. Be ready to give me an update.'

Your cushy existence is over, Jane. The late starts, the early marks, the continual sick days. I'm back, and I'm not putting up with that crap. You're going to have to put in as much as the rest of us.

I nod at my new assistant, Hannah. 'I'd love a coffee. There's a good place across the road. White skinny latte, thanks. I'll be in my office.'

Start as I mean to go on, that's always been my motto. It's important to establish authority from the beginning; it isn't something you can go back and demand later on. Anyway, I've never believed in becoming best friends with the people who work for me. It's a conflict of interest. I need to be tough, able to lay down the law, make the hard decisions. I'm sure Jane has revelled in telling Hannah all about me, how horrible and unreasonable I supposedly am. Hopefully, Hannah is mature enough to make up her own mind.

My office. Full of memories of a stronger, indomitable me. The blinds are shut, and I tug on the drawstring, lifting them up to reveal the cityscape – blocks of concrete and glass separated by thin pillars of blue sky – a view I've always enjoyed. A cardigan that I assumed I had lost

44

somewhere is draped over the back of my chair. My monitor has a thick film of dust on it and there's an open packet of gum next to the keyboard. No framed photographs. I've never been overly sentimental.

I'll take it easy, pace myself, not go too hard (my mistake the last time I tried to return to work). Already, my head is filling with things – how to handle Jane, what work to assign Hannah, a review of all open projects – other than my pain levels. Dr White was right. This is exactly what I need: a shift of focus. This will help more than any medicine can.

Hannah arrives with my coffee. My new assistant is medium height, medium weight, has nondescript, mid-brown hair and is plainly but neatly dressed. Her face has a harried look about it – as though there are a million things racing through her mind.

'Did you transfer from another department?'

She's one of those women who blush easily. 'No.'

'I'd forgotten just how good this coffee is,' I murmur, taking a moment to savour the taste. 'Grab a pen and paper and we'll get to work.'

I take another sip of coffee, and a sense of deep contentment – of belonging – infuses every part of me.

It is so fucking good to be back. This time will be different.

7

Hannah

Sophie McCarthy. Sophie McCarthy, *of all people.* I couldn't believe it when she walked up to us outside the kitchen. I recognized her straight away – she hasn't changed that much – but she seemed to have no idea who I was. It must have shown on my face, how shocked I was, but her mind must have been elsewhere because she hardly gave me a second glance.

Sophie's return was announced at last week's department meeting.

'What position is she coming back to?' Jane groaned.

'The same position,' Alyssa, our HR manager, replied. 'Pricing Manager.'

'So I'll report to her?'

'You did before, didn't you?'

Jane is one of four senior pricing actuaries in the Motor department. Maybe she felt that the department was functioning fine without Sophie. Maybe she thought that she was experienced enough to manage her own workload. It was clear that Alyssa, who started just before me, found Jane's attitude perplexing. She gave her a quick frown before turning to me.

'Hannah, you'll be supporting Sophie as well as Peter. You'll be with Sophie three days and Peter two.'

Jane caught up with me after the meeting.

'We don't need Sophie McCarthy three days a week, or even one day a week. Nice that she's feeling better and everything, but we got along just fine without her. Maybe she'd be of more use in another department? Another subsidiary? Another insurance company altogether?'

I hadn't seen this caustic side of Jane before. She had been nothing but friendly and helpful since I started.

'Why don't you like her?'

'Because nothing I do is ever good enough for her . . . And she's one of those managers who counts every minute you're late.'

Jane is one of the few women in our department who's like me: a mum. Most of our female colleagues have put children on their to-do list, wanting to get ahead with their careers before starting a family (not that there's anything wrong with that). I try not to let my kids interfere with my work but, even with the best intentions, I am sometimes – like Jane – late to the office and need to leave early.

Of course, I never associated the Sophie McCarthy who Jane was moaning about with the Sophie McCarthy I knew from school. The name that was awarded dux – the highest-ranking pupil for academic achievement. The name that has stayed in my mind, even though everything else about high school is a far-distant memory now. The name that still, all these years later, makes me question and loathe myself.

I get off the bus at my usual stop and hurry down the hill towards the apartment block that is now our home.

Mum's car is parked directly outside – parking is notoriously tight around here and she would have been pleased to snatch such a convenient spot.

'Helloooo!' I call out, opening the door to our two-bedroom unit and manoeuvring my way past the shin guards, football boots and one rather muddy soccer ball that have been abandoned in the minuscule hallway. 'Who has left all this gear out for me to fall over?'

No answer. I walk further into the apartment, and there they are, two heads of ruffled fair hair, dirty knees stretched out in front, mesmerized by whatever is on the TV.

I position myself directly in their line of view.

'Aw, Mum . . . we were watching that!' they exclaim, in almost perfect unison.

'Hello, boys. It's your mother here . . . Just in from a hard day's work and looking for a simple greeting. *Hello, Mum* would be lovely. A hug would be a bonus.'

Finn, the more affectionate of the two, jumps up and loops me with his skinny arms. He smells of dirt and biscuits.

'Hi, Mum. Sorry. We're just watching a really good show.'

Callum rises more slowly, his eyes still on the TV as he imparts a token hug, before cunningly steering me to a spot where I'm not blocking his view.

'We're not long home ourselves,' Mum says, emerging from the balcony, her arms full of clean laundry. We're not actually allowed to hang laundry out there – apparently it's unsightly, and there are shared washing lines in the garden below which we're meant to use – but no one has complained yet. I hate the thought of hanging our laundry in a communal place, where everyone can see it, and anyone can take it, for a laugh, or just because they can, but I suppose it's one of the compromises that comes with apartment living.

'How was training?' I ask the boys.

New home, new suburb, new school, new soccer team. It's been a tumultuous six months.

'The other kids were really friendly,' Finn says, looking away from the TV to smile at me. 'Some of them are in our year at school.'

Despite being considerably smaller and skinnier, Finn has always been the more gregarious and confident of the twins. Callum is a darker personality, more introverted, harder to engage. He's the one who's feeling the change more keenly. Not that he'll show it.

Mum takes my arm and steers me towards the kitchen. 'The coach mentioned that the boys' registration fees haven't been paid . . .'

Rumbled. By the coach and by my mother. 'I'll pay them next week . . . when my salary comes in.'

Yes, I can pay next week, but that means I won't pay something else: the car insurance, or the electricity bill, or the school-camp fees. To be honest, I was hoping to get some leeway with the soccer fees, to stretch them out to my next pay cheque. No such luck, obviously.

'Technically, the coach shouldn't have allowed the boys to train. He said they aren't insured, should they hurt themselves, or anything else. He was a nice man. Very

49

good with the kids. He's just following the club's rules, that's all. "No pay, no play," he said.'

'Flipping heck, Mum. It's not as though they're doing anything dangerous. They're just kids, it's just football, they shouldn't need to be insured. The world's going crazy.'

'How much is it, Hannah?' Mum asks, seeing straight through my bravado.

I bite down on my lip. 'Between the two of them, the best part of four hundred dollars.'

'Good grief.' She looks shocked. If it had been a smaller amount, she would have offered to pay. Four hundred dollars is out of her reach too.

'Look, I'll pay it next week,' I say, even though I'm not sure I can. The electricity is already on a payment plan, and I've had three reminders about the school camp. 'It'll be fine.'

It'll be fine. I'm blue in the face from saying that phrase. *It'll be fine.* It's not fine. Not at all.

Mum stays for dinner, as she often does. It's a warm evening and we eat outside, spaghetti bolognese on our third-floor balcony. Our view is of other apartment blocks, separated from us by a major arterial road. The traffic never stops, roaring past at all hours of the day and night. Squealing brakes, revving engines, hooting horns. Despite the noise and the inevitable breeze, it's nice out here. It can be stuffy in the apartment, particularly on warmer days. The boys shovel the spaghetti into their mouths, scraping their bowls clean. Their appetites seem to grow by the day. *What's for dinner, Mum? What're we having for lunch? Can we have a snack? There's nothing to eat,*

Mum. Sometimes I have nightmares that the fridge is empty and there really is nothing to eat, that the boys are hollow-eyed and starving, and I've failed to provide their most basic need.

'I'll be off, love.' Mum gathers her bag and jacket when dinner is over. She lives only a short drive away, which is one of the reasons I decided to move back to this area, where I spent my own childhood. The other reasons were financial: a house that had fallen in value and was worth less than its purchase price; an already tight cash flow made impossible by the sudden reduction to one income; the existence of high-density, slightly more affordable accommodation in this part of the city.

'I'll see you after school tomorrow, boys,' Mum continues, then, with a little laugh, 'Same time, same place, eh?'

'Bye, Nan,' the boys chime. They're back in front of the TV. I really need to do something about how much they watch.

'Bye, Mum.' My hug is tighter than both of us expect.

'Are you all right, love?' she asks, peering at me more closely. 'You've been a bit quiet tonight . . . Did something happen at work?'

Yes, Mum, something did happen at work. Sophie McCarthy happened. And I feel like I'm sixteen all over again. Sixteen, with no clue about life, about people and what they're capable of. Timid, naive, insecure, that was me. Clever, confident, unstoppable, that was Sophie McCarthy.

'I'm fine, Mum. Just tired. It's been a busy day.'

I allow the boys fifteen more minutes of TV before discovering that their homework is only half done. Then there's some sternness from me, some push-back from them, before the homework books are opened on the dining table and the apartment is silent as they work.

Afterwards, it's showers and bed. They fall asleep within minutes of their heads hitting the pillow. I wish it were the same for me.

The next two hours are frantic. Throw dirty clothes in the washing machine. Assemble lunchboxes for the morning. Sign various school permission notes. Sew a button on Callum's school shirt. Check bank balance. Toy with the thought of ringing the soccer club and claiming financial hardship. Discard idea. By the time I get to bed, my mind is whirring. The soccer fees, the car insurance, the clothes the boys are growing out of, Sophie McCarthy, Sophie McCarthy, Sophie McCarthy.

I remember you, Sophie McCarthy. I have never, not for one moment, forgotten you.

Stop it, for God's sake. I'm thirty years old. I'm the mother of twin boys who need me so much that I often feel completely overwhelmed. I'm a widow – a hateful word I used to associate with my own mother, but now it applies to me too. I'm a woman who has gone through the profound shock of losing her husband, a man she assumed she'd grow old with. I am a good administration assistant: efficient, professional and calm under stress. This is who I am, and I can't let Sophie McCarthy get in the way of any of it because *I need this job.*

So what if Jane doesn't like her? So what if she's not the easiest to work for? Toughen up, Hannah, get on with it. Buy her coffees from across the road, type up her letters, manage her diary, enter her expense claims. You're not scared of hard work, are you?

I need this job. That's the bottom line here. *I need this job*, and I can't afford to jeopardize it in any way.

Sophie McCarthy, Sophie McCarthy, Sophie McCarthy.

Stop it, Hannah. She doesn't remember you anyway. There's no problem here.

8

Dee

'Would you like more potato, Aidan?'

'Thanks, Mrs McCarthy. That'd be great.'

I prefer to be called Dee and have told him this, but either he's forgotten or he wants things to stay on more formal terms. I can't really say it again: I don't want to come across as one of those impossible-to-please mother-in-laws. Not that Aidan and Sophie are actually married. Still, Richard and I need to come to terms with the fact that this isn't an ill-considered fling and that Aidan Ryan may be sitting at our dining table for many years to come. Despite everything that has happened, despite our disapproval – Richard has barely said a word to him – it's obvious that Sophie and Aidan are very serious about each other.

'Here you are.' I pass the casserole dish to him. 'Help yourself.'

'Thanks, Mrs McCarthy,' he says, and I'm annoyed all over again.

When Aidan is done with the roast potatoes, he offers the dish to Sophie, who puts an extra two on her plate. She's slightly overweight and I care only because I know *she* cares. Sophie always took great pride in her appearance, and approached her diet and exercise with the same gusto and dedication as everything else in her life. What's changed is that she doesn't seem to have the same will-power when it comes to food, which is exacerbated by the fact that she's not in a position to do any kind of exercise. I'm her mother, her weight doesn't have any effect on how much I love her, but someone needs to remind her – gently – not to overeat. Still, this isn't the time or place. Maybe I'll get an opportunity later on.

'How is work going, Sophie?' Richard booms across the table.

His voice seems to be getting louder lately, and I'm beginning to think he might have a problem with his hearing. Again, not the time or place to suggest that he gets it checked out. There's so much left unsaid at this table. Are other families like this?

'So far, so good.' Sophie looks across at her father, her face adopting the intense look she always assumes when talking about her career. 'I'm getting back into the swing of things. A few bad habits seem to have crept in while I've been away, so I've spent most of the time resetting standards.'

'Good on you,' Richard declares. 'Everyone will have to watch their Ps and Qs now you're back. Right, sweetheart?'

I wish he wouldn't talk to her like that, like she's the best and everyone else is rubbish. We've spoken about this before. Many times. It's like an itch in our marriage.

Stop making her think she's so much better than everyone else, Richard.

But she is better than everyone else, Dee. It's a fact.

Everyone has something to offer, Richard. Intellect isn't the be all and end all! You build her up too much.

And you seem bloody intent on pulling her down, Dee.

'And how has it been physically, Sophie?' I ask in a pleasant tone that – I hope – shows no trace of all those old arguments between Richard and me. 'How have you been feeling?'

'Tired. So tired at night that I can hardly move. And sore. My back has been tighter, probably from all the sitting down.'

It shows in her face: pale, drawn, frail, despite the extra weight. All of a sudden I feel ashamed of myself. My daughter is a battler who has defied everything that has been thrown at her. She has had to fight for her life not just once, when she was born prematurely, but *twice*. Sophie is brilliant and brave and truly remarkable. I am the bad one here, the villain. As Richard says, I seem intent on pulling her down, always finding fault.

'I've been talking with the physio,' Aidan interjects quietly. 'He's given me some extra tips on what I can do to help Sophie in terms of back massage and exercises. And I've worked out a special diet, with lots of complex carbohydrates to boost her energy levels.'

Despite the fact that he's directly responsible for the pain that Sophie is in, and the fact that this is a man who *left his wife and child* to pursue a relationship with my daughter, a tiny part of me has to admit that I could like Aidan Ryan if I allowed myself to. I can see why Sophie is attracted to him. That quiet sense of authority he has. His strength – more than once I have found my eyes drawn to the swell of muscles on his upper arms. How obliging he is. Massaging Sophie's back. Helping her around the house. After this meal, he'll get up from his seat and clear the table. Aidan Ryan is a doer. He gets on with the job, whatever it happens to be. It's something they teach them in the army, I suppose. He says, 'No problem,' a lot, and I get the impression he means exactly that: nothing is insurmountable, everything – ultimately – can be fixed.

'Jacob and the kids are coming at Easter,' I say, changing the subject. 'We should organize something while he's around. A barbecue would be nice.'

Sophie chews on her food, looking uninterested.

Aidan answers on her behalf. 'That sounds good. We don't have any plans for the Easter weekend. Just name the day and we'll keep it free.'

Sophie remains noncommittal, and I sigh, a brief emission of air and disappointment. It's an area where I have failed as a mother: I dearly wanted to instil a sense of closeness, of kinship, between my children. Jacob lives in Newcastle, a couple of hours' drive away, where he works for the local government as a communications officer: press releases, advertising, council newsletters, that sort of thing. I know – from speaking to friends who have grown-up children of similar ages – that other siblings manage to talk on the phone, or Skype, or catch up for coffees, meals or drinks on a regular basis. If I didn't insist on a family occasion every time Jacob's in town, I don't think he and Sophie would lay eyes on each other at all. It saddens me – *puzzles me* – this lack of closeness between the two of them. When they were little they would play together, and now I'm trying hard to remember when that stopped. OK, there wasn't much love during their teenage years, but that's pretty normal with all the angst and hormones getting in the way. As adults, I fully expected them to rediscover each other. I've questioned them both. Sophie seems apathetic (*Why do we have to be close, Mum? We've nothing in common. At least we're civil – that's more than can be said for many siblings*). And Jacob seems overly wary of his sister . . . he seems to remember a lot more childhood squabbles than I do.

Sophie's distant with Milli and Hugo too, and that's inexcusable. She's their *aunt*, for goodness' sake. How can she not feel a connection? How can her heart not melt at the thought of their chubby faces, their devilish smiles, their developing personalities? I find myself asking: *Who is she, this daughter of mine? What is going on in that head of hers? Do I really know her?* And you know what makes me even more upset? Aidan's daughter, that's who. The fact that Sophie sees more of that girl – Jasmin – than her own niece and nephew. Jasmin seems like a lovely girl, and none of this situation is *her* fault, but I can't help feeling jealous on behalf of Milli and Hugo. All I can hope for is that Sophie will find her niece and nephew more interesting when they're older and will form a relationship with them then.

As predicted, Aidan stands up and begins to clear the table when we've all finished eating. He rinses the plates before stacking them in the dishwasher.

'Do you want to keep any of this, Mrs McCarthy?' he asks, his gaze sweeping across the pots – some with left-over vegetables in them – sitting on the stove-top.

'It's Dee!' I snap, before I can help myself. 'I don't like being called Mrs McCarthy. Dee is fine. And the pots are fine too. I'll take care of them.'

There's a stunned silence. Sophie and Richard are shocked because this sort of behaviour – being caustic and bad-mannered to anyone, let alone a dinner guest – is so out of character for me. I'm shocked, myself. I'm the easy-going one in the family, the peacemaker, but everything seems to have got on top of me today: Sophie and Aidan, Richard and Sophie, Sophie and Jacob.

It all comes back to Sophie. That's why I'm so disgruntled. I feel like I've failed her in some way, but don't ask me how.

Aidan is the only one of us who isn't rattled by my outburst. 'No problem . . . I'll take out the rubbish, Dee.'

9

Chloe

'Go back to bed, Jasmin.' My voice is as calm as I can muster at this time of night.

'I've lost my tiredness, Mum.'

From the corner of my eye, I see her walk from the doorway, where she hovered for the first few moments, to the side of the armchair where I'm sitting. Don't look at her. Don't engage. Minimal communication. That's what all the experts say.

'Bed. *Now.*'

'I'm not tired, Mum.' Her voice gets progressively louder with each word. 'I'm . . . not . . . tired . . , any . . . more.'

My eyes veer from the TV programme I've been trying to watch. Jasmin's face is red, her hands fidgety. Not good signs. 'Don't you raise your voice to me, Jasmin Ryan. Go back to bed this instant.'

'I can't sleep. I . . . can't . . . sleep.'

Oh, for pity's sake. How many times have I heard that phrase tonight? How many times over the last few months? The last year?

'Of course you can sleep. Telling yourself that you can't isn't helping, you know that. You must tell yourself that you *can* sleep . . . Now, back to bed.'

'Can you tuck me in?'

'I've already tucked you in. Twice.'

'Please tuck me in. Please . . . Please.'

'No.'

'I'm . . . really . . . sorry . . . I . . . just . . . can't . . . sleep.'

'You *can* sleep,' I insist. 'Off to bed now. Goodnight.'

My acting skills are quite amazing. I sound fully confident that my child is going to trot off to bed, hop under the covers and fall into a deep sleep.

She turns, walks rather promisingly towards the door, then stops dead. 'Can you tuck me in, Mum?'

'For goodness' sake. We've just had this discussion. Stop asking the same questions over and over again. Just go to bed, Jasmin. *Go to bed.*'

That wasn't good. It wasn't calm. Not calm at all. Deep breaths. Deep breaths. You can still save this, Chloe.

'I'm trying,' she wails. 'I'm trying. Why are you being so mean to me?'

'Because I'm tired,' I wail back at her. 'OK, I'll tuck you in. I'll tuck you in – even though I know it'll make no difference whatsoever. You'll be back down here in ten minutes.'

Grabbing her by the arm, I march her out to the hall and up the stairs.

'I need to go to the bathroom.'

'You've already been, remember? The last time you got out of bed.'

'I need to go again.'

'Go, then. Just go.'

Calm down, Chloe. Calm down. You're doing all the wrong things. Again.

'I'm sorry for shouting,' I say when she emerges. 'Shouting doesn't help.'

'I'm sorry too, Mum.' Her face crumples with fresh tears.

'Come here, darling.' I give her a brisk hug, and plant a kiss on her forehead, which feels hot under my lips. 'Now, we're going to start again, OK?'

Ushering her into the darkened room, I pull back the covers. She obligingly gets in, curls up on one side, and yawns. Maybe this will be it for tonight. Dear Lord, please let this be it.

Downstairs, instead of waiting tensely for the next instalment in the bedtime saga – as I often do – I try to be proactive and make myself a cup of herbal tea. The programme I was half watching earlier has finished, and I pick up one of my sewing magazines instead. There are a number of patterns I want to try – a pretty skirt for Jasmin, a kaftan-style dress for myself. Just when I think she's actually done it, fallen asleep, I hear a thump overhead, then the creak of the floorboards, before the sound of her bedroom door opening. She lasted fifteen minutes. That's a long time for her, at this stage of the night.

She's trying, Chloe. Don't get cross with her. She's trying.

Then the same conversation happens again. *I'm not tired, Mum. You are tired, Jasmin. Can you tuck me in? No.* She starts crying, I start shouting, we both say sorry.

By the time she's back in bed, my tea is cold. What I'd give to finish a cup of tea, to watch a late-night TV show from start to end, to make a start on one of the patterns in the magazine, or read a book. What I'd give to be able to call my parents, who are on an extended trip to Europe, or one of my interstate friends for a long chat. These are the things I used to do at night, before Jasmin lost faith in her ability to fall asleep.

There's another thump upstairs and suddenly I'm furious, more furious than ever, tonight or any other night, or any other point in my life that I can remember.

'I can't take this any more, Jasmin. *I am too tired.*'

She doesn't progress past the doorway. 'Are you going to move out, like Daddy did?'

'Of course not. Just go to bed. *Go to bed, for pity's sake.*'

And she goes, running up the stairs, sobbing hysterically. How have you let it get to this, Chloe? You're hopeless. This wouldn't have happened if Aidan were here. Jasmin would be in bed by now; it would be over for the night. But Aidan's not here. *He's not here, damn him.* He'll text tomorrow to ask how the night went. *A text doesn't count him in.* I hate him. I hate him. No, I *wish* I hated him. It would be so much easier if I did.

Jasmin has stopped at her bedroom door. 'Can you please tuck me in? Please, Mum.'

Nothing works. Being patient. Being firm. Having consequences. Not having consequences. Explaining the impact of her actions. Making light of it. Engaging. Not engaging. Tucking in. Not tucking in. Having a screaming match the entire neighbourhood can hear. Nothing works.

'Please, Mum?' Her face is blotched, her nose running, her entire body trembling. What am I to do with this child? Tomorrow morning, after I've dragged her out of bed, she will be contrite and cooperative and generally delightful. What is the answer? *What is the answer?*

It's well past midnight. That's the only thing I know.

I trudge up the stairs and walk her back to bed. Then, completely defeated, I lie down next to her, one arm tight around her thin, shaking shoulders.

'I'm sorry, Mum. I'm sorry . . .'

'Ssh, Jazz . . .'

For the next twenty minutes, she's too overwrought to lie still, jerking and twitching against me. Finally, just as I'm losing sensation in my arm, her breathing becomes more even, the twitches less frequent. She's asleep. Carefully, I adjust the angle of my arm to ease the pins and needles, but I don't dare to move any other part of me in case it wakes her up. More than once I've woken her as I tried to creep out of the room. The very thought roots me to the bed. Twenty more minutes pass by, and I lie next to her in the dark, thinking of all the things I could have done differently tonight.

Bit by bit I move my arm away from her and edge my way off the bed, stopping when it creaks loudly and waiting a few moments until I know it's safe to continue. I tiptoe across the carpet, and spend a few moments on the door, trying to open it as noiselessly as possible. She tosses and turns in the bed. Fighting sleep. Even now.

What is it? What is wrong with her? Because it's very clear that *something* is wrong. This isn't normal. Nobody can tell me this is normal. Yet that's what all the questionnaires have come back with: Jasmin is a normal nine-year-old girl. She doesn't have ADHD, ADD, OCD, ODD,

Asperger's, autism, anxiety or any other recognizable disorder. She's attentive and focused at school, listens when she is spoken to, and her ability to follow instructions is in fact at a level much higher than usual for her age. Except when it comes to bedtime.

Downstairs, I turn off the TV, pour the remains of my tea down the sink and switch off all the lights.

As I stand in the dark kitchen, a sob erupts from deep inside me. I am the worst mother in the world. A dreadfully cruel mother who yells and loses her temper and who is damaging her child – a precious, unique, truly marvellous girl – for life.

I'm sorry, Jasmin. I'm so very sorry. We can't go on like this. We can't.

10

Aidan

Dust billows in my face. Rubble crunches underfoot. One of my men – on my nod – kicks in the door and we swarm inside. The walls, as with most of the traditional dwellings, are made of mud, and the room has a serious deficit of air and light. Mattresses and pillows line the perimeter. How many live here? Ten? Fifteen? There's a sound. We all hear it and train our rifles towards that corner of the room. My men are seeking my go-ahead to open fire. I hesitate. What if there's a child behind that sound? Or an old man, quivering with fear? A dark-eyed young woman, too scared to breathe? Then another sound: an unmistakeable click.

I wake to the burst of gunfire. My heart's racing. I'm sweating as hard as if I really were in Kabul, and the terror is just as palpable. I check the clock for reassurance rather than a need to know the time. I always wake early, even on weekends. It annoys Sophie, who likes to sleep in. It used to annoy Chloe too. Even when Jasmin would have us up half the night, I still woke early the next morning. Yeah, I was tired, so tired it was a struggle to get ready for work, to get through the day, but my eyes opened bang on 5.30 a.m. and, no matter what, even if it was a weekend and there was nowhere to go and nothing pressing to do, I simply couldn't fall back asleep. My body point-blank refused. Maybe this is how it is for Jasmin. She's tired and wants to sleep, but her body simply won't allow it.

I slip out of bed as unobtrusively as I can, deciding to forego my shower until later, when Sophie is awake. The kitchen is shrouded in bluish predawn light. I fill the kettle with fresh water, throw a tea bag into a mug and wonder how Jasmin got on last night. It's too early to text Chloe to ask.

My tea's ready, and I take the mug over to the glass-topped dining table where I left my iPad last night. The psychologist's report, the last thing I was reading before going to bed, opens up on the screen. 'Dr Matthew Wheatley' is emblazoned across the top. Chloe seems to trust Matthew. When she's feeling positive, she believes that he can genuinely help Jasmin. When she's feeling negative, well, like me, all the worst scenarios come to mind: Jasmin being like this for ever; Jasmin beginning to do badly at school; Jasmin not being able to hold down a job as an adult, not being able to maintain any meaningful relationships, being a social outcast.

OCD was my greatest fear, because there *is* something compulsive about how Jasmin repeatedly gets out of bed. She knows she shouldn't, but she does it anyway, can't seem to stop herself. Chloe relayed my specific concerns to the psychologist, and he has addressed it in his report. Now I read back over the relevant paragraph, reassuring myself again.

OCD is an anxiety disorder that usually stems from an obsessive fear: fear of contamination or illness, excessive concerns about symmetry, exactness, morality, religion, to name a few examples. Compulsions are repetitive actions carried out to try to prevent the obsessive fear from happening: excessive hand washing and cleaning; repeated checking of locks and appliances; applying rigid rules and patterns to the placement of objects; touching, tapping or moving in a particular way or a certain number of times. Jasmin presents no signs of the obsession (excessive fear) or compulsions (compulsions usually happen all day, every day, not just at night).

But despite being somewhat reassured, Chloe and I are still in the dark: we don't know what's causing this. You could say that we know more about what it *isn't* than what it *is*. Some anomalies did pop up in Jasmin's results. The report refers to something it calls her 'low registration', which apparently means that she doesn't have a strong sense of self-awareness. The report also states that our daughter has relatively high sensory sensitivity – whatever that means. Last night, I wrote down both terms – 'low registration' and 'sensory sensitivity' – on the back of an envelope, which is still next to the iPad. Later today, when my brain is switched into gear, I'll spend some time on Google and try to educate myself.

I switch screens from the report to the news headlines. A scandal involving a politician I used to admire. Wild weather in Far North Queensland. A rugby player involved in a nightclub punch-up. The breaking stories provide enough distraction to get me through to six thirty. Still too early to text Chloe?

Almost by telepathy, my phone beeps with a message: *Are you up?*

Yeah. How was last night?

Dreadful.

Damn it. Not what I wanted to hear.

Want to talk? I type, after only the slightest hesitation.

A few moments later my phone begins to ring.

'Hey,' I say.

She's crying. 'I was horrible to her . . . Horrible.'

'Ssh . . . It's all right.' Consoling Chloe is second nature to me. I can see her right now, sitting up in bed, knees pulled against her chest, the phone cradled against her ear, her sun-bleached hair and year-round tan, her cheerfully coloured pyjamas contrasting with the white bedlinen . . . but it's not a good idea to dwell on those kinds of details. 'You tried your best . . . I know how frustrating it can be.'

'I don't know what to do any more . . .' Her voice shudders with each sob. 'I wake up feeling so guilty, already dreading the next night . . .'

'When's your next meeting with the psychologist?'

'Thursday, after school.'

'I'll come with you.'

'But your work . . .' She knows that my job isn't flexible, that arriving late or leaving early – no matter what the family occasion – is frowned upon.

'It's no problem. I'll talk to the colonel. He'll understand.'

She cries even harder. 'It's not only Jasmin who turns into a monster at night . . . it's me too.'

'You're not a monster, Chlo. Far from it.'

'You didn't see me yelling at her last night.'

'You need a break, that's all. A night off.'

She sniffs a few times, then sighs. 'You're right, I think I do. For her sake and mine.'

'Leave it with me, OK? It's time we sorted something out . . . Is Jasmin awake?'

'No. She was exhausted by the time she finally fell asleep. I'm going to leave her as long as I can.'

I'm not sure if it's wise, allowing her to sleep in. Won't that put her even more out of her routine, make her less tired when she goes to bed tonight? Still, I have no right to object. Not from here, from Sophie's house.

'Hey, I'll get the bus over later on, take her for a kick-around at the park, burn off some energy.'

'If only it was as simple as needing to burn off energy.' She has stopped crying, but she sounds hollow, defeated, and it's almost as bad. Chloe is colourful, loud, effervescent – even when she's angry or upset – and I always find it especially disconcerting when she's flat.

'I know . . . I'll see you later, OK? We'll talk properly then.'

A small sound by the kitchen door causes me to swing around on my seat. Sophie, wearing very short pyjama pants and a skimpy vest, is standing there, glowering. To be fair, I can see how this looks from her end: Chloe and I having an obviously intimate conversation in the early hours of the morning, when everyone involved should still be in bed.

'Your phone woke me up.'

'Sorry.' I stand up from the table, stretching. 'Look, we needed to talk about Jasmin.'

'And you're telling me it couldn't have waited until later?'

Normally I would put my arms around her, give her a hug and a kiss to show her that she has no need to be jealous of Chloe. But Chloe sobbing like that, the thought of the scene that happened last night, the guilt I feel at leaving her to deal with Jasmin on her own, makes me less contrite. Instead I am becoming aggravated at an unjustifiable and alarming rate. My hands tense by my sides. That urge again, to hit, to strike out, to find release. 'I'm going for a run.'

She frowns at me. 'Didn't you do a big run yesterday?'

Sophie retains detail in a way Chloe doesn't. I'm still getting used to this aspect of her personality. Sometimes it feels like she is trying to catch me out, even though I know that's not the case.

'I'll be back in an hour.'

Yesterday's run was fitness training in preparation for Operation Panther. Ten kilometres in full uniform and boots, with twenty kilos of equipment on our backs. Upstairs, I change into shorts, a sleeveless T-shirt, and trainers – infinitely more comfortable than yesterday's running attire – and within a matter of minutes I'm outside. I set a punishing pace from the outset, one I can't hope to maintain for long, but soon the rhythm and sheer exertion take almost all my concentration. My aggravation and guilt, Sophie's jealousy, Chloe's tears and disappointment in herself, the ongoing mystery of Jasmin's sleeplessness, are all temporarily left behind.

11

Hannah

Jane is having a rant about Sophie. 'It's exactly how it was before. Phone calls after hours. Emails twenty-four/seven. The constant pressure. The knowledge that she's *never* going to let up on me and, no matter how hard I try, I'll never measure up.'

Jane and I are having lunch in an old-style café a few streets away from the office. Conversation is pretty one-way today; she's letting off steam. I feel sorry for her, I really do, but I'm getting caught in the middle. The truth is, the two of them clash. Jane thinks the worst of Sophie, and Sophie thinks the worst of Jane. If both of them backed down just a little, there wouldn't be this constant warfare.

'Of course you measure up, Jane. You're a qualified actuary with years and years of experience. I think these problems are happening because Sophie relies on you so much. Maybe you should send her an email telling her how much pressure you're under. Putting it in writing would give you the opportunity to choose your words carefully, to let her know that —'

Jane isn't listening to a word I say. 'It was Sunday night, for Christ's sake. And it was a complex report that deserved more than a rush job.'

The incident that triggered Jane's rant is a report that Sophie wanted ready for this morning. Apparently the report was needed for a board meeting that Jane didn't seem to know about.

'I was just going to bed when I got her email. I had to turn around and go downstairs and spend a couple of hours importing historical data and statistical assumptions, fleshing out the best- and worst-case scenarios . . . Exactly what you need late on a Sunday night! Then, just as my brain was getting foggy from all the numbers, there was a cry from upstairs: "Mum." I thought it was another nightmare . . . the girls seem to be going through a phase. They *never* call for their father. They haven't worked out that he's considerably larger than me, and if there are monsters under the bed he's obviously the one to call for help . . .'

Jane pauses, finally, to fork some food into her mouth. She looks extremely pale. Zara, her youngest, had a vomiting bug, not a nightmare. Poor Jane was up most of the night with her.

'You're looking peaky,' I tell her. 'I hope you're not coming down with the same bug as Zara.'

She rolls her eyes. 'To be honest, some sick leave would be a relief – a break from Sophie . . . She must be the same with you, right? I bet she thinks she owns you.'

Sophie *is* exacting to work for, but I've also found her to be quite reasonable. Her manner is businesslike, very direct and clear, and I quite like that . . . I know where I stand. Some of her workload eats into the days I'm meant to reserve for Peter, but I've been able to manage. I've made a conscious effort to focus on the here and now, rather than ancient history from school, and so far, it's been fine.

'She's been OK, actually . . .'

Jane pushes away her half-eaten plate of food. 'Maybe I should resign,' she says with a dramatic flourish of her hand. 'I almost did, last October, when she came back the first time. I even typed up a draft resignation letter when the reality of working for her again became too overwhelming: the constant deadlines and stress, never being able to trust that my family time was not about to be interrupted or completely hijacked. Then she collapsed, was carted off on a stretcher, and the problem went away.'

Now she is being downright callous. I've heard from other people what happened when Sophie collapsed. Apparently she was out cold on the kitchen floor – they had to call an ambulance. It was all very dramatic. Paramedics circling around her on the floor, the stretcher being carried through the office, some of the staff (especially the graduates, who are really just kids) getting upset.

Jane continues obliviously. 'The first thing I did after she was gone – while everyone else was still standing around talking about whether she would be OK, and how we should have a whip-round to send some flowers – was to rush back to my desk, open up the draft of my letter of resignation and press the delete button.'

I feel uncomfortable talking about Sophie like this. As though her collapse was something to celebrate.

'Do any of yours play soccer?' I ask, in a blatant attempt to change the topic of conversation.

'Lily does. They've just started training. Mick is the coach this year.'

Lily is the middle of Jane's three girls, Zara is the oldest, and Madison is the baby (my favourite story about Madison is her first swimming carnival, when she was overly optimistic about her swimming abilities and had to be rescued by the lifeguard halfway through the fifty-metres freestyle). Jane had her girls late, and they're all quite close in age. I know a lot about her kids because that's what we used to talk about before Sophie came back to work: how special and talented and terrible (some of the time) our children are, and trivia about sicknesses and behaviour and schools. With everyone else, I need to watch what I say. They're all very polite and always enquire about my children, but they expect a one-line response, nothing more, and I have to be perpetually careful not to overdo it. With Jane, I don't have to rein myself in. Neither of us can remember what life was like before our children existed. I find myself gazing at my younger colleagues in bafflement and harbouring nanny-like thoughts: *Why on earth are you wearing so much make-up? Those heels you're teetering around in are going to wreck your back. Are you really going out again tonight?* I vacillate between being intensely envious of their freedom and pitying them for their shallow, purposeless lives. Jane is exactly the same. I don't know who she used to talk to before I started at Real Cover.

'How much are Lily's soccer fees?' Maybe I've chosen a particularly expensive club for the boys. I should have done some research before registering them.

She shrugs. 'I don't know. Mick takes care of that stuff.'

Mick is Jane's husband. He's an electrician and works mainly in the building trade. I get the impression that Jane's salary is more than his but, with two incomes, I imagine that Lily's soccer fees are no big deal.

Jane's phone begins to ring. She glances down at it. 'It's her. Jesus Christ, her ears must be burning.' She turns off the phone and throws it back on the table with unnecessary force. 'Mick says I should tell her to get stuffed . . . He works hard, but when he clocks off, he clocks off. No after-hours calls or emails or expectations. If he needs to work overtime, it's agreed weeks in advance and he's paid double time. He doesn't understand my job. Yeah, the salary is good, but not so great if averaged out over all the hours I put in.'

Jane's words are tumbling out on top of each other. I've never seen her so agitated, but I guess I haven't known her that long, in the scheme of things. I reach across the table, put my hand over hers.

'Breathe, Jane. You need to breathe . . .'

That's something I tell myself at night, when I'm trying to sleep and all my money problems are whirring around in my head.

'That's the problem, Hannah. I can't breathe. Not when that pinched, disapproving face of hers is looking over my shoulder, judging me, finding me lacking, demanding more and more and more. Jesus Christ, I even dream about her at night.'

'You're overtired from being up with Zara . . . I bet things won't seem so black tomorrow.' She snorts at this. 'Come on, we'd better get back.'

Outside the café, on the walk back to the office, she starts up again. 'You know, Hannah, it might not sound like it, but I love my job. Coming into the city every day, the fulfilled feeling that comes from using my brain, having a life away from my kids and all the domestic humdrum. I loved the nice vibe we had in the department, the feeling that I was appreciated and valued, but all that disappeared as soon as she came back.'

Flipping heck, it's actually a relief to return to work. I know that Jane is stressed out, but she's being completely over the top. We catch the lift up to the third floor and, after a quick smile to the receptionist, proceed through the security door. It seems ironic that Sophie is the first person we see when we set foot in the department.

She has obviously been waiting for us. She looks upset. 'I've been trying to call you, Jane . . . Please come into my office.'

12

Sophie

'There are mistakes all over this report. The assumptions are inconsistent and, on top of that, there are typos . . . *everywhere*. It was John Greenland who spotted the error in the assumptions. *John Greenland!* I had to apologize to him and the other directors. You put me in a very awkward position, Jane.'

'Sorry,' she mumbles, looking out the window instead of meeting my eyes.

'"Sorry" isn't good enough. We're professionals. We can't hand in substandard reports and follow up with an airy apology. They *rely* on our analyses, make decisions based on *our* accuracy. We have to –'

'You didn't give me enough notice!'

'What?' I'm speechless for a moment. 'You're blaming me now? Come on, Jane. *Seriously?*'

'There wasn't enough notice,' she persists, slowly turning her eyes from the window to me. 'I thought the report wasn't due until later in the week, but when I saw your email last night, I dropped everything and tried my best to give you what you wanted. In retrospect, I should have said no, it wouldn't be ready on time. That would have been the more professional thing to do, I realize now. Obviously, working so late at night didn't help my accuracy. And Zara was sick in the middle of it . . .' Jane pauses, as though regretting mentioning her daughter, as though I am the kind of person to blame a sick little girl.

Finally, she seems to come to her senses and properly apologizes. 'I'm sorry, Sophie, I really am. I'll reissue the report right away, and send a written apology to John and the rest of the board.'

I nod, and she makes a move to leave, no doubt contemplating where she can go to lick her wounds before facing her colleagues.

'Stop. Wait a minute.'

She stops in her tracks, her expression hardening, becoming mutinous. I think she knows what's coming.

'This is a warning, Jane. A *formal* warning. Your performance is not up to the standard we require from employees of your experience and standing. Your report reflected badly on the whole department. I need to be able to rely on the quality of your work, and I feel I can't. It's not just this particular instance. If it were, I'd be prepared to let it go. Quality seems to be an issue across all areas of your work, and I see a distinct lack of commitment on your part, as though this job is a means to an end and nothing more. This warning will be put in writing and entered in your employment record . . .' I clear my throat, and then, because we both know it's required by law, ask, 'Do you have any response?'

She doesn't even hesitate. 'Yes, I do have a response, actually.' She raises her chin, takes a deep breath. 'Don't bother with the warning letter, save yourself the trouble. I resign.'

'Oh, come on, Jane. Don't be rash!'

There is no stopping her. 'I can even make things easier again and leave right this minute. There'll be no risk of any more substandard reports, or supposed quality or commitment issues. Does that make you happy, Sophie?'

For God's sake. 'No, it does not. I think you –'

'I'll tell you what . . . it makes *me* happy. Imagine, I'll have my *life* back. How will that feel? I won't have to monitor my emails twenty-four hours a day. I won't have to drop everything to tend to your short-notice demands. So fuck you and your warning, Sophie McCarthy. *I resign.*'

The wooziness starts when I'm on the bus, about halfway home. The voices around me recede, as though someone has turned down the volume. It's one of the warning signs (the others being dizziness, sweating, tunnel vision) before I collapse into whatever heap gravity pulls me into. Afterwards, there's the terrible feeling of having lost control, a mortifying loss of dignity, as well as the bruising, often on my face.

Come on, Sophie. Not here. It'll only cause a scene. Come on, fight it. You're on public transport, for God's sake. They'll stop the bus. They'll call an ambulance. You'll delay all the other commuters. It'll be all so much more complicated if you faint here. Hold it together, Sophie.

And I do hold on. By taking deep breaths, dragging oxygen into my brain. By not giving in to the urge to slide down, to close my eyes. The fresh air when I get off the bus revives me further but, within moments, I feel weak again. The exertion of the five-minute walk to the house when I'm already so tired. The slight incline, an incline I used hardly to notice when I was fit and well. The weight of my laptop bag biting into my shoulder, an extra burden when I can hardly hold myself up straight.

Aidan's already home, in the kitchen, making a start on dinner.

'Hey,' he greets me. 'You're late.'

I hurry past him, heading for the safety of the couch, the one place where I can't do myself any harm if I do pass out.

'Sophie?' In my mind I imagine Aidan putting down the knife, drying his hands on a tea towel. If I turn my head, I could actually see him doing all this, but moving my head wouldn't be good right now, not when every-thing is already so wobbly. 'Are you all right, Soph?'

Deep breaths. I'm safe, I made it home. Deep breaths.

He crouches down in front of me, takes one of my hands. 'What is it?'

My voice is slurred. 'Thought I was going to faint.'

His face is full of concern. 'Did you overdo it?'

Yes, you could say that. The stress of getting ready for the board meeting. John Greenland glaring down the length of the table – directly at me – declaring, 'Assump-tion three doesn't make any sense.' Then that awful scene with Jane.

Maybe if she had been at the board meeting, on the receiving end of John's biting criticism, been the one who had to take the brunt of the responsibility – even though the errors belonged to someone else — she might have understood how compromised I was, and why I got so angry with her.

Fuck you and your warning, Sophie McCarthy.

I know she was upset, but I did nothing to deserve *that*. It wasn't as if I *wanted* to give her a formal warning. I did it only because I felt I had no other choice. I had to be seen to act. Otherwise, John Greenland would think that substandard work was tolerated by our department — by *me*.

Jane didn't have to resign. She could have gone off somewhere to cool down and gather her thoughts. And, if she was determined to hand in her resignation, there was no need to walk out like that, on the spot. She could have worked out her four weeks' notice, like everyone else does. But no, she lost her temper, her job and her notice pay, all in one fell swoop. If it had been me in her shoes, on the wrong end of a formal warning, I would like to think that I'd be mature, stoic, dignified.

Aidan, as always, wants to make it better. 'What can I get you? Water? Tea? A cold sponge?'

'Water. Thanks.'

Thank God I have tomorrow off, a chance to recover. And thank God I kept my head and didn't yell back at Jane. Of course I had to go straight round to Alyssa in HR to explain what had happened. Alyssa took notes while I relayed my version of events. I was clear, unemotional and tried to be fair. I'm sure she has called Jane by now and got her version on record too. God only knows what Jane said about me.

'Here.' Aidan hands me the water and sits down next to

me, his hand resting lightly on my back as he waits for an explanation.

'One of my staff resigned. In fact, she walked right out the door. After she told me to fuck myself.'

Aidan is visibly shocked. He struggles to understand the corporate world, the lack of discipline and respect, the frequent breaking of ranks. Today is one of those days when I wish my work environment was more like his. Respect is underrated at Real Cover Insurance. Everyone, even the graduates, has an overblown sense of self-importance.

'And it was so *unnecessary* . . . Really, *really* stupid of her.'

I can see Jane at home now, trying to explain to her husband, realizing the enormity of what she's done.

The worst thing – for her – is that she won't be able to get a reference. *Fuck you, Sophie McCarthy*. There's no going back from that, no smoothing things over, no ending on a nice note. It would be a farce, not to say downright dishonest, for me (or anyone else at Real Cover) to recommend Jane Dixon as a potential employee.

'Well, it sounds like you're better off without her,' Aidan says with a wry smile.

Yes and no. I will miss Jane, in some respects. She had years of experience and knew her way around complex actuarial concepts as well as the minefield of office politics and policies. Now I'll have to hire someone new and invest lots of time in teaching them all the things Jane already knew.

Just the thought of this makes me feel even more tired.

Sometime later I wake to the clatter of crockery. Aidan is setting out plates.

'What time is it?' I mumble.

'Seven. You've slept thirty minutes or so. Feel any better?'

His voice is clear, as is my vision, which I test on various items around me: the coffee table, a picture frame, the TV.

'Yes.' I yawn and stretch, then sniff. 'Is that curry?'

'Yup. I'll dish it up now, if you're ready.'

'Just give me another ten minutes, to wake up properly.'

Ten minutes later, punctual as ever, Aidan drags the coffee table closer to the couch.

'Special privileges for the sick and tired.'

'Lucky me.' I smile up at him, grateful for how he's always thinking of me, taking care of me, making things easier when and where he can. I know Mum and Dad don't understand why I'm with him, especially after what he's done to me. They can't see past all the months in hospital, the rehabilitation, the ongoing pain, the fact that I'll never be the same again.

I can. I see the caring, considerate man underneath that controlled exterior. I see that his core is one of kindness, despite the aggression that's often required of him in his job. He is not a perfect man. He has made mistakes and I'm sure will continue to do so. But he is the sort of man who will do anything – anything in his power – to rectify his wrongs. Hurting me was a colossal mistake. But he's making up for it. He's doing everything he can. And that has to count for something, right?

He sits next to me on the couch, balancing his plate on his knees. For a while we eat in silence. The curry is good, just the right level of spicy, the chicken melt-in-my-mouth tender. Aidan is a very competent cook. Self-sufficiency is one of the many things they teach them in the army: cooking, cleaning up, laundry, ironing, sewing on buttons and taking up hems. I can't remember how it was when it was just me living here, not being able to enjoy the benefit of Aidan's many skills.

'Soph?'

'Yeah?' My mouth is full. I'm hungrier than I thought I'd be.

'I need to ask you something.'

'What?'

'It's about Jasmin.'

My heart drops. This is one of his drawbacks: his family. Chloe's bad enough, but at least she's an adult and can be kept at a distance. Jasmin is harder to shut out. She's always there, between us. Kids are like that, ever present, needing constant attention. Parents can never *switch off*. This is the very reason I decided not to have kids: because I need an OFF button. Luckily I came to this decision long ago, as I'd never be able to get through a pregnancy the way I am now, and it would be yet another thing that I'd need to forgive Aidan for.

'Yes?' I prompt warily.

'I know this is your house, not mine. And I know you're especially tired with the return to work, and Jasmin isn't your child, or your responsibility . . .'

'But?'

Aidan puts his plate down on the coffee table and turns to face me. 'Chloe is feeling overwhelmed . . .'

85

'She is?'

'I need to give her a break . . .'

'And how are you going to do that?' I ask, even though I know I won't like the answer.

'Jasmin needs to stay with me some of the time. Every other weekend, to start with. And maybe some weekdays too . . . later on, of course.'

My fork slips from my grip, clanging on to the plate. It's not that I'm shocked. This was always on my risk radar. I was just – foolishly? – hoping it wouldn't eventuate. 'You want her to sleep over here?'

'Yes.' He takes a deep breath. 'It's not just about Chloe, and giving her a break. I miss Jasmin terribly. At the start, it seemed like the right thing to do, keep her with her mother, minimal change to routine, maintaining some distance between you and her. But we're at a different stage now. It's been a few months and we need to evolve to a more long-term arrangement. One that's fair. To everybody. Including you.'

I don't want Jasmin in my house. A nine-year-old child to feed, to entertain, to navigate my way around. *I'm not good with kids.* Not even my own niece and nephew. Just ask Jacob, he'll tell you. The truth is, I don't know what to do with them, how to speak to them, how to relax and be myself around them. It doesn't help that the rules seem to change vastly depending on the exact age of the child . . . What delights a twelve-month-old – peekaboo, clapping hands – doesn't seem to impress a two-year-old so much. It's all too hard, too demanding, and – if I'm honest – too boring. I hate how some people – including my own mother – act like it's the crime of the century not to be infatuated with kids.

Aidan leans forward, his head bowed, his hands clasped together. He looks like he's waiting for a verdict of some sort.

It's only because I love him so much I say, 'OK, if it means that much to you.'

His smile lights up his face. At least one of us is happy.

13

Richard

A date has been set. At long bloody last. The sentencing has been adjourned several times, mainly due to excuses relating to Aidan's job. This or that drill or major operation that happens to be on the proposed date. Everything can seem urgent and super-important when it's related to the army. What's urgent is that bastard being held to account by a court of law. Of course Sophie doesn't see it like that.

'I wish we didn't have to go through this. I wish we could just put the whole thing behind us.'

I have to bite my tongue. It's downright ludicrous, the idea of putting it behind her when she is living with the consequences every moment of every day. I don't want her to be one of those pathetic women. The ones who forgive – again and again – the men who hurt and violate them. The ones who believe all the excuses.

She doesn't look at all well today: white in the face, dark circles under her eyes, that hunched-over posture she has when she's struggling.

'Are you all right, sweetheart? You look washed out.'

She shrugs, tries to make little of it. 'It's been a full-on week ... But some good news, Dad. Aidan and I have bought a car. It's a Golf. I took it for a test drive and it felt right, you know?'

I don't know. I've never been a fan of VWs, but she didn't even ask my opinion. I've helped her buy all her cars, right from her very first set of wheels, when she was eighteen.

'How did you manage the test drive?'

She gives a small laugh. 'You forget all the little movements involved, checking the mirrors, looking over your shoulder, pulling up the handbrake. But I tried not to do anything too suddenly and, overall, I felt great. So you won't need to be my chauffeur any more . . . You must be happy about that!'

'Now I wouldn't say that, sweetheart.'

Despite the terrible circumstances, driving her around has been an absolute pleasure. We've had some great chats while we've been getting from A to B. I like hearing her opinion on things, seeing that fierce intelligence come to the fore. I feel like I've got to know her all over again: her likes and dislikes, what makes her laugh, what ticks her off.

'I'm not planning on driving every day,' she continues. 'It's not practical to take the car into work . . . my muscles would seize up, sitting in the traffic. But it'll be great to zip down to the shops and over to you and Mum. They're just finishing off the paperwork and giving it a clean. It should be here tomorrow.'

I should be happy for her. This is good news, another step forward. It's just the thought of Aidan and Sophie buying a car together. Their lives becoming even more entangled. And hearing this on the same day that I hear about the date for the sentencing.

'I was just popping in to say hello,' I say, unnecessarily. More often than not I call over on her days off. 'Can I do anything for you? Have you had lunch yet?'

'I'd love a sandwich, if you're making one.' She glances towards her laptop, which she was working on when I came in. 'I just need to make a quick call for work.'

There's no bread in either the pantry or the freezer. In the fridge, I find the end of a packet of cold ham and a hunk of cheese. I add this to a plate with some crackers. It's the best I can do.

Sophie is still on the phone. 'The file is on my desk, Hannah. The document should be near the front . . .'

I pop the kettle on and make two cups of strong tea. After five minutes or so she finishes the call.

'Who's Hannah?'

'My new assistant.'

'Is she good?'

Sophie thinks about it. 'Yes, she is . . . She's *obliging*, and I feel quite grateful for that, given that Jane was so hostile all the time.'

Jane is the one who walked out earlier in the week. Sophie told me all about it. Good riddance, in my opinion.

She joins me at the table and sighs appreciatively as she picks up her cup. 'I needed this. Thanks, Dad.'

'Your fridge is empty . . . Will I run down to the shops for you?'

'Less temptation if the cupboards are bare.' Her smile is a self-deprecating one. 'No, I'll go with Aidan tomorrow when we get the car. Thanks, anyway, Dad.'

'Any gardening that I can help with?'

'No, thanks. Aidan caught up with it over the weekend.' She puts some ham and cheese on a cracker, then stalls. 'Actually, if you're looking to pass some time, there is one thing you could do for me . . .'

'Just say it.' Something I can get stuck into. At last.

'The spare room. I need to clear out the boxes from the wardrobe, create some space.'

'Are you having someone to stay?'

'Jasmin.'

Sometimes we can talk for ages without Aidan popping up, and I can almost forget about him. Today is obviously not one of those occasions. Aidan and the new car. Aidan doing the gardening and the groceries. Aidan's bloody daughter coming to stay.

It makes me want to shake her, to shout: *Wake up, Sophie! Aidan's the one who did this to you. How can you ignore that? How can you have him, and now his daughter, under the same bloody roof as you? How can you act like this is a normal relationship, when everything it's built on is rotten to the core?*

Of course I said all those things, and more, at the start. She refused to take heed – it's like he's brainwashed her – and now she won't even allow me to bring up the subject.

'Right,' I say instead. 'Where do you want the boxes to go?'

'In the laundry, behind the door . . . if you can fit them in. Thanks, Dad.'

The boxes don't fit in the laundry because there are too many other things in the way: other boxes (mostly empty), sporting equipment (bats, tennis racquets, mitts, all thrown in haphazardly), and backpacks of every shape and size. I end up clearing out the whole area and running down to the hardware store for a four-by-two storage unit to make better use of the space.

All the while, Sophie takes and makes calls on her phone, talking about files and reports and meetings, working as hard as she would if she were in the office. Three days a week, my arse. Sophie isn't capable of clocking off. She's a workaholic, like me, or at least how I used to be, before I retired . . . the biggest bloody mistake of my life. But Sophie doesn't want to hear my reservations, doesn't want to be told to slow down, to hold back for the sake of her health. And in many ways, it's good to see her like this – busy, focused, in charge. I just can't help worrying. Another relapse would be a terrible blow for us all.

At 2.30 p.m. I stop to make a call to Dee. 'Do you mind making your own way home today, love?'

'Not at all. What're you up to?'

'Helping Sophie with something.'

The new storage unit is missing some screws, and another visit to the hardware store is required. By five o'clock, the unit's assembled, but everything needs to be sorted through before it's put away.

'I'll come back another day to finish this off.'

'There's no rush, Dad. It'll probably be another week or so before she stays over. Aidan and Chloe are still sorting things out.'

Once again I have to bite my tongue, keep what I really think inside.

Sophie stands up from her laptop and comes over to

give me a hug. 'Thanks for today, Dad. You're very good to me.'

'I know. Too good.'

I spot Aidan on the main road, getting off the bus. My brief glimpse of him is oddly clear: one hand on the strap of his backpack, his eyes staring straight ahead as he strides away from the bus, those deceivingly clean-cut features set in concentration. He looks healthy and strong and purposeful. It makes me furious. So insanely angry I want to turn the car around and chase him down. Ram into him over and over again until *his* sternum is fractured, *his* nerves are permanently damaged and *he* doesn't know what a day without pain feels like.

Calm down, Richard. You'll give yourself a heart attack. Calm down. He hasn't got away with it. The date has been set. With any luck, the judge will have a daughter of his own and will be able to imagine the horror of what we've all gone through.

The date has finally been set. I thump my hand against the steering wheel.

If there's any justice in the world – any at all – they'll put him behind bars.

14

Hannah

I had to plead financial hardship to the soccer club. There was no way I could scrape the money together, not with all the other bills. I dreaded the phone call, but the lady I spoke to was so kind. Initially, she suggested a payment plan, but when I told her that my husband had died unexpectedly and explained all the upheaval the boys had been through, she waived the fees altogether. Her kindness moved me so much I started crying. Linda, her name was. Lovely Linda. Let's hope I never meet her face to face. I don't know what's more embarrassing: the fact that I needed to claim financial hardship in order for my boys to have the simple pleasure of playing soccer, or that I broke down and bawled my eyes out to a complete stranger.

The team – the Cheetahs – is warming up down at one of the goals, going through a drill with their coach, Davy. Mum has been impressed with Davy. She likes how he doesn't let the kids get away with much.

'They respect him,' she said after training last week. 'Any fooling around and they have to run a lap of the field. It's a great way to discipline them, and they get fit in the process. Right, boys?'

Apparently both Finn and Callum had to run laps this

week. Does this man – Davy – think that my boys are badly behaved? Does he know that they've lost their father and their home? Does he know about the club fees being waived? I can feel my face getting hot, even though the rest of me is rather cold. Fooled by the blue sky, I decided against a jacket when I left the apartment this morning.

'There's a bite in the air,' the woman next to me comments.

'Yes, there is, isn't there?' My voice sounds stilted, even though I was aiming for friendly.

'Which one is yours?'

'The twins. Callum and Finn.'

She squints in the direction of the boys. Like the other parents, she's dressed well: a trendy jacket and designer jeans in strong, contrasting colours. No evidence of financial hardship there. Can she tell by looking at me? Do my clothes give me away?

'And which one is yours?' I ask politely.

'The girl. She's hard to miss.'

The referee – a dad in shorts and T-shirt, who, like me, must have overestimated the blue sky – calls the teams into position. Callum is centre back and Finn is right forward. The two of them look smart in their new playing gear – red shirt, black shorts and socks – and they fidget as they wait for the whistle. My heart aches. For them. For Harry. For all the upcoming tackles and passes and goals that will remain unacknowledged. It's not fair. It's just not fair.

The whistle blows.

'And we're off,' the woman says. 'Another soccer season under way. Smelly socks and muddy boots. Hooray.'

She's being friendly, and I'm grateful for the effort she's making because nobody else has spoken to me. They're clustered in little groups, chatting and laughing like they've known each other for years. Younger and older siblings are ganged up in similar groups, playing games, weaving between the adults.

'Clear it!' the woman shouts. 'Clear it. Look up. Find a player.'

Callum mistimes a tackle and the opposing team make an early shot at goal. The goalie fumbles before getting a firm hold of the ball, and we all breathe a sigh of relief: there's nothing worse than conceding a goal in the first thirty seconds.

'It's fine, Callum!' I call, because it's obvious he's berating himself for the mistake. 'Next time you'll be ready.'

The goalie, quite a small boy with surprising strength, kicks the ball out over the halfway line, where Finn picks it up and makes a good run forward. He dodges and weaves but forgets to pass – his weakness – and loses the ball to an opposing player.

'Don't forget to pass, Finn!' I yell, louder than I intended, my voice so shrill Davy glances my way.

Harry used to do this. Calling out to the boys to find space, to pass, to jockey. He could project his voice without shouting, unlike me.

I turn to the woman. 'I think I'm in trouble with the coach.'

She waves one hand dismissively. 'Davy's used to us

shouting. He doesn't expect us to stand here completely mute. Anyway, he tells the kids to listen to him and him alone.'

Twenty-five minutes are gone in a flash and we're one goal down at half-time. Davy gathers the kids around to give them a pep talk. They hang on his every word. I can see what Mum meant about him having their respect.

My phone rings in my bag. Sophie. Flipping heck! It's Saturday morning, I obviously have family commitments – I have two young boys, for God's sake. This is exactly why Jane quit, but I'm not going to let it get to me, like she did. I'm going to be level-headed, matter-of-fact and clear about my boundaries. There's no need for it to become acrimonious.

Besides, I'm enjoying the work. Sophie has been giving me some of the more junior parts of Jane's job. I have nowhere near Jane's experience or qualifications, but I like the challenge. I do miss Jane, though. Work isn't the same without her. I miss her seeking me out for quick chats throughout the day. I miss being able to ask her questions freely about how things work around the office. Jane is shrewd and sassy, and I miss the security of having some-one like that looking out for me. I've left numerous calls for her but I don't think she's ready to talk about what happened. There's a rumour that she told Sophie to 'Fuck off'. Given how worked up she was at lunch that day, I have a horrible feeling it's true.

The team goes back on the field and puts everything they have into evening up the score. Luck is against them. The ball whizzes past the post, missing by a whisker.

Again and again it soars over the top of the goal. Then it hits the crossbar with such force the whole structure shakes, it boomerangs down into the goal face but – unbelievably – does not go over the line.

'Come on!' I can't help yelling.

'You can do it!' my new friend shouts, a lot louder and less self-consciously than me. 'Get one back, Cheetahs.'

They're running out of time. The referee is looking at his watch.

Callum makes a clearance at the other end. The ball flies through the air, a midfielder picks it up, passes it forward, and then, miraculously, the ball is in the net. A goal. Finally. Finally. Finally.

Celebrations worthy of the Premier League ensue on the field, the players jumping on top of the skinny boy who scored the goal. The whistle goes, and the first game of the season is over: one all, a draw.

The sun has got a little warmer, and my boys, their faces flushed and sweaty, are in the midst of their new team, celebrating the last-minute comeback. It has been a good morning. There were even a few stretches of time when I lost myself in the game and forgot about Harry and the waived soccer fees and everything else.

The woman, my new friend, is grinning. 'The draw feels like a win.'

She's right. Sometimes, just surviving is an achievement in itself. A dead husband, a repossessed home, a new school and suburb, a mortifying phone call to the registrar of the club. But we're here. We got to play. And, for the moment at least, it does feel like a win.

It suddenly occurs to me that we've talked all this time without properly introducing ourselves.

'I'm Hannah, by the way.'

She smiles, flicking a strand of naturally highlighted hair away from her face. 'And I'm Chloe.' Her daughter comes to stand next to her. 'Also known as Jasmin's mum.'

Jasmin's a pretty girl, her face open and smiling.

'Nice to meet you, Chloe and Jasmin.' My boys are still out on the field, doing some practice penalty kicks with each other. I'll have to go and persuade them that we've had enough soccer for one day. I give Chloe and Jasmin a small wave. 'See you both next week.'

15

Jasmin

I wish Daddy was here. I wish he'd seen the goal. And my tackle on that really good kid. Daddy doesn't care about winning or losing. All he cares about is everyone trying their hardest and 'fighting the good fight'. He would've been proud that we didn't give up.

'You played so well, Jazzie.'

Mum squeezes my shoulders. She looks happy. She's made friends with Hannah, the twins' mum. Mum doesn't have many friends because we've only been living here a year and a half, and it takes a long time for grown-ups to make friends. We've lived in lots of different places because of Daddy's job, and Mum's got friends in all those places, and so do I. I've lived in seven houses, but I can't remember three of them. Daddy's lived in more places than us – East Timor, Iraq and Afghanistan.

'Say thank you to Davy.' Mum gives me a little shove.

This is my second year in the team. Davy was the coach last year too. The twins are the only new people this season. I know what it feels like to be new. At least they have each other. I wish I had a sister, or even a brother. Davy is bent over, packing up the kit bag.

'Thanks, Davy.'

'See you on Wednesday, lass.'

Davy is Scottish. He comes from Aberdeen, which is the third biggest city in Scotland, after Glasgow and Edinburgh. Davy calls all the boys 'son', but I'm the only 'lass' on the team. I used to giggle when he called me lass, but now it makes me a little bit sad because I automatically think of Daddy. I'm really *his* lass. He couldn't come today. Last year he was at all my matches.

'I think you've earned a slushie,' Mum says. 'What do you think?'

'Yeess.'

I get an orange-and-blue slushie at the canteen, and Mum gets a blue-and-red one. We sit on the wooden fence at the side of the field. Another soccer game has started. The kids are older than me. There are no girls on the team.

'What age are they, Mum?'

'Twelve or thirteen, I'd say. Look how well they pass the ball, Jasmin.'

Davy says we need to focus on passing the ball sooner, before we lose it. I tried today, but one time I accidentally passed to the other team. Davy says that we need to work on our fitness too. The best soccer players can keep running and running and never get puffed.

'The sun is lovely now, isn't it?' Mum says, lifting her face to it.

The sun *is* nice and warm, but it's making me sleepy. I was really tired this morning. Mum had to call me three times, and eventually she whipped back the blankets. We were ten minutes late for warm-up. Davy doesn't like us being late so I had to do extra laps. The cold air and the running woke me up.

'Did I play OK, Mum?'

'I told you, you were great.'

'Do people know I didn't get much sleep last night?'

'No, darling. I'm quite sure nobody could tell. Everyone has their own problems to think about.'

Mum and I had high hopes for last night because of the new diet. The 'sugar diet', we call it. It's every kid's dream: two jelly snakes before bed each night. Matthew said that sugar makes most kids hyper, but for a small percentage of kids it has the opposite effect, it actually calms them down. Mum looked sceptical ('sceptical' is one of our extension words at school). Then she said she would try anything at this stage, even something that goes against every rule in the book.

'The jellies didn't work last night, Mum, did they?'

'No, darling.'

'Am I going to have them tonight?'

'Yes. Two weeks, minimum. Then, if it hasn't worked, we move on to the next thing on Matthew's list. That's the plan.'

Daddy came to see Matthew with us, and he was sceptical too. Daddy puts no bad food into his body, and he runs or goes to the gym every single day. He has huge muscles on his arms. Sometimes he would lift me up over his head and hold me up there, pretending to groan under the pressure.

'Careful,' Mum would warn. 'Don't drop her, Aidan.'

She would be grinning, though, and I would be laughing, and Daddy would still be pretending to groan.

One of our other games was when he'd pretend to be a criminal and I would have to try to escape from him.

'What are you going to do, Jazzie?'

'Poke you in the eye.'

'What if you can't get close enough?'

'Kick your kneecap as hard as I can.'

'Anything else?'

'Slam my hand against your nose. Pull your ears. Scream.'

Then I would scream my best scream, until Mum begged me to stop.

'What's your best weapon, Jazzie?'

'My brain. My brain is my deadliest weapon.'

It feels like some of those things will never happen again: him lifting me up in the air like that, our self-defence games, me not having to think twice about whether he'll be at my soccer game.

'Jasmin,' Mum says, in the voice she uses when she has to tell me something serious.

'Yeah?'

'Dad and I have been talking . . .' She runs out of breath. This often happens when she's talking about Daddy. She's really sad too, but she tries to hide it. 'We've been talking about how much he misses you, and how he wants to see more of you . . .'

'Is he coming back to live with us?' I ask hopefully.

'No, he's not. Sorry, darling.' She takes another raggedy breath. 'But he does want you to come and stay the night with him. Maybe every second weekend. What do you think?'

'No.' My eyes fill up. Then my face gets red because I'm

embarrassed. I hope that the older boys playing the game don't notice that I'm being a baby. 'No.'

'I know you'd like to see more of Dad,' Mum continues, as though I haven't spoken. 'This is a way for you to spend some time together.'

'I don't want to stay with him and Sophie,' I say, louder, so she can't pretend not to have heard. 'Sophie doesn't even like me.'

'You know that's not true.'

'It *is* true . . . It *is* true.'

'No, Jasmin, the truth is the other way around. You don't like Sophie because you want Daddy to be with me. It's very normal to feel like this.'

Mum is right. That *is* the truth.

'You can't make me do it. *Nobody can make me.*'

'Jasmin, darling . . . Don't get upset. Take some deep breaths.'

'I'll be better, Mum,' I sob, not caring any more about who is watching. 'I promise I'll go to bed for you. I'll try very hard. I promise.'

I will not get out of bed tonight. Not once. Even if I am awake all night long. I'll prove to her that I can be good.

'It's not that, Jasmin. It's not about the sleeping,' she says, even though we both know it kind of is. 'This is about me and Daddy sharing you. It's what happens when parents separate.'

'Are you and Daddy getting a divorce?'

She bites down on her lip, and I'm sorry I asked the question and wish I could delete it. 'I don't know. Maybe. Eventually.'

Jessica Zang's parents are divorced. She's always forgetting whose house she's going to after school, and last week she was wearing her school uniform on mufti day.

'Daddy and I thought we'd start the new arrangements after Easter,' Mum says. 'That should give you time to get used to the idea.'

I'll never, ever, *ever* get used to the idea.

We walk back to the car and I fling my slushie in the rubbish bin. I'm too sad to drink the rest of it. I'm sadder than I've ever been in my life. I'm *bereft*. Even more than the day Daddy moved out because, even though I cried and cried, I still thought he'd come back. Now I know he isn't ever coming back. I will have to go to him and stay the night, like a visitor.

I don't want to go. They can't make me.

Actually, they *can* make me.

Now I understand how Daniel Morgan must feel when he's cornered by Nathan Finnerty at school.

Trapped. Not able to say the right thing to stop it. Knowing that it's going to hurt.

16

Dee

Sophie has always been Richard's favourite. I'm not saying he doesn't love Jacob. He does, let's be clear on that, as well as the fact that he's a good father to both of them: dependable, practical, caring, in his own blustery way. But he has a different chemistry with Sophie. It's like he comes alive when she's around. He talks more, laughs more and is more interested, engaged, intense. It's always been obvious, even when Sophie was little, that he's completely in awe of how clever and accomplished she is.

Seeing Sophie like *that* – with machines keeping her alive and doctors grave about her prospects of making it – was devastating for both of us. Richard's way of coping was to devote himself to her care and recovery. He also devoted himself to driving her around, keeping tabs on all the medical nitty-gritty and hating Aidan Ryan with all his being. Now, he's *excited* that the court date has been set. This morning, he phoned Dr White and some of the other specialists to see if the prosecution has been in contact. He even intends to do some research on the magistrate, to see what kind he is.

'I hope he's as tough as they come,' he declares when we sit down to dinner.

I sigh. 'And what will that achieve? Sophie has forgiven Aidan. The last thing she wants –'

'She doesn't know what she wants.' He's shouting at me, though he doesn't realize. It's his hearing. 'He's *fooled* her –'

'She's *always* known what she wants, Richard. Have you ever known anyone so clear-headed and decisive?'

He can't argue with this and flounders for a few moments.

'Life has just gone on for him,' he says finally, pain etched in every word. 'Life has just gone on, and you know that isn't fair, Dee.'

I can see where Richard is coming from, I really can. It *is* unfair: Aidan's life being normal while Sophie's will never be. She'll carry this with her for ever – pain management will be part of her life until the day she dies. But she has found it in her heart to forgive Aidan and, if she has forgiven him, then we must too.

'Who knows what was going through his head at the time,' I say gently. 'I imagine that soldiers see some terrible things that must affect –'

He comes back, shouting again. 'Why am I the only bloody one in this family who wants him to be held to account for what he did?'

Richard scowls at his food before attacking it with his fork. I hate it when he's like this: vengeful, furious, bloody-minded. It's like Sophie's pain is his pain. It's like he's living through her. There's a reason for this: he doesn't have enough going on in his own life. He should never have retired. Sophie has become his sole focus, and as result he's stunting her recovery rather than helping it. But he refuses to step back or give her the chance to be more independent.

'I spoke to Jacob today,' I say, steering the conversation to a safer topic. 'It's all systems go for Easter. We'll have to organize an egg hunt for the kids.'

Just thinking of my grandchildren is enough to make me genuinely cheerful: Milli and Hugo in our garden, squeals of excitement on finding the eggs, chocolate smears on their little faces. Oh, I cannot wait to get my hands on the two of them. I just wish they lived closer, so that we could see them a few times a week, be as familiar to them as their own parents. Instead, all we get are a few days here and there.

'Maybe we could have Milli and Hugo stay on,' I say, the idea just occurring to me. 'Just for a night or two extra. What do you think, Richard? A little adventure with Grandma and Grandpa. You could drive them back home at the end of their stay.'

At first, Richard seems too distracted to give the idea any serious thought.

'We could take them into the city,' I persist. 'Catch a ferry, or a train. Children of that age love transport of all descriptions. We could go to Darling Harbour, have an ice cream at Circular Quay. Oh, it would be fun, Richard.'

He seems to perk up, come out of himself a little. 'What about your job, Dee?'

'Oh, I'll take a few days off. Things are so quiet they'll probably be relieved . . . Will I call Jacob after dinner? Suggest it to him?'

He shrugs. 'Why not?'

Jacob seems open to the idea when I phone him up. 'I just need to clear it with Carolyn. She's giving them their bath at the moment. Are you sure Dad won't mind driving them home? It's a four-hour round trip . . . It might be a bit much.'

'Oh, Jacob, your father is looking for ways to fill his time. I can assure you it won't be a problem. Actually, why don't you have a think if there is anything around the house he can help with while he's there? He put in a new storage unit for Sophie last week. He can do the same for you, or even some gardening . . .'

'Mum, you'll be hiring him out next!'

I laugh. 'Oh, he comes free, Jacob. And there aren't many things in life that are free, are there?'

We talk for another few minutes, until one of the children starts howling and Jacob says he has to go.

Richard has already cleaned up the dinner things by the time I hang up. He is a good husband, a good man. Just under-utilized at the moment. Under-utilized and unhealthily obsessed with Sophie: her pain, her career, her house, her relationship with Aidan. Not a good thing, not when your daughter is an adult and should be living her own life.

At least now I have a short-term answer to the problem. Richard can transfer his attention to Milli and Hugo, become more involved in their lives, obsess about them instead. There's no reason at all why he can't make the journey to Newcastle once a week. Two loveable, unpredictable toddlers to focus on. Some badly needed support for Jacob and Carolyn. Sophie's back at work and driving again. She doesn't need Richard as much as either of them thinks.

I'm not being mean. I'm doing this for Sophie's sake as much as anyone's. She's my daughter, and I love her dearly. But her independence is crucial for her future happiness, and, just like the physical parts of her, it needs to be nursed back to health.

17

Hannah

'It was a stupid thing to do,' Jane confesses when we meet for lunch at a café that's a safe distance from the office. She seems relieved to admit that she's made a mistake, a huge professional error her career might struggle to recover from. 'Mick is wonderful, totally supportive, but he works in construction: people walk off the job all the time, apparently without any long-lasting consequences to their career. He doesn't really understand all the protocols I've broken.'

It's good to see her at last. I've missed our daily chats, exchanging updates on our kids, the easy similarity of our lives.

'Are the rumours true? Did you really tell Sophie to fuck off?'

She looks sheepish. 'It was "Fuck you" actually ... Jesus, just thinking about it makes me cringe ...'

I shoot her a sympathetic smile. 'You *were* a little crazy that day. I think it was because you were so tired from being up with Zara.'

Jane nods. 'At the time it felt like an epiphany. As I stood in her office, I remember thinking, *I don't need to put up with this.* The invasion of my home life, the tense atmosphere in the office, the feeling that nothing I do is good enough. The pressure, the bullying, the daily humiliation. *I don't need to put up with it.* Of course I realize now that I was delirious with exhaustion, closer to a breakdown than a breakthrough.'

Our meals arrive. Jane's having a burger and chips: comfort food, she said when she ordered. My chicken salad (the cheapest thing on the menu) looks like an advert for healthy eating by comparison.

Jane chews on a chip and continues berating herself. 'She'd only been back a couple of weeks, for Christ's sake. Surely I could have lasted longer, stuck it out while I figured out an exit plan? I wish I could press the rewind button and put myself back in her office. I would keep my mouth shut. OK, maybe I would put on record that I thought the warning was unfair, but that would be it. I certainly wouldn't resign . . .'

'Or tell her to fuck herself,' I suggest in a diplomatic tone, and we both burst out laughing.

She smirks. 'Then again, it felt *so* good to say it, to let it out . . . I'd been dying to say it for years.'

We laugh again, and then concentrate on our meals for a while. My salad is fresh and flavoursome, but I can't help gazing longingly at Jane's chips. Maybe I should have ordered some comfort food too. Work is busier than ever. Jane has left some big shoes to fill.

'So, Mick was fine about it?' I ask eventually.

She snorts. 'He actually laughed, the idiot. The financial consequences didn't register . . . They might next month, when my salary is missing from our bank account.'

Thank God for Mick. Jane has his income to fall back on, as well as his moral support. She doesn't realize how lucky she is.

'So, what's the plan now? Are you looking for something new?'

She shakes her head. 'I went as far as updating my résumé, and clicked through a few job search websites, but I still feel too raw to be going for interviews, to be putting myself out there. I think I need some resolution before I can look for something else.'

I glance up from my food. 'Resolution?'

'Yes . . . Look, I know that I was the one who actually said the words, who resigned, but I feel like Sophie was deliberately trying to catch me out. Her email on the Sunday night, when she knew it was too late for me to be able to do anything but a rush job. The warning she gave me straight after the board meeting. Jesus Christ, she wouldn't have had that much time to think it through. And it was only an inconsistent assumption . . . It happens all the time. Embarrassing that John Greenland picked it up, I get that. Anyone else but Sophie would've had my back, though. Isn't that what bosses do? Take the flak? It's as though Sophie had been waiting for the right opportunity to teach me a lesson . . .'

'So how, exactly, are you going to get resolution?' I enquire, pushing my plate – with quite a lot of green leaves left on it – to one side and resting my elbows on the table.

'By hiring a lawyer . . . and lodging an unfair-dismissal application . . . Want some of my chips?'

I pop one in my mouth. As I suspected, it's infinitely

nicer than lettuce leaves. 'But you weren't exactly dismissed, were you?'

'Dismissal can include resignation if the resignation was forced by the conduct of the employer,' she says, then grins, 'That's a quote directly from the Fair Work website.'

Interesting. But I don't know if I agree that her resignation was forced.

'I see. Well, I –' My ring tone interrupts me mid-sentence. I glance down at the screen. 'Speak of the devil.'

'You shouldn't answer that. You're on your lunch break, for Christ's sake.' Jane seems to realize how harsh she sounds and smiles, to take the edge off. 'Sorry, Hannah. I don't mean to be bossy. It's your business how you handle Sophie.'

True, it *is* my business. Sophie has certainly upped the ante these last few weeks, my phone ringing more at night and weekends with requests that supposedly can't wait. But I'm managing it, managing her. At least, I think I am. More often than not I do what she asks, because I'm still enjoying the work. Besides, it's a short-term thing: the recruitment process has started for Jane's replacement and everything should revert to normal when the new person starts. Then I'll be lamenting how boring my job is again.

'Actually, I seem to be getting on OK with her,' I say awkwardly.

Jane looks slightly miffed at this. 'Well, there's no problem, then.'

The waitress comes and asks if we'd like coffee.

'Have you got enough time?' Jane checks, obviously keen.

'I'll have a quick one.'

The waitress goes again, and Jane apologizes. 'Look, I'm sorry if I've overstepped the mark. You obviously have a different relationship with Sophie. We're toxic, me and her. Too much has happened between us. Too much history.'

Almost by agreement, we change the subject. For the next few minutes we talk about our kids. Jane's youngest, Madison, winning the school cross-country, showing grit and stamina that her parents didn't know she had. Jane is particularly thrilled she was at the finish line to jump and cheer.

'I'm always at work for school cross-country. I took about five hundred photos, although the poor thing was beetroot and so tired she could hardly stand on the podium.'

My phone rings again. I turn it off and toss it back on the table. I want Jane to see that I am setting boundaries, that I can manage this.

Jane stares at my phone for so long it's as though she's gone into a trance. Then we're right back to where we left off: Sophie. 'Once, when I was at the funeral of a friend, she tried to phone me four or five times. She knew where I was that day. I distinctly remember telling her that Alice had died from breast cancer and I would need to take a day off for the funeral. I remember crying in Sophie's office. Alice had gone downhill so fast I was in shock. Sophie – surprisingly – was quite sympathetic. "Take whatever time off you need," she said, or something along those lines. The funeral mass was in one of those lovely old churches in the city. The family had asked me – one of her closest friends – to do the eulogy. As I was standing at the lectern, sharing with the other mourners what I loved about Alice and why I would miss her so much, trying to keep my tears and nervousness in check, my phone vibrated in my pocket: Sophie. Later, when we walked behind the coffin to the waiting hearse, my phone started to go again. And then, in the function room of the pub where we shared stories, cried some more, and got very drunk, Sophie tried to get hold of me several more times. In the end, Mick lost patience, grabbing the phone out of my hand, and bellowing, "We're at a bloody funeral, Sophie. Whatever it is can wait until tomorrow."'

'That's awful, Jane. She must have forgotten where you were.'

'Obviously,' Jane concedes. 'But that doesn't change how she made me feel that day: hounded, harassed, like my grief didn't matter to her.'

I wonder who gets to decide about the unfair dismissal. How much weight will be put on incidents like this? I know Sophie must have forgotten that Jane was at a funeral. If I can arrive at this explanation, then whoever decides the unfair dismissal will too. They'll see a boss who works her staff very hard, trying to get the best out of them. They'll see a staff member who feels badgered and constantly under pressure. But more than anything they'll see a clash of personalities, two women who are refusing to meet in the middle, to cooperate with each other.

I stand up, leaving my half-finished coffee behind.

'I'd better get back . . . I'll tell everyone you said hello.'

Jane nods, bites down on her lip. 'I miss them . . . I miss

my job . . . Jesus, I wish I'd kept my mouth shut and put a complaint through HR instead.'

'I know, I know. But maybe it's not a bad thing it came to a head.'

'The adrenaline was short-lived,' she admits, close to tears now. 'I felt like throwing up afterwards.'

I wish I could stay longer, give her the reassurance she needs that it will all be OK, that things have a way of working out. But I've been gone almost an hour and have stacks of work to get through before I can go home this evening.

I take my purse from my bag, getting ready to leave my share of the bill.

She waves me away. 'My treat.'

'Flipping heck, Jane. You're unemployed, if you hadn't noticed.'

This makes her laugh. 'It's a thank-you for allowing me to bend your ear. As I said, Mick doesn't get it.'

When she rang to make the arrangements for today I initially suggested a sandwich in the park. She snorted, saying she didn't want to come all the way into the city for a boring old sandwich. Her offer to pay makes me suspect that she knows I don't have the means for too many lunches like this.

I bend down to kiss her on the cheek. 'Let's do it again soon. My treat next time.'

I weave my way through the tightly packed tables in the café, my thoughts still on Jane: how funny and generous and smart she is, and how Sophie is her Achilles heel.

Once outside, I turn on my phone again. Only the two missed calls from Sophie. See, nothing to get stressed about.

18

Richard

'Have you checked the shed . . .' Dee prompts, when the kids, their baskets full of Cadbury mini eggs, wrongly assume that the hunt is over.

'The shed,' Hugo parrots, and lunges in that direction.

'Great,' Carolyn mutters. 'More chocolate.'

Jacob takes her hand in his. 'Don't worry. We'll sneak some for ourselves.'

It's good to have them here. Dee is right, we should do this more often. I think the car trip has put them off. Two small children, only fifteen months apart, with at least one of them – if not both – likely to scream the whole way down the motorway. Two hours of driving is not much. I suppose two hours of screaming is.

Jacob seems to read my thoughts. 'It wasn't so bad this time . . . They were pretty good in the car.'

'Yes, they were.' Carolyn's gaze falls on Milli, who's frowning in concentration as she endeavours to unwrap the foil from one of the eggs. 'Hopefully, they'll be just as well behaved tonight.'

It's obvious that Carolyn is anxious about leaving the kids with us. According to Dee, she's never had a night away from them. What's the worst that could happen?

One of them getting hurt. Or being sick during the night. Or getting out of bed and somehow escaping the house without Dee or me hearing. Truth be told, I'm a bit anxious myself.

Milli has figured out the foil wrapping and is already on her second egg.

Carolyn drops Jacob's hand. 'OK, that's enough. We'll put the rest away for later. After lunch.'

Hugo reluctantly delivers his basket into his mother's outstretched hand but Milli isn't so easily persuaded.

'No.'

Milli says no even when she means yes but this time she's saying exactly what she means. She has a formidable look on her face, and it's clear there's no way of recovering the basket without forcibly prising away each one of those stubby, chocolate-stained fingers.

'No,' Milli repeats, in case there is any doubt.

'Yes,' Carolyn and Jacob say, in perfect unison.

'Noooooooo. No. Noooooo. No. Noooooo.'

'We call this the "No" song,' Jacob says cheerfully. 'It has a catchy melody and beat. Milli needs to work on the lyrics.'

I laugh. It's not right to encourage Milli's defiance, but I can't help being delighted by her.

Jacob sweeps his daughter into his arms, Carolyn swipes the basket from her loosened grip, and then Jacob pivots her so she's upside down. 'The best thing about this manoeuvre is that it not only distracts her but gives me the satisfying illusion of emptying all those negative thoughts out of her stubborn little head.'

Milli squeals, I laugh again, and then the garden gate rattles. Sophie and Aidan are here.

Two stuffed toys – rabbits – are propped in each of Sophie's arms. Buck teeth, floppy ears and oversized, glassy eyes that seem to stare at us all. 'Happy Easter,' she says.

Milli kicks until Jacob turns her the right way up and sets her down. 'Bunny . . . Bunny.'

Hugo jumps up and down on the spot. 'The Easter Bunny's here. The Easter Bunny's here.'

Milli moves fast for such a sturdy girl. Within seconds she's at Sophie's legs, her chubby hands reaching up.

'Bunny, bunny, bunny,' she chants.

'Hello, Milli.' Sophie bends down to hand the rabbit to her niece.

'Say thank you,' Carolyn instructs, sounding unnecessarily terse.

'Dank you,' Milli says, in a rare moment of obedience, and toddles off, the rabbit almost the same size as she is.

Hugo receives his bunny and prances around the garden with it.

Well, this should make Dee happy: she's always going on about how Sophie should make more of an effort with the kids. She even complains when Sophie puts money in a birthday or Christmas card.

'Money means nothing at this age.'

These rabbits would've taken some thought; they're clearly not something Sophie happened across at the newsagent's or chemist's. She must have gone shopping with Hugo and Milli specifically in mind.

Aidan comes to shake hands with Jacob and me. Jacob looks every bit as awkward as I do. When was the last time these two met? Have they seen each other since the hospital?

'Now, who'd like a drink?' Dee asks.

Aidan nods. 'A beer would be good.'

'Sophie, would you like anything?'

'No, thanks . . . I'm driving.'

I should ask how the Golf is going, but I can't seem to find the words. I suppose I'm still hurt that she didn't consult me.

'Carolyn? Jacob? Richard?'

Jacob asks for a beer, Carolyn a wine, and I decide to stick to water. My mood seems to have plummeted since that bastard walked through the garden gate as though he had a right to be here.

By the time Dee's distributed the drinks, Milli has found Aidan. She and her rabbit are perched on his hip. Her eyes are fixed on his face, studying him, as though he is the most fascinating man she has seen in her life. Milli is a funny little thing, given to strong likes and dislikes. She has obviously decided that Aidan falls into the former category, and has staked her claim on him early. I can see Dee watching closely. Later on she'll say to me that children are a good judge of character. Rubbish.

'She's pretty heavy,' Carolyn says to Aidan. 'Feel free to let her down.'

'I don't mind.' He hoists her higher. 'I miss it. Jazzie is nine now . . .'

'Time for lunch,' Dee says briskly. She finds it insulting

that Aidan's daughter gets to stay in Sophie's spare room, when her own niece and nephew have hardly set foot in the house. At least we're agreed on that.

Lunch is roast beef and dessert is strawberry meringue, Dee's speciality. I have flashbacks to other Sunday dinners around this same table, realizing that we were happier then. The split (Jacob and Dee in one camp, me and Sophie in another) has become more distinct over the years, the differences of opinion more pronounced. Now, with Aidan in the picture, tension levels are at an all-time high. I want to say something about the court date, but both Dee and Sophie would be furious.

Jacob gets up midway through the meal to help himself to another beer.

'The food will absorb it,' he says, in answer to my frown.

Then he has a second helping of lunch and it's Carolyn's turn to frown.

'You'll have no room left for our dinner tonight.'

Dee asks where they're going for dinner. Carolyn tells her about the posh restaurant she's booked but I can't catch all the details because it's difficult to hear when there are a few conversations going on at once. Hugo is blabbering on about Spiderman, mainly to Aidan, who's sitting next to him, and Jacob is talking quietly to Milli, coaxing spoonfuls of mash into her mutinous mouth. Sophie isn't saying much. I don't know if it's because she isn't feeling well or because of the lack of rapport between her and Jacob. They don't really get along and, like Dee, I struggle to understand why. Sophie likes to admire people, and maybe she thinks – quite wrongly – there's nothing she can admire about Jacob. Or maybe she gets annoyed because she feels that he doesn't admire *her* enough or doesn't give her any credit for her achievements. The need to admire and to be admired is wound in there somewhere, I know that for sure, in addition to the fact that they used to squabble a lot when they were kids. Let's just say that they don't bring out the best in each other, Sophie and Jacob. It's upsetting for both Dee and me.

Carolyn and Jacob leave straight after lunch.

'Bye, Mum! Bye, Dad!' Hugo yells cheerfully, holding Dee's hand as we all stand by the kerb to wave them off.

Milli doesn't look happy to be left behind, but at least she's not bawling her eyes out. She and her rabbit are re-installed on Aidan's hip.

'Well, it looks like we were worrying for nothing,' Carolyn says through the open window of the car, sounding a little put out about the children's nonchalance.

'It's good, right?' Dee says brightly. 'We don't want tears.'

'Yes, it's good . . . Is it silly to miss them already?'

Jacob takes off before Dee has the chance to answer.

'We should get going too,' Sophie says, when Jacob's car is out of sight. 'Thanks for lunch, Mum.'

It takes some time to extract Milli from Aidan. She starts sobbing when he puts her down, turning on a waterworks show that was strangely missing for the departure of her parents. Sophie starts the car. The engine sounds gravelly and I can't help noticing some scratches on the paintwork. Why the bloody hell didn't she ask me to look it over?

As we go inside with the children my thoughts – without warning, without my permission – jump from Sophie's current car to her previous one, a dark-grey Mazda 3. Brand-new, it was. I negotiated a great price with the dealer and Sophie and I went for a drink afterwards, to celebrate. When I think of it: clinking our wine glasses, laughing gleefully about the discount, no inkling at all that only a few months later the Mazda would become a mangled jumble of metal holding up peak-hour traffic on Anzac Parade.

19

Sophie

It was an accident. I was minding my own business, driving to work. He was driving his wife to a doctor's appointment, I heard later on. Traffic was moving, for once. Maybe it wouldn't have happened if the traffic had been going at its usual snail's pace. Or – if it was destined to happen – then at least it would have been less serious. Sadly, it *did* happen, and at relatively high speed, *and* it was serious. The first I knew was when I saw a flash of silver loom in front of me. And I had a moment when I thought, *That's odd, where has that come from?* The very next moment my little Mazda was crushing into it – a silver four-wheel drive – and I was flung against the steering wheel, the air bags bursting open all around me, and the pain . . . I can't properly describe it. *I'm dead*, I thought. *There's no way I can survive this kind of pain. I'm dead.*

Aidan's car came out much better than mine. It was stronger and larger, and both he and Chloe were able to walk away from the accident. I was still conscious when he tried to open the buckled door of my car, to see if I was OK. Apparently I asked him if it was my fault. Then I blacked out.

Every day at work we analyse the statistics of such

accidents. We set car-insurance premiums on the basis of driver history and age, car make and model, the mileage of the vehicle, the postcode where it's garaged, and all sorts of factors – including data on accidents – that we consider relevant. But the fact is, most accidents happen for no obvious reason, or due to a series of unlikely events culminating in disaster. Wrong place, wrong time. In Aidan's case it was a momentary lack of concentration. We all have those, don't we? We've all gone through a red light, or a stop sign, and laughed nervously on the other side about how stupid we are. Aidan simply didn't see me, pulled out right in front of me, and I hit him full force at seventy kilometres an hour. Almost a year later I'm still feeling the reverberations of the impact, and I've only really just grasped that I will for the rest of my life. Aidan's momentary loss of concentration has cost me a lot: two months of my life in hospital, nine months out of work; my confidence in my appearance; my fitness and agility; my faith in having a successful career and future. Not to mention the on–off boyfriend I had at the time of the accident.

But Aidan got it. He understood the enormity of what he'd done to me. How he had wrecked my body, and my life as it was. And he was apologetic, so genuinely apologetic that he got under my skin. I'm quite sure his legal counsel would have advised against any contact, but he stuck to his principles and faced up to me, turning up at my hospital bed, begging me to allow him to make good what he had done. He admitted full responsibility. There was no shirking, or twisting facts, or glossing over the truth of what had happened. He brought me books, games and flowers. Chloe came once, with some magazines.

'We're so sorry,' she murmured. 'Both of us. You did nothing wrong, yet you are here . . .'

I had no interest in listening to her apologies, and I feigned sleepiness. She didn't stay long.

Aidan would come to the hospital after work, in his fatigues. Handsome, commanding, exotic in my sterile hospital room. I saw how the nurses sized him up, and I began to look forward to his visits. He apologized over and over again, to me, to Mum and Dad, to Jacob, to the doctors who were treating me, to anyone who would listen. This was a man who couldn't bear to do wrong, who was completely tortured at the thought of the hurt he'd inflicted on me.

It was an accident, even though 'accident' seems too tame a word to describe it. Calamity? Catastrophe? The worst day of my life? But some good did come of it. I met Aidan. Granted, not the most romantic way to meet my future partner. Certainly not the most straightforward, with police and doctors and distraught families to contend with. He continued to stay in contact after the hospital, calling around to my house, doing what he could: changing light bulbs, mowing the grass, before moving on to more intimate chores, like hanging out my washing and making meals (and every now and then he would stay on and eat with me). It was months before I admitted to him that I loved him, and another few months before he reciprocated, saying that he had feelings too, and more months again before he was prepared to leave his family (he moved in with a friend for a few weeks before moving in with me). The guilt he still carries over that fateful morning is now combined with the guilt about leaving Chloe and Jasmin. I have never met such an honourable man. It was one of the things that attracted me to him – the honour, the honesty, the strength of character. Now I can see that it's both a good thing and a bad thing. Aidan's guilty conscience is a weight on our relationship. Chloe and Jasmin are never far from his thoughts. Sometimes it feels as though they're in the house with us, forever hovering in the background, silently urging Aidan to come back to them.

But I love him, and he loves me. Yes, we met in terrible circumstances. Yes, it's unfortunate that he was married. And, yes, everyone seems to have an opinion about our relationship: that it's doomed, that I only fell for him because I was terribly vulnerable, and that his feelings were spawned from guilt. I've heard it all before, hundreds of times, mostly from Mum and Dad.

'He has a *family*.'

'It won't last.'

'You were at your lowest, your weakest.'

It *will* last. Aidan isn't the first man to leave his family because he's fallen in love with someone else. He fought his feelings, tried to deny them for Chloe and Jasmin's sake, but in the end they were simply too strong to suppress. And my feelings are just as powerful. Not only do I love Aidan, I *admire* him. He maintains high standards in all aspects of his life. He's smart. He's extremely competent and can-do. He has determination, self-discipline, courage. There's a lot to admire. And come on, aren't I entitled to some happiness? Aren't I entitled to him? Haven't I sacrificed more than Chloe has ever had to sacrifice? Not to mention the role fate has had in all this. Now I'm not big on fate, or destiny, or any of that psychic rubbish. But seriously, you have to ask yourself, what are the chances? Of him pulling out exactly when he did. Of me being in that stretch of road exactly when I was. Of our cars colliding. Of the undeniable, powerful chemistry between us as we got to know one another.

Another thing I feel like telling all the detractors is: *Don't underestimate our strength.* We're fighters, both of us. We'll get through whatever ups and downs are ahead. Aidan and I have endurance beyond what anyone can even begin to understand or imagine.

20

Chloe

I was there when it happened, the moment we cut off Sophie McCarthy on her way to work, the moment our marriage fell apart. I was there, but I wasn't looking. My thoughts weren't on the cars whizzing past on the main road we were trying to join. My thoughts were elsewhere: the fertility clinic on the other side of town. If we were going to be late for our appointment. If the transfer would work this time. If the embryo they'd chosen had XX or XY chromosomes, and Jasmin – nine months from now – would have a little brother or a little sister. I remember feeling jittery with excitement – we'd been waiting such a long time for this. I was apprehensive too – what if it didn't work again? I couldn't bear the disappointment. And I was annoyed that we were behind schedule – Jasmin had been particularly hard to coax out of bed and we'd been slightly late dropping her at her friend's house (the mother was going to take both girls on to school). The very last thing on my mind was Aidan's driving.

That's what's so maddening: I normally look whenever Aidan pulls out, and I almost always say something: *Go. You're all right. Wait. Hurry up.* It's an automatic reflex and, even though I know it's annoying, I can't seem to help it.

It exasperates Aidan, the fact that I can't shut up and let him drive. But I didn't look that morning. I didn't tell him to stop, to wait. I didn't warn him that there was not enough space, not nearly enough time, or that the oncoming car was practically upon us. The first I knew was the violent jolt, my ear belting against the side window and Aidan yelling out.

'Fuck ... I didn't see it ... Fuck, fuck ... Are you all right, Chlo?'

'Yeah, I'm –' He'd already flung open his door and was halfway out of the car.

As soon as I had a full view of the other car – the concertinaed bonnet, the shattered windscreen, the inflated air bags, the girl slouched forward – I realized that this was no everyday accident. This was serious. The girl was hurt. Because of us.

Aidan had wrestled open the door to her car and seemed to be talking to her. She had dark, glossy hair. That was all I could see of her.

'Call an ambulance, Chlo.' Aidan turned his head around to face me. There was blood trickling down his face from a nasty-looking gash on his scalp, but he seemed to be unaware of it. The colour had leached from his face, leaving it a sickly shade I'd never seen before.

'Are you all right?'

'Damn it, never mind me, she's losing consciousness.' He dug in the trouser pocket of his uniform, extracting his phone, which he tossed my way. 'Tell them it's urgent.'

My fingers were shaking so much it took two attempts to dial. Then the operator fired questions at me: what, when, where. I held the phone to Aidan's ear so he could answer what I couldn't.

'No, she isn't conscious at the moment. She was at first . . . Yes, she has a pulse but it's weak . . . No, I won't move her. I think she's broken some ribs. Her breathing sounds laboured, so maybe some lung damage too . . . No fuel leakage that I can see.'

His army training had kicked in. Even though he was as shocked and devastated as I was, he could still function and do what was required. He gave information on the severity of the injuries and stabilized the young woman until the ambulance got there. Aidan's a good person to have around in an emergency: level-headed, practical and trained in first aid, as well as many other things.

The ambulance seemed to take an eternity and, in the end, two arrived. One of the other witnesses must have made a call too. Aidan's cut obviously needed attention, and my ear was really hurting at that point, so Aidan and I were taken to the hospital in one of the ambulances; the young woman went in the other. I caught a brief glimpse of her on the stretcher before we left: her deathly white face under the dark hair, bruising and blood around one eye, an oxygen mask sealed over her mouth, and one arm hanging lifelessly over the side. I realized that our lives were changed for ever.

'I pulled out right in front of her,' Aidan explained to the police when they took his statement at the hospital. 'I can't believe I did it . . . I just didn't see her.'

The police officer – a man in his fifties who had obviously been around a while – seemed somewhat startled by his honesty.

'Any drugs or alcohol in your system, sir?'

'None.'

Aidan's cut needed four stitches, and he had to give blood and urine samples. They sent me for a CT scan. It turned out I had a temporal bone fracture and a ruptured eardrum. It wasn't severe, and surgery wasn't required, but it hurt . . . a lot. I felt I had no right to complain, though, not when the young woman's injuries were obviously so much worse.

Both Aidan and I were discharged from the hospital by noon. We caught a taxi home. Very little was said on that journey. Both of us were feeling utterly shocked and miserable.

'Why does Daddy have a bandage on his head?' Jasmin asked when one of the other mothers dropped her home from school. 'What happened to him?'

She asked the question of me, even though her father was standing right there with us. Probably because she could sense how shell-shocked he was, how incapable of answering even the most basic question.

'Mum and Dad had an accident in the car,' I replied, when Aidan didn't, then I pulled my daughter into my arms, hugging her with a ferocity that surprised us both. 'Thank goodness you weren't with us.'

Aidan was like a caged animal for the next few weeks. He dissected that morning, the series of events that preceded the crash, agonizing over what he could have done differently. He rang the hospital several times – we knew that she'd been taken to Prince of Wales, like us – asking for updates. He discovered her name: Sophie McCarthy. Two weeks later, when the news came through that she was starting to show signs of recovery, he said he wanted to visit, to apologize in person for the hurt he'd caused. He actually asked for my opinion.

'Do you think I should go to see her?'

He was a wreck at that point, hadn't slept properly for nights.

'I think that's a marvellous idea.'

I wish I could take it back, that permission, just as much as I wish that we had left earlier for the fertility clinic that morning, and that I hadn't been so distracted in the car.

We never went back to the clinic. The thawed embryo that was due to be transferred into my uterus was refrozen, on our instructions. It didn't seem right to be starting a new life when we were unsure if Sophie would survive. Then, when it became clear that she would pull through, there were other consequences to be dealt with: Aidan's torment over what had happened, having his driving licence suspended by the police, the fact that he insisted on pleading guilty to negligent driving. Then waiting to be sentenced, to be punished for that tiny moment of inattention. And still waiting (Aidan has now been given a new date, in May, which looks like it'll go ahead). Needless to say, with all that going on, the myriad emotional and legal consequences, there was never the right time to talk about our frozen embryos, about when one of them might be thawed again and given the chance to be part of our family.

The army has a lot to answer for when it comes to

babies and having a family. Months on end without seeing my husband at all, and then months of readjustment when he got back from whatever godforsaken place they had sent him to and we felt as though we were falling over each other. Even when he was in Australia, on home soil, they still moved him around. Seven different houses since Jasmin was born. A horrendous cycle of packing and unpacking, some items never even making it out of the boxes before it was time to move on. Not to mention the exhausting process of making new friends, putting yourself out there, only to turn around and leave just as those connections are starting to take hold and mean something.

On top of being so unsettled, there was also a bit of complacency about our second child, because Jasmin had been conceived so easily. It took us a while to wake up, to realize that number two was going to need a little help: specialists, examinations for both of us and a surgical procedure for me. Then Aidan got posted to Afghanistan and everything was put on hold. We were living in Canberra when I finally accepted that it wasn't going to happen naturally and we needed to go down the IVF path. I found a clinic and a specialist and had some eggs harvested. Then we moved to Melbourne. We implanted one of the Canberra embryos in Melbourne, but it didn't work. Maybe it was angry with us for leaving it there, in storage, for almost a year. Maybe it, like us, didn't appreciate being moved from one city to another. Before I had the chance to rally myself, to go for round two, the army sent us back to Sydney again.

So you can see where my head was at that morning on our way to the clinic. I was thinking: *This is it. At long last. We're on our way. Our embryo, our baby-to-be, is waiting for us. Sorry that we have kept you waiting all this time, but we will make it up to you. We will love you so very much, darling.*

Not once did I think we would hit another car. Or that my husband would eventually fall in love with the driver of that car. Or that he would leave me and Jasmin for her. When did I lose him? At what point, exactly? That first visit to see her at the hospital? Or one of the later visits, when he realized there was something happening between them. Or maybe it was even later, when he would go to her house and do odd jobs around the place, desperate to make it up to her, to make good the wrong he had done. What does it matter, anyway? Whether I lost him in a gradual way, bit by bit each and every time they met, or if it was a sudden and definite moment in time, an epiphany that startled them both. All that matters is that those confused and often miserable months following the accident led to the night he sat me down, admitted that he had 'feelings' for Sophie and thought he should move out for a while, to think things through. '*I haven't cheated on you. I promise I haven't cheated on you. But I can't deny that I have these deep feelings for her. I'm sorry, Chloe. I don't know how this happened. I wasn't looking for it. But I have to be honest with you, with myself. I can't hide it. I'm so sorry.*' A few weeks of limbo followed, when he slept on the couch of one of the officers at the barracks. Sorting through his feelings, striving to do the 'right thing', to be as moral as he could be in the circumstances, when it had become painfully obvious – even to me – that he would eventually choose Sophie.

Aidan was the most loyal and trustworthy of husbands. Him leaving me was as inconceivable as me leaving him, so I never saw this coming. But I was dreadfully worried about him after the accident. He wasn't the same man. He was plagued by what he had done, couldn't come to terms with it. Control – everything is about control in the army. Accidents are hard to understand for men like Aidan. He was at fault, so he had to take responsibility, he had to make good. And of course he is not the kind of man who lets himself off lightly. Aidan would go to lengths that no one else would dream of to make things right.

Every month I get a bill for the storage of our embryos. It was always strange – even when Aidan and I were together – paying for the embryos to continue to exist in whatever form of life they are at. When I got a bill last week it felt like the saddest moment of the last year, and that's out of so many dreadfully sad moments I don't know how or where to start cataloguing them. I paid the bill. I cried on and off for the rest of the day, for those three poor little embryos, waiting to be thawed, to be transferred, to be born, to be loved, to be part of a family.

I was there, right beside him, when it happened. Jasmin could have had a brother or sister by now, if only I had looked.

21

Hannah

Today I'm going to make more of an effort with the other parents. I'm determined, so determined that I suspect it shows on my face and I probably look more scary than friendly.

'Helloooo. I'm Hannah, Callum and Finn's mum.'

'Oh, the twins,' says one of the dads. His tone implies that my boys already have a certain notoriety and my determination is instantly punctured, making me want to slink into the background.

'Which is which?' asks one woman politely.

'Callum is the bigger one. Much to Finn's disgust.'

They smile at that. Nobody has offered their name yet. The men all look similar. Board shorts, surf T-shirts and baseball caps. None of them seems to feel the chill in the air. The women, by contrast, are overdressed: stylish scarves, padded jackets, jeans, boots.

'So who belongs to who?' I ask, forcing myself to soldier on.

Various children are pointed out to me, and I try to retain whatever names I can. Some of the parents tag on their own names to that of their offspring, and within moments all the names are tangled in my head. Is Josh the name of the dad or the kid?

A young child comes up, sobbing and holding out her arm. The parents crowd around her, examining her injury.

'Let's see. Only a scratch.'

'What happened, love?'

One of them produces a lollipop. 'Look what I found in my bag.'

They're nice people. It's just that they've known each other for years. I can't expect to infiltrate their group in one measly go. I move away as unobtrusively as I can. Job done. I made the effort. Next week I'll chat to them again. That's all I can do.

My phone rings, and I don't even have to look to know who it is. It wouldn't be Saturday morning without a call from Sophie. Sometimes I can laugh it off, call her a workaholic and leave it at that. On other occasions, like now, I get a tight feeling in my chest. What does she need? How long is it going to take? How am I going to squeeze in the time?

I know Sophie's intentions are good – she wants everyone in the department to be the best they can be – but in her enthusiasm she forgets what time of the day or night it is, the fact that weekends are meant to be a time of rest, and that some of us have children who need to be cared for.

My phone rings out. I'll pick up the message later, at home. Hopefully it won't be anything too complex.

The game is about to kick off when I notice Callum on the bench with another kid. His head is down and, even though his face is hidden, I can picture the scowl on it. He was busting to get on the field this morning, and would hate not being on the starting team.

Please, Callum, don't make a scene. You'll get your turn.

'Run, Jasmin. Don't just stand there.'

I hear Chloe before I see her. There she is, further down the sideline, standing beside a tallish man. Her husband? Something in how they're standing sets them apart from the other parents: remarkably straight, heads high. My eyes fix on her husband. Short hair, tanned, very handsome for this rather ordinary Saturday-morning setting. Lucky Chloe.

It's a tough game. The other team are significantly bigger and are using it to their advantage. The goal, when it comes about fifteen minutes into the game, has an air of inevitability. Our goalkeeper – his actual name is jumbled up with all the others I've heard this morning – looks as if he's about to burst into tears.

'Head up, son,' Davy, the coach, shouts in his thick Scottish accent. 'It's all right. Don't worry.'

Davy continues to bellow instructions, and the kids nod to show they understand. They put up a good fight, but the opposition step and weave around them and score another two goals. Finn has hardly touched the ball; all the play has been down at the other end. Callum's still on the bench, busying himself kicking dirt with his boot. Davy must have forgotten about him.

Chloe comes to stand next to me. 'We're under a bit of pressure this week.'

'Looks like it.' I smile, grateful that she came to say hello.

'Goodness me, those kids are huge. I can't believe they're under ten.'

'I was thinking the same thing.'

'What are they feeding them?'

She stays next to me, shouting the odd direction but not as vocal or as loud as she was last week. Maybe her husband doesn't encourage it.

Half-time comes and goes without Callum going on the field. Quite a few other substitutions have been made by now, and suddenly it becomes obvious to me that Callum is being punished. Something must have happened before the game. His bravado – the scowl, the anger – has dissipated and he looks smaller now and suspiciously close to tears. What did he do to deserve this? What could have been so bad? Does Davy have any idea what he's been through? Tears prick my own eyes just from watching him.

'What's up with Callum?' Chloe asks, no doubt seeing my repeated glances towards the bench. 'How come he hasn't been on? Is he injured?'

'I think he's in trouble with the coach,' I mumble, feeling embarrassed on his behalf. Callum's ten years old. Sitting out a whole game seems rather extreme, whatever he's done.

Chloe stays with me for the rest of the game. She's definitely more subdued than last week. I probably seem different too. I'm feeling increasingly upset, and finding it hard to disguise it. I should have gone up to Davy at half-time and found out what was going on. Typical me, avoiding confrontation. Now I've let Callum down.

'Well, that's it,' Chloe announces when the whistle goes. 'Five–nil. A thrashing.'

'They might've had a chance if he'd let Callum play,' I say, unable to contain myself any longer. 'Excuse me, Chloe.'

Davy is crouched on the grass, the team circled around him, spouting something about marking players and not giving up.

'Sorry for interrupting.' I'm not really sorry at all, and the kids can tell because I can sense their shock at my obvious rudeness. 'I just want to know what happened. Why Callum didn't get to play today.'

Davy regards me through his glasses, which have thick, old-fashioned glass that magnifies his eyes. Then he runs a hand through his hair, which is white and thinning. 'Callum knows why he didn't play. Don't you, son?'

I turn my eyes to my child, who is just fifteen minutes older than his brother, yet so significantly bigger, stronger and more challenging.

'Just leave it, Mum,' he mutters, hanging his head in embarrassment.

'Don't talk to your mother like that, son,' Davy admonishes, in a tone that makes all the kids sit up straighter. 'Apologize now.'

'Sorry, Mum.' Callum's face is burning. He looks completely miserable.

'Tell her why you didn't play, son.'

'Because I was disrespectful.'

Davy nods. 'I run a tight ship. I have rules, and they know I have rules, and there are consequences when those rules are broken. Now that Callum is clear on what the consequences are, I don't expect any more trouble.'

Trouble? I would like to know what his definition of 'trouble' is. A smart remark by Callum? A push or a shove or fooling around? Not listening? Small things, minor transgressions for a child who has endured the worst loss imaginable.

'Rules?' I'm trembling from head to toe. I know I should shut up, walk away, not make a scene. All the things I tell my boys to do when they get angry. But I can't. Because this isn't fair. None of this is fair. And the sheer and utter lack of fairness spurs me on, gives me courage when I'd otherwise have baulked. 'He's lost his father. Did you know that? Callum and Finn lost their father, and they'll spend their whole lives without him there to back them up. What are the rules for that? Tell me –'

'Hannah.' Someone has taken hold of my arm. Chloe. 'It's OK, Hannah. Come –'

'No!' I cry, trying to shake her off. 'I want to talk about rules, and what's fair.'

Davy stands up and brushes some grass off his jeans before speaking. 'You're right, it's not fair these lads lost their dad. But it wouldn't be fair either if I let young Callum here get away with things because of that. Respect, rules and love – that's what they need at this age. You can trust me with them.'

And with that he ambles back to the bench, where he begins to pack up the stray cones and balls into the kit bag.

'Who owns this?' he asks, holding up an abandoned drink bottle.

'Me!' One of the boys jumps up to claim it.

The children and parents, who were all watching the scene with open mouths, suddenly remember that the game is over and it's time to go home and resume the rest of their weekend activities.

Chloe hooks her arm through mine. 'Let's go for a coffee.'

22

Jasmin

Mum takes Hannah to the café down the road. She keeps Hannah's arm hooked through hers until we get inside. It's busy, mainly with the soccer crowd. I recognize some kids from the team we just played. They're grinning and laughing, and you can tell just by looking at their faces that they won. 'Jubilant' is the word that describes them.

'Hannah and I will sit at this table,' Mum says. 'Why don't you kids sit over there?'

They obviously want to have a private conversation, one that we can't hear. Anyway, the tables are really small so it makes sense that we sit apart.

Mum goes to the counter and orders for everyone: coffees for her and Hannah, and strawberry milkshakes for us.

'When did your dad die?' I hope the boys don't mind me asking. Only it would be stupid to ignore it after what just happened with their mum and Davy.

'Last year,' Finn mutters. 'In September.'

Everyone thinks that Finn is the nicer twin because Callum looks angry most of the time. I would be angry, too, if my dad went and died. Maybe their dad had cancer. That happened to one of the girls at my last school. Her mum got cancer in term one and lost all her hair in term two. By term four she was dead. All the mums made dinners for the family. Then there was another mum who got injured in a car crash. She was in hospital for a long time, but she didn't die. The mums made dinners for that family too. Dinner times could be a bit weird, thinking of those other families eating the exact same food as us, imagining how it would feel to have your mum dead or paralysed.

'How did he die?'

'He got a virus.'

'It must have been a really bad virus.'

'It was . . . It made his heart stop beating.'

I'd better check with Daddy to make sure he doesn't have any viruses and his heart is OK. I'll ask him later, when he comes to pick me up. Daddy went home after the match because he had something to do this afternoon. He's coming back to get me at four and I'm staying the night with him and Sophie.

'Was your dad fit?' For some reason I look at Callum. Maybe because he doesn't talk enough.

'Yeah,' he answers. 'Dad used to play soccer at the weekends, on Saturday afternoons. We always went to watch him.'

I don't like the sound of this virus at all. My dad is *really fit*, but that's obviously no guarantee.

I can't think of anything else to say. I don't have a lot in common with the twins, other than soccer. They're always getting time-out tickets at school and having to do extra laps at soccer training. I prefer kids who don't break the rules. But it's harder not to like them now that I know what's happened to their family. My dad isn't dead, but I know exactly how it feels to have him missing. Not seeing him in the morning when I come downstairs. Not chatting with him at dinner time. Not saying good-night to him.

'My dad doesn't live with us,' I offer, hoping this will make them feel better.

'Where does he live?' Callum asks, after taking a loud slurp from his milkshake. His table manners aren't very good. My mum would glare at me if I made a noise like that.

'He lives with his girlfriend. My mum is very sad about it. She cries nearly every night.'

'Our mum cries a lot too,' Finn says.

The three of us look over at the mums. Their heads are bent close, and they look like they're having a Really Serious Discussion. Mum has her arm around Hannah's shoulders.

'Do you have two bedrooms? One at each house?' Callum's being more talkative now. It's funny how he says nothing at first.

Some kids at school have two bedrooms. They spend one half of the week with their mum and the other half with their dad. Or they stay with their dad at the weekend. Their homework and their sports uniform always seem to get left behind in the wrong place.

'I'm staying tonight for the first time ever. I don't want to go . . . My dad's girlfriend doesn't even like me.'

If Mum could hear me she'd tell me that's not true, that

it's *me* who doesn't like Sophie, not the other way round. Mum and Dad were standing very close together at the match. I kept looking at the two of them, hoping they would suddenly realize that they loved each other again, and that Dad's arm would curl right around Mum's waist, the way it used to, and Mum's head would tilt back to rest on his shoulder. Then Mum went over to stand with Hannah, and I felt like bursting into tears, which was really stupid, but I couldn't help it.

Callum is grinning. 'How can you tell she doesn't like you?'

I shrug. 'She always looks either really, really bored or really, really annoyed.'

He laughs. 'All grown-ups look like that . . . Anyway, I bet your dad will spoil you tonight . . . You'll get lots of treats and stay up late, watching telly. Nathan Finnerty's dad lets him go to bed whenever he wants.'

'Nah, my dad's strict about bedtime and I'm not allowed lollies or fizzy drinks when I'm with him . . . My dad's in the army.' I'm proud that Daddy's in the army and keeps people safe. The only thing I don't like about the army is how we had to move house all the time.

'Really?' Callum looks impressed, which makes me even prouder.

'Yeah. He's a captain. He's the boss of lots of soldiers!'

'Wow. I'd like to be a soldier when I grow up.'

'Me too,' says Finn.

There's another silence. The boys have finished their milkshakes. I'm trying to make mine last.

'I wish you got to play today,' I say to Callum. 'We wouldn't have lost as badly. You're our best defender.'

148

He looks pleased. 'Yeah, well, no one is going to get past me next week.'

Everyone will be happier next week. Especially me.

I won't have to worry about staying with Dad and Sophie because it'll be Mum's turn to have me. Sophie won't be annoyed because of my bad sleeping (I already know she's going to get really annoyed). I don't want to go. I don't want to stay in Sophie's house. Maybe she will tease Daddy the way Mum used to. Maybe they will kiss in front of me. Yuck. Yuck. Yuck. I don't want to go. But Mum says I have to. She has to share me with Daddy. I bet she wants a night off from me. She is *exhausted* from me.

'Yeah, bring on next week,' I say.

23

Aidan

I didn't have high expectations for tonight: new bedroom, new house, an entirely new dynamic, combined with Jasmin's sleeping history. Hey, it would've been stupid to expect anything but a challenging bedtime, and that's precisely how it's playing out.

'Is this normal?' Sophie asks, after I order Jasmin back to bed for the third time.

'Normal for her . . . Chloe has been taking her to see a psychologist in the city, but they don't appear to be making much headway.'

'Is it anxiety?' Sophie presses. 'Is she worried about something? School? Some kid who's being mean to her? You and me?'

'She doesn't seem to be overly worried about anything, that's the perplexing thing.'

'Maybe she's picked up on the tension about the court date?'

I have taken great care not to discuss the court date around Jasmin. I've every intention of being upfront with her, when the date is closer, but I can't see the point in worrying her now.

'I'm pretty sure she hasn't overheard anything . . .

besides, this sleeping problem has been going on long before any of that.'

'A mystery, then,' Sophie says.

I slip my arm around her shoulders. 'Thanks for being so good about this.'

She shoots me a smile. 'Will I put the documentary back on?'

'Yeah, do,' I say, even though I suspect that it's only a matter of minutes before we're interrupted again.

Chloe, like me, didn't have high expectations for tonight.

'Maybe we're not ready for this,' she said, when I came to pick Jasmin up.

'We've got to do it sometime . . . And don't tell me you don't need the break, Chlo.'

She looked worn out. She was wearing a floaty green top that seemed to suck the colour from her face. Her feet were bare, as they often are, her toenails painted an interesting shade of orange. Sophie doesn't paint her toenails. Maybe she thinks it's frivolous, or maybe having to bend right over to reach them is painful for her. Sophie tends to avoid colour in her clothes too, while Chloe's mantra is, the brighter the better. I usually try to avoid making comparisons like this.

'Will you text me to let me know when she's fallen asleep?' Chloe asked.

'That's not a good idea. You need to let go . . . Hey, try not to think of us at all.'

Jasmin emerged from her bedroom with her backpack. She came towards us, showing a distinct lack of enthusiasm, which I tried not to take personally.

'Come on, darling,' Chloe urged. 'Daddy's been waiting. Give me a kiss. Be good now.'

She was trying to be brave, and this made me want to give her a hug, but of course that was out of the question. Jasmin and I headed for the bus stop, and Chloe, a forlorn figure standing in the doorway, waved us off. I knew she would cry her eyes out as soon as the front door was shut behind her, when she was on her own.

Jasmin's natural chattiness eventually reasserted itself on the bus. Back at the house I showed her the spare room, and then we went to the park to do some penalty practice. Dinner was home-made burgers, and after that the three of us sat down and watched a PG movie. It felt strange – the dynamics between Jasmin and Sophie and me – but that was to be expected, and I would go so far as to say that everything had gone relatively well. Until bedtime, of course. The real test.

There's a thump, indicating that she has got out of bed again. Sophie sighs. Within moments Jasmin is standing in front of us, obscuring our view of the TV.

'I can't sleep.'

'Move out of the way, please. We're watching something . . .'

She takes a token step to the side. 'I can't sleep, Daddy. I need help.'

'Jasmin, I told you that you were on your last chance, and if you got out of bed again you would have no screen time tomorrow. I was really clear with you . . .'

I'm following Chloe's directions here.

'Three warnings,' she said earlier. 'Then one day of lost technology for every single time she gets out of bed.'

Apparently the psychologist – after a few interesting weeks experimenting with Jasmin's diet – has moved on to behaviour, and having a closer look at how Jasmin reacts to consequences. This is old ground. Consequences were the first thing we tried when this problem started, but they had no impact at all. No matter what we took away from Jasmin (play dates, sports, technology) or what punishments we imposed (chores around the house, time-outs, extra schoolwork), it made no damn difference at all. Chloe knows this too, but she pointed out that those initial consequences might not have been imposed early enough in the night – when we were all still thinking rationally – and that they should be cumulative.

'That's not fair, Daddy,' Jasmin implores. 'Please don't take away my screen time. Please, please . . .'

'You were warned, Jazzie. That's the end of it.'

'But Daddy, I can't sleep. It's not fair. I can't sleep. And now I have no TV or iPad tomorrow . . .'

She's crying now, really crying, and it's a sad sight because she is too old to be behaving like this. Sophie looks completely horrified. OK, so I didn't have high expectations for tonight, but a small part of me secretly hoped that the combination of the new environment and her wanting to save face with Sophie would have a positive impact and keep her in bed long enough to fall asleep.

'Stop it, Jasmin. You got three warnings. There's no negotiating here. No technology tomorrow. And if you get out of bed again, you'll have no technology the day after that. So think twice before you throw back those covers . . .'

'But Daddy . . . I can't sleep. You have to help me.' It's as though she's in another zone and didn't hear a word I just said. And this is why consequences don't work . . . She's not rational when she gets like this.

'Jasmin! Back to bed. *Now.*'

I'm deliberately keeping my eyes averted from Sophie. I can't expect her to take on this problem.

'I'm sorry!' Jasmin shouts, her eyes wild, her arms and legs fidgeting like crazy. 'I can't help it. I'm sorry.'

There is obviously no way my daughter is going to return to bed of her own accord. I don't know if it's the fact that she's so worked up she can't listen to reason, or that her willpower is in fact stronger than mine and her mother's, but nothing will budge her when she gets like this.

'Come on, I'll go with you this time. But that's it, Jasmin. I've had enough for one night.'

We're not meant to do this, escort her back to her bedroom, but after all my years in the army I know a losing battle when I see one.

The atmosphere is tense by the time I get back to Sophie. I have no sooner sat down when there's another thump.

Sophie stands up. 'This is exhausting . . . I'm going to bed.'

'I'm sorry,' is all I can say.

Jasmin gets up five more times and has lost a full week of technology before I give in and lie next to her on the bed.

She's distraught. Sobbing, shaking, saying sorry over and over again.

'It's all right, Jazzie.' I put my arms around her and hold her tight. 'It's all right. We'll talk about it tomorrow. Go to sleep now.'

But it's easier said than done, getting this child to sleep. I know what Sophie is thinking. That Jasmin is doing this for attention. Or perhaps because she's clingy and wants me or her mother close. If that's the case, then why isn't she asleep by now, having got what she supposedly wanted? Instead, it takes a good half-hour for her to wind down, to stop jerking and twisting and to stay still for any length of time. Once or twice, I think she's almost there, then she jumps in my arms again, fighting until the very end. Damn it, Jasmin, you'll be the undoing of me. I'm a captain in the Australian Defence Force, in charge of the daily activities, emotional welfare, qualifications and fitness of a hundred and twenty grown men. Some of them have drinking problems, marital issues, depression, post-traumatic stress . . . you name it. I deal with all their problems. I lead them and train them and discipline them when needed. So why is a nine-year-old girl, my own daughter, so difficult to fathom, to resolve, to get to conform?

As a baby, she would sleep within moments of being cradled in my arms. I remember the day she was christened, the service in the barracks chapel, the christening font an old First World War helmet mounted on a stand. Jasmin slept through it all. She grimaced a little when the water was poured on her head but didn't wake. We laughed, Chloe and me. We were already imagining the other babies we would have – at least another two or three of them – who might be christened in that same chapel, over that same metal helmet.

Where did we go wrong? How did that sleepy baby turn into this girl who has somehow lost the art of falling asleep? Was it all the moving around we did, all those different beds and bedrooms and houses? Or maybe it's a symptom of Jasmin being an only child, and Chloe and I are being obtuse by not recognizing that this problem – at some complex level that is hidden by Jasmin's outwardly sociable nature – is an extreme form of clinginess.

Finally she's asleep, and the twitching and jerking has eased. I could extract myself now, tiptoe from the room, and get into bed with Sophie. I know I shouldn't stay here with her – both Sophie and Chloe would disapprove – but still I do exactly that.

I'm sorry for leaving you, Jazzie. I'm so sorry. I've made things worse by not being there. We will fix this problem. We will. I promise you.

24

Sophie

I tried really hard to be understanding, but *seriously*! A
nine-year-old behaving like that? Up half the night,
screaming and crying, running rings around her mother
and father, and now me? It's downright ridiculous. Aidan
stayed with Jasmin all night. Then we started Sunday
morning with an argument, a hissed exchange in our bedroom so that Jasmin, who was awake and reading in the
spare room, wouldn't hear.

'You slept with her ... How on earth does that help
things?'

'She was upset, Sophie. That was as bad as I've ever
seen her, and it took ages to calm her down. I risked waking her if I left the room. I don't think any of us could face
the whole saga starting all over again.'

Aidan looked awful: pale, tired, stressed.

'I think you're handling this all wrong.'

'And what would you do differently?' he asked, with a
touch of sarcasm, which – given my sabotaged Saturday
night – I did not appreciate.

'I think you should put a lock on her bedroom door.
That's what I think.'

To me, it seemed like the obvious fix, but Aidan looked aghast.

'Lock her up?'

'Lock her *in.*'

'That's cruel, Sophie.'

'What's cruel is that you and Chloe allow her to get away with this behaviour . . .' Aidan's face darkened. Perhaps I had gone too far. 'Come on,' I said, using a nicer tone. 'It's not as though her bedroom is a prison cell. She's got a nice bed, books to read, her things around her. A lock would just stop her from opening the door and proceeding to upset everyone else's night, that's all. It seems pretty reasonable to me.'

Aidan, unfortunately, didn't see my point. 'How would you feel if I locked you in your bedroom at night? It wouldn't matter what things you had with you. That sense of being trapped, of having no control, knowing you can't get out. I know how that feels, Sophie. In Afghanistan I was –'

'And I know how it feels too,' I cut in, not interested in the war story. 'I spent two months bedridden in hospital, remember? And it *was* cruel, but I got on with it and I survived.'

I regretted the words as soon as they were out of my mouth. I could almost see the guilt gushing into Aidan, dragging down the corners of his eyes, his mouth, his shoulders. 'I'm sorry. That wasn't fair. Listen, you're Jasmin's dad. You make the decisions, not me. I'm just giving an outsider's view, nothing more.' I held out my arms, inviting his hug and the end of the argument. 'Love you, OK? . . . Now I'm just going to have a quick shower to wake myself up.'

By the time I was showered and dressed the kitchen was a hub of activity. Aidan was preparing breakfast and Jasmin was laying the table. She was deathly pale, her eyes red and gritty. Even her hands seemed to have a tremor. She was like one of those scare advertisements: this is what happens when you don't get enough sleep.

'I'm sorry about last night, Sophie,' she said, without delay.

'OK,' I replied, even though it was far from OK.

'I'm sorry I ruined your documentary.'

Jasmin looked genuinely regretful, very close to tears, and I felt a stab of sympathy for her.

'Never mind the documentary,' I said, injecting a cheerful note into my voice. 'What's for brekkie?'

On Monday morning I can still feel the effects of Saturday night. I'm quite exhausted when I wake up for work. Weekends are my down time, the only opportunity for my body to recover from the strain it endures during the week. A proper night's sleep, an undemanding environment, that's all I need. And Aidan knows this. He knows perfectly well how wrecked I am by the end of the week, and what it takes to rally myself for the week ahead. I can't sustain a Jasmin performance every second weekend. Aidan knows this, just as I know that he's conflicted by his responsibilities to me and to Jasmin.

I'm not long in my office when Hannah appears with my morning coffee. 'What age are your twins, again?' I ask her, taking the lid off the takeaway cup and letting some of the steam escape.

'They've just turned ten.'

'You had them young,' I comment, carefully sipping the scalding coffee, hoping the caffeine will do its job and perk me up.

'Yes, I did.' She shrugs. 'It just happened that way.'

Hannah's a year younger than me. I found this out a few weeks ago, when it came up in conversation, and it surprised me. She has a weary, harassed air about her, one which busy mothers seem to specialize in. Make-up and jewellery are kept to a bare minimum: there clearly isn't the time or the imagination or maybe the money. Peter told me she's a widow, and I presume it's tough raising two boys on your own. Hannah doesn't speak about it, though, and I respect that. I detest hearing the minutiae of my colleagues' personal lives, their partners' shortcomings – they never have good things to say about their husbands or wives – and their gifted children.

'What time do your boys go to bed?' I ask, breaking my own rules this once.

'Eight thirty.' Hannah grins before adding, 'Thereabouts.'

'Do they take long to fall asleep?'

She smiles again. She looks younger when she smiles. I suppose we all do.

'Not really. Ten, fifteen minutes. They play hard, fight hard and sleep hard . . . Why do you ask?'

'Oh, because of my partner's daughter. She stayed with us on Saturday night. Getting her to sleep was a nightmare.'

'Maybe it was the new environment?'

'No. Apparently she's always like that . . .'

'You could try some relaxing music, or a hot bath?'

'I'm tempted to try a good old-fashioned smack,' I say with a laugh. 'But that's obviously a no-no.'

'Wicked-stepmother territory,' she laughs back.

Well, if Hannah's boys are good sleepers, then it's unlikely she can enlighten me on what the problem is with Jasmin. I put down my coffee cup and train my eyes on my screen. Time to start work.

Unfortunately, Hannah doesn't take the hint and lingers. 'Sophie?'

'Yes.'

'Actually, there's something I wanted to ask you.'

'What?' It's almost nine o'clock. This is what I get for starting a conversation.

'Sorry.' Her voice has a slight wobble. Is she nervous? 'Look, I know that first thing on Monday morning isn't an ideal time to be asking a question like this. But seeing as we were chatting anyway, I thought I'd bring it up . . .'

'Bring what up?' I can hear the impatience in my voice.

'My pay. I was wondering if you would consider a review.'

'You mean a pay increase?'

'Yes.' She flushes. 'You see, I started here at an entry-level position, but my responsibilities have expanded since Jane left. I think my job should be classified at a higher level. Also, I hope I've proved myself by now, and that my work is worthy of a higher hourly rate.'

Hannah's right. Monday morning isn't the ideal time to be discussing such matters. She should have waited for her performance review, or made a special appointment with me to discuss this. But as she stands there in front of me, her face looking so much older than mine, wearing those chain-store clothes, along with an air of desperation that makes me suspect that her husband left her in a difficult financial situation, I can't help but be moved by how vulnerable she is.

'I'll review it and let you know the outcome. Now, can you please close the door on your way out?'

25

Chloe

Consequences don't work. They didn't work before, and they don't work now. I don't know why I allowed Matthew to convince me otherwise. Our next appointment isn't until late next week, but we can't hang on until then. We're at breaking point. Good Lord, even Aidan was rattled when he dropped her off on Sunday. He came in for a coffee, and we sat on the back deck and talked. Aidan had tears in his eyes, and seeing that made me even more emotional, and more at a loss about how to fix this.

'I was hoping for too much,' he said. 'I thought that something as simple as being in a different place could fix it.'

'I had a dreadful night without her . . . I couldn't stop worrying, didn't sleep a wink.'

Aidan's eyes locked with mine, as though he could see the misery of that night on my own, without my daughter, without my husband, without even a friend living in the same state as me who could drop round with a bottle of wine and the right mix of sympathy and pull-yourself-together tactics. One thing that had become clear was that I needed to think about my future, what I was going to do with my life. I have a degree in fashion and textiles, and work experience in retail and styling. For the last nine years there seemed little point in going back to work, not when there could be another baby at any moment. Moving house all those times also took its toll. It fell to me to make the transition smooth, to provide stability, and it seemed the only way to do that was by staying at home. Then along came the problems with Jasmin's sleeping, which left me too tired and dispirited to even think about my career. But one night of being completely on my own, in an achingly empty house, had brought things into sharp perspective. Something else was needed in my life. Something to sustain me when I was on my own. Something to give direction, fulfilment, distraction, an extra purpose.

'The first time was always going to be the hardest,' Aidan continued. 'But you need a break, Chlo, to keep up your strength, because you're the one who has to deal with this all week long. Somehow, we have to persevere.'

Neither of us said anything for a while. Aidan felt so close in that silence, and yet so painfully distant. More than anything I wanted to reach out and touch him. His bare arm beckoned to me. The stubble on his jaw taunted my fingers to brush over it. For a while I became fixated on his knee. Why couldn't I rest my hand on the denim? Just briefly? To show I cared? To ease the craving I had for him? It was just the two of us, on the deck of this house where we'd lived longer than any of the other houses, where we'd sat many times before, but never with this hopeless sadness, this horrible distance. Jasmin was in her room. She'd shut herself away almost as soon as she'd walked through the front door.

Then one of us – I can't remember if it was me or him – resurrected the conversation, and we talked about our fears for Jasmin, where this would all end up, what kind of life she would have if she couldn't get this problem under control. Even though what we were talking about was dreadfully upsetting, it was intimate too, and there were moments when I could fool myself into believing that I had my husband back. The only difference was that vital lack of touch. Not once did he reach out. No hug, no pat: nothing. I longed for it, the warmth of his touch, the roughness of his calloused hands, the weight of his arm across my shoulders. My eyes followed his mouth as he spoke; I was shamelessly fantasizing about him kissing me, suddenly and hard.

'What do we do from here?' he asked.

I sighed. 'I don't know what else to do other than stick to Matthew's plan. Keep going with the consequences until the next appointment, and then review the situation. I can't think of anything else. Can you?'

'No, no, I can't.'

But that was Sunday, and this is Thursday. Jasmin has now lost technology privileges for a whole month, and is still getting out of bed over and over again. *It hasn't worked.* If anything, it's made things worse; it has dragged the misery into our daytime. Jasmin is bored, withdrawn and resentful because of the lost privileges.

'I'm sorry, Mrs Ryan, he's with another client,' the receptionist informs me, not unsympathetically, when I phone Matthew's office.

'Please tell him it's urgent,' I plead. 'I really need to speak to him today.'

Matthew calls back later in the afternoon, and just hearing his voice is enough to make me break down completely. 'It's been dreadful . . . a disaster . . . She's miserable . . . I'm miserable. Losing technology is just one more thing for her to worry about, and it's stressing her out when I need her to stay calm. It's just not working, Matthew. I'm sorry for calling you like this, I know you have other clients, but we can't last another day, let alone another week.'

His response is the other extreme to me: calm and measured. 'It's all right, Chloe . . . So it's not working. I believe you, OK? You don't need to convince me any further.'

Silence fills the line. I take a deep breath, and then another. It's as if I'm breathing the silence, drawing it into me. My thoughts become more organized. More coherent.

'Matthew, did you ever get into trouble at school for something you didn't do? Something that was accidental, out of your control?'

'I'm sure I did.' He sounds amused. 'Many times.'

'Me too, and I remember how unfair it felt. I think this is something similar for Jasmin. She's being punished for something that's out of her control. That's why she feels so resentful.'

'You could be right . . .' Matthew is pensive, as though his mind has gone off in a different direction. 'Listen, Chloe, do you think you have the strength to try one more thing?'

I'm absolutely sure I *don't* have the strength. 'What is it you want to try?'

'Making the technology a reward rather than a consequence . . . This is what I think we should do. Tell Jasmin that all her technology privileges will be reinstated if she can stay in bed tonight. Just one night, that's all that's required, and she gets everything back. I want to see if she can do it.'

'She won't be able to do it,' I say with certainty.

'I think you're right. But it's worth a try. She misses her iPad and the TV, so there's a strong motivation there. And it's not as if she has to perform for a whole week . . . one night is all we're asking.'

He's doing it again, talking me into something that won't work. But what's my plan of action for tonight? What else is there left to try? And what's one more night of misery in the scheme of things?

'One night,' I hear myself agreeing. 'Anyway, it's not as if it can make things any worse than they already are.'

It's almost school pick-up time when I get off the phone. I hide my red eyes and blotchy face under big sunglasses and head out. It's a fifteen-minute, mostly flat walk to the school, and I'm startled to discover it's a lovely day outside. The heat from the autumn sun is gentle and restoring, and by the time I get to the school grounds I have regained my composure and some – albeit small – level of hope. Another mother whose name evades me – Lisa? Aleisha? Elisa? – sidles up, and we chat until the bell trills through our lightweight conversation.

Kids emerge from all directions. There's Jasmin, with Hannah's boys. The twins are bouncing a soccer ball between them, shouting and laughing and full of life.

Jasmin seems lethargic by comparison, ignoring the ball and the conversation.

She spots me and trudges in my direction.

'Hello, darling. How was your day?'

'OK,' she mutters.

This isn't the Jasmin I know. The girl who talks incessantly, her words gushing out and sometimes tripping her up. What work they did in class. What marvellous games were played at lunchtime. Who got into trouble with the teacher, who was praised and got an encouragement award. This sullen disengaged child is like a stranger to me.

'I talked to Matthew today,' I say as we walk away from the chaos, through the gate and past the dogs who have come to school as part of their daily walk but must wait outside the grounds.

Jasmin casts me a wary glance. 'Yeah?'

'He made a suggestion. A good one, I think.'

'What?'

'You can have all your privileges restored if you stay in bed tonight.'

Her face immediately brightens. 'I won't lose technology for a month?'

'Not if you stay in bed. Just for tonight. That's all. Think you can manage it?'

'Yeess . . . Really, Mum? I can have my iPad tomorrow? And TV?'

'Absolutely.'

'Hooray!' She punches a fist in the air.

Well, that's a good first reaction, but I'm a long way from being as optimistic as she is.

'Bye, Finn!' she suddenly yells out. 'Bye, Callum!'

Up in front of us, the twins are in the process of getting into a battered-looking hatchback. An older woman holds out the door while they scramble inside.

'Stop it, boys. Behave yourselves,' she commands, to what seem to be deaf ears.

It must be Hannah's mother. Should I stop and say hello?

Before I can decide, she has slammed the door shut and gone around the other side of the car.

Hannah has been on my mind this week. Her outburst after the game, her raw grief as we sat in the café, her face swollen from a combination of embarrassment and tears. I did what I could to comfort her, but there was little I could offer other than to listen and be there.

'Thank you,' she said, blowing her nose on one of the table napkins. 'You've been very kind. Your husband's not waiting back at the field, is he? I'm so sorry. I –'

'My husband and I split up a few months ago,' I said, trying to sound matter-of-fact but failing miserably. Then I was honest with her. 'I'm devastated about it, actually. It was dreadfully hard today, standing next to him at the game. Him being there but not being there, if you know what I mean. I know it's not as tragic as what happened to you, but I think I understand some of what you feel. The loneliness. The disorientation. The sadness every time I look at Jasmin and think of the impact on her.'

We have the potential to be good friends, Hannah and me. There's no retreating after a conversation like that. We can only go forward, and stand united on the sidelines, where all the other parents seem so happily coupled.

At home, we have a fairly ordinary afternoon. Jasmin reads her book, goes outside to kick her ball against the wall, does some spelling homework, kicks her ball again, tackles some maths, then has dinner. Next we start the lead-up to bedtime: a card game with me, a hot bath, some more reading time.

'I'm going to stay in bed, Mum,' she declares when I tuck her in.

'Of course you are, darling,' I reply, mimicking her confidence.

Downstairs, I turn on the TV and make myself comfortable on the couch. Then the loneliness hits. This is the hardest time of the day, when I'm brutally reminded that Aidan doesn't live here any more. He is not going to stretch out next to me on the couch, he is not going to debate what programmes we watch, and he is not going to step in and deal with Jasmin when she gets out of bed.

Don't expect the worst of Jasmin, I berate myself. *Believe in her. Believe that she can do it.*

For a while it's looking remarkably good. There's a home-renovation show on the telly and I lose myself in it for little periods of time. Then, at the thirty-minute mark, I hear the tell-tale thump of her feet hitting the floor. But she doesn't appear. Has she got back into bed?

I'm getting caught up in the plight of the home renovators. Structural damage, rising damp, dodgy electrical work . . . it's a disaster. It's been almost an hour now. I can still hear intermittent sounds from upstairs. She's trying, really trying, but she's still wide awake in there. For pity's sake, she might as well come out, get it over with. As though reading my mind, she does exactly that. I hear her door, her footsteps on the stairs, and next thing she's in front of me, as distraught as she's ever been.

'I tried, Mum, I really tried. How long has it been? Have I lost the chance to get my technology back? I'm sorry. I said I could do it. Has it been an hour? How long did I last?'

Questions and statements of self-disgust come out in such a torrent there is no opportunity for me to answer. My phone is next to me on the couch. Without really knowing what I'm doing, or why, I pick it up, go to the camera icon and hit the record button.

'I'm stupid for not falling asleep. *Stupid*. I hate myself . . .' She doesn't register the phone at first. When she does, she becomes even more hysterical. 'What are you doing? Are you recording me? *Why are you doing that?*'

The phone is capturing it all, the monster that my beautiful daughter transforms into every night.

'I'm doing it because I don't know what else to do,' I say, tears streaming down my face.

26

Hannah

This week alone, I have the water bill, the phone bill and my car registration. It's obvious that something will have to be deferred until next week, or the week after that, or – ideally – permanently. Which one, is the million-dollar question. We need water, obviously. The phone is an absolute necessity: I need to be contactable by Mum and the boys while I'm at work. The car? I guess we could hitch rides to soccer games and wherever else we need to go, or get the bus more often, or maybe I could talk to Mum about borrowing her car at weekends.

On the bright side, Sophie has agreed to review my pay. She surprised me, actually. I didn't feel optimistic asking the question, having already convinced myself it would be an outright no (for two reasons: I haven't been in the company the requisite time for a pay review, and because the extra work should ease off when we find a replacement for Jane). But the fact that Sophie didn't turn me down there and then makes me think she'll give it a really good shot.

I open the front door to the usual scenario: bags and boots in the hallway, preventing the door from opening fully, two less than clean children plonked in front of the

TV, my loyal mother – whose car I was mentally pilfering only minutes ago – out of sight in the kitchen.

'Helloooo. Nice to see you put your things away, boys. How was your day? How did training go?'

'Good.'

As usual, Finn is the one who responds, but Callum is who I want to hear from today. Were there any repercussions from Saturday?

'Callum?'

'It was fine.'

'Did you behave yourself?'

'Yes . . . Davy said I played really well.'

I hadn't been sure whether sitting out Saturday's game would make Callum sulky and uncooperative at training today, or have the opposite effect and motivate him to try extra hard. That's the problem with Callum: it could go either way. From what he's telling me, it's all good, but I'll still double-check with Mum.

I make my way into the cramped kitchen, where she's in the process of making bolognese, our usual Wednesday-night fare. 'Mmm . . . that smells lovely.'

She throws me a tired smile over her shoulder. 'I'm still twenty minutes away. We were late getting back from soccer.'

'Speaking of soccer, how did it go?'

She turns, spatula in hand. 'As a matter of fact, I've never seen Callum so well behaved. He did exactly as he was told, straight away, no mucking about.'

Mum received an abridged version of Saturday's events, a version that left out my own embarrassing outburst. What a relief that everything went smoothly today. One less thing for me to worry about.

'I'm thinking of getting rid of the car,' I say, testing the waters.

She gives me a hard stare. 'I'm not sure that's a wise move, Hannah.'

'It sits there for most of the week, while I'm at work.'

'You use it *a lot* at the weekends,' she points out, quite correctly.

'I do . . . but maybe I could be more creative about how we transport ourselves around.'

Even as I'm saying this, I'm mentally trying to fathom how we'd get to our soccer games on Saturday mornings, as they can be anywhere in the area. Wheedle lifts from the other parents? Become one of those annoying people who are always asking for help, so much so that people start to vet their incoming calls? The only alternative is to ask Mum if we can share her car. No, it's too much. Besides, she has walking club on Saturday mornings, and other commitments with her friends over the weekend. It wouldn't be fair.

'I don't know what else to do,' I say, and it's true. I'm running out of ideas on how to keep my family afloat on my meagre salary. I summon a smile. 'I've asked my boss for a pay rise, and she didn't tell me to get lost. So there's some hope.'

Maybe the pay rise will be enough to cover the insurance, the registration, the petrol and all the other costs that come with the car. I didn't mention a specific amount to Sophie. Was that a mistake? She might come back with a nominal increase, a token gesture that would make no real difference. Even if she comes back with something more substantial, it's not as if I'll get it all in one go. It will trickle in, month by month, when what I really need is one big cash injection.

While Mum finishes preparing dinner I start to bring in the washing from the balcony. It has been left out too long. Some of the T-shirts are so dry the cotton has gone hard.

'Oi!' someone calls at me from down below.

I look over the balustrade, the washing clutched against my chest. There's a man down there, frowning up at me. He's one of those obsessively neat older men, shirt tucked into his shorts, socks pulled up straight to his knees.

'That's not allowed,' he declares.

'What's not allowed?' I ask, pretending innocence.

'Hanging your washing out on the balcony like that. It's unsightly.'

'Oh, go and get a life,' I mutter, and move away from the balustrade, quickly unpegging the rest of the clothes from the drying rack.

'It's against the rules,' he rants on, the self-righteousness in his voice carrying to the back of the balcony, where I am practically hiding. 'Haven't you read the by-laws?'

I continue to ignore him, pretending I don't care, but my heart is beating wildly by the time I get inside.

'Your phone has been ringing, Mum.' Callum hands it to me as I dump the washing, unfolded, in the basket. 'I didn't answer in case it was work.'

It *is* work: Sophie. Who else would phone at this hour

of the evening, when everyone else is sitting down having dinner, talking about their day and winding down? I'll call her back later, after we've eaten. No, I'll call her straight away – she is reviewing my pay, after all. I usually step out on the balcony to make my phone calls, but I'm scared that Mr Fastidious is still out there ranting about by-laws, so I signal to the boys to keep the noise down and shut myself in my bedroom.

'Hi, Sophie. You were looking for me?'

'Yes. Sorry, I know it's dinner time. I'm just wondering if you've finished the packs for tomorrow's meeting.'

'No, I was planning on finishing them in the morning. The meeting isn't until eleven, right?'

'I'll need some time for review, then they'll need to be printed and bound. I don't think there'll be enough time.' She pauses. 'Unless you can get in here really early?'

Before-school care doesn't open until seven thirty. The earliest I can get to the office is an hour later, my usual arrival time.

Swallowing a sigh, I give her what she wants. 'I'll work on them later tonight, when the kids are in bed. I'll send through a copy when I'm done.'

This is the price of the pay review: having to say yes to her all the time. Not that I've said no very often.

Mum goes home after dinner. I switch off the TV and demand that homework is done, and bedtime – for once – is adhered to.

'Hurry up, boys. I have some work to do tonight and I can't concentrate until you're both in bed and fast asleep.'

'Why do you have to work at night?' Finn asks, quite reasonably.

'Are we going to sell our car?' Callum obviously overheard some of my conversation with Mum.

The answer to both questions is the same: money. I don't tell them this, avoiding their questions as artfully as they sometimes avoid mine.

Finally they're in bed, the flat is quiet, and I sit on the couch with my laptop on my knees, the closest I'll come to relaxing today. It takes an hour to finish off the information pack. The hardest part? Knowing that it could have waited until the morning, and that I could have spent that hour with the boys instead of rushing them off to bed.

Once I've emailed the pack to Sophie, I log on to my bank account and spend an inordinate amount of time staring at the balance, hoping for inspiration. In the end I don't pay any of the bills. I can't choose between the water, the phone and the car. If I make a payment now, I could regret it tomorrow, when it's too late to change my mind.

It's when I'm turning out the lights that I see it, the envelope in the hallway, lying among the boots and socks that never got cleared away in the end.

Notice of Contravention of a Body Corporate By-law.

Flipping heck!

I open it, my eyes skimming the contents before I place it on top of the pile of bills. It's annoying and inconvenient, but at least it isn't something that needs to be paid.

27

Sophie

I am not a bully! I cannot believe this. Jane walked out of here. For God's sake, she told me, 'Fuck you.' And now she's trying to pretend that she was forced into it, that she was being harassed and bullied, and she snapped that day because of the pressure. *Come on!*

'I'm shocked,' I say to Alyssa. 'Actually, words fail me.'

The unfair-dismissal claim is still in my hand. I would like to read it again, more slowly and with a highlighter, so that I can illuminate all the inaccuracies and exaggerations and misunderstandings.

The funeral. OK, that was a mistake. Of course I wouldn't have called her if I had remembered – I am not that heartless or unsympathetic. There was a board meeting, and I needed to know where to find something, and Jane was the custodian of that particular information, and I forgot about the funeral. It's as simple as that. I know she told me about it, but that was a few days before and things move fast in our office. Sometimes it's hard to remember where everyone is, where they're up to in their work, so I phone them. Yes, I'm the first to admit I use the phone a lot, but I don't *harass* people, as she claims. I like to talk to people. In fact, I find conversing much more effective than email or texts: it's my preferred communication method, nothing more.

'Can you explain what happened with the leadership programme?' Alyssa asks, her pen poised to take notes. 'Why Jane was taken off the programme after being included on the initial list?'

For God's sake, she's dredging up ancient history now. When was the leadership programme? Two or three years ago? Twelve high-achievers, including Jane, were to be coached and mentored and have their careers fast-tracked. They all attended the kick-off, a two-day event in a swanky hotel in the city. Then the budget got squeezed and there were casualties, simple as that.

'There were only enough funds for ten people, so two had to go. The executive board made the decision on who would be dropped from the programme. I was the messenger, nothing more.'

'Jane says here that the decision was to do with her age?'

'It was ... The other candidates were significantly younger than her, at earlier stages in their career.'

'And that isn't being ageist?'

For fuck's sake, Alyssa should know this stuff. 'It's a fact that Jane's in her mid-forties and her career doesn't have the same runway as someone in their mid-twenties.'

Unfortunately, age does matter when it comes to career planning, and I was honest with Jane about that. HR avoided giving her a direct reason. Our department head was apologetic but vague. Everyone else sidestepped the issue, everyone except me, and look what thanks I get in return: being accused of age discrimination – along with bullying and harassment. Besides the fact that Jane's recent behaviour proves she should not have been on that list of potential leaders in the first place.

'Do you feel there's any basis to what she said about the lack of support for her family life?' Alyssa asks more delicately.

'No, I don't. Yes, I phoned her after hours and sometimes on weekends, but I feel that was balanced out by all the days she was late into work, or had to leave early . . . In fact, I kept a record of all the time she took off for her children, all the school assemblies, the sports days and the sicknesses. There were *a lot* of sicknesses . . .'

Alyssa raises one of her thinly plucked eyebrows. 'You kept a record?'

'Yes. Because it felt like a lot of time to me. But you're welcome to look at my notes and come to your own conclusion.'

It's obvious that, while I was keeping tally of the time Jane took off work, she was keeping a different count: all the times she wanted to be there for her children but wasn't. I get that she's the mother of three school-age children. Of course there are occasions when her children will need her, and when she may not be able to work as a result. But Jane being Jane, she took undue advantage.

There's something about situations like this – when there's a commission involved, and possibly lawyers too – that puts everyone on the back foot, on the defensive, as though we're all guilty, no matter how preposterous the allegations are. But just because she made a complaint doesn't make it true. Just because something is put in writing doesn't mean it's not pure fabrication.

'What happens now?' I ask, massaging the back of my neck, trying to relieve the build-up of tension there. The irony is that I arrived in work this morning feeling refreshed and more energetic than I've been for ages. Aidan and I had a quiet, restorative weekend together, and on Tuesday I was careful not to overdo things from home. But all that feel-good and energy has been singularly wiped out by *this*.

'Well, it's clear that you dispute some of the facts, so we need to document your version of events.'

'And then?'

Alyssa shrugs. 'Disputed facts usually lead to a conference or a hearing . . .'

Hopefully the hearing will show Jane for who she truly is: lazy, belligerent and spiteful.

'Could she get her job back?'

'If the commissioner finds that the dismissal was unfair or harsh, yes. But not if we can prove there is a lack of confidence and trust.'

'There *is* a lack of confidence and trust,' I say tersely. 'Would we have to pay compensation in that event?'

'Possibly. Let's dispute the facts and take it from there.'

Alyssa looks every bit as weary as I feel. It's obvious that dealing with these sorts of legal issues is not her favourite part of the job.

I stand up too quickly, and pain – hot and angry – cripples my chest. 'Argh.'

'Are you all right?' Alyssa is alarmed.

Gripping the edge of the desk, I straighten myself slowly, take a cautious breath. 'I'm OK, I'm OK . . . It's just sometimes I need to be more careful about how I move . . .'

'Shall I help you back to your office?'

'No, it's passed, I'm fine now . . . Listen, before I go, can I have Hannah Evans' file?'

'Sure . . . Performance review?'

'Pay review.'

One of those thin eyebrows moves upwards again. 'Isn't it a bit early for that?'

'Yes, but she's been doing a good job.'

Back in my office I sit for a while, trying to recover from another wave of pain, which seems to have come of its own accord and not as result of any careless movements I've made. To be honest, I don't feel very well. It's the stress, I suppose. The humiliation. The unfairness. Even though I did nothing wrong, I still stand accused.

I am not a bully.

I am exacting. I have high standards and expect the same from everyone else. What's the crime in that? How many pay increases did I give Jane over the years? How many bonuses and awards? Did she ever stop to think of those? Of how generous I've been? People like her never appreciate what they've been given. Their hard-done-by attitude blinds them to reality.

Sighing heavily, I open Hannah's file. She's only been with us five months: company policy is that a year's service is required for a general pay review. I'll have to see if I can upgrade her role, get her into a different pay band, and review her salary that way. As my eyes are scanning through her résumé, to see if her experience and qualifications qualify for the next pay band, I see it: *St Brigid's.* Under the education heading.

Hannah went to the same school as me? Now that I think of it, she did look vaguely familiar on my first day back at the office. Fourteen years ago, and the fact that she was in the year below me, that's my excuse for not being able to place her. But what's hers? I was school captain and dux of my year, for fuck's sake. Everyone knew my name. She must have known me. *She must*. So why on earth hasn't she said anything?

My head feels heavy. I can't seem to think straight. It's extremely odd that Hannah didn't mention she'd gone to St Brigid's too.

Is she hiding something?

No, of course she isn't.

But why not say something? Why miss the chance to have the rapport of being old girls from the same school?

Too shy. Too socially awkward. That's the reason why. Now stop thinking about it.

Thinking about anything is becoming impossible. My head feels weighed down. The black print on Hannah's résumé is bleeding into the white background: my vision is going.

No, no. Not here.

Cold sweat prickles across my skin.

No. Not here. Not now.

My breath thunders in my ears as I try to gulp back some air.

Come on, Sophie. Not here. *Come on*.

And that's my last thought as my desk comes rushing up to meet me.

28

Aidan

Sophie's recuperating on the couch, after sleeping most of the afternoon. John Greenland, the executive general manager, gave her a lift home. Apparently he popped into her office to check on something and found her slumped on her desk. When she came to, he refused to call her a taxi, insisting that he drive her home himself. I'm grateful to him. I hate the thought of her being weak and vulnerable like that, being at the mercy of some random taxi-driver.

She was fast asleep when I came in from work, and I sat next to her for a while, watching her breathe and reminding myself of all the reasons I love her.

It started with her first words to me. She had to take off her oxygen mask to talk, and that action made her words all the more startling and memorable. 'I hope you're here to say how fucking sorry you are.'

I don't know what I was expecting. Anger, definitely. Tears, quite likely. Some sort of forgiveness, if I was lucky. What I didn't expect was to be challenged like that, to be put in my place. Those words were spoken by someone who was strong, feisty. Her chest had been ripped apart, she was on oxygen and drips and all sorts of drugs, but she wasn't going to be weakened by any of that, she was going to hold me fully accountable, and she woke something up in me. You know that part of you that automatically responds when you meet a kindred spirit? Well, that's what it was like that first time in the hospital. In fact, I could have easily said those same words had our roles been reversed. *I know this girl. She is as familiar to me as my female colleagues. Tough, resilient, smart. Yet intriguingly different from them too.*

For reasons I couldn't fully explain, I continued to visit her at the hospital. Yeah, I was largely driven by guilt and a desire to make good, but there was an attraction too, not that I was prepared to acknowledge it at the time. When Sophie spoke, she was articulate, precise and completely mesmerizing. She told me where she worked and what she did for a living, and it seemed the perfect job for her because it was evident, in the structure of her sentences, in that assessing stare of hers, that she was driven by logic. Those hospital visits – given the circumstances – should have been awkward, but they were far from that. I found myself looking forward to them, wondering what we would talk about, what direction our conversation would take. I discovered we had some things in common: both of us were practical, resourceful, ambitious, and we had a liking for routine and order and discipline. She laughed out loud when I sheepishly admitted that I was dux of my school too.

Dux or not, Sophie is infinitely smarter than me. When we're shopping, I ask her to add things up in her head, just because I enjoy watching her, the way she scrunches her face when she's working something out. And it's not just maths – Sophie is extremely well read and knowledgeable about many things: the capital cities of obscure countries, scientific tables from school, history, politics, music (classical music, that is – she finds my taste in popular music quite hilarious).

I know she can be abrupt at times, and I would guess that she's hard to work for. Smart people often are. Tough people *always* are. I should know. I've had some difficult bosses in my day, especially in those early years when I was low down in the pecking order. But the tougher the boss, the more respect they earn from the soldiers. And the tough ones were nearly always fair, like Sophie. I'm as stunned as she is by the complaint that's been made against her. I could tell that something was bothering her as soon as she woke, that something had happened to cause this relapse. On my urging, she recounted everything: the claims of unfair dismissal, of harassment and discrimination. How she feels guilty even though she's done nothing wrong. It's the bullying thing that's distressing her the most.

'It wouldn't happen in the army, would it?' she sighs now. 'Not a chance.'

At various times over the last five years, when Chloe was having trouble conceiving and I was being moved from pillar to post, I considered leaving the army and trying to get a nine-to-five job in the corporate world. But when I hear things like this – the lack of order and reason, the lack of respect, the infighting and backstabbing – I know I wouldn't last there. I would become too frustrated with all the petty conflicts, all the politics. Anyway, as Chloe used to say, I was too institutionalized to become a civilian.

'Do you constantly take time off work for Jasmin? Do you go to every single one of her school ceremonies and sporting fixtures?' She rubs her eyes with the back of her hand. 'No, you don't. Because if we all took that approach, there would be nobody at work, for God's sake.'

She's right. I've never been involved with Jasmin's various schools. Whenever there was something important on, I was either overseas or had drills or operations I couldn't get out of. Actually, it's something I regret: the fact that I've been so absent from that part of her life. But it's difficult for Sophie to comprehend this. She doesn't realize how much it means to kids to have someone there to clap and acknowledge their achievements.

'I am not a bully,' she says again.

'I know . . . Hey, I wouldn't love you if you were.'

Chloe and I have wondered on and off if Jasmin's sleeping troubles have been caused by bullying at school. She seems to have plenty of friends, she's happy to go to school every day, and her teacher hasn't noticed anything untoward, so we have no real evidence to go on. Bullying is notoriously hard to pin down, though. I've had a few cases come across my desk at work. Even in the most obvious case – a sergeant who intimidated a soldier so relentlessly that complaints were made by several witnesses – the perpetrator still didn't believe he had done anything wrong.

I'm about to stand up to make a start on dinner when Sophie puts her hand on my arm.

'Aidan . . .'

'Yeah?'

'About Saturday . . . I know it's your turn, but I don't

think I'm strong enough to have Jasmin here this week-end. I'm sorry.'

No, that's not how it works with kids.

'Look, I know you feel crap but that shouldn't impact on Jasmin. She's not some box to be ticked, an opt-in or opt-out.'

Her lips press together. 'These are extenuating circumstances, Aidan. I passed out at work, for God's sake. I need some time to recover.'

She doesn't get that kids are there on your bad days as well as your good days. When you are tired, fed up, disillusioned and sick, just as much as when you are happy, energetic and able to cope. I guess she's used to being selfish, not having to see beyond her own needs.

'Sophie, I know you need to rest, but Jasmin can't be put off every time you don't feel up to it. She needs consistency –'

'Seriously, it's just one weekend. That's all I'm asking. Why are you making such a big deal about it?'

I give in only because Sophie's weak and upset and not in the right frame of mind to see that children, and one's responsibilities to them, *are* a very big deal.

'I'll get the dinner on,' I say, standing up.

'I'm sorry I feel so tired,' she calls after me. 'I love you.'

'Love you too,' I reply, and I mean it wholeheartedly.

This is all a huge learning curve for Sophie. She's astute enough to know that I'll be standing my ground the next time we have a disagreement about Jasmin.

29

Richard

Milli reminds me of Sophie. This realization is a surprise, because they're so different physically. Sophie was small and slight at this age, whereas Milli is tall and thickset. Sophie has delicate features and almost black hair, whereas Milli has a squarish (often mutinous) face under that deceiving halo of white-blonde curls. Yes, starkly different in looks and physicality, yet so similar in character. Determined, focused, tenacious.

'Milli, don't take Hugo's toy. Give it back, sweetheart.'

'No.'

Milli, just like Sophie, will not be swayed.

'Be a good girl, now.'

'No, Gwand. No. Noooo. No. Noooo.'

That's what she calls me: Gwand. Her mouth can't quite manage the two syllables in 'Grandpa', or the 'r' sound. I like it. *Gwand*. Dee was right. It's good to see more of the grandchildren. Once a week I drive up to Newcastle, and sometimes I stay overnight. I help where I can: gardening, jobs around the house that Carolyn has saved up for me, babysitting, in the main. Dee tries to come along too, but her hours at the shop have been fluctuating and she's not always free.

'Milli, give the toy to Gwand, and I'll pass it to Hugo.'

'No. No. Noooo.' Milli decides that Hugo is too close for comfort and pushes him away. Her feistiness makes me want to laugh, but that would be setting a poor example. Hugo, who is used to being pushed around by his younger sister, steadies himself and barely complains.

'Right, Milli. You know the rules. Do you want to go to the naughty step? Do you?'

The naughty step is at the bottom of the stairs. The children are sent there for a one-minute time-out if they misbehave. They get three warnings, three chances to back down and make amends, then off they're marched. You'd think they were being sent to a hellhole the way they scream and carry on. I don't believe in naughty steps, or naughty corners, or any of that ridiculous newfangled parenting stuff, but if Carolyn catches me being lenient with the children I could well end up on the dreaded step myself, so I'd better stick to the bloody rules.

'One . . . Two . . . Th—'

At the very last minute Milli throws the toy on the floor. You've got to admire her gumption. She seems to know exactly how much to push the limits.

'You'll go far, Milli,' I tell her. 'You'll go far.'

She has no idea what I'm talking about, of course. No idea that she's a natural leader who knows her own mind. No idea that she has an innate strength and confidence that people will defer to when she gets older. No idea that one day she will have a career and undoubtedly hold a position of authority – maybe chief executive of a major organization, or a headteacher, or a political leader. I used to play this game when Sophie was small, imagining what she would be when she grew up. I thought she could go all the way. Prime Minister, if that was what she wanted. She had the brains, the confidence, the work ethic to get there.

Peace has been restored between Hugo and Milli when my phone rings in my pocket. It's Dee.

'Sophie . . . work . . .'

'Sorry, Dee. I can't hear you. The children are babbling. What did you say?'

'I said Sophie isn't well.' Dee always sounds sterner when she has to repeat herself. 'She had to come home from work . . . Apparently the head honcho gave her a lift.'

'You mean John Greenland?'

'I don't know his name,' Dee says, vague as usual.

'John Greenland is a busy man – driving Sophie home would've been a major inconvenience. This is not good, Dee . . . Sophie's been doing too much, pushing herself too far. She doesn't know how to hold back. She never did, that's the bloody problem. Now she's had a relapse. Of course this was going to happen. Of course.'

'Now don't get upset, Richard . . .'

Don't get upset? Is she mad? Our daughter, who could have gone all the way to the top, is barely able to hold down a job at the moment. She is dangerously exhausted, spends her days off – which are a bloody joke, by the way – recuperating and trying to muster enough strength to face another week. It's a vicious circle.

'How is she now?'

'She's feeling better. Aidan said she had a good sleep and ate dinner.'

'Bloody Aidan . . .'

'Richard!' Dee's reprimand is so loud I have no trouble hearing it.

'This is all his fault, Dee. *All his fault.* I hope the bastard ends up in prison. If there's any justice –'

'Richard! *Stop it.*'

'I'm just giving my opinion, that's all.'

'Well, don't give your opinion, thank you very much. We're past that, do you hear me? They're a couple now. You can't go around saying things like that.'

Dee is worried about me. She's worried about my hearing (she's booked me in for an ear test next week). She's worried that I don't have enough things to occupy my day (she wants me to join the local bowling club, despite the fact that I've never displayed the slightest interest in bowling). She's worried that I might be depressed (I've told her that being chronically bored is quite different from being depressed). And she's worried that I'm too involved in Sophie's life, and too harsh on Aidan. I don't care what she says, I cannot accept that man into our family. *I just can't.* Not after what he's done. Doesn't matter how hard he tries to make up for it. Call me bitter, call me vengeful, call me anything you want, but he should have to face some consequences for the pain he's caused. Losing his licence? Not enough. Helping Sophie around the house? Again, just not enough. The consequences must be severe – even prison seems too kind, but I'd settle for it – because what's happened to Sophie is severe. I think the whole situation wouldn't plague me so much if I could be guaranteed some justice.

I don't know, maybe I am a bit obsessed and depressed and Dee is right to be worried. It's hard, that's all. *Really bloody hard.* Just being with Milli – so young, so full of promise, so adoringly indomitable – makes me realize the full extent of what Sophie has lost: her health, her confidence, her career, her future. But, more than anything, she's lost her strength.

I have this question to ask: *What can you become if you aren't strong?*

Nothing, that's what.

Sophie, who could have been anything in the world she wanted to be, will end up nothing, a nobody. It's enough to make a grown man cry.

30

Jasmin

I'm not going to Daddy and Sophie's this week. Daddy said we're going with Plan B instead. He'll pick me up after my soccer game tomorrow and then we're going out for the afternoon. We'll either do laser tag or some rock climbing, whichever I prefer. Laser tag, I think. Then we'll have something to eat before he drops me home. Pizza, although Daddy might need to be persuaded. I hope he comes in when he drops me off and sits outside on the deck again, chatting with Mum.

'Jasmin!' Mum's voice cuts in on my thoughts. 'Are you listening to Matthew?'

'Yes, Mum.' I sit up straighter in my seat. Matthew's eyes are looking straight into mine, as if he can see that I've just told a lie.

'I believe it's been a tough couple of weeks,' he repeats.

Yeah, it has been tough. Really, really, *really* tough. My sleeping problem has got way worse. I couldn't stay in bed in Sophie's house, even though I tried my hardest not to let Daddy down. Sophie got really annoyed and the next morning I could hear her and Daddy having an argument about me. Then I couldn't stay in bed when Mum offered me the chance to get all my technology privileges back.

Even worse, I got into trouble with Mrs Stanley today for not paying attention. I *never* get into trouble with Mrs Stanley. It's just that my brain felt too fuzzy for maths and I had already gone to the toilets and the bubblers, so I was out of excuses and ways to wake myself up. What's wrong with me? Why can't I fall asleep, like everyone else? The weird thing is, when I go to bed at first, I really believe I can stay there, and I'm tired, I really am. But then my body won't stay still, and I toss and turn until I'm wide awake again and have to get up.

Matthew clears his throat, reminding me to answer him.

Too embarrassed to look at him, I stare at my feet instead. 'I wish I could delete the last two weeks.'

'How do you feel today?'

'Tired . . . Stupid . . .'

'Jasmin!' Mum is cross. *'Don't say that.* You are not stupid, OK?'

I *am* stupid. I can't fall asleep. I am the only person I know who doesn't know how to do it. That makes me stupid.

'I recorded her,' Mum says. 'When I was at my wits' end, when I didn't know what else to do, I got out my phone and recorded her. Do you want to see it?'

When I look up, I see that Matthew is nodding. 'Yes, I'd like to see. You OK with that, Jasmin?'

I'm not OK with that. I'm angry and I'm even more embarrassed, and I'm lots of other things too: *dismayed, appalled, sickened.* Mum showed me the video the next morning when I came downstairs and said I was sorry (that's what normally happens the next morning). My face was red, and I was crying and shouting and swaying. I was acting like a retard – I know that's not a nice word, but I can't think of any other word that describes how bad I was.

Matthew is still staring at me, waiting for my permission. I don't want him to watch it. I think he likes me, but he won't after seeing that video. Crying like a baby, shouting at my mum. But part of me wants him to see it so he can understand how bad I get, and maybe then he'll know how to help me. So I nod, and look down at my shoes again – one of my laces has come undone – while Mum fiddles with her phone before handing it to Matthew.

My voice fills the office, high and whingeing. Matthew's probably as shocked as I was. It sounds dumb, but I had no idea I was that awful. The next night I tried to remember the video, to make myself stay in bed, but it only worked for a little while.

Matthew gives the phone back to Mum. 'Thanks for that. It was very helpful.'

Then he gets up from his seat and opens the cupboard behind his desk. It's full of brightly coloured toys.

He turns to face me, a purple, cushion-like thing in his hand. 'Here, Jasmin. Put this on for a while.'

He drapes the cushion around my neck. It's heavy.

'What is it?' Mum and I ask at exactly the same time.

'It's a weighted cape.'

'What does it *do*?' Mum is frowning, as if the cape is something bad.

'It's used in autism sensory-integration therapy. It provides deep-pressure sensory input –'

'Autism? Are you saying Jasmin is autistic?'

I don't exactly know what 'autistic' means but, judging from Mum's voice, it isn't good.

'Not at all,' Matthew says, and I feel very relieved. I'll ask Mum later what 'autistic' is, just so I know, even though I don't have it. 'But her state of agitation in the video – the twitching and jerking and rocking – is not dissimilar to the symptoms of autism. The cape promotes self-calming through proprioceptive feedback.'

Mum glares at him. 'Proprioceptive *what*? I don't know what that means. I don't know what *any* of this means. Can you just tell me, in plain English, please . . . Do you know what's wrong with Jasmin?'

He puts up his hands, as though to say, *Slow down*. 'Look, Chloe, you know that I don't like to make snap diagnoses. Let's just say there's a certain area that I want to look closer at now I've seen the video, especially when I consider it in conjunction with the sensory analysis we did way back at the start –'

'And what is that area?' Mum interrupts again. She's being a bit rude – she would kill me if I didn't let someone finish speaking like that. 'Just tell me. I'm going mad here.'

She does look a bit crazy. My sleeping problem has done this to her.

Matthew is very calm, by comparison. 'It's sensory-processing disorder. I'll need to refer Jasmin to a physiotherapist who specializes in the area . . . I'll write you a referral now.'

The office is strangely quiet in the next few minutes,

the time it takes Matthew to type up the referral – a letter of some sort – on his computer. He calls out some suburbs to Mum, trying to find out which one is closest to where we live so he can find a physiotherapist nearby. One of the boys in my soccer team had to see a physiotherapist when he hurt his ankle. I thought they took care of broken bones and sore muscles. Have I broken something I don't know about?

Sensory processing disorder.

When we get home Mum will go straight on the computer and google it. Then she'll ring Daddy (because he couldn't come with us today) and tell him everything she's found out. Later on she'll give me a simplified version, as though I'm not capable of understanding to the same level as Daddy.

This is *my* problem. I want to know the full truth, not some baby version. Maybe I'll google it myself. I'm smarter than she thinks.

I just hope it isn't bad. I just really, really, *really* hope they can cure me.

31

Hannah

It's been two weeks since I asked Sophie for a pay increase, and those two weeks have been hell. The phone calls never stop, any time up to eleven at night, and starting again from six in the morning. Every waking hour, actually. Most of the time they're unnecessary. There's no emergency, only Sophie's lack of patience and complete disregard for my family life. Flipping heck, I can't even look forward to a reprieve on Tuesdays and Thursdays, when she's supposed to be at home and I should be concentrating on Peter's work. If anything, she's more relentless on those days, and sometimes she even turns up at the office, catching me off guard.

I've been thinking more and more about Jane and feeling guilty that I didn't understand quite how much pressure she was under. This is exactly how she felt. Resentful. Harassed. Powerless. This is what made her snap. I can see now how it happened because I've fantasized about handing in my resignation. But that's all it is: a fantasy. I need this job as much as ever, so for now I'll have to be at Sophie's beck and call, and put up with whatever she throws at me. I keep telling myself that it'll be fine, that it'll all work out OK, that things will improve when we find a replacement for Jane. And I've got to believe that. It's the only way I can cope.

It's the start of another working week and everything feels like a chore: dragging myself out of bed, getting the kids ready for school, catching the bus to the city, buying Sophie's skinny latte from the café across the road. I arrive in her office dispirited and aggrieved. She looks up from her computer screen and beams at me.

'Good news, Hannah. I've put in an application to have your role regraded to Administration Assistant Level 2. I'm waiting for John Greenland's approval, but I don't expect any issues – he generally goes with my recommendations.'

'Thank you.' I set down her morning coffee on her desk with a smile that's prompted by both surprise and gratitude. I had kept my expectations low, so this is good news, even though I'm not sure what it means in terms of cold, hard cash. I'm reluctant to ask for fear of sounding ungrateful.

'The midpoint salary is $7,500 more than what you're currently on,' she says, and I'm thankful for that practical side of her, that she calls things as they are and doesn't beat around the bush. $7,500: not enough to stabilize my finances but enough to give me hope that once a few months' worth has trickled through to my bank account, it will ease some of the pressure.

'Thank you,' I say again.

'You're welcome.' She pauses, and I think that's it, my cue to leave, when she adds, 'I saw in your file that you went to St Brigid's.'

Heat fills my face. Flipping heck! Thirty years old and

still blushing like a schoolgirl. Talk about making myself look guilty. 'Yes.'

'I went there too . . . I was in the year above you, I believe.'

'Yes, I know,' I say, trying, belatedly, to be in some way honest, because she obviously thinks it's odd that I haven't mentioned this before now. She had such a high profile at school, she would expect to be remembered. 'I half recognized you when I first met you but I missed the moment to say anything. You know how that happens?' Her nod is almost imperceptible. 'And then it feels irrelevant to bring it up afterwards.'

There's another silence. Once again, I'm at the point of leaving when she speaks, stalling me.

'Do you keep in touch with any of the girls?' Her smile is so forced it looks like it's hurting her. Maybe I am imagining things.

I shake my head. 'I lost touch pretty quickly. I went to the UK for a gap year – that's when I met Harry. A year turned into two, and when we came back here we lived on the other side of the city . . . Then I got pregnant, which was as good as putting me on another planet. No, I don't see any of them . . . Do you?'

'A few.' Her response sounds exceptionally abrupt, even for her. After a long pause, she adds, 'It was a long time ago, wasn't it? Feels like a completely different life.'

For a moment I'm transported back. The light-blue cotton blouse that always felt too tight around the neck. The knee-length A-line skirt that was so unfashionable. The assemblies, the much-hated double-science classes, the dreaded PE lesson every Wednesday afternoon. I didn't love it, but I didn't hate it either. Not until that maths camp in Year 11, which seemed to tarnish everything that went before and after. Now my overriding feelings about St Brigid's can be summed up with a great big question mark.

I could easily say, *Do you remember the camp we went on? The maths one? Years 11 and 12 together?*

But of course I'm not going to say that. For the same reason I didn't tell her I went to St Brigid's in the first place. All it would take is a few further questions and my face would give me away. She would know, then. She would know that I know something, although I am still, to this day, not sure what it is that I know, other than the fact that she's a liar.

'Yeah, a different life indeed,' I agree, my words starkly different from what's running through my head. 'Wouldn't it be lovely, though, to keep to school hours, to clock off at three thirty? Or the holidays ... Who wouldn't love eight weeks off over summer?'

She's laughing as I leave her office. Back at my desk I start my working week, reading emails, catching up on paperwork and making a Herculean effort to dwell on the here and now and not on what happened at maths camp more than fourteen years ago.

It turns out to be one of those days when I'm pulled in opposite directions by the demands of my two bosses. Peter usually takes the back seat, allowing Sophie to dominate, but not today. He has a valid reason: a major bid response that's due and one key member of staff off sick. Sophie maintains that her need for me is just as urgent, and the pay rise seems to have made her extra possessive with regards to how my time is split. The tug of war culminates in terse words as the two of them go head to head in front of my desk. Sophie eventually gives in – there is nothing more important than a bid response, after all – but she is like a petulant child for the rest of the day.

Much later I arrive home to face another battlefield. There's a letter in Callum's school bag, asking me to make an appointment to see his teacher.

'What have you done?'

'Nothing.'

'*Tell me.* You must have done *something.* Have you been respectful? Have you been trying hard? Are you nice to the other kids?'

'*Yes.*'

'Don't shout.'

'I'm shouting because you always think it's something bad.'

In the middle of this heated exchange there's a knock on the door. Finn, who has been unusually quiet and obviously knows *exactly* what this proposed teacher meeting is about, goes to answer it.

'It's one of the neighbours,' he calls out from the hallway.

'I'm not finished with you,' I warn Callum before going to see who it is.

It's that man, Mr Fastidious. His hands are clasped behind his back, and his head is jutted forward so he can peer into our hallway, into our lives, undoubtedly noting all the discarded shoes and sporting equipment and making judgements. What does he want? My washing has been hung out on the communal lines since early this morning, and once I've finished this argument with Callum I'll go and retrieve it. Does he have something else to complain about? Of course he does. Complaining is his hobby.

'Can I help you?'

'The noise.' He holds one hand to his mouth as he coughs. 'It would be great if you could keep it down.'

It's too much, after the day I've had.

'You know what would be *really* great? If you could go and get a life, that's what.' Even the door is refusing to cooperate with me: it slams rather than shuts, the bang so loud it feels like it has reverberated through the entire apartment block.

Finn and Callum burst out laughing as I burst into tears.

'Stop laughing . . . It isn't funny. That was extremely rude of me. Now I'll have to say sorry to him.'

I whip open the door, ready to apologize, because we *were* being loud, and there is no excuse for bad manners, but he is gone, out of sight.

'Oh God. Now I'm sure I've breached some other flipping by-law.'

The boys start laughing again.

'Come on, Mum. Stop stressing. It's cool.'

It's not cool. And it's *not* funny. Where is their respect? I must do better with them. I *have* to do better, be tougher, set boundaries, or there will be many more letters from school.

'Stop laughing. Stop it. *Now.*' The laundry basket is

among the array of items clogging up the hallway. I pick it up, thrust it at Callum – the one who's laughing the hardest, the one who'll always be more susceptible to getting into trouble and who needs a good example set. 'Go and get the washing from the line. Both of you. Don't look so stunned. Hurry up.'

I'll give them more chores, that's what I'll do. And once and for all, I'm going to put time limits on how much TV they watch. There are going to be changes around here. Starting now. Starting with me.

They're late going to bed, and it's later again by the time I sit down with a glass of wine. I try not to drink too much during the week. There's the cost, for a start, and let's face it, someone in my predicament, drinking alone . . . it can be a slippery slope.

The wine has the desired effect. Calm creeps over me. My thoughts begin to assemble.

Mr Fastidious. An apology is owed and will be delivered, with the boys as witnesses.

Callum. A long discussion with his teacher, and maybe the school counsellor too. Do I worry too much? Should I have more faith in him, in the young man he can become? He will change, of course he will. He isn't set in stone, he can develop into an open and positive young man, I know he can. That's part of the journey of life, right? People changing, growing, evolving as they get older and wiser. I am not the same person I was at school. Neither – I hope – is Sophie McCarthy.

It's harder to assemble my thoughts when it comes to Sophie.

The pay rise. I'm sincerely grateful to her for that, I really am. The application to HR would have taken time and thought on her part, and because it was outside normal procedures she would've had to fight my corner. It proves that she's not all bad. Yes, she's extremely difficult to work for. She harasses me, pressures me, demands nothing short of excellence from me, as she did with Jane. And let's be realistic, the pay rise is her licence to be even more demanding and possessive. But that doesn't necessarily mean she's an evil person, does it?

The fact is, people are complicated. They can have conflicting facets (Harry being the perfect example . . . but my head can't go there right now). Sophie's meticulousness and hard-work ethic is one part of her. The fact that she can be an outright bully at times is another. But there's obviously generosity and empathy in there too, and that's a good thing, a positive thing.

The girl she was at school. How much of that girl is left in today's Sophie? Does it even matter? I caught her out in a lie. *A gigantic lie.* But the truth is, I am not a hundred per cent certain of even that, so what's the point in driving myself crazy over a question mark?

I'm confused. Sophie McCarthy has *always* confused me. I've never known what to think of her. Not then. Not now.

32

Dee

This is what happened at the school, or, to be specific, the school camp. There was an accident, and a girl got injured, badly injured. It was awful, terribly upsetting for everyone involved: all the Year 11 and 12 kids at the camp, the parents and the wider school community, and the poor girl and her family, obviously.

Sophie was distraught. The first I knew was when I went to pick her up from the bus. I could tell straight away, from her red eyes, that she'd been crying. I assumed it was something trivial. Not enough sleep, someone who had been unkind, maybe even a touch of homesickness.

'Kristina Owens fell,' she began, and starting sobbing.

'What, sweetheart? Kristina who? What happened?'

'She fell from the ledge. We were orienteering. I was *with her*. She was just ahead of me.'

It was the first time I had heard the girl's name, Kristina Owens. Richard, though, knew exactly who she was.

'She's the tall, gangly girl. You should know her, Dee. Strawberry-blonde hair? She's smart, always gets awards at the school ceremonies. It's usually her and Sophie on the stage together.'

I didn't know her, much to his amazement. I never

took notice of who got what award, not in the way Richard did. He would keep a running commentary throughout the ceremonies.

'She got that writing award last year too . . . Mmm . . . that's an interesting choice. I wouldn't have picked her for that . . . I would have thought Sophie would have been in the running for that one.'

In my view, Sophie was a very fortunate girl. She always got at least one award at those end-of-year ceremonies, but that never seemed enough for Richard. He wanted her to blitz it, for her name to be the one that was announced the most frequently. Sophie McCarthy, star of the show. I prefer to see these things shared around. One child shouldn't be made to feel superior to everyone else. And what about the kids who never get anything? Kids like Jacob, who performed solidly but never shone enough to be recognized, to have his name put on a plaque or a certificate.

Anyway, I'm digressing. The point is that Richard knew who Kristina was straight away, whereas I didn't have a clue. Maybe I wouldn't have been so shocked by the accusations that followed if I'd known who she was: Sophie's rival.

'Thank you for coming in, Mr and Mrs McCarthy.' I remember thinking that the headmistress – Mrs Jones – looked exactly right for the role: her silver-grey hair cut in a no-nonsense bob, her light-blue blouse and navy skirt quite similar in style to the school uniform, and her tone of voice so unyielding that I felt myself sit a little straighter in my seat. 'We have some rather serious allegations we need to discuss. It's not the first time we've had two girls providing different versions of the facts, and it's probably not the last, but given the injuries sustained by Kristina Owens – broken leg, hip and collarbone, concussion – this is a very serious matter, and the school, and possibly the police, must investigate it thoroughly.'

Richard immediately jumped in. 'Sophie saw it all, if that's what you need to know. Kristina was too close to the edge. She was trying to see over –'

'Mr McCarthy, I'm quite aware of Sophie's version of events. The reason you are here today is that it differs from what Kristina says. Kristina is quite adamant that she didn't lose her balance . . . According to her, she was pushed.'

Richard jerked forward in his seat. 'Pushed? By who?'

Mrs Jones looked down at her notes. It seemed to take ages before she looked up again, meeting our eyes in turn. 'By your daughter, Mr and Mrs McCarthy. By Sophie.'

I felt automatically guilty, as though Sophie *had* done it – pushed the girl – and we – me and Richard and even Jacob – were all in some way responsible.

Richard was as shocked as I was, but it seemed to have the opposite effect on him. While I had completely lost my tongue, he – normally a relatively quiet man – had found his. He was furious, as angry as I have ever seen him. 'That's preposterous . . . ridiculous . . . My daughter was the one who climbed down to help. She was very distressed by what happened. I cannot believe she is being accused like this. This is defamatory. I will *sue* –'

'I can assure you that this is not defamatory in any way.

Nobody else in the school knows what Kristina has said . . .'

'Try convincing our lawyer of that!'

'Richard!' I cried, finding my voice. Threatening legal action was hardly helping the situation. 'Mrs Jones, you say the girl – Kristina – had concussion. I am not sure you can give any weight to her recollection of what happened. All I can tell you is that my daughter was genuinely upset and I find it impossible to believe that she was in any way responsible. She is not a violent or vindictive girl . . .'

As I uttered these words – 'vindictive', in particular – I felt my resolution waver just a little. A memory from years back replayed in my mind. Jacob holding up bruised fingers.

'She hit me.'

'I did *not*.'

'I was winning, and then she hit me . . .'

I couldn't remember what he was supposedly winning at, or what happened afterwards. Did we punish Sophie? Probably not. After all, it was her word versus his, and how could we tell which one of them was lying? Jacob wouldn't intentionally lie, I knew that, but he was certainly capable of mistaking an accident for a deliberate act. And Sophie, well, she was a hard nut to crack. No matter how hard I pressed or questioned her, she always stuck to her story.

But it was normal brother–sister stuff. A squabble that went too far, that was all. Kristina Owens was a different matter altogether.

'It's unbelievable, isn't it?' I said to Richard on the way home from the school.

'Outrageous. I won't allow it. The girl obviously wants someone to blame for her own mistake. I won't let her or the school sully Sophie's name like this. I know you think it's over the top, threatening to sue, but I bloody well will, if it comes to it.'

I sighed. 'That's the problem with these school camps. Anything can happen. Too many kids and not enough teachers to watch them all. And why were they orienteering, anyway? It was a maths camp, for heaven's sake.'

In my mind I tried to imagine the scene of the accident. Sophie wearing her trainers and her favourite denim shorts, holding a map, earnestly working out the coordinates, or whatever they do in orienteering. Kristina Owens leading the way through the rocky terrain. Why had she been paired with Sophie? Were they friends? Or were they the leftover kids who no one else had chosen to be with? Was Kristina a bit of a daredevil? I can picture her – this faceless girl with the strawberry-blonde hair – stretching her pale neck to see what lay beyond the ledge. Did she misjudge her footing, or lose her balance? Sophie seemed to think it was the latter. I could hear her scream in my head, see her body hurtling down the steep sides of the gorge, bouncing against tree trunks and boulders before coming to a stop in the undergrowth.

Then the image of Kristina's broken body was replaced with that of Jacob's bloody hand: *She hit me*. A tiny part of me was questioning Sophie now, and I wished that I could be as adamant, as loyal, as Richard.

Kristina Owens didn't come back to St Brigid's. From what I heard, she saw out the rest of Year 12 in the local public school. Richard wrote to Mrs Jones a few days later, outlining his disappointment at her handling of the matter, the obvious lack of supervision at the camp, and once again implying that he would take legal action if necessary. The school backed down. Nothing further came of it, and Sophie graduated later that year, awarded the highest of honours: dux.

I'm sure Richard has forgotten about Kristina Owens. I still think of her. Occasionally. What happened still niggles at me. Even after all this time.

33

Richard

I think about Kristina Owens every now and then. More often in recent times, since Sophie had her accident. She seems to pop up in my mind whenever I think about blame. The need to lay blame is almost like a human reflex. Something bad happens and our immediate reaction is to point the finger at someone, to find a focus point for our anger, to yearn for the perpetrator to *pay a price* for what they did. That's exactly how I feel about Aidan Ryan, why nothing less than prison will suffice, but at least my feelings are legitimate: he was the one behind the wheel, the one who wasn't paying attention that morning, the one who walked away from the accident while Sophie was left shattered in every way. Kristina Owens had only herself to blame – she went too close to the edge – but she was too immature to come to terms with the harsh truth of what had happened. She wanted to blame someone, anyone, and poor Sophie was in the wrong place at the wrong time.

'Hey, Dad. How's it going?'

My thoughts are so far away I don't notice Jacob until he's practically right in front of me. His hands are stuffed deep in the pockets of beige chinos. His shirt is open at the collar. The dress code at the council seems fairly relaxed.

'Good,' I respond. 'How's work?'

'Oh, nothing exciting . . .' He sits down next to me on the garden wall. Milli and Hugo are playing amicably in the cubbyhouse. Ten minutes ago they were fighting like cat and dog. 'How were the kids today?'

'The usual ups and downs.' I laugh fondly. 'Milli is the boss. She reminds me so much of Sophie.'

Jacob frowns at me. 'Don't let Milli get away with things, Dad . . . You always allowed Sophie to get away with murder.'

I frown straight back at him. 'That's uncalled for,' I say sternly. 'I was very fair with both of you, just like I am with Milli and Hugo.'

Jacob is silent for a while. I'm getting the impression that he's out of sorts: maybe his day at the office wasn't as unexciting as he claims.

'Do you remember the time Sophie almost broke my fingers with her tennis racquet?'

'What?'

'I was about eleven. I remember the plastic rim coming down on my knuckles – the burst of pain, the shock – before she did it again, and again. I remember bawling my eyes out as I ran off to tell on her. I remember Mum trying to kiss it better, sending you to get some ice, but most of all I remember that Sophie got away with it.'

I don't remember the incident at all. 'We must've thought it was an accident . . . Sophie wouldn't hurt you on purpose. You know that, Jacob.'

'But she did hurt me on purpose. There was nothing accidental about it, nothing at all. I was winning the tennis game and she couldn't stand it. She couldn't stand losing.'

There might be some truth in that. Despite being a year younger, Sophie was a faster runner and swimmer than Jacob, and he didn't come anywhere near her academic ability either. Tennis was the only thing he could beat her at. His reflexes were faster, it was as simple as that, but I'm sure it must have annoyed her. She was fiercely competitive.

'I used to concede points to make the games closer than they were because there was always a backlash if I completely thrashed her: a pinch, or a kick to the shin, or she'd hide my books or my soccer ball. But you and Mum couldn't see that side of her. Everyone loves the clever, talented kids, and it takes imagination and perseverance to look beyond that and see what's really beneath.'

Bloody hell, Jacob can hold on to a grudge. He's talking about stuff that happened twenty-odd years ago. Normal brother–sister scuffles and disagreements. Take Milli and Hugo, for example. Their constant tussles throughout the day, their cute little fights. How Milli invariably has the upper hand. How Hugo takes it, takes it, takes it, before finally cracking and pushing her away.

'Look, Jacob, Sophie didn't do anything to you that Milli won't do to Hugo. It's normal for children to fight and hurt each other and for one of them to come out on top. One day Milli will be infuriated about something and there will be a tennis racquet or a cricket bat nearby, and what do you think will happen?'

He crosses his arms. 'If that happens, then Milli won't get away with it. Carolyn and I will punish her accordingly.'

I frown at him again. 'Do you think your mother and I were bad parents? Is that what you're saying?'

'No, no, I'm not saying that at all.'

I'm not sure he's telling the truth. I'm bloody annoyed, to be honest. Has he ever put himself in our shoes?

'How would you and Carolyn feel if Hugo and Milli were barely speaking twenty or thirty years from now?'

That makes him pause for thought. Of course he'd be upset – like Dee and I are – if his grown-up children didn't get along. Isn't that the whole point of having more than one child? The belief that they'll be there for each other? That they'll form their own little unit and pull together in the good times and the bad?

'Like I'd failed as a parent,' he admits. 'I'd be heartbroken.'

'Exactly. You're a grown man, a father of two children with vastly different personalities. There will be many, many altercations ahead . . . You must understand that holding grudges is just about the worst thing one can do.'

Sophie might have been overly competitive and at times spiteful as a child, but Jacob was far too sensitive and always wanted to believe the worst of her. Jacob was in his first year at university (studying communications and media) when Kristina Owens made those shocking allegations.

'Are you sure she didn't do it?' he asked me one night when it was just the two of us at home. Dee and Sophie were at training of some description – Sophie was involved in a lot of extracurricular activities. I had come into Jacob's room in search of dirty laundry, and he was lying on his bed, reading a book. He was an avid reader back then.

I looked up from the laundry basket to give him a withering stare. 'That isn't nice, Jacob . . . And how do you know about it, anyway?'

'I overheard you and Mum talking about it.'

'It's a serious allegation that's been made, a black mark against Sophie's character, and we're not going to take it.'

I gathered some dirty clothes from the basket and made to leave the room.

'She *is* capable of lying, you know,' Jacob suggested quietly.

I turned around and glared at him again. 'Jacob McCarthy! What's got into you tonight?'

I feel like saying the same to him right now. *What has got into you today?*

'You know, Jacob, your sister has been through a horrific experience . . . It makes me and your mother incredibly sad that you haven't truly supported her.'

Jacob looks a bit ashamed of himself then. 'Sorry, Dad, you're right. The thought of Milli and Hugo potentially falling out one day does make me want to do better with Sophie.'

Carolyn calls us in for dinner, which is a chaotic affair. The children have reached that time of the day – arsenic hour – when they can't be reasoned with. I say my goodbyes straight after the meal and commence the drive back to Sydney. The freeway is fairly quiet and I have the pleasure of being able to drive faster than usual. My thoughts are on Sophie and Jacob and the hope that our chat will bring about some improvement in their relationship. I had no idea that Jacob felt so aggrieved. Now that I think about it, holding a grudge is very closely connected to laying blame and, just like that, I'm back to Kristina Owens again. Of course the poor girl wanted to blame someone – other than herself – for her awful injuries. Of course she wanted to believe someone else was responsible. She was just a teenage girl, and of course her mind immediately latched on to the girl who epitomized all she had lost: Sophie.

The headmistress, if she was any bloody good at her job, should have figured this out. That woman pointed the finger at Sophie without stopping to think of the alternative: *Kristina being the liar.*

34

Hannah

I was on the other side of the gorge when the accident happened. I was with Felicity Harrison, my assigned partner for the orienteering exercise, and she had asked me to stop because she wanted to take yet another photo.

'Wow. Look at that tree. Amazing.'

Felicity Harrison was one of those overly enthusiastic girls. Fine in small doses, but harder to take over extended periods, like this two-hour trek. We were way behind schedule because we kept stopping to take photos of the trees, the wildlife, the view to the other side of the gorge and Felicity herself, in various poses in front of the very same trees, wildlife and view. In fact, we still hadn't reached the halfway mark, and I could see that some groups had crossed the infamous rope bridge – I could only imagine how many shots Felicity would want to take of that! – and were heading home along the far side.

So, while Felicity was zooming in on one of the strangler figs – it *was* rather impressive, I had to admit – I was staring into the far distance across the gorge. There were two girls almost directly across and they had stopped, like we had. I was about to raise my hand to wave and call out to them – as we had been doing with other groups – when one of them, the girl in red, seemed to disappear suddenly. My eyes followed her down the ravine, an ominous flash of red bouncing through the undergrowth and rocks, in what felt like slow motion. Then the echo of her scream reached my ears.

'Oh my God! Someone has fallen.'

Felicity lowered the camera from her face. 'Who? What?'

'I can't see who . . . we're too far away. Give me the camera. Quick.'

Felicity obediently lifted the camera strap over her head and handed it to me. I zoomed in and found what I was looking for: a red shirt among the brown-green undergrowth and grey rocks.

'She's not moving.'

'Who is it?' Felicity asked breathlessly.

'I can't see her face.'

I brought the camera up so that I was looking straight across again.

'That's Sophie McCarthy at the top. It must be her partner who has fallen. Do you know who she was with?'

Felicity shook her head. 'No.'

'Sophie looks like she's about to climb down there.' I handed the camera back to Felicity. 'Come on. We have to turn back and get help.'

Felicity and I retraced our steps, covering the return journey at a much greater speed. We didn't talk much, concentrating on moving as fast as we could, jogging along the narrow and sometimes treacherous path, our breath panting in our ears. Back at the camp we found the first available teacher and blurted out a teary account of what had happened – shock was beginning to set in.

Within an hour or two everyone knew about the accident and the name of the girl who had fallen: Kristina Owens. She was a well-known face at the school, captain of both the netball team and the senior band. I didn't know her personally – she was a year ahead of me – but I felt as though I did. I had passed her in corridors, seen her taking books from her locker and witnessed her laughing with her friends. It was unfathomable to think that she had been stretchered out of the ravine by rescue paramedics, and that now she was unconscious in a hospital far from home when she should have been here, sitting around the campfire with the rest of us, drinking hot chocolate and trying to pretend that maths wasn't fun.

The next morning there was counselling offered to anyone who felt they needed it. Felicity went; Sophie too, or so I heard. I decided not to. I was still in a state of shock, and too young to understand the long-term impact an accident like that can have on you, how it can replay over and over in your head, as vivid as the day it happened, even though it's a lifetime later.

After some half-hearted maths tutorials – where no one could concentrate on the practical problems we were being asked to solve – the teachers realized the situation was irredeemable and organized for our buses to come a few hours earlier than planned.

'Oh, you're early,' Mum said when I came through the door. 'Had enough maths?'

It was a bit of a standing joke in our house: my love of

maths. Both Mum and Dad had been numerically chal-lenged at school – or so they claimed – and were half amused and half proud of my abilities.

But instead of giving her the grin she expected, I promptly burst into tears and launched myself into her arms.

'What is it, Hannah? What is it?'

I couldn't answer right away, I was too distressed. We stood there in the kitchen, and I cried for Kristina Owens. I cried as hard as I imagine I would have cried if she'd been my sister, or my best friend.

'What is it?' Mum kept asking, and it was quite some time before I could string together a coherent answer and give her an outline of what had happened.

'I thought you were at a maths camp. What were you doing orienteering?' she asked, pragmatic, as always.

'To get some fresh air and clear our heads,' I hiccupped. 'Before doing more maths.'

'Were there teachers on the walk?'

'Mr King and Miss Curtis.'

'Where? At the end of the group? Or the start?'

'The middle, I think.'

Mum was only asking the same questions all the other parents would ask over the following days. The school convened a special meeting to deal with the distraught children and angry parents.

Mrs Jones addressed us all from the podium. 'We are here tonight because we have been affected by the unfortunate accident that occurred during the orienteering activity ... And you all have questions and concerns, which is perfectly understandable. Questions about how such an accident could occur, and if there was proper supervision, and concerns over whether the activity being undertaken was a safe one . . . I can say that we have interviewed everyone involved . . .'

Not everyone. You haven't interviewed me.

'And there are differing accounts of what exactly happened – which is common in cases like this – but we feel that it is reasonable to conclude that the student in question, who was walking ahead of her partner, came across a dangerous section of the path and lost her footing, which led to the fall . . .'

Should I put my hand up? Tell her what I saw? That Kristina Owens was not walking ahead? That she and Sophie had stopped, like Felicity and me on the other side of the ravine. Had Kristina been about to take a swig from her drink bottle, or was I imagining that?

I had been very far away from it all. Maybe Kristina *was* slightly ahead. I could have sworn they had stopped, though. But I wasn't sure enough to put up my hand and draw attention to myself.

'A safety assessment is currently being undertaken at the camp, and the final report will be shared with all the parents and students involved. Kristina herself is – understandably – traumatized and must now concentrate all her energy on getting well. In the meantime, we have talked to everyone else . . .'

So they've spoken to Sophie? Well, obviously. Sophie would have been the key witness. And she had no reason to lie about who was standing where at the point of the fall.

Mrs Jones droned on for another fifteen minutes or so, and then took questions – of which there were many. I sat through it all, not saying a word, not even to Mum, who would have been a good sounding board.

Sophie had no reason to lie. That's what I thought, and that's the main reason I didn't put up my hand (the other reason was that I was painfully shy and simply didn't have the self-confidence required to stop the headmistress mid-flow).

Six months later I realized that maybe Sophie McCarthy *did* have a reason to lie, after all. It was when I heard her name being called out at the end-of-year ceremony. When I saw her triumphant smile as she accepted the plaque from the mayor: Dux of St Brigid's.

When someone behind me whispered: 'That should have been Kristina Owens.'

Until that moment I'd no idea that Kristina and Sophie were rivals. My imagination went into overdrive. I envisaged an ongoing feud between the girls, culminating in a dramatic wrestling match at the side of the ravine. It was complete conjecture on my part: like most teenage girls, I had a penchant for drama. The truth is, I saw nothing other than Kristina falling, and Sophie standing there, before starting to climb down to help. I didn't know what to make of it at the time, and I still don't today. These last few nights, lying in bed, I've found myself looking across that gorge and trying to make sense of it. How Kristina fell, and why, or even if, Sophie lied. And the answer is, I don't know. I just don't know.

Teenage girls can lie for no reason at all. Maybe she lied

out of panic because she thought she could get in trouble for something that wasn't her fault. Or maybe it was a knee-jerk reaction, a psychological reflex to distance herself from the trauma.

I don't know. I just don't know. And I will never know.

35

Aidan

Last night I dreamed that Jasmin was in Iraq, that she was one of a group of caramel-coloured children playing hide-and-seek in a bombed-out building. The children giggled as they darted to their various hiding spots, oblivious to the danger of the partially collapsed walls and the heavily armed insurgents nearby. I tried to warn them, to shoo them away, but it was as though they were in a different realm to me and couldn't hear me roaring at them. The insurgents attacked, as I knew they would, and bullets ricocheted off the crumbled walls. The children ran from their hiding spots, straight into the gunfire, and fell one by one. I dropped to my knees to cradle one of the dead in my arms. It was a girl, and when I pulled back her hijab to better see her face, I saw that she was my own daughter. I woke with a scream in my throat, my heart thumping with grief and terror. My dreams are often a macabre mix of the present and the past. Jasmin wasn't even born when we invaded Baghdad, and yet it had felt so real, real enough for my hands to continue to shake while I'm shaving, causing the razor to nick the underside of my chin.

This morning I'm meeting my solicitor, Barry Ford. Barry came recommended by one of the legal corps at the barracks. My first meeting with Barry was about two months after the accident. His office was on the fifteenth floor of a new building in Sussex Street and had a spectacular view of Darling Harbour. Barry wore an expensive-looking shirt and tie and had diamond cufflinks flashing on his wrists; he presented as one of those extremely well-groomed older men. I was in full uniform, my boots planted on the luxurious carpet, my beret in my hands. I felt – and looked, I am quite sure – completely at odds with my surroundings.

'I want to plead guilty,' I told him in no uncertain terms. I had received a court-attendance notice from the police. I intended to enter my plea at the first opportunity. The accident was my fault, my mistake, and I couldn't live with myself if I didn't take full responsibility. Being responsible also meant hiring a good solicitor. Someone who had a wealth of experience with cases like mine, and who could add their expertise to my principles (my need to admit culpability) to achieve the best possible outcome in court.

'I respect your desire to take responsibility, Captain Ryan. But you need to be aware of what this means . . . By pleading guilty, you're admitting to the necessary elements of the crime, including being of sound mind at the time. As soon as that plea is entered, there's no going back on either of these points. Are you sure this is how you want to proceed?'

My stare was unflinching. 'I wasn't paying due attention to my driving that morning. I was tired and distracted, but I was perfectly sane. To say otherwise would be lying.'

'Quite,' said Barry Ford, giving a little cough.

I entered my plea, but then a number of adjournments (initially due to my attendance at a traffic offenders' programme, and then because of necessary military commitments) caused the usual timelines to stretch out. Finally we have a firm court date for the sentencing and here I am, back in Barry Ford's swish fifteenth-floor office, the cut on my chin stinging slightly as Barry explains, once again, the relevant laws and penalties.

'A person must not drive a motor vehicle negligently on a road or road-related area. If the driving occasions grievous bodily harm, the maximum penalty is imprisonment for nine months, or disqualification for up to three years, or both ... There's the fine – $2,200. This is all for a first offence ... It gets more serious after that.'

The prospect of nine months in prison sounds serious enough to me.

'What're the chances I'll get put away?' I've asked this question before and, for Jasmin's sake, I feel compelled to ask again. A flash of last night's dream comes back to me – the horror of seeing her lifeless face behind the hijab, the crushing grief that still hasn't quite gone away. Jasmin knows about the accident, that I made a mistake and will be punished – just like she is when she does something wrong – but I haven't yet broached the fact that a court date has been set, or that prison is a possibility. Should the worst case eventuate and I'm locked up for however many months, what kind of toll would that take on my daughter? Would the added anxiety and embarrassment cause her sleeping to deteriorate even further?

Would other behavioural problems begin to manifest? What would happen at school, with her friends? Once or twice, I've deluded myself with the notion that maybe the shock of having her father incarcerated would push a reset button in her brain, her sleeping miraculously correcting itself.

This time it's Barry whose stare doesn't flinch. 'In all probability, you'll be ordered to enter into a good behaviour bond, and that's all. There are so many factors in your favour, Captain Ryan. No criminal history, no traffic history, your being an indisputably worthwhile member of society and a person of good character, the accident occurring because of a momentary lapse of attention rather than a sustained period of reckless driving, and you showing *great remorse* for your actions . . . A good behaviour bond and a fine, that will be it.'

I hope it's that straightforward, I really do. 'And my licence?'

'The judge may extend the disqualification, but it's more likely that he'll be happy with the twelve-month suspension you've already had.'

It seems odd to have to go to court – to pay for medical reports, expert opinions, solicitor and court fees – when the outcome seems almost predetermined. I suppose the police need to push cases like these through to their full conclusion – predictable though it may be. Otherwise, there would be no accountability, no consequences, no structure in place to stem the recklessness – and terrible damage – we're all capable of every time we sit behind the wheel of a vehicle.

Barry continues speaking. 'Now, our main objective today is to expand on your background and other subjective factors. I'll need details of your upbringing, your responsibilities at work, stable family circumstances, that sort of thing. I'll also need some character references for –'

I cut him off. 'There's something you should know . . . about my family circumstances . . . Sorry, I should've mentioned it earlier . . . You see, something rather fundamental has changed since we last met. The victim – Sophie McCarthy – and me . . . well, we're in a relationship . . .'

Barry's mouth drops open. A few moments pass before he collects himself to ask, 'What kind of relationship, exactly?'

My grip on my beret tightens. 'We're living together.'

'I see . . . And your wife?'

Chloe's face – hurt, shocked, blotched from crying – flashes in front of my eyes. 'I've separated from my wife.'

My solicitor temporarily abandons his notes and pushes back from his desk. 'How did this happen, if I may ask?'

'We fell in love,' I say, as though it were that simple.

'You fell in love,' Barry repeats slowly. 'When? I mean, how long after the accident?'

It's hard to pinpoint the exact timing. At what point did my concern for Sophie, and my remorse, morph into attraction and love? At the hospital, when she was so helpless yet so feisty? When I started to visit her at home, helping wherever she needed my help and in the process seeing how clever and determined and resilient she was? When she declared her feelings for me and forced me to acknowledge my own? Would it put things in context for

Barry if I explained that I fought my feelings as hard as I've fought in any battle? That I did everything in my power to defeat them, to kill them off? Would it help if I told him there was a period of transition, a few weeks when I slept on a colleague's couch, confused and distressed, until it became clear that everyone involved – even Jasmin, who was the most vulnerable – deserved my honesty, if nothing else? And what would Barry make of the fact that everything is still far from clear-cut and resolved? That Sophie and I have argued about Jasmin, and that not a day goes by when I don't think about Chloe? When I don't miss her?

'A few months ago.'

Barry pulls his chair in close to his desk again before he mumbles, more to himself than me, 'Well, that certainly puts a different spin on things.'

'Does it?' I ask. 'Will the fact that Sophie has forgiven me make any difference to the outcome?'

'Sorry, I was speaking more from my own point of view,' he clarifies. 'The judge may take it into account when he's considering special circumstances . . . But at the end of the day, the law is the law, and negligent driving is a crime, no matter how forgiving the victim might feel.' He picks up his pen, poised to make further notes. 'Now, the other thing we need to do today is organize a psychiatric assessment for you. It's pretty standard in cases like these.'

A psychiatric assessment for a soldier is like a car crash of a different kind. Scratch the surface and you don't know what the hell you'll find.

'No problem. Just tell me who to see.'

36

Jasmin

They put me in a swing and asked me if I liked it. I did. I was allowed to swing for as long as I wanted to. That never happens in the park; there's always someone else waiting – younger kids – and Mum makes me get off so they can have a turn.

Then they put me in a hammock and asked what I thought of that. I liked it too. Actually, I nearly fell asleep in there (I was really tired from last night). There were two of them, a woman and a man. The woman – Rosemary – was in charge. The man was training to become a physiotherapist. He took lots of notes.

There was a gym, with monkey bars and ladders and climbing nets. I explained to Rosemary that I'm bad with heights and she asked me to try my best, so I did. She taught me a new word, *acrophobia*, and gave me a high five each time I managed to climb to the top. Next, we did trampolining, tug of war, push-ups and wrestling. The wrestling was my favourite. The man did it with me. He said I was super-strong, tougher than most boys.

Mum and Dad were sitting close together on the red couch in the waiting room. They looked like they were having a Really Serious Discussion, and I wished we hadn't come out right then and interrupted them because they could've been talking about getting back together.

'Jasmin did really well today,' Rosemary said, pulling up a chair so she was opposite Mum and Dad. I stayed standing, even though my legs were tired. 'We did a lot of specific activities that should help self-regulate her level of arousal and prevent sensory overload at bedtime.'

'There was a swing and a hammock and a trampoline . . .' I said. My voice was breathless.

Rosemary gave me a smile. 'Sit down, Jasmin. You must be worn out.'

I sat next to Daddy, and he pulled me close. He was in his uniform. He had taken some time off work again.

'Based on what we observed today, we've prepared a sensory diet for Jasmin,' Rosemary said, handing Mum a document to read.

'A sensory diet?' Mum asked, wearing one of her sceptical expressions.

Rosemary nodded at Mum, as though she had been expecting this reaction. 'A sensory diet is like a plan, making sure the child has enough of the right activities to regulate their level of alertness. Activities that involve heavy resistance and input to the joints and muscles are particularly effective. Pushing, pulling, bouncing, jumping, climbing, that sort of thing. This is why a tight hug can be so calming if one is feeling upset about something . . .' Rosemary went on, using lots of words I've never heard of: 'vestibular', 'tactile', 'cognitive'. 'Oral activities can be particularly effective too. Chewing gum, blowing up balloons, sucking drinks through straws. I've enclosed a list of crunchy foods . . .'

'Is it really going to work?' I asked Mum and Dad when we got outside.

I didn't want to be sceptical, but the sugar hadn't worked. Neither had the 'consequences'.

'Let's hope so,' said Mum in a tired voice.

'It'll be fun.' Daddy grinned, obviously trying to make up for Mum's lack of enthusiasm. 'I foresee many great wrestling matches.'

'You'd better watch out,' I told him.

'No, *you'd* better watch out. I'll be using all my dirty tricks. Such as this . . .' He gave me a sloppy kiss on the cheek.

I wiped my face. '*Yuck*.'

He laughed. 'I'd better go. I'll see you at the weekend, OK?'

'OK, Daddy. Bye.'

I'm having another try at staying over with him on Saturday night. I just hope all the jumping and bouncing and pushing is working by then. Otherwise, Sophie will get really, really annoyed again.

37

Chloe

I finally brought it up with him. At the physiotherapist's, while we were waiting for Jasmin. It took every ounce of courage I had, to take the bill from my handbag and offer it to him, to force the issue like that, to demand a decision, to pretend our unborn babies amounted to nothing more than money that needed to be paid, or money that could potentially be saved, depending on what we decided.

'This came last week . . . It's the storage costs . . . from the clinic.'

Aidan took the invoice from my outstretched hand and stared down at it. Neither of us said anything. I regretted it then. I wanted to snatch it back from him, and say, *Forget it*. We were alone, but still it was the wrong place for this kind of discussion. Not that any discussion was happening; we were like mutes, both of us. But it needed to be dealt with, and I had gone this far. Aidan looked completely at a loss, and so it was up to me to say the unspeakable.

'It doesn't make sense to keep on paying . . . We're not a couple . . . These babies are not going to be born.' My voice broke, and a few moments passed before I could trust myself to speak again. 'I can't believe it has come to this . . . It breaks my heart, it really does, but we need to be practical about this.'

Still no response. I could see the pulse throbbing on his neck, and I knew how hard he was working to contain his emotions.

'I'm sorry,' he whispered, finally meeting my eyes. 'I know how badly you wanted those babies . . .'

'*We* wanted them, Aidan,' I corrected him furiously. 'Not just me.'

'Yes.' He hung his head again. 'I know . . . I know.'

It was hard to stay angry when he was so obviously upset. I softened my tone. 'So what are we going to do?'

'I don't know, Chloe. I just don't know.'

And it was hard to watch him – usually so decisive and sure of himself – flounder like this.

'We can't keep paying it month after month . . . You're living with someone else, for pity's sake.' Another flash of anger from me.

He looked at me again. 'What would they do with the embryos if we don't pay?'

'Destroy them,' I whispered.

'How?'

'I'm not sure I want to know.'

And that's where we were at when Jasmin bounded in. Her face was flushed, her ponytail askew, her words tripping over each other; she had never been so absolutely perfect. Were our unborn babies genetically similar? Did they have her dark hair and honey-brown eyes? Did they have the same big heart, ingrained conscientiousness and unfailing enthusiasm? Potentially, the same difficulties falling asleep at night?

Jasmin sat down next to Aidan and he put his arm around her shoulders; our eyes met over her head and I knew the exact same thoughts were crossing his mind. These were *our* babies we were talking about, Jasmin's brothers and sisters.

Rosemary started to run through the sensory diet with us. I felt jaded listening to her. We've tried so many different things it's hard to maintain any kind of optimism or enthusiasm.

We said goodbye outside. Aidan gave Jasmin one of the sloppy kisses she loves to hate, then he took my hand and squeezed it.

'I need some time to think about what we discussed . . . Can I sleep on it?'

Jasmin was watching us closely.

'Sure.' I used a brisk tone, to stop our daughter from getting ideas. 'I'll see you on Saturday, at the game. We'll talk then.'

Today, I need to be brave all over again. Aidan's coming to soccer, and Jasmin is going home with him afterwards. My husband and daughter will leave the soccer pitch, hand in hand, and I'll be left behind. The whole afternoon, evening, night, and most of tomorrow on my own. I need to look as though I'm not devastated at the thought. Even better if I manage to look excited. Pity I was never any good at acting.

'Jasmin, your laces are undone . . .'

My daughter looks down, surprised. She shouldn't be; this is a regular occurrence. She is often too busy talking or looking around to apply herself properly to the task.

'Come here.' I bend down and pull the first pair tightly before tying a double knot.

'Do you think we'll win today, Mum?' she asks from above.

Despite the promise of the first game, we haven't yet managed to secure a win. It's hard to pinpoint why. The Cheetahs are a good little team, gritty and quite skilful for their age. I guess it's luck . . . it hasn't been on their side. And I know how that feels.

'It's not about winning. It's about trying your best. Other foot.'

'There's Daddy . . . And Sophie.'

Sophie? Oh Lord, I guess she gave him a lift. I imagined him coming here on the bus, not with *her*.

The second lace needs to be unpicked before I can tie it properly.

'There.' I stand up too quickly, blood rushing to my face. Aidan and Sophie are right in front of me, holding hands. For pity's sake, why rub my face in it? Couldn't they pretend, just for my sake, just for one measly hour, that they're not intimate with each other? Spare me some degree of humiliation?

'Morning.' Aidan ruffles Jasmin's hair. 'How did you sleep?'

Jasmin shrugs and looks to me for an assessment.

'Better than usual,' I say a little breathlessly. 'She only got up four times.'

I'd been looking forward to sharing this news with Aidan, but Sophie standing here – with that perpetual unimpressed expression and my husband's hand clutched possessively in hers – has sort of taken the moment away and made me question what I thought of as a definite improvement.

Jasmin darts away, joining the circle around her coach to receive a last-minute pep talk. Sophie, Aidan and I are left alone, not knowing where to look or position ourselves. We'll never be able to pull this off. We'll never be able to achieve that amicable, easy-going camaraderie that other separated couples manage to achieve when new partners and new children are added to the mix. I feel anything but amicable.

'Here's her bag.' I thrust the backpack at Aidan. 'She wanted to do her own packing, so goodness knows what's in there.'

'Thanks.' He sets it by his feet. 'So last night was better?'

'Yes. A little.'

I desperately want to elaborate and give a blow-by-blow account, but it's impossible with Sophie. She radiates disapproval and lack of interest in equal measure.

The game starts, and the three of us form a line: Sophie, Aidan, then me. It's a relief to have something to focus on, something other than the fact that my husband is standing right next to me with another woman. At least they've stopped holding hands.

'Come on, Cheetahs!' I call out, my voice sounding as hollow as I feel inside.

About ten minutes into the first half, Aidan leans in

closer to me, so close that his breath is warm on my face. 'About that issue we discussed . . . I'm not ready . . . I need more time.' His voice is barely audible.

I watch some play before I murmur, 'Take whatever time you need.'

I did some research last night. Apparently we can donate the embryos, but that's only barely more acceptable than discarding them. They're our babies. They belong with us, in *our* family, not in another. Of course I can't say any of this right at this moment, unless I want Sophie to hear. Does she know about this dilemma we have? Has Aidan discussed it with her?

Hannah is here. She catches my eye and gives me a smile. It's a lifeline, that smile of hers.

'I just need to catch someone,' I say to Aidan. 'A friend . . . I'll be back later . . .'

As I make my way towards Hannah, a ball comes whizzing over the sideline, narrowly missing my head.

'Sorry, Mrs Ryan.'

The culprit is Finn, one of the twins.

'That's all right,' I say cheerily. 'No brain damage . . . This time.'

Everyone laughs, and I hand the ball to the opposing team for the throw-in.

Never mind brain damage, it's heart damage that's the problem here. *I have lost the man I love, my soul mate, the father of my children (yes, I am counting the ones who haven't been born).* I can make jokes, I can tie laces, I can walk and talk, I can function. But my heart is torn to pieces. I am not sure it will ever be whole again.

38

Hannah

Flipping heck! I don't believe it. Sophie McCarthy. Again. At the soccer field, of all places. I thought I was hallucinating at first but, no, she's for real. There she is, wearing a beanie and one of those big, puffy jackets. She's going to be too hot in all that gear. It's only the first half-hour or so that's cold, then the autumn sunshine kicks in. Is that Chloe's ex she's talking to? Talk about six degrees of separation! Is there no getting away from her? I was still getting emails when I went to bed last night, at 11 p.m. At least she hasn't seen me. Not yet.

'I know that woman, the one standing next to Aidan,' I say to Chloe, when she comes over a few minutes later. 'I work with her.'

She looks taken aback. 'You work with Sophie?'

'She's my boss,' I say, trying to keep a neutral tone.

'Oh.'

Chloe shoves her hands in her pockets. The action feels defensive, and it makes me look closer at her face. Her mouth seems to have a slight tremble. She's upset. About Sophie? Or her ex-husband? Or maybe it's something else entirely. Even though I'm bursting with questions – Are Sophie and Aidan a couple? It certainly looks like it. Does Chloe get on with her? Maybe Sophie's a lot more agreeable socially than she is at work – I make myself shut up and concentrate on the game.

For the next fifteen minutes or so we stand mostly in silence, other than the odd word of encouragement called out to our kids, who're being run ragged by the opposition but – somehow – haven't yet conceded a goal. After another few close calls, the whistle blows for half-time.

'Get your drinks, team.' Davy is standing right next to us, his white hair standing up from the breeze. 'Gather round.'

He waits until they all have their drink bottles, then crouches down so he's at their level.

'Now, the good news is that youse haven't conceded a goal . . .'

'What's the bad news?' Callum asks.

'Trust Callum to be negative,' I say sotto voce to Chloe, and she smiles.

'The bad news is they're dominating us,' Davy answers bluntly. 'They're making us run, and we're getting tired . . .'

It sounds like my work. I'm being dominated too, being made to run around and chase my tail, and I'm fatiguing.

'What's Sophie like to work for?' Chloe asks, with uncanny timing.

I hesitate. I don't like to be indiscreet but, after the stress of the last few weeks, it's hard to conjure up an outright lie. Dishonesty takes energy, something I'm completely out of.

'Tough.' There, that was honest, and not too derogatory.

Chloe grimaces. 'Yes, I imagine she'd be a hard taskmaster.'

'How do you get on with her?' I ask, turning so I can fully see her face.

'To be fair, I think I'd find it hard to like anyone who's in a relationship with Aidan ... I'm too emotionally involved ...' She sniffs, then plucks a tissue from her pocket and blows her nose. 'Sorry, I think I'm coming down with a cold.'

I feel her misery so keenly it could almost be my own. She's a pretty girl, Chloe, but this morning – with her red nose and drawn face – she looks worn out, trampled on.

'How long have they been together?' I ask sympathetically, hoping for her sake that it turns out to be a short-lived fling.

'A few months ... I'm as bad now as I was at the start. I can't accept it, Hannah. It's doubly hard, given the circumstances ... I can't stop blaming myself for how things have turned out.'

'How exactly did they meet? Was she a friend of yours?'

'No. Never.' Chloe's response is vehement. 'We crashed into her car one morning. Aidan was driving, we were both distracted ...'

Suddenly I can picture the scene. Two mangled cars. Fates intersecting. The guilt, the responsibility, the consequences. 'Oh my God ... the accident that caused her to miss all that time from work ...'

'Yes, that was because of us ... Aidan and me.'

'Did it go to court?'

'Yes. Aidan pleaded guilty. He's going to be sentenced in a few weeks' time. We're all on tenterhooks, waiting.'

'And when did . . . How did they . . .' I'm making a mess of this, but she knows exactly what I'm asking.

'When did they fall in love? Afterwards . . . He saw a lot of her. He wanted to help her out. And it just happened, his feelings changed, or so he says . . .' Chloe tries to smile, but once again it looks more like a grimace. 'And if it's not hard enough seeing her here with him today, or them *living* together, I also have to grapple with Jasmin being drawn into it. She stays with them every other weekend now. She's with Sophie when she should be with me.'

The game resumes. Despite Davy's pep talk, the other team continues to dominate, resulting in two quick goals. The game looks irredeemable and the team is clearly disheartened.

'I'd better go back,' Chloe says. 'I don't want them to think I'm being antisocial.'

'Of course.'

Slowly she makes her way down the sideline, coming to a stop next to Aidan. He turns towards her and says something. I should stop staring.

I feel sorry for her. How could I not? I know just how lonely she'll be tonight, and tomorrow. When Harry died, I felt the same. The weekends were like an abyss, insurmountable, never-ending. But at least I didn't have to watch him holding hands with another woman. I can only imagine how agonizing that would be for Chloe.

'Come on, Cheetahs!' Callum shouts from the far side of the field. 'Let's get one back off them.'

He's been very vocal this game, calling out to his team mates, shouting, 'Time!' and 'Man on!' and 'Well in!' It must be something Davy is trying to instil at training. It's good.

For once, it's Finn who's the despondent one.

'We're not going to win any games this season,' he moans in the car on the way home. 'We're going to come last.'

'We *are* going to win,' Callum counters fiercely. 'That team is top of the league, and we only lost by two goals . . .'

'It's not about winning,' I say, wondering how many parents across the city, across the country, are bandying about that exact same phrase on their way home from Saturday sport. 'Callum's right . . . They were a good side, and your team made a valiant effort.'

'What does "valiant" mean?' Finn still sounds sulky.

'Brave. Fearless.'

Speaking of bravery, it was decidedly cowardly of me not to go over to Sophie. She obviously didn't see me, but I *did* see her, and the grown-up thing to do would have been to say hello, at the very least. Something came over me there on the sideline: as one part of my brain was telling me I should approach her, another, stronger, part was resisting with all its might. I'm a grown woman. Why should I have to be sociable with people I just don't like? What is the point?

The thought stays with me for the rest of the drive home: *I don't like Sophie McCarthy.* It has taken me quite a long time to arrive at this conclusion, because I was trying so hard to be positive, but now that I'm here I feel quite definite about it. I don't like how Sophie behaves at work, how she creates deadlines almost for sport, how she huffs and puffs and harasses her staff. I don't like how she backed Jane into a corner – goading her into a resignation – and I don't like how she has no respect for other people's partners, or children, or private lives. Yes, she got me a pay rise, and for a while that distracted me, fooled me into believing that perhaps there was a better, nicer, kinder side to her. The truth is, the pay rise wasn't about generosity on her part, or an acknowledgement of my efforts and hard work, or even sympathy about my financial situation. The pay rise was about keeping me in line, *indebted*, putting me in a position where I couldn't say no to her demands, which have been coming in thicker and faster than ever.

Another thing I don't like about Sophie McCarthy, although it is absolutely none of my business, is her relationship with Chloe's ex. Poor Chloe is obviously heartbroken. Jasmin left directly after the game, with Aidan and Sophie on either side of her. She had a bright pink backpack on her shoulders, presumably her overnight bag, and she looked every bit as reluctant about the sleepover as her mother did.

A conversation comes back to me, from Sophie's office, a few weeks ago. Didn't she say something about her partner's daughter being a nightmare to get to sleep at night? Is it because Jasmin feels anxious, intimidated, threatened? All the things I feel when I'm around Sophie? Oh my God, I remember now: Sophie made a joke about giving Jasmin a good old-fashioned smack. *Was* it a joke? She wouldn't go as far as hitting Jasmin, would she?

Back in the early days with Harry, when we'd talk late

into the night, exchanging our innermost thoughts and fears and dreams, I told him about Sophie. About what I saw that day at the ravine.

Harry had laughed. 'So what are you saying, Hannie? That the girl was pushed? By her walking partner?'

I remember getting annoyed with him. 'It's not a joke. She lied. Why would she lie if she didn't have something to hide?'

Harry tried to pull me close for a kiss. I shoved him away.

'So why didn't you say anything at the time?' he asked, taking me more seriously.

'Because I didn't have the confidence to speak up. That's why. And it's not as if I saw the push. All I knew was that she lied. And I convinced myself that I didn't even know that for sure, that my eyes could've been playing tricks on me.'

It feels like centuries ago, that conversation with Harry.

But what if Sophie *did* push Kristina Owens down that ravine? What if she's genuinely dangerous? What if she saw Kristina as an impediment to her aspirations to be dux? And what if she sees Jasmin as an impediment to her life with Aidan?

The boys are fooling around in the back of the car, wrestling each other, arms and legs everywhere.

'Stop it, you two. That's an order.'

We get home, have lunch and get stuck into a school project. Then we have dinner, showers and watch a movie. It's late when I get to bed and I'm extremely tired. I yearn for sleep, oblivion, but instead I find myself back at the ravine. Looking across to the other side, trying to reconstruct the scene and who was where, trying to get my head around what actually happened. But it's useless. If only I had some certainty. If only I could be sure of what I saw, and what it meant.

I turn in bed, adjust the positioning of my pillow, and now I'm in the school hall, clapping as Sophie receives her plaque for dux, seeing a close-up of her flushed face and triumphant smile. How far was she prepared to go in order to secure that plaque?

I'm being melodramatic. There was never a suggestion by anyone at school that Kristina was pushed. Why am I being like this? Why am I so on edge?

It's because of Jasmin.

Her obvious reluctance as she left the soccer field sandwiched between Sophie and Aidan. How young and vulnerable she'd seemed. Knowing how downright intimidating Sophie can be at times. Knowing that Sophie regards Jasmin as an inconvenience, *at the very least*.

I can't help but be deeply troubled by it all.

39

Sophie

It's odd having a child in the back of the car. It makes me feel off balance, and a little irritable, if I'm honest. All Aidan's attention is directed at Jasmin, as though I'm not even here. It's not that I need to be the centre of attention. I'm old school, that's all. The 'children should be seen and not heard' school.

'Hey, are you all right back there?' Aidan enquires in an overly cheerful tone. 'It was a good game . . . A close one.'

From what I could see, it wasn't close at all. Why do parents feel compelled to lie? What's wrong with the truth? *The other team were better than you were. That's why you lost. End of story.*

'You played well . . . I was proud of you.'

As a matter of fact, Jasmin did play well. I was surprised; she was as good as any of the boys out there. It made me see a different side to her: tough, gritty, determined. She got a ball in the face once, and it obviously hurt, but she blinked away the tears of shock and refused to come off when the coach gave her the option. I liked that. Aidan seemed surprised when I offered to give him a lift to the game. Obviously, I would have preferred to spend my Saturday morning sleeping in, but the thought of the three of them being all cosy together urged me out of bed. Chloe seemed shocked to see me there, which was the whole point. I made sure Aidan and I were holding hands.

Aidan is constantly checking the rear-view mirror, smiling back at Jasmin, and looking over his shoulder whenever we stop. 'I thought we might make some pasta tonight . . . You can help . . . and we'll watch another movie . . .' The distraction level is phenomenal. I'm just glad I'm the one who's driving; I can see how children cause car accidents. Speaking of accidents, the police contacted me yesterday, looking for further medical reports, which I faxed through straight away. I'm dreading the hearing, reliving the horror of the accident while at the same time worrying myself sick about Aidan. What if the judge comes down harder than Aidan's legal-advice team are expecting? What if he's incarcerated and I have to walk out of that court room alone? Unlikely, I know, but it's hanging over me, hanging over both of us. It'll be such an enormous relief when it's over. To make matters worse, Jane's hearing has been scheduled for the week before. It'll get thrown out, of course. An extraordinary waste of time, money and – especially for me – energy.

We get home, and everything continues to revolve around Jasmin.

'Hey, Jazz, what would you like for lunch?'

'Want to go to the park for a kick-around?'

'You want a snack? No problem.'

'Which movie should we choose, Jazz?'

'You're hungry? Again?'

'Sure, I'll just find a deck of cards and we'll have a game.'

It doesn't stop. All afternoon, on and on and on. Aidan radiates contentment. This is normal to him, the constant consultations with his daughter about food and entertainment. I can't stand it. Peace and quiet, that's all I ask for at the weekends. Nothing too strenuous or taxing. Just Aidan and me, pottering around the house, recharging our batteries, spending time together. Instead, I get this *onslaught*.

By late afternoon my head is beginning to throb and the need to get away from them has become urgent.

'I need a rest . . . I'm just going to lie down.'

As soon as the bedroom door is shut and there's a firm distance established, some of my tension eases. I lie on the bed, eyes closed, my favourite music – *Clair de lune*, Debussy – filling my earphones. I don't know how mothers do it, how they keep their sanity, barraged by broods of children and constant demands. One thing I know for certain: it's not for me. There's only one of Jasmin, and that's unbearable enough.

Once I've re-established my equilibrium, I pull out the earphones, stack some pillows behind my back and reach for my laptop. People regenerate in different ways: exercise, reading, or – like Aidan – spending time with children. For me, it's work. Firing off emails, making snap decisions, ticking things off my to-do list, has always been cathartic.

An hour flies past, and it's time to resurface, unfortunately. The kitchen is chaotic. Aidan is one of those parents who like to cook with their kids. Ingredients are strewn across the countertop. Pots and pans and plates are piled in the sink. Jasmin has a smear of flour on her face that would be endearing if I were in any way maternal. She seems to be munching on something.

'What's that you're eating?'

She sticks her tongue through her teeth to blow a bubble. 'Chewing gum.'

I raise one brow at Aidan. 'Isn't she a bit young for that?'

'The physiotherapist recommended it. Chewing's good for sensory regulation.'

Oh, for God's sake. What rubbish!

'I've opened a bottle of wine . . .' He's tentative, because I don't often drink, at least not since the accident. It seems to bring on headaches; even one glass is enough to make me feel quite dire the following morning. But if there was ever a night I needed it, it's tonight.

'Yeah, pour me one.'

The pasta is delicious, and what's even better is that I keep my portion small, showing a reassuring flash of my old self-control. I've been trying to work on my diet, to cater for the fact that I can't really exercise. Being back at work has been both a great distraction (I have plenty to think about other than food) and motivator (my work clothes were uncomfortably tight at the start, but already there's been an improvement). The wine isn't exactly healthy, but it has mellowed my mood. Aidan puts on the movie. It's one of those PG-rated family ones, riddled with corny jokes, which Jasmin finds hilarious. After tolerating an hour of it, I retrieve my laptop from the bedroom and shoot out some more emails.

Finally the movie is over – the ending was obvious in the first five minutes – and it's Jasmin's bedtime. But, of course, that's not the end of anything. It's the start of an extraordinarily long pre-bedtime routine that involves frog leaps, bunny-hops and push-ups.

'Come on, Jasmin. Press back on your hands. That's right. Now tuck your feet in . . . Two sets of ten.'

What is Aidan trying to do? Wake the child up?

'Shouldn't Jasmin be winding down at this hour, rather than jumping around the place?'

'This *will* wind her down,' he says, choosing to ignore my sarcasm. 'It's part of her sensory diet.'

Sensory diet? *Seriously?*

Finally he finishes with the aerobics class and puts her to bed.

'Thanks for today,' he says when we're finally alone. 'You were great.'

Great? I hardly spoke to Jasmin. Didn't he notice? Of course he didn't. He's so fucking focused on her he can't see what's right in front of his nose.

'Fingers crossed she'll fall asleep straight away. Chloe says she's seen an improvement.'

I don't share his optimism. I give her twenty minutes. At best.

He pulls me closer, drops a kiss on my head. Then our lips meet and for a few minutes I forget about Jasmin, at least until the thump coming from her bedroom pulls us apart. Moments later she floats in front of the television, her face as white as her pyjama top. Here we go.

'Daddy, I can't sleep . . .'

'You obviously need more pressure work.' Aidan pulls his arm away from my shoulders, leaving a cold draught behind. 'Come on, down on the floor. Twenty push-ups.'

He gets down next to her and does his own set, the veins on his neck straining from the effort. 'Eighteen, nineteen, twenty . . . Right, that should do it.'

It doesn't do it. Ten minutes later she's up again, and they each do another set of push-ups, puffing and grunting on my rug. And ten minutes after that she reappears yet again, and, hey, it's another set of twenty. He sends her back to bed, and we wait for the tell-tale thud. Ten minutes pass, then twenty, then – a fucking record! – a whole hour.

Aidan is actually pleased. 'Only three times in all. That was pretty good.'

'She couldn't bear the thought of doing any more push-ups!'

'Don't be like that.' He's smiling, but there's an underlying edge to his voice. 'The push-ups are part of her treatment plan.'

Seriously? Don't talk to me about treatment plans. What it feels like to spend months in a hospital bed, to endure multiple operations, to face the agonizing prospect of physiotherapy day after day, not to mention the cocktail of painkillers and drugs that puff up your face and somehow manage to make you both irritable and lethargic. *That's a treatment plan.* Not all this airy-fairy stuff about sensory diet, chewing gum and jumping around the place at bedtime.

The bedtime behaviour has nothing to do with sensory

overload. It's attention-seeking, plain and simple. It's been going on all day – in the car, in the kitchen, during the movie, when she kept glancing at him every time she found something to be funny, making sure he laughed when she did – but Aidan's completely blind to it. All parents are blind: the kids have them running round in circles. It's the same with Jacob and his two. But at least they're younger and the manipulation isn't so blatant.

'She's done so well. I'll reward her in the morning . . . Let's go out for breakfast . . . Pancakes. She'll love that.'

Great. Now breakfast – like everything else – will be centred around Jasmin. Suddenly it's all I can do not to scream at him. *Stop it!* She deserves a smack, not a reward. Stop being reeled in by her. And stop making her the centre of everything. This is *my house, my weekend* and I've had enough. She's in bed now – at long last. Can't we talk about something fucking else?

We can't go on like this. I refuse to play happy families with Jasmin. Aidan is the one I want. Just Aidan. Is that too much to ask? After everything I've been through? So many times today I wanted to shake her. Hard. Scream in her face: *You're not part of the deal.*

40

Aidan

Jack's door is closed. My knock is tentative; there's a high possibility he's in the middle of something much more important than my own troubles.

'Come in,' he calls, his voice muffled.

I open the door halfway, and he's surprised to see it's me. It's usually the other way around: he comes to my office rather than me to him.

'Hey, do you have a minute?'

He pushes his glasses — small lenses, silver frames — further up his nose. 'Of course, Aidan . . . Take a seat . . . How can I help you?'

I sit down across from him. His office is smaller than mine and the floor-to-ceiling bookshelves make it feel even more enclosed. It's dark enough to warrant a light being on, even though it's the middle of a sunny autumn day. There's a distinctly musty smell, and an atmosphere — quiet, reflective — not so different from a real confessional box. Like many before me, it's hard to know where to begin.

'Is it about the sentencing?' he prompts. 'It's coming up, isn't it?'

'The court date's in a couple of weeks. But no, it's

not that. It's something else . . . I'm in a bit of a moral dilemma . . .'

He takes this in for a moment. 'Regarding one of your men?'

I'm sure my smile looks every bit as wry as it feels. 'Nothing to do with my men – for once. It's about me . . . and my wife . . .'

He nods, his expression carefully blank. I suspect that a generous proportion of the people who sit on this very seat come to unload about their wives, or their husbands, or their long-suffering partners . . . the unseen casualties of the army. 'Go on.'

There's an open Bible on his desk, sitting to one side, and I find myself gazing at it, wondering if Jack was reading it before I came in. I'm tempted to ask. I'm stalling, wasting the man's time.

'Well, I think you already know that Chloe and I have separated . . .' I look up in time to catch him nodding again. 'The thing is . . . the problem is . . . we have this situation . . .' I'm stumbling like an idiot. Just say it. 'Chloe and I have embryos . . . Three of them . . . left over from IVF.'

Jack takes this news without altering his expression in any way. 'I see,' is all he says.

But does he see? Does he know what happens to embryos when the people who create them separate or don't want them any more?

'Chloe and I need to make a decision about what to do with our embryos,' I clarify.

'And what are the options?'

'They can be destroyed, or donated, or we can continue to pay for their storage, knowing they will never be born.'

'And you're here because none of these options sit well with you?'

My first answer is a sigh that leaves me strangely short of breath. Then: 'Damn it, Jack, we wanted those babies so much. The embryos went from Canberra to Melbourne with us, and then back to Sydney . . . We were on our way to the fertility clinic when the accident happened . . .'

'I remember,' Jack says, and our eyes meet across the desk. He was a rock after the accident, popping up in my office on a regular basis, often under the guise of other business, but I knew at the time that he was watching out for me, concerned about my frame of mind.

I try to explain, as much for myself as for Jack. 'If things had turned out differently that day, I could be the father of a newborn baby. Hey, I'd be sitting here moaning about arsenic hour and broken sleep. So, yeah, in that context, especially when I think of those embryos as babies, all the options feel equally wrong. Destroying them is out of the question. Donating to another family is only slightly more palatable. Those embryos are our genetic material, Jasmin's brothers and sisters . . . Then the thought of doing nothing, leaving them there, permanently in deep freeze . . .'

My eyes stray back to the Bible. Where does scripture stand on IVF and leftover embryos? Which of the ten commandments could stretch itself to cover egg harvesting and fertilization, pre-embryo incubation, embryo transfer, freezing and disposal?

Jack clears his throat. 'As you know, Aidan, my brief as chaplain is to foster faith, character and conduct, which in turn inspire courage and self-sacrifice in adversity. I see this dilemma of yours as a form of adversity, and the answer to it lies in your own character and moral compass.'

Jack's a great listener, but there is always that moral high ground, an unshakeable belief that doing the 'right thing' will ultimately win the battle. But the 'right thing' by who? By the embryos? By Chloe? By Jasmin? And what about Sophie? She doesn't even know these embryos exist. Where Chloe and I were going that morning, what we were doing, ceased to matter. In the aftermath of the accident, all that mattered was Sophie, and if she would recover.

'That's not what you want to hear, is it?' Jack says, his eyes searching mine.

I stand up. 'It's just that none of the options we spoke about feels morally right, so I have no damned idea which way my compass should be pointing.'

'Then don't make a decision. Defer it, if you can, and I'll pray that things will become clearer for you.'

Back in my office, I pick up where I left off before I went to see Jack. Months in the planning, our major training exercise – Operation Panther – is now only three weeks away. While most of the men are being transported to the location by coach, some are parachuting in, and others will be scaling the cliff face – in the pitch dark. All units must converge on the 'enemy' and attack before daylight. The potential for things to go wrong is astronomical: unfamiliar territory, lack of light, blank bullets. It keeps me awake at night, the fear that someone will get hurt on my watch, on this training exercise that I've planned and am ultimately responsible for.

One of my tasks this morning is to arrange for all the ropes to be checked by the climbers, to make sure they're in good condition. Then I have to organize some extra unarmed-combat training for the men. This afternoon will be mostly taken up with a ten-kilometre run, with the men carrying twenty kilos of equipment on their back. The last time, thirty per cent failed to complete the run within the allotted time. Today – with Panther only weeks away – we need a hundred per cent success rate.

It's while I'm on the run – my equipment dragging down my shoulders, sweat sticking under my clothes, my boots cutting into my feet – that it comes to me. Something an instructor said, in the early days when I was in military college. He was cut from the same cloth as Jack: strong on character, conduct and morals.

'The Australian Army protects our country and our national interests, but most of all we exist to protect our people. People of all ages, all religious denominations, all sexes and all ethnicities . . . In a nutshell, we're here – all of us in this classroom – to protect human life. That's our overriding purpose. If you keep that in the back of your mind, you'll make the right decisions, do the right thing.'

Maybe the question I should be asking myself is if those frozen embryos are 'human life'.

The part of me that imagined cradling those babies in my arms, holding them closer, to inhale that 'baby' smell, pulling on their toes and watching their eyes light up, says, *Yes, they are.*

41

Hannah

Jane and Mick are drunk. They've been at the pub since lunchtime, when the hearing finished. Jane lost. She texted me to let me know, but I had already heard the outcome from Sophie, who returned to the office afterwards.

Jane stands up when she sees me come in. Using a grandiose voice, she reannounces the verdict. 'On the facts presented by both parties, the commission finds that the applicant, Mrs Jane Dixon, resigned of her own free will and was not in any way forced into tendering her resignation. The unfair-dismissal claim before the commission is hereby dismissed.'

Mick bangs his fist down on the table, mimicking a judge's hammer, and the two of them laugh their heads off. You could be fooled into thinking they're celebrating rather than commiserating. Sophie told me that the decision isn't usually announced then and there, but because the case was so 'clear cut' the member of the commission didn't see any point in reserving his decision.

'It was a long shot,' Jane slurs when she sits down again. 'Now I've wasted weeks when I should've been job-hunting.'

'Never mind, love,' Mick says. 'You tried your best.'

Mick is exactly how I imagined him: shortish, thickset, salt of the earth.

But Jane, who was laughing two seconds ago, now looks as though she might cry. 'The fact is, I shouldn't have resigned. It made me appear impulsive and hot-headed rather than the victim of sustained bullying. When I think back to all those times I held it in, when I didn't utter a single word of retaliation while she was walking all over me . . .'

Mick slings a heavily tattooed arm around her shoulders. 'I know you're disappointed, love. But you did achieve something today. You documented everything that happened, made her sit there and be accountable for it . . .'

'But they found in her favour!'

'Yes, they did. But today must have taken something out of her. And that HR person was there too, the one who was representing her . . .'

'Alyssa,' I supply.

'Yes, Alyssa. The next time someone makes a complaint she'll be on to it straight away.'

I hope so, for all our sakes. 'I feel so bad, Jane. I didn't fully realize what you were going through until Sophie turned the focus on *me*. I thought I could handle her . . . I needed to believe I could . . .'

She clasps my hand in hers. 'Poor Hannah. Don't feel guilty. I'm out of it. I don't have to set eyes on Sophie McCarthy ever again. I don't have to speak to her, justify myself to her, or even allow myself to think of her . . . But I can't bear that she's going to continue to get away with it, I really can't. I can't bear that now she's doing exactly the same to you.'

'She won't get away with it,' Mick says confidently. 'There's a dent in her reputation now. They'll be watching her.' He drains his drink. 'I'm going to the bar . . . Hannah?'

'I'll have a quick one . . . I need to get home to Mum and the boys.'

'It was a long shot,' Jane says again when he's gone. Then she slaps herself on the forehead. 'Jesus Christ, why do I keep saying that? I didn't make up the things she did to me. I didn't lie or exaggerate. Everything happened just as I said in my claim. The only thing I did wrong was resign, and it feels deeply unfair that one action should undermine my whole case.'

'Oh, Jane, I'm so sorry it didn't work out.'

'She was clinical, Hannah. She stood up on that witness stand and rebutted each and every point. High standards, strong work ethic, only wanting the best, blah, blah, blah. A bully? Out of the question. No fucking way.'

Does any bully ever regard themselves as such? Do they know what they really are? I suspect not.

Jane gulps back the last of her wine. 'I'd better get my act together. Tomorrow I'll start looking for a job . . . Although any potential employer will run a mile if they hear about this.'

'You'll get something, Jane. Somewhere that will appreciate all your experience *and* respect your home–life balance.'

'I hope so, I really do.' She looks wistful now. 'I want a boss who understands that children are an important part of the society we live in. Who understands the odd time when their needs must come before work. Who gets how precious my family time is to me.'

Mick comes back with a beer for himself and a bottle of wine for Jane and me.

'This is like the old days,' he pronounces, plonking himself down on the cushioned seat.

Jane's smile is nostalgic. 'We used to go to places like this when we first met. I would arrive in my work suit and high heels, and Mick in his overalls and dirty boots. I found him so much more rugged and handsome than the bankers and accountants my colleagues hooked up with.'

'I loved her for her money,' Mick jokes. 'Her salary was double mine.'

They're a great couple. Mick makes Jane laugh. He bolsters her when she's down. His support is rock-solid, no matter if Jane's in the right or wrong. I can't help feeling envious.

'Good thing you found more things to love about me than my salary,' she says.

He raises one bushy brow at her. 'Who says I have? You'd better get another job quick smart or I'll be looking for a divorce.'

'Oh, fuck off.'

I nudge her so hard she falls on top of Mick. 'When will you learn that saying the F word gets you into a lot of trouble?'

We're all laughing hysterically again, and no one looking would ever guess that Jane had just lost her case with the Fair Work Commission across the street.

Boots, balls, bags; it's almost impossible to get inside the front door. Again.

'Who has left all this stuff here? *Why can't things be put away?*'

264

Callum comes running, but it quickly becomes clear that the state of the hallway is not on his agenda. 'Mum, Mum . . . Guess what happened at training today?'

Something good from the look on his face, and the fact that he left the lure of the television to greet me on my way in.

'What?' I ask, rolling a dirty soccer ball out of the way with my foot. Grass shavings and clumps of mud speckle the carpet. I'll have to get the vacuum out later.

'Davy made me *captain*.'

I stop despairing about the carpet and drink in the proud grin on his face. 'That's great. For this weekend?'

'For the rest of the season . . . He said I was good at talking to everyone on the field and keeping spirits up when we're losing.'

Thank you, Davy. Thank you, thank you, thank you. You knew what you were doing that day you kept Callum on the bench. Respect and rules and love, you said. This will be the making of Callum.

'That's the loveliest news I've heard all week. Davy is right – you'll make an excellent captain. Oh, I am so proud of you . . . Come here. This news deserves a hug.'

He moves awkwardly into my arms. His body feels bulky against mine. He has grown, I realize with a start, and not just in height. His shoulders are filling out, and his face is beginning to mature too. He is so much like his father it takes my breath away; it's precisely why I worry about him so much. But there's no sign of that underlying broodiness today. His face is completely open, his eyes bright. He's had a badly needed shot of self-confidence. I can see now that this was what Davy was working towards. But Callum had to earn it first, to deserve it.

Callum is just stepping back from my embrace when there's an officious knock on the door, a knock that I recognize from the last time: Mr Fastidious. If it weren't for the fact that he was obviously watching out for me to get home from work and probably knows I'm on the other side of the door, I would consider not answering it. What now? Nothing good, if our previous encounters are anything to go by. I move some of the sporting paraphernalia out of the way with my foot so I can get the door open.

'Good evening.' I force a smile, trying to make up for the fact that I was unforgivably rude the last time we met. Is it too late to apologize? Callum's stare bores through my back; no doubt he's hoping for a repeat performance.

'Good evening,' Mr Fastidious parrots. He's as immaculately turned out as ever: pressed shirt, chinos with a razor-sharp crease, freshly polished brogues. 'Your boys . . .'

First it was the washing on the balcony, then it was the noise, and now, apparently, it's the boys.

'Your boys have been playing soccer in the driveway . . .'

'Is that a problem?' I feign surprise, even though I know perfectly well that it is a problem, at least to the killjoy portion of the population.

He stretches his neck in a way that reminds me of a turkey. 'Of course it's a problem. Cars are coming in and out. The ball entered some flower beds in the garden. Then it hit the wall, causing a noise disturbance.'

'Did you ever play soccer when you were a boy?' I ask, weariness overcoming me.

'Of course,' he bristles. 'We played in the park, the appropriate place for such games.'

'Never in the driveway, or on the street, or somewhere it wasn't strictly allowed?'

'Never ... We had rules, and we kept to them. Your boys need to learn a thing or two about rules, I might add. And you do know that children are not allowed to play on common property unless accompanied by an adult exercising adequate control?'

'Yes, I do know that, but I think that particular by-law is intended for very young children. Ten-year-olds need a little more freedom and lenience –'

He cuts me off, obviously not agreeing. 'And you know that an owner must not cause damage to plants or lawns on common property?'

'Yes, of course I know that. Hopefully nothing was actually damaged?'

He doesn't even acknowledge my question. 'And an owner cannot interfere with the peaceful enjoyment of other owners and occupiers.'

A sarcastic laugh erupts from deep inside me. 'Peaceful enjoyment? Give me a break! You don't know the *meaning* of that phrase ... You thrive on issuing complaints and finding fault ... Can't you just leave us alone?'

His face reddens. 'Now, listen here, there are rules, and we must all keep to them ...'

I've had enough. I'm sick of being trodden on. Of being constantly hassled at work and now at home too. 'Please stop. You're harassing me. Stop.'

'Harassing you?' he splutters. 'I'm most certainly not. I'm just pointing out –'

'I am just in from work. I haven't seen my children all

day. They're hungry, I should be making them dinner instead of standing here arguing like this. I am *not* a bad person. My husband died last year – I'm a single mother who's trying to make ends meet, that's who I am. And all my energy is devoted to keeping my head above water, not your flipping by-laws. Can't you understand that? . . . Now, good evening.'

Making sure to close the door as softly as possible, I turn around to see Mum and Finn shoulder to shoulder with Callum.

'You stood up to him.' Mum has a proud, surprised look on her face.

All my life I've been timid, slow to speak up for myself, chronically lacking in confidence, believing that my opinions were inferior to everyone else's. Mum and Dad used to despair over me.

'Must be Dutch courage from that glass of wine I had with Jane . . . The downside is that we're probably going to get another contravention notice as a result.'

Mum gives my arm a squeeze as we all finally leave the confines of the hallway. 'Will I stay on for dinner?'

I give her a wobbly smile. 'You can answer the door if he comes back.'

Dinner is weird. Everyone is on edge to the point of being giddy, especially Mum, whose high-pitched laugh makes the rest of us laugh too, though we're not clear on what's so funny. Every time there's a sound from the other units, a slammed door, a voice, we freeze, waiting for another knock, which doesn't come, and then Mum gives a nervous giggle and we all start laughing again.

Later, when I see Mum out, I'm half expecting to find an envelope inside the front door, another stealthily delivered contravention notice. But nothing's there, other than clumps of mud and grass that I'm too tired to vacuum up.

The boys are late going to bed – it takes a strength I don't have tonight to keep them on schedule – and when they're finally down, I check my phone (which, due to the strangeness of the night, never made it out of my handbag).

Four missed calls, two voice messages, and numerous emails in my inbox. All from Sophie. More harassment.

Stand up to her. Say no. But it's not that easy, is it? Standing up to her will have consequences – that much is clear. And look what happened to Jane. Jane, who is a hundred times more confident and more qualified than me. Jane, who has the indestructible Mick to cushion her fall, and who was prepared to go all the way to the Fair Work Commission. If Jane can't stop Sophie, who can?

Sorry. Have things on tonight. Will get to this in the morning.

I look at my reply for a long time before pressing send.

42

Sophie

It's going to be one of those bad days. I know, even before I open my eyes, that every hour, every minute, will be infused with pain. Getting out of bed will hurt. Getting dressed. Commuting to work. Sitting down. Standing up. Opening doors and filing cabinets. If I were still keeping my spreadsheet, I would rate this morning's pain as an eight: the worst it's been in a long time.

Aidan, as usual, has left long before I make it to the kitchen and I feel a stab of resentment at the thought of his energy, his fitness, and the fact that the possibility of pain doesn't even cross his mind.

'This is because of you,' I mutter, with as much viciousness as I can muster. 'You did this to me.'

Sometimes I do this when I have a bad day: turn on Aidan. Not for long — a few minutes of a one-sided tirade at most. I'm offloading, that's all, finding an outlet for my frustration and helplessness, and because he's not actually here and can't hear, it doesn't hurt his feelings, so no harm done. I love him, he knows that, *I* know that. I'm allowed to lash out every now and then. It's only fair.

'You too, Jane, you stupid bitch.'

On the contrary, I would be thrilled if Jane could hear

what I have to say about *her*. The fact that I feel so crap today is mostly her fault. Dragging us both in front of the Fair Work Commission. Wasting hours and hours of everyone's time. Me having to sit there and listen to all her whining and exaggerations, and then swear on a Bible before defending myself. How demeaning. How wearying, exasperating, infuriating. It's no wonder the strain of it has caught up with me today.

'I hope you never get another job, Jane Dixon. And if I'm ever asked for a reference, I'll take great delight in telling the truth, you lazy, vindictive cow.'

To think that, next week, I have another hearing to go to, another ordeal to endure: Aidan's sentencing. It's too much at once. My body is saying, *Enough already*. But there's no way the judge will allow another adjournment and, anyway, despite feeling dangerously exhausted, I really need to get this over with – *we* need to get it over with. Aidan's been really tense. He's worried that he'll get a term in prison, despite all the assurances that it's unlikely.

'How will I explain to Jasmin?' he said last night, just as I was about to turn off the light. 'Her dad going to jail . . . Imagine the shame she'd feel.'

Jasmin, Jasmin, Jasmin. What about me? I'm the real victim, remember? I'm the one who had her chest crushed, the one who'll never be the same again. I've forgiven you, but now I have to suffer through another day at court while work is piling up back at the office. And the stress of having to relive every little detail of the accident: the photographs, the medical reports, the statements from the various witnesses. Not to mention having to see your stupid ex-wife sitting there with her sad eyes.

Stop, Sophie. Enough. You're just making yourself feel worse now. You'll get through today. You always do.

First, a fresh cup of tea (the one Aidan made for me is still on the bedside table, untouched, cold).

Breakfast: two chocolate digestives (I crave sweet things when I'm like this). The junk food is stashed at the back of the pantry, where Aidan can't see it, and where it takes a little extra effort to retrieve, so there's time to change my mind. But I can't seem to stop myself this morning. I used to be so scathing of binge-eaters and people who couldn't control their weight, and look at me now. It's only a few biscuits, and it's only a few kilos; still, it's getting me down, and is yet another reminder that *I am not the same*.

With the biscuits filling the void in my stomach and the comforting taste of chocolate on my lips, it's time for some hardcore pain-relief tablets, which – please, *please* – should kick in by the time I get to work.

'Hannah, have you finished the new product report?'

Hannah glances up from her screen, her face unattractively flushed. 'Still working on it, Sophie.'

'I need it . . . I needed it *hours ago*, in fact.'

'I'm going as fast as I can.' Hannah is staring at her screen again, deliberately not meeting my eyes.

'That's why I messaged you last night. Because I needed the report *early* today.'

No answer. She's ignoring me, refusing to explain, to apologize.

I'm about to turn on my heel – even though I know that the abruptness of such a movement wouldn't be a good idea in my fragile state today – when she finally opens her mouth.

'Stop it.'

'Excuse me?'

'Stop bullying me,' she continues, her voice sounding wobbly and strangely young.

Oh, for God's sake. She's as pathetic as Jane. Nobody can take the pressure any more. 'What are you talking about? I'm not bullying you . . . I'm merely asking you to perform your role.'

'My role does *not* involve working after hours . . . or receiving texts, emails and phone calls every waking hour.'

'This is a busy department. Everyone has to put in more than nine to five.'

'I'm paid for nine to five,' she retorts, quite unbelievably, considering I've only recently given her a pay rise.

'You're paid very well,' I snap. 'Thanks to *me*.'

She swallows. 'I had other things on last night, that's why I didn't start on the report. I'm allowed to have a life outside work . . . You don't own me, Sophie.'

'I never said I did! Now, can you finish that *fucking* report so I can send it to John Greenland?'

Back in my office my anger immediately fizzles away. I shouldn't have lost my temper. Hannah is a solid worker, even though she isn't as flexible as I'd like her to be. I'll apologize when she brings in the report. I don't want another Jane-type situation. Anyway, John Greenland isn't expecting the report today; I wanted to surprise him, impress him with our efficiency.

My chest. It's not any better. I'll have to take more painkillers. 11.30 a.m. – *still too soon*. At least another hour before I can pop some more. *Fuck it*.

'Here's the first section.' Hannah's face is still rather red when she slides the document across my desk half an hour later. She avoids my eyes. 'I'm still working on the rest.'

'I'm sorry. I shouldn't have got angry with you. I know you try your best.'

My apology is met with silence and I can't help sighing.

'Look, Hannah. I know I can be demanding . . . To be honest, I'm in a lot of pain. It's hard to be nice when my chest feels ready to explode. Some days I can't think straight, let alone remember my manners and be pleasant with people.'

The set of her face relaxes before my eyes. 'I'm sorry . . . I didn't realize.'

I shrug, and then regret it because even that small movement hurts quite badly. 'That's part of the problem. Most people don't realize because they can't see it. Pain is a terrible thing, you know? It can completely change your personality, make you quite nasty at times. But people don't know it's there, and so they assume that you're just not a nice person.'

It's true. Every word I'm saying. Today more than any other day, because I think my initial rating of eight is now an eight point five and I'm struggling to maintain focus.

Hannah's face is full of sympathy. Does she understand some of what I'm talking about? Most people don't. They have no idea.

'Was your husband in pain? Before he died?'

A few moments pass before she answers. 'Yes, you could say he was.'

Now she looks as though she might start crying. She's a sorry sight with her quivering mouth, harried demeanour and cheap clothes. She makes me think of someone who's been kicked to the ground and pummelled repeatedly. Maybe this is the reason I'm prompted to ask, 'There was life insurance, wasn't there?'

Her eyes remain downcast. 'They didn't pay out.'

There are a number of reasons this could happen. Non-disclosure of a known condition. Alcohol or drug use. Dangerous or illegal activities.

Which one was it, Hannah?

I'm on the verge of asking. She's on the verge of telling me. Then the moment is over and she has turned to leave, hopefully to finish off the product report.

43

Dee

Richard has lost weight. His suit jacket looks baggy and the trousers are practically falling down. This time last year, I would've teased him if he'd put on something so obviously ill-fitting. But my husband is a tenser, surlier man than this time last year, and I don't think he'd be amused.

'Maybe you should wear your grey one instead,' I suggest tactfully.

I haven't given any thought to what I'll wear myself. It is a sombre matter, a sentencing hearing such as this. We've been told to expect some graphic photographs and potentially upsetting medical reports. We've been told, repeatedly, that it's unlikely Aidan will be incarcerated, and yet it is disturbingly evident that this is what Richard is holding out for, pinning all his hopes on. I'm blue in the face from talking to him, from trying to make him see sense.

I spoke to Jacob on Sunday. Told him how concerned I was about his father.

'The last twelve months have had an enormous impact on him. The shock, the grief, the readjustment . . . He isn't the same man.'

There was a tell-tale pause before Jacob asked, 'Do you think I should come down for the hearing?'

This was exactly what I wanted him to ask. 'It would be wonderful if you could . . . Can you get the time off?'

'It's not easy. There's a lot on next week, and I haven't really given adequate notice.' His excuses came embarrassingly easily. 'How long will it take?'

'A couple of hours. But we don't know the exact start time. Depends how the hearing before us goes.'

'Pity. If you were first up, I might get away with taking only a half-day. As it is . . .'

Then I had to ask myself if it was worth the hassle with Jacob's work. I want my entire family present, supporting each other, but at the same time the hearing is nothing more than a formality: we're not expecting any surprises.

'What will we do about Dad?'

'Oh, Jacob, I'm worried about him, you know that. But I'm sure the hearing will be a turning point and he'll start to improve. Don't say a word, but I've been looking at a little get-away for us. North Queensland, I think. Somewhere that's tranquil and beautiful, somewhere he can reset himself, get back on track.'

'Sounds like a good idea, Mum. I'll see what I can do about getting off work, but don't expect too much.'

'You can only try,' I said, forgiving him already because I knew, as did he, that he wouldn't be there.

Richard isn't the only one I'm worried about. Sophie looked positively ill when she called round yesterday: deathly pale, haggard in the face, purplish shadows under her eyes. She'd been at a Fair Work Commission hearing earlier in the week, and it had obviously taken a lot out of her. Apparently the employee involved – Jane someone – had resigned of her own free will and had later regretted her impulsiveness, claiming that the resignation was coerced due to sustained bullying.

'Nonsense,' Richard said.

'A total waste of time and energy,' Sophie agreed, pulling out a chair to sit down on. Because I was watching her closely I noticed how she winced at the movement, her mouth emitting a soundless gasp, her eyes momentarily shutting. 'But I still had to go up on that witness stand and defend myself. It was exhausting. Physically and emotionally.'

The hearing was emphatically decided in Sophie's favour, which was good news. I listened in as she recounted further details to Richard, something about a funeral and some sort of misunderstanding. I was relieved that Sophie's name had been cleared but found myself wondering about this woman, Jane, and her side of the story. Then I felt that traitorous niggle again. The same one I had when we sat in the headmistress's office all those years ago.

I come back to the present as Richard re-emerges from the bedroom in the grey suit.

'That's much better,' I say cheerfully, even though the difference is only very slight.

Three more days to go. Like everyone involved, I just want to get it over with. Richard will buck up as soon as it's behind us, as soon as he realizes that not even a court of law is on his side. A small holiday, a few days away together, will help get him back to his old self.

Aidan

'Jazzie, Daddy is going to court tomorrow, and the judge is going to decide my punishment for crashing into Sophie's car.'

The three of us are sitting around the weathered table on the deck, and the setting has strong echoes of the night when I told Jasmin that I was going to move out. It's even possible that we're sitting in the exact same positions, with me at the head of the table, Jasmin to my left and Chloe to my right. Just like then, Jasmin's eyes instantly fill with tears.

'Is the judge going to send you to jail?' Her question ends in a wail.

Those watery brown eyes are demanding honesty and nothing less. 'There's a very small chance I'll have to go to prison. But only if I get a *really* strict judge.'

'But you've said *sorry*.'

I lean across to hug her, calm her down.

'Yes, I have. I've said sorry to Sophie and to the police and to everyone who has been affected by my careless driving. And hopefully the judge will be happy with my apology.'

It takes some time to reassure her, to curb the tears and deal with the hiccupped questions (Can you Skype from prison? Will you have a telly? Will you share your room with someone else? Can you take any of your things with you? How long can visitors stay?). Finally, she runs out of things to ask and slumps in her seat.

'Time to go upstairs and start getting ready for bed,' Chloe interjects. She sounds incredibly tired, as though she's yearning for bed herself.

Jasmin goes without a murmur, and then I embark on my second big task for the night. The envelope is in the inside pocket of my jacket. I place it on the table between us.

'What's that?' Chloe asks warily.

'Bank details. My computer login and passwords. Some phone numbers, including Jack's. And I've organized a Power of Attorney.'

I have a similar envelope for Sophie, which I'll give to her when I get home.

Chloe makes a yelping sound. 'You don't seriously think . . .'

'Hey now, of course I don't. This is all precautionary . . . There's something else, Chlo, something I need to tell you, to be honest about, in case we're not going to see each other for a while, or be in the position to talk privately . . .'

She's wary again. 'What?'

Last night's dream had me digging frantically in the debris of a freshly bombed building. A baby's wail, faint, heartbreakingly vulnerable, could be heard beneath the mounds of shattered stone, timber and roof tiles. My hands were cut to shreds, my arms ached, but I continued to fling the rubble to either side of me. But the hole I was digging with my bare hands kept filling up again. The baby's cries got fainter and fainter until I could hear nothing at all. When I woke my body was drenched with sweat and dread and sadness.

'The embryos, our babies . . . They're constantly on my mind. I want you to know that.'

'Me too,' Chloe says.

'When this is over, I think we should go for a drink, or out for dinner, to talk it through some more, to make sure we do the right thing and make a decision we can both live with.'

Her smile is shaky. 'It's a date . . .'

Jasmin, dressed in very cute Dalmatian-print pyjamas, reappears in record time.

'Right, young lady.' My chair scrapes the deck as I push it back. 'Let's get to work.'

I briefly rest my hand on Chloe's shoulder as I pass. She takes a sharp, surprised breath. Then Jasmin and I go inside, get down on the floor and begin lifting ourselves up and down to my count.

Jasmin

I'm really, really scared. Daddy might go to jail for a few months. It's not fair. Daddy is not a bad person. He doesn't belong in jail. There are lots of bad and mean people in there who might hurt him. And he'll be lonely, because we're only allowed really short visits.

Dad tucks me in and kisses me goodnight. I pretend, for his sake, that I've gone straight to sleep, but as soon as

I hear the front door – about half an hour later – I go downstairs.

'I can't sleep. I'm too worried.'

Mum doesn't look surprised to see me. Her eyes are red. She's been crying, like me.

'Back to bed now, Jasmin. Daddy doesn't want you to worry.'

I go back upstairs, climb into bed and try really hard to lie still. My body is all twitchy and it's really soon before I'm up again.

'I'm sorry, Mum. I need some help.'

She gives me a tired, unenthusiastic look. 'Some extra push-ups, then. Come on, me too.'

We do fifteen extra push-ups, I go to the toilet and then I go back to bed. Amelia's mum is taking me to school in the morning. Should I tell her what's happening? Should I tell my other friends? What about Mrs Stanley? What if I get teased? What if people think my dad's a real criminal, when all he did was make a mistake? That's mean of me, thinking of myself when I should be thinking about Daddy.

I'm feeling ashamed and upset when I go downstairs again.

'I'm sorry, Mum. I'm really, really sorry. I'm just wondering if I should tell Mrs Stanley?'

Mum sighs. 'Let's see what happens first. Let's say nothing and hope for the best. Happy with that plan?'

'OK . . . What time is it?'

Mum's sigh is louder. 'Getting stressed about the time doesn't help, Jasmin.'

Back into bed. The blankets are annoying my toes. I move my foot around, trying to get comfortable. I am not sleepy. Not one little bit. I'm *alert*. I like that word. It sounds the same as what it means.

'I'm sorry, Mum. I really can't sleep tonight. My brain is wide awake.'

I'm expecting her to get really cross now. Because I've been up four times. This is my worst night in ages.

But she doesn't get cross. 'I'm worried about tomorrow too, Jazz. Come on, I'll take you up.'

Mum lies on the bed next to me and hugs me so tight I can hardly breathe.

I don't want to go to Amelia's in the morning. I want to go to the court, to see what happens. No, I don't want to go to the court, because what if Daddy gets a Really Strict Judge? I'm really, really, really scared that he'll go to jail. I'm *petrified*. I'm *frantic*. I wish I could delete the accident, make it go away.

'Shush,' Mum whispers every time I jerk.

She keeps holding me really, really tight until we fall asleep together.

44

Sophie

We're here. We're finally here, at the finish line. I catch Aidan's eye and give him a nervous smile. The last few weeks have been unbearably tense.

The magistrate enters the court room and everyone stands. He's a grandfatherly type: portly, balding, a gentle face. He doesn't seem the sort to send anyone to prison, least of all Aidan.

Ford, Aidan's lawyer, introduces himself. 'Your Honour, a plea has been entered on an earlier occasion and the matter is to proceed to sentence.'

'Indeed, it is,' the magistrate says. 'Are there any additional documents?'

There are a surprising number of additional documents. The police approach the bench with the agreed facts and some further medical reports, and the defence hand up some character references. Silence (tense and strangely devoid of the soft coughs, sniffs and sighs which are the usual waiting sounds) descends while the magistrate reads the paperwork. I try to catch Aidan's eye again, but he is staring straight ahead, sombre and upright in his army uniform.

'Does Mr Ford wish to be heard?' the magistrate asks.

Mr Ford does wish to be heard. He launches into a well-rehearsed speech, focusing on what he calls the subjective facts. Aidan's lawyer is confident, articulate and very persuasive; Aidan is in good hands. While he listens, the magistrate looks around the room, studying the faces before him and no doubt matching them to the relevant names. His eyes seem to linger on Chloe before finally turning to me.

Ford is now talking about mitigating factors, something I am familiar with from the insurance industry. 'On the morning in question, Captain Ryan and his wife were on their way to an appointment at a fertility clinic, where Mrs Ryan was scheduled to be inseminated with a thawed embryo . . .'

What? I believed they'd been on their way to a routine doctor's appointment. Why am I finding this out now? I frown at Aidan, but he isn't looking my way. Chloe wipes her face with her hand. Is she fucking crying? Seriously?

'I'd like to draw Your Honour's attention to the psychiatric assessment submitted to the bench,' Ford continues, and I tell myself that the reason they were in the car is irrelevant. I must concentrate on what Ford is saying. 'Captain Ryan was suffering from stress on a number of fronts: he and his wife's fertility problems, concerns for his daughter, who has trouble sleeping, and of course flashbacks of certain traumatic, job-related incidents.'

Ford sits down and then the police make their submissions, putting an emphasis on the gravity of the injuries. 'The various medical reports describe the injuries in graphic detail: the chest bone was ripped apart, the lungs punctured, various ribs were broken . . . but the worst effect has been the nerve damage. Unfortunately, nerves don't heal as well as bones do, and the full impact can be hard for everyone here today to grasp, because we can't *see* it. By all accounts, Miss McCarthy has spent the last year in a great deal of pain.'

The magistrate nods sympathetically. He obviously understands the insidious nature of invisible, everyday pain that is virtually non-existent to everyone but the sufferer. 'Does Miss McCarthy have a victim impact statement she can read to the court?'

The police sergeant looks uncomfortable. 'Your Honour, Miss McCarthy has asked me to point out that the victim impact statement was written several months ago, and doesn't reflect her changed personal circumstances . . .'

The magistrate clears his throat. 'Yes, indeed. Miss McCarthy is now in a relationship with Captain Ryan.' There is a worrying note of incredulousness in his tone. Chloe actually flinches at this point. 'But I still believe it beneficial for Miss McCarthy to read the statement aloud to the court.'

Dad, who hasn't been in my direct line of view, gives me an encouraging smile when I stand up to speak. Someone from the prosecution table hands me a copy of the statement. Somebody muffles a cough. It's the only sound in the court room.

'Every morning, even before I open my eyes, I feel pain. Even though many of my injuries have essentially healed, it is now clear that the residual pain is never going to go away, and that my life is never going to be quite the same, and that I will never go back to the way I was.' My voice is assured and remarkably clear. Everyone seems to be listening intently. 'What was I before the accident? Well, I was healthy. I was fit. I had a demanding job that I loved and could throw myself into. I was a young woman who didn't know what it felt like to be in constant pain, who didn't realize how debilitating pain can be, how it can lead you to the very depths of depression and affect not only your physical abilities but your mind too, which is worse, really. This accident has taken so much away from me. My confidence, my fitness, my relationship at the time, not to mention my career, which I can't pursue with nearly the same vigour as I used to.' I stop, glance at the magistrate, then across at the defence table, to Aidan. Our eyes meet for what feels like a long time. 'Your Honour, a lot has happened since I wrote this statement. I now know that Captain Ryan is not a negligent person – in fact, he is quite the opposite. I can also attest to the remorse he feels for what happened that day, and how he has done everything he practically can to make up for it. In my opinion, Captain Ryan has suffered too. Just like me, he will never be the same again. If I am dogged by pain for the rest of my life, he will be dogged by guilt . . . And I know this fact for certain: if Your Honour sentences Captain Ryan to the maximum penalties, it will only hurt me even further. Thank you.'

I have another brief glimpse of Mum and Dad as I sit back down again. Mum is dabbing her eyes with a tissue. Dad looks livid. He wants Aidan to suffer. An eye for an eye, a tooth for a tooth: he wants the punishment to match the injury. But, seriously, what did he expect? I love Aidan. Of course I'm going to plead for leniency. Dad is delusional to think otherwise.

The police sergeant makes his concluding remarks. 'Your Honour, we believe that the seriousness of the offence warrants a custodial sentence . . . The range of penalties being imposed by the courts for cases like this are clearly inadequate and fail to reflect the long-term effects of the injuries sustained . . . Leniency should *not* be afforded on the basis of the offender's good character . . .'

It's the prosecution's job to call for a custodial sentence. Just because it's called for doesn't mean it will be given. Aidan and I must keep calm. Hopefully the magistrate is a reasonable man.

The magistrate looks down at his notes for a few long moments. When he looks up again, his gaze fixes on Aidan. 'The offender, Captain Aidan Patrick Ryan, is presented for sentence, having pleaded guilty to the following charges: For that he, on 18 May 2017, at Randwick, did negligently drive a motor vehicle on Anzac Parade, thereby causing grievous bodily harm to Sophie Elizabeth McCarthy. The prosecution is brought under section 117(1) (b) of the Road Transport Act 2013, which provides, relevantly, for present purposes: a person must not drive a motor vehicle negligently on a road or road-related area. Maximum penalty, if the driving occasions grievous bodily harm, twenty penalty units, or imprisonment for nine months, or both.'

He pauses to take a breath. 'For the purpose of these remarks on sentence, I will provide my own brief summary of the salient facts . . . The offender is thirty-five years of age and a captain in the Australian Army. He has served his country in East Timor, Afghanistan and Iraq and is currently responsible for the welfare of his company, which amounts to one hundred and twenty men. At the time of the accident, the offender resided with his wife and eight-year-old daughter in a house in Randwick. He now resides with Sophie McCarthy, the victim in this case . . .' Another flinch from Chloe. I must stop looking in her direction. 'Despite the strange personal circumstances, this is a relatively straightforward case. None of the usual aggravating factors so often present in serious collisions: speed, drugs or alcohol. The weather conditions were clear, and there was nothing to obstruct the view of either vehicle. No mechanical defects or failures were found . . . It is clear that the offender appears before the court as a person of good character. Testimonials have been tendered from Captain Jack Malone, senior chaplain and colleague of Captain Ryan, and Colonel Trapuzzano, Captain Ryan's superior and mentor. These are people who've known the offender well over many years and are in a position to make an unbiased and level-headed assessment of his character. Mrs Chloe Ryan, the captain's estranged wife, has attested to her husband's deep remorse about the accident, his difficulty sleeping, his lowered mood and heightened anxiety, and his determination to "make good" his mistake. I accept that the offender is remorseful and has suffered emotionally. I accept that he made no attempt to avoid responsibility and pleaded guilty at the first available opportunity.'

The magistrate coughs and takes a sip of water. 'Nevertheless, as the police have demonstrated, the offence is a serious one and the injuries are long-term in their nature. The courts must be tough with cases like these. We need to do all we can to stop these awful collisions, where people die, or permanently lose their ability to think for themselves, or to walk for themselves, or to resume their life as it once was.' He pauses again, and glances in my direction. 'Miss McCarthy is an actuary, obviously good with numbers, and she may have a better understanding of the physics behind the collision than I do. How fast she was travelling – below the speed limit, according to the accident investigators, but possibly too fast for the level of congestion – at what point she braked, what her speed was at the point of impact. Miss McCarthy was on her way to work, her thoughts full of the day ahead. Then a car pulled out in front of her, and suddenly she had to fight for her life.'

So many times, I've gone back to those crucial moments just before the impact. I've driven slower on approach. I've been more vigilant. I've swerved at the last moment. I've braked sooner, harder. Of course no amount of reimagination will undo the violence and devastation of his car hitting mine.

The magistrate resumes with his remarks. 'I turn now to consider the question of "special circumstances". Special circumstances are a discretionary finding of fact, and even if special circumstances are found, the court is not obliged to vary the statutory ratio . . . That said, I am prepared to find special circumstances due to the age of the offender's daughter – who is currently nine years old – and the impact it will have on this young girl if her father is in custody. I understand that the girl – Jasmin – already has some behavioural issues in relation to sleeping at night and that her mother will have difficulty coping entirely on her own. I even suspect, though this cannot be tested, that Captain Ryan's momentary lack of attention on the morning of the accident may have been caused by fatigue, due to his daughter not sleeping well the night before . . .'

Fatigue. It's like being in another collision. Being hit at full force, out of nowhere. Driver fatigue: the underlying cause of so many car accidents. Why didn't I think of it before now? The statistics speak for themselves: twenty to thirty per cent of serious accidents involve fatigue. I work in motor insurance, for God's sake. *It should have been obvious.*

'The offender is convicted and ordered to enter into a good behaviour bond under Section Nine for a period of twelve months. The offender is to be of good behaviour and appear before the court if called upon to do so at any time during the currency of the bond. The offender is to notify the registrar of this court of any change of residential address during the currency of the bond . . . The disqualification period for driving will be twelve months in total, most of which has expired.'

Everyone stands as the magistrate leaves the court room. I'm dazed. Only half aware of the handshakes at the defence table. Of Dad glowering from his seat. Of Chloe slipping away.

All I can think about is Jasmin.

What were the chances? That's what I've been asking myself, over and over, since it happened. What were the chances of me being on that precise stretch of road? What were the chances of Aidan being at that intersection at the exact same moment as me — it wasn't as if it was his regular route to work. What were the chances that a man who is so exact in all areas of his life, so disciplined, would suddenly lose concentration, pull out in front of another vehicle and crumple both the vehicle and the driver?

The chances were low. So low that I felt they were almost unquantifiable. So low I had to accept that freak accidents do happen, and get on with my life as best I could.

I didn't factor in Jasmin. Even when she was up and down out of bed when she stayed over with us, even when Aidan was obviously tired and stressed the next day from dealing with her, I never factored *Jasmin* into the equation.

'Captain Ryan's momentary lack of attention on the morning of the accident may have been caused by fatigue, due to his daughter not sleeping well the night before . . .'

So obvious, in hindsight. Fatigue results in the impairment of driver decision-making and reaction times. I should've figured it out long before now.

Fatigue: the underlying cause of so many car accidents, including *mine*.

Jasmin: the underlying cause of Aidan's fatigue.

Aidan hadn't had enough sleep. The accident happened because he was tired and not paying proper attention.

The accident happened because of Jasmin.

45

Richard

A good behaviour bond. This is our justice system. This is the best it has to offer: a bloody good behaviour bond. Waiting almost a whole year for that – for *nothing*. The man who broke my daughter's bones, who stretched and tore her nerves, who stunted her career, who turned her into a shadow of her former self, who inflicted pain on her for the rest of her life, gets to walk out the door, free. A bloody good behaviour bond. It's a disgrace. A horrendous waste of time and resources for everyone involved. An insult to those victims who are genuinely hurt by the careless actions of others, and to their families – their fathers and mothers and siblings – who feel that pain as their own. Every time I look at Sophie's face, the anguish in her eyes, the press of her lips as she contains her pain, the flinch that seems to accompany almost every movement, I feel a stabbing sensation of my own, deep down inside me.

A bloody good behaviour bond!

It makes me want to kill someone.

Chloe

It's over. Thank goodness the nightmare is finally over. I don't need to go home to face my daughter and break the news that her father is going to prison. I've been spared that. My eyes filled with tears as soon as I heard the sentencing. I wanted to hug Aidan, to hold him in my arms, to sob openly with relief. I had no right to do any of those things. I left the court room without touching him, without speaking a single word to him. I slipped away discreetly. I didn't want him – or Sophie – to see how emotional I was. I've had enough humiliation for one day. Hearing the judge refer to their relationship in his remarks – validating it in front of the court – was like a slap in the face. Then Sophie speaking about Aidan in her victim impact statement, the sense of intimacy she portrayed, the sense of knowing him, what kind of man he is, all made worse by the glances that were darting back and forth between the two of them.

I've no doubt that Sophie will experience pain for many months – or years – to come and that her life and her career will never be quite the same. But at the end of the day, it wasn't all for nothing. She met Aidan. She took him from me and Jasmin. And it can be argued that our pain, albeit a different kind of pain, will be just as enduring as hers.

Aidan

I'm relieved. Of course I am. It didn't matter how many times Barry Ford assured me that prison was an unlikely outcome, there was still that question mark hanging over me, as well as the deep-down feeling that I *ought* to be locked up. I had, after all, almost killed someone. In some ways, I relished the inconvenience of having my driver's licence suspended. The pain of leaving Chloe and Jasmin was well deserved. Punishment seemed like the only salve for my guilt. But now that the punishment is more or less over, how will I manage to keep my guilt in check? Sophie is right. She's destined for a life of pain, and I'm destined for one of guilt. It's a sobering thought.

'Congratulations,' said Barry, shaking my hand after the judge had left the room.

I'm relieved, yeah, but I'll never be at the point of wanting to be congratulated. For what? For getting off so lightly? For being another example of how lenient the courts are with matters such as this?

'I'm glad that's over.' Sophie came over to join us. 'Can we go home now, please?'

Her face was strained, extremely pale.

Chloe didn't wait around afterwards. I wanted to catch her, to thank her for the character testimonial, and for turning up to support me, even though it must have been difficult to hear some of what was said about Sophie and me.

'Let's go.' Sophie started walking towards the door.

As soon as we were alone in the car, I discovered that her haste to leave wasn't because she was in pain; it was because she was enraged.

'Was the magistrate right?' Her voice was shrill, accusing, as were the tyres of the car as we rounded each ramp in the car park. '*Were* you tired?'

At first, I wasn't sure what she was getting at. 'What?'

'Did it happen like the magistrate thought it did? Jasmin had kept you up all night and you were sleep-deprived the next morning?'

'What are you saying?' We pulled up at the boom gate. I handed her the ticket.

'I'm just trying to determine Jasmin's part in all this.'

I waited until we were outside, on the main road, before I answered, enunciating each word clearly. 'Jasmin had no part in this. Don't blame her.'

'Really?' I didn't turn to see her expression, but her voice was cold and sarcastic, and that told me enough.

'Yeah, really.' It had been a draining morning, to say the least, and the last thing we both needed was an argument, certainly not an argument of the magnitude this could be.

She laughed humourlessly. 'You're forgetting . . . I've seen her in action, Aidan. And I've seen you the next day. Tired. Stressed. Not your normal self . . . I should have put two and two together before now.'

'I don't like where you're going with this, Sophie. I've already told you: blame me. I was the one behind the wheel. It was my mistake.'

'You were tired. *Because of her.*'

'And I was tired countless other mornings too . . . I didn't cause an accident any of those times, did I?'

'It was waiting to happen, can't you see that? Sooner or later, the tiredness was going to catch up on you and cause a mistake . . . *and it did*. What other explanation is there?'

'Stop it, Sophie. Just . . . stop . . . it.'

'And you should stop defending her and making excuses for her appalling behaviour.'

Even though I wanted to end the argument, I couldn't let her get away with that. 'Appalling behaviour? What are you talking about? Jasmin is a great kid . . .'

'She should know that her actions caused the accident . . . She might stay in bed at night if she knew the truth.'

'How can you accuse her like that? She wasn't even in the car when the accident happened!'

'She didn't need to be *there*. She'd already done the damage, making you so tired you couldn't see what was right in front of you – my car, *me*!'

'Jesus. You're unbelievable . . . You really don't like Jasmin, do you?'

'*I'm not saying that!*'

'It's pretty fucking obvious.'

'I won't allow myself to be manipulated by a child, that's all.'

'Manipulated? Just shut up, Sophie. If you say another damn word, I'm getting out of the car.'

She shut up and drove the rest of the way home in a jerky, furious manner.

How could she accuse Jasmin like that? To lay the blame for my mistake, for her horrific injuries, on Jasmin's young, vulnerable shoulders. What kind of person does that? Blames a child when things go wrong? Thinking it is bad enough. Saying it aloud, pressing home the point, is something else again. Yeah, I probably was tired – from memory, it had been a pretty bad night with Jasmin – but I could've asked Chloe to drive, I could've called us a taxi, I could've acknowledged my tiredness and made a conscious effort to be more alert with my driving. The decision to drive that morning, to pull out when I did, was all down to me.

Sophie's obvious dislike and vindictiveness towards Jasmin has left me reeling. It's like the explosion in Iraq. I didn't see it coming, the utter shock when it happened, the pain cascading down my arm, damn well furious with myself for being complacent and not spotting the signs.

46

Hannah

Sophie has been in an especially filthy mood since her court case. It's as if that discussion in her office – when she admitted to being in terrible pain and I almost told her the truth about the life insurance – never happened. All week, she's been snapping instructions at me and everyone else, stomping to and from her office, slamming doors whenever the opportunity presents itself. Today, she commandeered my lunchtime with a supposed emergency. And now she stops me in my tracks as I'm on my way out the door, my head full of how the twins got on at school today – they were both excited about the try-outs for the school soccer team – and what I can rustle up for dinner.

'What about the risk analysis? Have you finished it?'

My face fills with colour. How does she do it? How can she make me feel so totally in the wrong when I know for a fact that I am not? 'I didn't know you needed that today, Sophie.'

'Well, I *do* need it today.' Sarcasm drips from every word.

Don't let her bully you. Don't let her bully you.

'You should have said so. I'm sorry, I really am, but I

299

have to go now. My kids need their dinner . . .' I laugh in an attempt to lighten the mood, but her expression stays as mutinous as ever. In fact, she looks furious enough to fire me right here and now, and realizing this fact is enough to make my resolve quickly disappear. 'I'll log in later tonight and make a start on it.'

She doesn't move from where she's standing, forcing me to walk around her to get past. Oh God, this is as pissed off as I've ever seen her.

'I want it ready first thing in the morning.'

Well, that's telling me. How many hours will it take? Three? Four? Another late night, and another groggy start to tomorrow. But anything to make her happy . . . or should I say, *less unhappy*. Anything to secure my next pay cheque.

Callum's mood is as bad as Sophie's. I can tell the instant I see his face.

'What's up, love?'

He scowls, mutters something that ends with 'not fair' and stalks off to the room he shares with Finn.

His brother is left to explain. 'He didn't make it to the next round of try-outs.'

'I see . . . And how did *you* get on?'

'I got through.' Now Finn is scowling too. 'I don't know why they picked me. Callum's better, everyone knows that.'

It's true, Callum is the stronger player of the two. So why wasn't he chosen? Didn't he play well today? Or was it more to do with his behaviour? He isn't popular with the teachers (uncooperative in class, poor concentration and participation rate, his teacher said when I was called in recently). But this is soccer, the very thing that brings him out of himself. Should I have a word with whoever ran the try-outs, plead his case? Oh God, another battle to face. I'm not sure I have it in me.

'You look exhausted,' Mum says as she gathers her coat in her arms. She's going for a meal with some friends tonight and she's flushed with excitement.

'I am.'

'I had some leftover casserole. I put it in the fridge in case you were stuck for dinner.'

'Thanks, Mum.' My eyes fill up unexpectedly. Her face becomes blurry.

'Come here.' She pulls me in for a fierce hug. She's quite a bit smaller than me, and hugging her always feels odd, unnatural. 'You're doing a good job . . . with everything. Do you hear?'

'Not at work, Mum. Not at home either. I –'

'Stop it now. You're doing well, all things considered. Chin up, love.'

She gives me another squeeze – so tight it takes the air out of me – before letting go. 'I'll be off. Try to get an early night.'

She would be horrified if she knew what I have ahead of me tonight, so I don't say a thing and nod as if going to bed early is exactly what I'll do.

Callum is sullen for the rest of the evening and nothing I do or say can change his mood. It frightens me, this dark side to his personality. It frightens me to the point where I am quite rigid with fear.

'Do you want me to talk to the teacher?' I ask, sitting on the side of his bunk as he settles down to bed.

'No, Mum. It'd make no difference.'

'It's unfair, but life is unfair sometimes, and we just have to deal with it. Right?'

'Right, Mum.'

'And you're the captain of your club team. It's a big responsibility, you know. Focus on that and forget about the school team.'

I kiss him on the forehead, then stand up to demand a kiss from Finn, who's on the top bunk. He has been less than his usual sunny self today as well. Hopefully we'll all – Sophie included – have a better day tomorrow.

It's one in the morning by the time I finish the risk analysis and send it off to Sophie. Messages have been flying in from her all evening, asking for updates on where I'm at, loading on more work – more demands – for tomorrow. It's relentless. *She's* relentless.

Don't let her bully you. Don't let her bully you.

But how can I stop her? And what is bullying, anyway? What is the difference between being assertive and being intimidating, between persistence and harassment, between high standards and unreasonable demands? Is it bad to strive for perfection when standards can so often be disappointingly low? Where are the lines in today's world, a world of 24/7 access and connectivity, a world where no one wants to wait, a world where there is no clear start or end to the working day? And is pain an adequate excuse for Sophie's sometimes appalling behaviour?

Or maybe it's me. Maybe I can't handle the pressure. Maybe I just don't have the capacity for a demanding role like this. Maybe I'm not tough enough, quick enough, clever enough. Maybe I'm the flipping problem, not Sophie. But Jane thinks Sophie's a bully too. Jane, who had Mick to pick up some of the slack at home but still couldn't keep up with Sophie's demands. Jane, who was there before Sophie's accident, before she was in constant pain, and *still* thought her behaviour was horrendous.

Is there anyone out there, other than Jane and me, who thinks that Sophie McCarthy's a bully?

Kristina Owens. The name pops into my head unbidden.

Oh, for God's sake. Now I'm raking over something that's entirely different. It was a lie that Sophie told. Fourteen years ago! Just a lie.

Stop thinking. Go to bed. You're tired enough, Hannah.

But my brain is racing. I know I won't be able to sleep. What happened to Kristina Owens? Did she get married? Have children? Go on to have a happy life? Has she more or less forgotten what happened at the maths camp, put it behind her as an unfortunate accident? Does she keep in touch with any of her old friends from St Brigid's?

Kristina Owens: I type the name into Google.

There's a string of Facebook and LinkedIn results. I haven't been on Facebook since Harry died. At the time, I couldn't face reading all the messages on his timeline: *Rest in peace, Harry*; *Hope you are somewhere happy, Harry*; *Take care, mate*. I hesitate, my finger hovering over Enter. Stop being such a coward, Hannah.

One click and I'm in. There's a Kristina Owens who's

fundraising for cancer, and another who runs marathons. There's a Kristina Owens in Adelaide, and one up in Brisbane. None of them seems to match. I search for St Brigid's, and after a few minutes I come across a Kristina Nolan, whose maiden name was Owens. The photograph – a woman with large sunglasses and a puffy face – is inconclusive.

Before I know it, I've sent her a message: *My name is Hannah Evans. I'm looking to make contact with students who graduated from St Brigid's in 2004/2005. Please let me know if I have the right person.*

It's two in the morning by the time I fall into bed. At three, I'm still wide awake. Worrying about Callum. About my job. About money. About Harry's timeline, and what other messages have been written on it since I last looked.

My alarm goes off at six and another day starts. It's not just Sophie being relentless. It's life in general.

47

Aidan

She's already here. Sitting at one of the rustic outdoor tables, a multicoloured scarf wound around her neck, a glass of red wine set down in front of her. Her head is bent, her eyes downcast, her arms folded tightly around herself. She presents as a sad and lonely figure, despite the jaunty scarf. Chloe has always liked colour. From her handmade clothes and jewellery to her rainbow nail polish, to the cushions and throws and furnishings in our home. Even when bland palettes were fashionable, and celebrity designers were appealing for restraint, Chloe happily ignored them, splashing colour wherever she could. She looks up and sees me. Her smile is reserved.

'You're early,' I say.

She shrugs. 'I dropped Jasmin off at a friend's. There was no point in going home for fifteen minutes so I came straight here.'

'Which friend?' I ask because in other circumstances Chloe and I would've had a discussion about who was taking care of our daughter.

'Amelia . . . Jasmin's new best friend.'

'Jasmin's obviously not staying the night?'

'Obviously . . .' Chloe's smile feels more natural this

time. 'She's improving, but she's still a long way from going on a sleepover.'

I indicate her glass of wine, which has been hardly touched. 'Hey, should I get a bottle?'

She shakes her head. 'I have the car.'

At the bar I order myself a glass of red, to match hers. Then I sit down next to her, close enough so we can have a private conversation, far enough to ensure there's no risk of accidental touch. Is it obvious to the other patrons that we're not a couple? Is the polite distance a giveaway? Chloe had a habit of stretching her legs across my lap, using me as her personal ottoman. Maybe that's why the distance feels more significant than it probably is.

'Have you thought about it?' she asks now, her eyes searching mine.

'Yeah . . . constantly.'

'And?'

Heat is blasting from a nearby outdoor heater. My face is warm but the rest of me is cold, shivery. 'I don't want to have them destroyed. And maybe it's selfish of me, but I don't want to donate them either. They're our embryos. It doesn't feel right to give them to another family.'

'But it's not as though we're going to have the babies ourselves, is it?' She's trying to be pragmatic but all I hear is bitterness.

'No, it's not,' I acknowledge with a weary sigh.

There's a stand-off. An impasse. A rigid silence. How can we agree on anything with this unnatural stiffness between us? I reach for her hand and the effect is instant. Her face softens, becomes more conciliatory, reflecting the changes I feel in me. It's like a homecoming, having her hand in mine.

'Please, Chlo, let's just keep paying the storage bill. There'll come a time when this will all become clearer, I know there will. But please, let's give those embryos every chance we can.'

Her hand moves in mine, and for a moment I think she's going to pull it away. Instead, her grip becomes ever so slightly firmer.

'OK.'

We stay like that – linked – for an indeterminate amount of time, our conversation fragmented but familiar, until our glasses are almost empty.

'I should go . . . I told Jasmin I wouldn't be long.'

'Is Amelia a good friend?' It doesn't feel right that I've never set eyes on my daughter's best friend. I don't know where this Amelia lives, or what her parents are like. I don't know how much Jasmin has said about me, if anything at all.

Chloe's smile is indulgent. 'I think so. She seems like a nice girl.' Then her hand squeezes mine, her face lighting up with an idea. '*Come with me*. We can pick up Jasmin together. You can check Amelia out. Oh, Jasmin would be so thrilled to see you. You can even stay for bedtime.'

Dangerous territory. Yeah, it would be great to see the surprise on Jasmin's face, to hear her chatter in the back of the car, and be there for bedtime and whatever that entails. She's my daughter, I have every right to see her, so why this terrible guilt? Because my ex-wife's hand is still in mine. Because it's all I can do to keep it to that, and not give in to the temptation to gather her fully into my arms. Because of Sophie.

Things haven't been good between me and Sophie this past week. I've been sleeping on the couch, and we're still barely speaking. I can't get past the argument in the car, I don't know if I can forgive her for blaming the accident on Jasmin. The warning signs were there: Sophie being unsympathetic about Jasmin's sleeping problems, callously suggesting I put a lock on the bedroom door, always so quick with excuses not to have Jasmin to stay over. *Sophie dislikes Jasmin. Perhaps even hates her.* Now that this fact has become clear to me, and now that I've seen her vengeful side, I'm not sure I can trust her the way I did before. Or love her.

It's a mess, a terrible mess, and going home with Chloe has the potential to make it an even bigger and more complicated mess.

Chloe's face is glowing from the heater. Warmth radiates from her skin, her eyes, even from that ridiculous scarf, as she waits for my answer. I've never stopped loving her, not for one minute, and if leaving her and Jasmin was an attempt to punish myself in the most brutal way possible, then I have succeeded, job done.

'OK.' I drain the rest of my wine. 'Am I on push-up duty, or are you?'

Chloe's laugh manages to be both sardonic and affectionate. 'You. Definitely you.'

48

Sophie

We're still not speaking. The odd frosty monosyllable – 'yes', 'no', 'please' – nothing more than necessary. He's waiting for me to apologize, and I'm considering it only because it looks like he won't relent unless I do. I admire that about him. That he won't give in. That he's tough and stands his ground. That he's not prepared to roll over for an easy life.

Jasmin is one of his few weaknesses. He can't see the truth about that child, can't see how he's being manipulated, doesn't believe the girl is capable of doing wrong. The trouble is, I'm one of those forthright people who get to the nub of the issue and say what they think. I guess we'll have to find a middle ground about Jasmin. I'll have to pretend to be a bit more understanding than I actually am. Aidan will need to be more objective about his daughter's behaviour and hold her accountable. We'll sort it out, I'm sure we will. But it still makes me mad. What that child needs is to be taught a lesson. If her parents won't do it, then maybe I should. After all, I'm the one who's suffering here. *Tired people make mistakes and cause accidents.* That's why going to sleep is a *must*. Maybe I can get Jasmin on her own and stress this fact to her. Maybe she'll listen to me. I'll resist the urge to smack her and we'll have a sensible talk, a real heart-to-heart. Something to think about. I'd have to work out how to get some alone time with her, though. Aidan is fucking stuck to her side when she's at our house.

There's a knock on my door and John Greenland sticks his head in.

'Got a moment for a quick chat, Sophie?'

'Sure.' I force a smile. I'm not strictly meant to be in the office today – it's Tuesday – and I was just about to leave, but the executive general manager is not someone to be put off until tomorrow.

'I wanted to have a talk about this report on the new car-insurance product.'

'Yes?' My hackles are up. John's chats are usually prompted by errors he's found. I've never known anyone – certainly not at his level in the company – with such an eagle eye. Nothing escapes him, which can be both good and bad.

He puts the relevant document on my desk. 'Page four. Assumption two.'

He has highlighted the assumption and put a question mark beside it. He looms over me while I read – he's intimidatingly tall, and our difference in size is not helped by the fact that I'm sitting down. My heart sinks as it becomes apparent that he's found something wrong: the assumption is flawed and not appropriate for the scenario we were looking at.

'I'm sorry, John. You're perfectly right. I think this was something Jane was working on before she left . . .'

I'm not actually sure if it was Jane, but I may as well use her as the scapegoat: it's not as if she's here to defend herself, and it's not as if she doesn't deserve to have her name blackened. But that's not to say I won't reprimand the real culprit if I discover the error originates with someone else.

John's sigh has a ring of disappointment. 'Look, that's the point, Sophie. Maybe it was Jane, or maybe it was someone else. Mistakes will be made. But it's the manager's job to pick them up. *Your* job. And I feel I can't quite trust what's coming through from your department at the moment.'

Seriously? That's so unfair. Of course he can trust my department, trust me. I check everything to the nth degree. Come on, everyone knows how scrupulous I am.

My face burns under his gaze. 'I'm sorry, John. I've been tired lately. I'll try to be more vigilant.'

There it is again: *Tired people make mistakes.*

'Good.' His smile has an edge to it. 'That's why I came round. I knew you'd be right on to it.'

The house is dark and empty when I get in from work. Aidan is out somewhere (there was a polite note on the counter when I came down this morning, saying he would be late). The note felt as short as our recent conversations: he didn't specify where he was going or what he was doing.

My neck is aching, my head throbbing, and the first thing I do, after turning on the lights and the heating, is take some pain relief. The container is almost empty – I need to renew my prescription. More drugs, just so I can make it through the day. And for what? To be brought down to size by the executive general manager, to be told – more or less – that I'm not doing enough. So fucking unfair. I work hard, too hard. I'm meant to be part-time, for God's sake.

I fall on to the couch, my jacket still on, while I wait for the medication to take effect. I'm so tired I could vomit. So angry I could scream (in fact, I did scream earlier, at the graduate who made the error that caused the trouble). And so disappointed I could cry. John Greenland has been like a mentor to me since the day I started at Real Cover Insurance. He's heaped praise and encouragement on me at every juncture, and taken a keen interest in my career. He's included me in many senior-management initiatives, making it clear that one day he expects me to be in the top echelons of the company. Everybody knows I'm his protégée. Never, in the six years I've been working with him, has he been as openly critical as he was today. He obviously thinks I'm not as good as I was before, that I'm slipping. And the hard thing to take, to admit to myself (if not to him), is that it's true. Of course I'm not as good as I was before. I'm broken, limping from day to day, gulping back painkillers to keep myself going. And we know whose fault that is, don't we? Fucking Jasmin's.

I'm cold. My jacket, the heating – nothing's working, I can't get warm. One of Aidan's hoodies is folded over the back of the couch, within arm's reach. I grab it with the intention of draping the fleece interior across my legs, which are quivering. Something's hanging out from one of the pockets: white paper, folded over a few times.

Probably rubbish. No, not rubbish. An invoice. From a fertility clinic.

Embryos. Three of them. In deep freeze. Aidan and Chloe's fucking embryos. Of course that's where they were going the morning of the accident: they were on a fucking baby-making mission. It shouldn't matter where they were going, but *oh, it does*. It makes me furious. Really, really furious. Suddenly I'm ripping the invoice, shredding it with my fingers, snow-like flecks floating to land on the cushions and rug.

There. Destroyed. *Like me*.

The pain is starting to dull – thank you, pills. But something tells me it's going to refuse to go away fully, that it'll loom in the background, ready to pounce. I stay on the couch, waiting it out, the battle of the pills versus the pain. I'm both hungry and sick to the stomach. 8 p.m. Sitting, waiting. 9 p.m. Still waiting. Where is he? Who's he with? What's he doing? I send him a text: *When are you coming home?*

No reply. Nothing. It's almost 10 p.m. now. I should be fed and in bed, rallying myself for tomorrow. Instead I'm still on the couch, hungry, fuming, waiting.

Finally my phone beeps: *With Chloe and Jasmin. Going to stay the night. See you tomorrow.*

He's with Chloe. For all I know, they're discussing their unborn babies – *their fucking embryos* – making plans to reunite.

All my rage and disappointment pour into the scream. It fills my mouth, my ears, the whole house.

I can't bear it. My hands shake uncontrollably as I try to work my phone.

313

'Dad . . .'

'What is it?' He must be able to tell from my tone that something is wrong. I feel like a little girl again. Hurt, angry, but so relieved to have him, to be sure of his unconditional love.

'Do you need me to come over?'

'Yes,' I sob. 'Please come and get me. I want to come home.'

49

Chloe

He stayed the night, slept in my – I mean *our* – bed, and we fell asleep holding each other. Nothing happened. Everything happened. I couldn't be happier. It's not even six in the morning, and here I am, grinning from ear to ear, so absolutely thrilled I could jump up and dance around the room. The light is grey and shadowy, and more than once I turn my head to gaze at him, to reassure myself that he's really here and this is not a dream.

I'm impatient for him to open his eyes, to hear his validation that something significant has occurred. *This is the way things should be, Chloe. Me and you in this bed. Jasmin safe next door. This is normal, this is real. The last year has been nothing but a cruel aberration.*

He stirs. Then his eyes flutter. At last.

I roll over on my tummy and prop myself up on my elbows. 'Good morning,' I beam.

His return smile is more like a grimace. He is a man of principle and, even though nothing physical happened between us last night – which took great restraint on my part, and I assume his too – there is that sense that we're cheating. Which is nothing short of ludicrous. Aidan is my husband.

315

'Good morning,' he replies, after a pause that speaks volumes.

'Don't be glum,' I implore him.

Unfortunately, he doesn't agree. 'I've made things worse.'

'How, exactly?'

'Sophie will be furious with me.' He sighs, sounding incredibly tired, despite the fact that he's only just woken up. 'I haven't been fair to her.'

'Oh, for pity's sake. Nothing happened. We slept next to each other. Is that a crime?'

'In Sophie's eyes, yes.'

'Well, I don't care about Sophie's eyes.' My tone is petulant, but my hand – when it reaches out of its own accord to touch his face – is oddly gentle. His morning stubble prickles my fingertips. His breath is warm. He groans and turns his head away from my touch. He doesn't want this. He's right: it will only make things worse than they already are. Still, my head fills with other potential moves I could make from here. I could lower my lips to kiss the hollow of his neck; I can already imagine how warm his skin would be. Or I could slide my leg over his, push myself against him. More brazenly, I could drop my hand down under the covers and claim his early-morning erection. So easy, any of these moves. So very tempting. Things I've done a thousand times before without a second thought. 'I want to be crystal clear, Aidan. I love you, and I want you to come home. We're your family. We were here before Sophie. This is where you belong.'

His hand finds mine and our fingers interlace in what feels like a pledge. I feel so close to him now, so deeply intimate that my sexual urges have been momentarily satiated. 'I love you too.' His voice breaks. 'I always have, and always will. But I need to fix this mess, and I need to do it in such a way that I can live with myself . . . Will you give me some time?'

This is the same as what he said last night, when we talked and talked and talked. He still loves me, but he needs time to sort things out. What choice do I have? He is a man plagued by his conscience. It's vital – if we're to have any chance of putting this behind us – that he extracts himself from Sophie in a way that he feels is honest and fair.

I tighten my fingers around his. 'Just don't take too long.'

Channelling all my willpower, I pull back the covers and get out of bed. 'I'll get some coffee on.'

Downstairs I turn on the radio, fill the kettle and pop two slices of wholegrain bread into the toaster. It's all I can do not to break into song. He loves me. I love him. He needs time. I can give him time. Am I being a complete walkover, welcoming him back with open arms, no questions asked? Should I hold out on him, even just a little? Make him pay for leaving us, for choosing Sophie over us? No. He wasn't himself. The man who decided to leave us was a stranger, anguished beyond recognition, and making him pay feels futile, even cruel. I've seen enough army couples try to reunite after a split to know what works and what doesn't. Holding on to the bitterness, the hurt, the anger, is the worst thing you can do. It festers, you see. It may well be only a small residue of bad feeling to start with, nothing more than a slight desire for the offender in the marriage not to get off that lightly, but it always seems to grow much bigger than that. Until the couple splits up again. As far as I'm concerned, it's start with a clean slate or not at all.

Jasmin is still sound asleep when Aidan comes downstairs, his hair wet from the shower. The whole scene feels achingly familiar.

'Big day today?' I enquire conversationally, sliding his coffee mug – a Father's Day present from Jasmin with DADDY hand-painted in uneven bubble writing – across the counter.

'Huge.' He sits on one of the bar stools and sips his coffee. 'We're going up the mountains on a night-time training exercise.'

'Ah, an overnighter.' I smile. 'I remember those.'

Aidan would be incredibly tense in the days leading up to an exercise – all the planning was his responsibility. Then I would hear nothing while he was away, and I would worry for him and his men because things can go wrong on expeditions like that; they sometimes use live bullets, for goodness' sake. But he always came back in one piece, dirty, exhausted and deeply satisfied that everything had gone to plan.

'Panther's one of the most challenging I've been involved with,' he says now. 'Coaches, helicopters, boats, climbers – it's a logistical nightmare. I should get going. I wanted to get in early this morning to sort out a few last-minute details.'

'Will I call you a taxi?'

He shakes his head. 'I'll flag one down on the main road. Do you mind if I stick my head in on Jasmin first?'

'Of course not. She's had enough sleep. For once!'

'Last night went OK, didn't it? Only three times. She's definitely improving.'

'Yeah, she is.' My eyes meet his and there's so much conveyed in the look we share: the memory of all the bad nights over the last few years; the dreadful worry that there was something drastically wrong with our daughter; the tiredness, the despair, the rows, our dwindling hope as theory after theory and plan after plan proved not to make the slightest difference; now there's sheer relief and a rather unexpected *pride* – in Jasmin, in ourselves – that we seem to have found the answer and we're beginning to see a real improvement. Sensory overload. It sounds so plausible, so obvious. In hindsight.

Aidan goes back upstairs, and I'm draining the last of my coffee when my phone beeps so loudly I almost drop the mug with fright. The text is from Hannah.

Sorry for the early morning intrusion. Just wondering if you can fit in a coffee after school drop-off? Need to discuss something with you.

That's odd. I wonder what Hannah needs to talk about. Something to do with soccer? And what's so urgent that it can't wait until the game at the weekend? Doesn't she have work this morning? Won't this coffee make her late?

Sure. Let me know when and where.

Aidan reappears. 'She's awake, and full of questions about why I'm still here.'

I shrug. 'That's to be expected. She's a smart girl.'

Our eyes meet again in another look that seems to say a thousand things.

'Right, I'm off. I'll see you soon. Very soon.'

'Bye, Aidan.' Quite suddenly, I'm scared to let him go. What if this exercise is especially risky? What if he gets seriously injured? It would be too cruel that, just as we're beginning to pick ourselves up from the last accident, another should occur. *Be safe*, I implore him silently. *Keep yourself and everyone else safe*.

He lets himself out, and I resist the urge to run to the front window and steal one last glimpse of him.

50

Aidan

The house is empty and cold. Sophie's nowhere to be seen and the bed hasn't been slept in, but I'm too short of time for even a brief phone call to establish where she is. Change into my uniform. Quick shave. Don't forget the bag I packed before I went to see Chloe last night, with extra clothes and toiletries for the exercise.

I leave a note on the counter.

Sorry about last night. Back late tomorrow. Talk then.

My guess is that she's at her parents' house. I can't think of a friend she would turn to. Sophie's friends are groups rather than individuals. Some girls she knows from school, another group from university, a small knot of similarly minded colleagues from work. Nobody close enough to be in daily contact. Richard is invariably the one she calls when she's upset, or in need of anything. The dynamic of their relationship has bothered me at certain points over the last few months, and now it strikes me – just as I'm heading out the door – that Richard's more like Sophie's best friend than her father.

Another taxi. It's only a matter of days now until the twelve months are up, when I get my licence back, and I'll never take the privilege of driving for granted again. The ease of going straight from front door to car. No more jerky stops, no more foul smells, no more delays from buses that have come and gone too early, or arrive unapologetically late.

The traffic is heavy and progress is slow, despite the short journey. I could call Sophie now – it looks like we'll be at this particular set of lights for a few minutes – but it's still very early. She tries to stay in bed as late as she can in the mornings so that she's had enough rest. And it's not as if I can offer her any assurances. I'd be waking her only to upset her even further.

Staying with Chloe last night was cowardly, an act of weakness, and Sophie – despite our stand-off about Jasmin, despite the fact that we're barely speaking to each other – deserves much better. It's obvious now that she's blindingly jealous of both Chloe and Jasmin, and that's why she has been so terribly callous, so quick to lay blame. And there's no doubt she would have assumed the worst when she got my text last night. The fact that Chloe and I didn't have sex means nothing. What we did – admitting that we still loved each other, my promise to extract myself from Sophie – was far more dishonest. It was cheating.

Sorry, Sophie. I'm sorry to hurt you yet again. It's such a mess. All my fault. Blame me for all of it. What am I? A man who ping-pongs between women? Tells them he loves them, only to change his mind? What is wrong with me? I'm a walking disaster zone.

One thing I know for sure: I've always loved Chloe. It's the Sophie part I'm struggling to understand. Our argument in the car was liked being doused with a bucket of icy-cold water. *I couldn't love Sophie if she felt like that about Jasmin.* And once I had reached this stark conclusion, I then started questioning if I had ever loved Sophie to begin with. I thought it was love, I really did, but now I can't comprehend how I arrived at that particular label. If it wasn't love that I felt, what was it? Attraction? Admiration? Pity? Concern? A need to take action, to make good, along with a generous measure of guilt and the desire to punish myself? All of the above? Whatever it was, it was incredibly strong, something I couldn't fight, something I felt compelled to act on.

The coaches are already outside the barracks when I get there. There are three of them, their engines running, even though we're not meant to depart for another thirty minutes. I have some last-minute paperwork to complete and a hundred and twenty men to organize and keep safe over the next twenty-four hours. There's no choice: I must leave Sophie, Chloe and this fresh layer of guilt, remorse and confusion behind me, at least while I'm on this operation. Nothing can go wrong. There's no room for distraction or error.

I lock my phone in my desk drawer. The only technology allowed on Panther is the radio and satellite equipment.

Hannah

Here's Chloe now, a few minutes early, which is a bonus. I texted Sophie to say I have an emergency at home and won't be in until ten. She'll be annoyed. If she knew what

I was really up to, she would be considerably more than annoyed. Suffice it to say, the 'less late' I am, the better for everyone.

'Hey.' Chloe smiles as she sits down across from me. Her highlighted hair is tied in a high ponytail, and her skin is shiny with moisturizer. She's obviously a morning person; happiness seems to radiate from her.

A waitress appears with much appreciated efficiency. Once we've ordered, Chloe rests her elbows on the table and asks, 'What's up?'

A perfectly reasonable question, but where do I start? Back at St Brigid's, or the present day? With my gut instinct, or the proven facts?

'You know how Jasmin stays the night with Sophie and Aidan sometimes?'

Chloe blinks in surprise. 'Yes?'

'Well, I wouldn't want my twins doing that . . . I wouldn't want them staying with Sophie McCarthy, day *or* night . . . I wouldn't want them spending a single minute with her.'

Chloe stares at me, speechless. After a few moments, her questions come piling out on top of each other. 'What? What do you mean? Why?'

'Because she's spiteful and dangerous.'

The waitress brings the coffees. I've lost the appetite for mine. I assume Chloe has too, because she doesn't even glance down at the frothy cappuccino that has been set before her.

'How do you know this? From working with her?'

'Partly. She's a bitch at work. She's a bully, a tyrant who

makes life miserable for her staff. But the real reason I'm here is because of something that happened at school . . .'

Chloe looks taken aback at this further connection. 'You were at school with her?'

'I was in the year below. She hurt someone, Chloe. A girl at camp. The girl, Kristina, was a threat to Sophie. She was smarter than her, and Sophie couldn't stand it. She pushed her down a ravine. Sophie pushed this poor girl *down a ravine*, and she spent weeks in hospital. Here, I have some messages. I found the girl on Facebook . . .'

My bag is on the floor, and I reach down to pull out the pages I printed late last night. My first message to Kristina. Her short response saying that she had spent her life trying to forget St Brigid's and didn't want anything to do with a reunion, if that's what I had in mind. Then my reply admitting that I had seen something the day of the accident, and that I knew Sophie had been lying about her exact whereabouts on the track, and how much I regretted not speaking up at the time. Then Kristina's response, validation of what I'd suspected all along.

She pushed me. I did not lose my footing. She pushed me because she couldn't bear that I was better than her. But nobody believed me. The school said it was 'natural to want to blame someone' after such a terrible accident.

Chloe's reading slowly, thoroughly. What would I do in her situation? Jump into action, or take some time to mull it over? Take Sophie to task, demanding an explanation, or simply remove Jasmin from her vicinity?

All I know is that a weight has lifted from me: the self-loathing that came with knowing I had done nothing, kept my mouth shut for fear of drawing attention to myself, talked myself out of my concerns and allowed Sophie to lie through her teeth. Things would have turned out differently if I'd just opened my mouth. Sophie would've been challenged. It would always have been a case of her word against Kristina's. It's not as if I saw the push – my evidence was only to do with where she was on the path at the time Kristina fell – but at the very least Sophie would have been on notice. She might have realized that it's not so easy to get away with things. Her tendency to bully and get her own way at all costs might have been tempered, instead of going completely unchecked.

'What are you going to do?' I ask Chloe when she finally looks up.

'What you suggested . . . I'm not going to allow Jasmin anywhere near that woman.'

'Good.' I breathe out. My latte is cold when I take a sip. A waste of money, but time well spent. 'Now, I'd better get to work.'

'How can you face her?' Chloe asks, her eyes following me as I stand up and hitch my handbag over my shoulder.

My smile feels rather shaky. 'Because today is the day that Sophie McCarthy is going to be held to account. In more ways than one. As soon as I get into work, I'm going straight to HR to make an official bullying complaint.'

I can hear Sophie's excuses when she hears about my complaint. *I have high standards – what's wrong with that?* Her standards are not just high, they're deliberately impossible. *I may have been bad-tempered but I'm in a lot of pain.* Pain is

326

no excuse for anything. We're all in pain, in one way or another. How we react to it is a measure of who we truly are.

Do you hear me, Harry? It's not OK to give in to pain. It's not OK to use it as an excuse.

Chloe

I'm shocked. On many levels. That something so dreadfully serious should occur – a girl being pushed down a ravine! – without any consequences. That Sophie could live with herself afterwards. That she could get away with it. That she could be so vindictive, so callous, so cruel, so *dangerous*. We had no idea who it was we crashed into that morning. We assumed it was someone worthy of our guilt and remorse. How were we to know it was a monster?

Back at home I tackle some essential housework – a clean-up after breakfast, a load of washing, then a quick vacuum – before sitting down at my sewing machine. One of the mums from soccer admired my dress last week, and I impulsively offered to make her one the same. It's already half done: floral chiffon, fitted on top, then falling in soft folds to just above the knee. A dress that can be worn in any season (I had leggings and boots on with mine).

The rhythm of the machine soothes me, clears my head. What to do about Sophie? Apart from the obvious – making sure that Jasmin is never alone with her again – what other steps should be taken? This accident at the ravine happened fourteen years ago, but shouldn't the police be informed? Is there a time limit on such things? More pressingly, how should I broach this with Aidan? *The woman we crashed into, the woman you live with, is a complete psychopath*. What will he make of these emails – Hannah said it was OK to keep them – when I show them to him? Will he believe Hannah and Kristina, two people he hasn't even met? Has he seen any evidence of Sophie's vindictiveness and cruelty? If only he wasn't away on this stupid operation. He won't even have his phone with him. No technology. The army is infuriating at times.

Sophie doesn't like me.

How many times has Jasmin said these words? How many times have Aidan and I passed it off as being a natural sentiment on her part, to believe that her father's new partner didn't like her, when in fact the truth was the other way around? It strikes me now that I should have asked more questions. Why do you think Sophie doesn't like you, Jasmin? Has she said something to you? Done something? Has she hurt you in any way? If Sophie was evil enough to push a girl down a ravine simply for the crime of being too clever, what could she potentially do to Jasmin? Jasmin, whom her father adores, and who could be deemed a much bigger threat to Sophie's obvious aspirations to have Aidan all to herself?

But it was such a long time ago. They were all so young. Maybe it *was* an accident. Hannah and I are united on one thing: we don't like Sophie. Maybe that's blinding us, making us want to believe the absolute worst of her and take Kristina's side. My head is beginning to feel significantly less clear now.

The dress is ready by mid-afternoon. I fold it reverently and place it in a carrier bag by the door so I won't leave without it. Maybe custom-made clothes are something I should consider doing more of. With everything that's happened, it feels time to reassess my much-neglected career. I can see now that I put too much on hold while I was waiting to get pregnant again. Having something else to focus on would have helped in so many ways.

Wednesday is my day for getting things done. Jasmin goes straight to soccer after school, and that gives me an extra hour and a half that I wouldn't usually have at my disposal. I prepare some vegetables and meat for dinner and bring in the washing from the line. There's not a lot because it's just Jasmin and me. Soon Aidan will be living with us again. I'll be catering for his appetite at dinner time, washing his clothes, and everything will feel more substantial, more *right*. Now I'm making him sound like one of those men who needs to be waited on, which he most definitely is not (Aidan does more than his fair share of household chores). It's only that I feel his absence more keenly when I'm doing these everyday tasks, like laundry and cooking dinner.

At four thirty I shrug on my warmest jacket and my new scarf – the one Aidan laughed about last night – for the short walk to the training fields. The light is dwindling by the time I get there. I can see the kids in the distance, and my eyes automatically search for Jasmin. She's the only girl, so she's easy to pick out. I can't see her. Strange. Maybe she's sitting down or having a drink.

I'm closer now. Davy is putting them through their

paces, shouting instructions in his booming accent. 'Inside foot. One touch. Find space.'

'Where's Jasmin?' My eyes skim the far side of the field, where a few parents and siblings are watching. The woman who ordered the dress isn't here yet.

Davy stops mid-stride and turns his head to stare at me. 'She didn't come today. I assumed the lass was sick.'

There is a horrible moment of realization. Jasmin isn't here. For the last hour and a half, when she should have been here training, she was somewhere else. Where? *Where?*

Davy bellows at the children. 'Come in, lads . . . Has anyone seen Jasmin?'

The kids respond to the urgency in his voice and converge around us, their heads shaking, one by one. The training fields are directly across from the school. The kids make their own way here. It's such a short distance, perfect to practise a little independence. There's even a volunteer at the pedestrian crossing to see them across safely.

'Where is she?' I appeal to Davy, even though he clearly doesn't know the answer and is every bit as clueless and helpless as I am. '*Where is my daughter?*'

The kids hear the panic in my voice and now they're scared too. Other parents begin to walk towards us, no doubt wondering what all the commotion is about.

'Have you seen Jasmin?' I ask them frantically. 'Has anyone seen Jasmin?'

Their replies offer no hope.

'No.'

'She didn't come today.'

'No. Sorry . . . Maybe check with the school?'

'The school office is closed by now. The staff will have gone home.'

Davy swipes out his phone from his pocket. 'I'm calling the police.'

The police? Oh Lord. What am I forgetting? I must be forgetting something. *Focus*. Was there something special on after school? Was she meant to go to a friend's house? No, nothing is coming to me.

My phone. Has she been trying to call? No. Nothing. No missed calls or texts.

Oh dear Lord. This can't be happening. Where is she? Did she forget about training? Has she been waiting for me outside school all this time?

Where is my daughter?

51

Sophie

My cheeks sting. I've never been so humiliated in my life. Or so violently angry. Or so liable to burst into tears.

'*I am not a bully.*'

John Greenland and Alyssa are sitting across from me. Neither of them looks as though they believe me.

'I'm exacting.' I direct my appeal to John, my mentor, who knows how much I strive for perfection. 'Some people find that hard to take, and to keep up with what I expect from them.'

'Phone calls at eleven o'clock at night? Work demands all through the weekend? Sophie, there's a line between being exacting and harassing your staff.'

What a hypocrite! He has called me after hours and over the weekend, and I haven't gone around calling him a bully, have I?

My desk phone begins to ring. I glance at it meaningfully, because it's 6 p.m. and, technically, we should all be at home by now. 'We don't work in a nine-to-five environment, John.'

'Yes, I understand that. And we're all guilty of expecting after-hours input from our colleagues. But on one occasion – on Monday night, I believe – you made four phone calls, and sent two texts and numerous emails to Mrs Evans. Requesting a complex piece of work to be completed by first thing the next morning. Is that true?'

He looks at me with his most intimidating stare, and my head scrambles back to Monday. Yes, the risk analysis. 'Hannah didn't complete a certain task by the time she left for the evening . . .'

'How did you expect her to get sufficient sleep? To spend any time with her family on this particular evening?'

Seriously? Come on, John. How many times have I worked late for you? How many times have I come into the office early the next day on only a few hours' sleep? OK, so you didn't specifically ask me to work around the clock, but I *knew* – without being told, I might add! – when it was *necessary*, when a special effort was required to get the job done.

'I'm committed.' My chin rises as I return his stare. As though to prove my point, my phone begins to ring again, and I raise my voice to talk over the trilling. 'I put my job first, and I expect the same of my staff. I needed that analysis to be completed.'

Now he looks sceptical, which is even worse than when he's being plain intimidating. 'The risk analysis? It *was* the risk analysis, wasn't it? The one for me? Something that wasn't due until later in the week, if I remember correctly.'

'Yes . . .' Give me strength! I shouldn't have to justify myself like this. 'I needed to review it before it got to you and, as you mentioned previously, the standard of work coming out of my department has been an issue . . .'

'Sophie, you don't need *three days* to do a review. Stop making excuses. There was no urgency, no reason to make Hannah work extra hours. *None at all.*'

If I were Jane, this would be the point when I'd resort to saying, 'Fuck you.' I can understand now what motivated her, how it must have felt like the only appropriate response. Fuck you, John Greenland, you big, fat hypocrite. And fuck you, Alyssa, with your clipboard and fake concern.

Alyssa clears her throat. 'Look, Sophie, as you know, this isn't the first complaint we've had about your behaviour towards your staff. For this reason, we're taking swift and firm action. This is your first and final warning. It will be put in writing . . .'

A warning? Me? I'm a *senior manager*. One day – soon, I hope – I'll be an executive. And now my fucking phone has started ringing *again*.

Alyssa glances at it, and then at me. 'Do you have a response?'

'Are you serious?'

'Very serious,' she says, the bitch. 'I know this is a shock to you, Sophie. Nobody likes to think of themselves as a bully. Sometimes the truth can be harsh.'

'I approved Hannah's pay rise, for God's sake. Do bullies give a shit about what their victims get paid? Do they? Of course they don't.'

'Calm down, please,' John commands, in a voice that tells me everything has changed. There will be no more mentoring, no more career acceleration, no more talk of an executive position.

Calm down? I could strangle Hannah with my bare hands. Alyssa and John too. And Aidan, the bastard, for not coming home last night. Jasmin and Chloe too. I could strangle each and every one of them.

But Hannah! How could she? After all I've done for her? She's playing the victim – can't they see that? I bet her husband was addicted to prescription drugs or something, and that's why the life insurance didn't pay out. I bet she's blaming the doctor, the pharmacy, the health system, anyone but him, or herself. *Stupid, stupid bitch.*

There's a knock on the door. *What now? What the fuck now?*

The receptionist sticks her head in. I can't remember her name; I never did get around to formally introducing myself.

'I'm so sorry for interrupting,' she murmurs, looking nervous.

We're in the middle of something here. We're in the middle of a formal warning. *Go away!*

'It's just that the police need to see you, Sophie. I've been trying to phone to let you know.'

I can see them through the gap in the door. Two blobs of navy, male. Is it something to do with the sentencing? Some residual paperwork? Couldn't it wait? But before I have the chance to protest, they've swarmed my office, their uniforms and weapons stark and out of place in the room.

'Excuse us, Miss McCarthy,' the older one says, advancing until he's right in front of my desk and uncomfortably close. The other one hovers by the door, as though preparing for someone to make a run for it. 'This is an urgent matter. We need to speak to you about Jasmin Ryan.'

'What about Jasmin?' I ask, my head whirling.

John and Alyssa seem rooted to their seats. Can't I have some privacy here? Is that too much to ask? Apparently it is.

'I believe Jasmin is well known to you?'

'Jasmin? Yes . . . She's my partner's daughter. What –'

'Jasmin failed to arrive at her soccer training this afternoon, a short walk from her school . . . Do you know anything about her whereabouts?'

Why is he asking me this? Is it because Aidan's away?

'I'm sorry, I have no idea . . . Has she run away?'

'When did you last see Jasmin?'

I feel dizzy, unfocused. *Can this day get any worse?* 'At the weekend . . .'

'You've been here in the office all afternoon?'

Everything about him radiates suspicion: his tone, his stance, his stare.

'*Yes* . . . What is this about? Why are you questioning me? Surely Chloe would have a better idea?'

'Jasmin's mother mentioned you as a person of interest.'

'She *what*? You don't seriously think –'

My phone starts ringing again, interrupting me, and everyone turns to stare at it.

'Maybe you should get that,' John Greenland suggests, reminding me that he and Alyssa are still here, watching, judging, and no doubt jumping to all sorts of conclusions.

I snatch the receiver from its cradle. It's Mum on the other end, breathless, panicked. 'Do you know where your father is? The car is gone, and there's been no sign of him all afternoon. His phone is switched off. This isn't like him. I'm quite concerned –'

'Jasmin is missing too,' I say, before it strikes me that this is an extraordinary coincidence.

Both Jasmin and Dad are missing. What are the chances?

He wouldn't, would he?

No, of course not. He was upset for me last night. That's all.

But how can they both be missing at the exact same time? And Dad wasn't just upset last night, was he? He was distraught. Kept saying, 'I can't bear this to go on any longer. This is killing me, Sophie.'

'Sophie, you don't think he . . .' Mum's voice trails away but it's clear she's also considering the possibility. This is not good.

I keep coming back to the chances. Both of them gone at the same time.

Oh, no. *The idiot*. The fucking *idiot*. Oh, no.

52

Richard

We've been in the car about ten minutes before she speaks.

'This isn't the way home.' A statement of fact.

I don't answer. Traffic is infuriatingly slow with the after-school rush. It would have been better if we'd left earlier in the day, but then it's not as if I bloody well planned this, so the traffic is what it is.

'Where are we going?' Curiosity now. And a thread of panic. 'Where's Mum? Is she at hospital?'

'Shush,' I tell her. 'I need to concentrate on the traffic.'

'*But where's Mum?* What's wrong with her?'

'I told you already it's nothing serious. Now shush. We'll be there soon.'

Ten more minutes of silence and horrendous traffic. My head is as clogged up as the roads. Am I really doing this? Is Aidan's daughter really here with me?

Then her small, scared voice behind me, confirming that this is real, as real as can be.

'You said we'd be there soon . . . Why won't you answer any of my questions? . . . I want my mum and dad . . . I shouldn't have got in the car with you.'

Smart girl. No, she shouldn't have got in the car but, to give her credit, she hesitated before getting in.

'Your mum's not feeling well,' I said when I intercepted her outside the school. 'Your dad asked me to pick you up today.'

'What's wrong with Mum?'

'Nothing serious. She just needs a rest, that's all.'

'But I have soccer training. I'm meant to go straight there. Daddy knows that.'

'He thought you could miss one week,' I said, keeping my tone light.

It was in the balance for a few moments. A slight frown came over her face as she tried to weigh up this unexpected deviation from her normal routine and all the stuff they teach them at school about stranger danger.

'I'm not a stranger. You know me. I'm Sophie's dad.'

She got in the car, at last, and now here we are, heading west, towards the mountains, because that's the only place I can think of going. I hear the click of the door handle.

'It's locked,' I snap. 'And the windows are locked too.'

'Are you going to hurt me?' she asks breathlessly.

'Of course not.'

'But Mum's not really sick, is she? So why are you doing this? Why have you taken me?'

Because I want to hurt Aidan Ryan. I want to hurt him as badly as he hurt Sophie. I can't smash open his chest – if I were young and fit, that's what I'd do, rip him apart – but I can get to him in a different way. *Through you, Jasmin*. A daughter is her father's weakness. We can be as strong and invincible as we like, but our daughters instantly reduce us to more vulnerable beings. I would do anything for Sophie. *Anything*. Seeing her last night, so

339

broken and distraught, one thing became clear to me: I couldn't bear to watch this go on any longer. I had to do something. Something drastic.

'It's not you,' I explain, as much for my own sake as hers. 'It's your father. I'm doing this because of your father and what he did to *my* daughter.'

She contemplates this for a little while. It doesn't take her long to work it out.

'You mean the accident?'

'Yes.' Plus the fact that now he's broken her heart as well as her body.

'But he said sorry for that. And he went to court, and the judge didn't punish him any more.'

My rebuttal is harsh. 'Sometimes being sorry just isn't enough.'

This upsets her. Cracks her composure, which has been admirable until now. She begins to sob, then tries to stop herself by sucking in her breath.

'So you're trying to get back at him?'

I decide not to answer that, for fear of upsetting her again.

'Retribution,' she says next, more to herself than me.

Her vocabulary is impressive. 'That's a big word for a small girl.'

'I do extension words at school.'

Yes, she's clearly a bright young thing, and I have a softness for intelligent girls. Stop talking to her, Richard. Stop getting sucked in. Focus on the traffic. And make a bloody plan, for God's sake.

'You need to be quiet. I need to concentrate. The last thing we need is another bloody accident.'

Another sob and gulping sound from behind. Then several – more desperate – clicks of the door handle.

'I've already told you it's locked. Now listen, Jasmin. You have two choices. You can keep trying the door, even though there's no point, and getting more and more upset. Or you can sit quietly and make the journey more pleasant for both of us.'

'The journey where?'

'Shush.'

'I want my mum and dad.'

'*Just shush.*'

Thankfully, she responds to the harshness of my tone and quietens down.

An hour later we've begun our ascent up the mountains, my ears popping as we climb. Jasmin has spent most of the time gazing out of the window. Every couple of minutes a sob or a sniff reminds me she's there, not that I could forget. She gives the impression that she's trying very hard not to descend into full-blown hysteria. Such a tough little thing.

More from instinct than anything else, I turn off the main road at one of the smaller towns. The road is narrow, tree-lined, and eventually the houses taper away and we're deep in the bush. Another half an hour and it'll be dark. I need to find somewhere before then.

Jasmin takes a water bottle from her school bag and drinks noisily, then puts on her jacket; she must be feeling cold.

'Do you have a house here?' Her voice is croaky. It's been a while since she's used it.

A house? Ha, that would be nice! Dee and I were on the verge of buying a holiday home – an apartment near the beach – when Sophie had her accident. Dee brought it up again only last week. *We should start looking again, Richard.* But the mountains would be too wild, too isolated, too cold for Dee. Her face flashes in front of me, her lips tightened in a line of anger and worry. She's been saying for ages that she's concerned about me, and now I've gone and proven her right. My wife's talking to me now, conducting a conversation in my head.

You're not thinking straight, Richard. You've let things get on top of you. You're depressed.

I'm not depressed, Dee. I'm angry. Plain and simple.

What are you hoping to achieve with this? You'll do yourself more damage than anyone else.

What am I achieving? Well, Aidan Ryan will know just how much it hurts to have his daughter taken away from him, for a start. I'm still working out the rest.

Turn back, Richard. It's not too late. Turn back now, and everything will be OK.

Nothing will ever be OK again, Dee. Sophie's life is ruined. And I've been looking on – doing bloody nothing – for the last year. I can't bear it. Do you hear me? I can't *bear it* any longer.

'Are we sleeping in the car?' Now that Jasmin's found her voice again, she doesn't seem to be deterred by the fact that she's getting no answers from me.

Yes, I suppose we are. When did I last sleep in a car? A long, long time ago, before I had children. At a rock festival, if I remember correctly. The sun is gone now, and dusk is setting in, dimming the vividness of the scenery around us. Jasmin changes position in the back seat. She's getting fidgety.

A few kilometres on I see a dirt track and I take the turn too late, the wheels skidding, orange dust billowing behind us. Jasmin yelps.

Shortly after, a declaration: 'I'm hungry.'

Well, I am too. But I didn't think to pack any food, so we'll both have to put up with it. The track narrows. The trees are high and slender, leaning in on the car, forcing me to drop speed. After five minutes I'm down to a crawl and in serious danger of scraping the car. I decide we've gone far enough.

'I need to pee,' Jasmin whispers when we come to a stop.

Me too. I get out of the car, locking the doors after me, and walk out of sight, relieving myself against one of the gum trees. What now, Richard? You've got this far. Aidan will know by now. They'll have got word to him (Sophie said he was away on some overnight operation). He'll be frantic, imagining the worst. Just the way I was when I got the call about Sophie.

Your daughter has been in a serious accident.

I was at home when the call came through and I remember picking up the phone carelessly, saying a jovial hello, expecting that it would be Dee or Jacob or even Sophie herself on the other end.

Your daughter is in a critical condition.

The world stopped for me when I heard those words, and it's never quite restarted again. I'm stuck in that

343

moment, when my dreams and hopes for my clever, talented daughter shattered around me.

What will they say to Aidan?

We're concerned for your daughter's safety.

Should they be concerned for Jasmin's safety? *Should they?* What's the plan, Richard?

If I were a bad person, I would hurt her. Then Aidan would really know what it feels like to be in my shoes. To see your child, your beloved daughter, and all her amazing potential *wither* in front of your eyes. Sophie could have been anything. *Anything!* How would he feel if Jasmin were crippled? Unable to play soccer, or go to school for full days, or lead a normal life. *Broken.*

I came here with no plan other than taking her from school and driving far away and causing Aidan to feel a fraction of the worry I felt about Sophie. But now that I'm here, in the middle of nowhere, with hours at my disposal before they find us, it doesn't feel as if I've done enough. I wasn't going to harm Jasmin, I really wasn't. But this rage I have, this terrible, helpless rage, seems to be growing instead of receding. The waste of what Sophie could have been. The waste of her talent and determination and her mind. It's killing me. Turning me into someone I don't recognize. But then again, this person – this man who abducts children and deliberates on whether to hurt them – *is* faintly familiar. Back when the children were young, I used to fantasize about killing anyone who threatened them: pummelling imaginary attackers to death, cracking their necks with my bare hands, gouging their eyes out. I used to fantasize about violence. I just didn't imagine it would be a child I'd have to hurt, that's all. A bright, intelligent girl. But she's the only way. The only way to get to *him*.

Then Dee is in my head again, admonishing me in that overly loud voice she reserves for me lately.

Don't do it. You don't need to do anything tonight, Richard. We'll talk about it in the morning.

53

Jasmin

Don't cry. Daddy always says that my brain is my best weapon. Crying will just get in the way of thinking.

Don't cry. Think. *Think*.

Richard has kidnapped me. That's bad. Very bad. He wants to get back at my dad. *Bad*. The car doors are locked. *Bad*. Nobody knows where we are. *Bad*. He obviously hasn't done much planning for this, that's the only positive I can think of. If he'd planned it, he'd have known where he was going and not made all those sudden turns.

I'm trying to make a plan, trying to imagine what Daddy would do. He's used to situations like this – they're always practising for emergencies in the army. And I've been trying to remember the book I read a few weeks ago. It was a fiction book from the library, about a boy lost in a forest. Lucky for the boy, he was able to survive because he had all the important things he needed: water, food, torch, warm clothes. My problem is that I only have what's in my school bag: my jacket, my drink bottle, a grain bar and an apple I was meant to eat before soccer training. I don't have a torch, and that's a BIG problem because it's getting dark and we're out in the middle of the bush. Richard doesn't have a house here, so we're obviously going to sleep in the car . . . if I'm *alive* to sleep in the car.

Don't panic. Deep breaths. Daddy says that the first step in solving a problem is staying calm. I need to get out of this car. I'll tell Richard I need to go to the toilet. Then I'll make a run for it. But I'm not going to be able to run carrying my drink bottle and my jacket and my apple. And if he sees me with my bag on my back, when I'm just meant to be having a pee, he'll guess what I have in mind. So I put on my jacket in the car, even though it makes me feel hot. And I gulp what's left in my drink bottle, hopefully enough water to get me through. I'll use some of my self-defence techniques if he catches up with me. Kick him in the kneecap. Smash my hand against his nose (he has no idea how strong I am after all those push-ups). I slip the grain bar into my jacket pocket, and a pencil – perfect for eye-poking, which Daddy says is the best self-defence technique of all.

'I need to pee,' I say when he finally stops the car. We're deep in the bush, on a fire trail, and the trees are grey and spooky in the dusk. No one is going to find us here. My only hope is to escape.

He gets out of the car without answering me, and walks until he's out of sight. I heard him lock the doors as he went, but I try them anyway. Trapped. Five minutes pass. Ten. Twenty. Don't panic, Jasmin. Don't cry. *Don't.* A few tears blur my eyes, and I rub them away. He'll come back, he has to. Keep planning. Am I going to run before or after going to the toilet? Am I faster than him? He's old, so I must be a better runner. And Davy has been doing

347

lots of fitness at soccer, so my stamina is good. I can keep going for thirty minutes, or an hour if I have to. Which way am I going to run? From what I can see, the trees and undergrowth are pretty dense. It'll have to be the track we came in on. Which will make it easier for him to come after me. But if I can run fast enough, he won't be able to catch me. And if he turns back for the car, I'll have a chance to hide.

Finally – when my watch tells me he's been gone fifty-five minutes – he returns, emerging from the dark and opening the driver's door, cold air coming in with him. Is my jacket going to be enough to keep me warm?

'I need to pee,' I say again, trying to sound teary, which isn't hard.

He completely ignores me.

'I haven't been since lunchtime,' I plead. 'Do you want me to go in your car?'

He sighs, gets out and comes around to open my door.

'Thanks,' I say, pretending to be friendly.

His grip on my arm is tight, too tight to wriggle free from. Once I'm outside the car, I realize it isn't as dark as I thought. There's a half-moon and some stars, and if I concentrate hard I can actually see a little bit.

Richard marches me to a nearby tree. 'You can go here.'

My eyes dart around, establishing the most direct route to the track. I can't afford to trip up, or stumble. As Mrs Stanley often says, *Time is of the essence.*

But Richard looks as though he's planning on staying right next to me, which is *not* part of the plan.

'I don't want you looking at me,' I tell him, my voice wobbly, which is good, *authentic*.

We stare at each other. Can he see how much I'm shaking?

'Don't you try anything,' he warns, before taking a few steps back so he's on the other side of the tree.

He's close, closer than I imagined he'd be. I have the advantage of surprise, though. And I have the pencil gripped in my hand, just in case.

I move my feet in the scrub, and rustle my clothes, pretending that I'm about to pee. Then, after one last shaky breath, I launch myself into the dark, towards the barely visible track. His voice calls out in shock, and then he comes after me, his legs much longer than mine, but slower, hopefully slower. I run faster than I've ever run in my life, my legs thrashing down hard on the uneven ground.

You're faster than him, Jasmin. Go. Go.

My breath is loud in my ears. I'm grunting with the effort. I can hear him behind me, panting in a ragged, old-man way.

'Stop, you silly girl.'

Never. I am never going to stop. Each breath burns in my throat. My legs feel heavy, but I keep going, through the almost-dark, with him calling out every so often, begging me to stop. All my energy is concentrated on running. I don't answer him, don't turn around to establish my lead, not once.

I can't hear him any more. He has stopped chasing me. This is where he's going to turn back to get the car. Which means I have another minute or so of running on the track, then I'll need to disappear into the bush, into the scary undergrowth where there could be snakes or spiders or a zillion other deadly things waiting for me.

Count, Jasmin. One, two, three . . . At sixty, even though I don't yet hear the sound of the car, I turn into the bush, charging through the brambles, wincing when a branch snaps back and slaps me on the face. Then I walk straight into what feels like a huge cobweb, and it sticks to my face and my hair and I thrash my hands, trying to get it off me.

'Yuck. Yuck. *Yuck*.'

Focus. Forget the cobweb, and the spiders living in it, and the fact that there could be one crawling on me right now. Keep going. Deep. Deeper. As far away from the track as I can, and in as straight a line as I can, because I need to be able to find my way out of here later, when he's gone.

Here he comes, the hum of his car filling the night. Now the headlights in the distance, extra light that I take advantage of, moving with greater speed for a short while, until he's closer and it's time to crouch down and hide. The car is going very slowly now.

The headlights move past me. Hooray! He thinks that I'm further along than I actually am. Should I go deeper into the bush? What's worse, the risk of getting lost, or being too easy to find? My school tights are torn, and I know, from my stinging skin, that I have lots of cuts on my legs, as well as on my face and hands.

Keep going, Jasmin. Go deeper. The deeper you are,

the safer. Don't be scared. Don't cry. Don't panic. Your brain is your best weapon.

Richard must have stopped further up the track, because I can hear his voice now, faint yet insistent.

'Jasmin! Jasmin! I'm sorry.'

I stop again, because moving makes noise and, even though he sounds quite far away, I'm scared he'll hear me and come in this direction. This is far enough. Here's a tree I can sit against. Hopefully there are no spiders living in it. Or ants. Are ants nocturnal? Kangaroos are, and koalas. I'm not sure about ants . . . or snakes. My upper body is warm, thanks to my jacket, but my legs are quickly becoming cold and I pull in my knees tight against me. Don't think about the animals. Or the cold. Think about Mum and Dad. Pretend that they're right here next to me. Mum's wearing her puffy red jacket and her purple jeans and she doesn't care that the colours clash. Daddy's in his uniform, of course. They have their arms around me, squashing me between them. Mum keeps kissing my hair and saying, 'I love you, I love you, I love you.' Daddy's voice is very serious, 'Keep your head, Jasmin. Stay calm.' Now tears are filling my eyes again, hot as they roll down my face. I will never be naughty or mean to Mum and Dad ever again. If only I could get them a message to tell them this. What if they think I'm dead? Mum will be *distraught*. Daddy will be trying to find me. He is looking for me right now, I know he is.

'Jasmin. Jasmin.' Richard is still out there.

But I'm safe. There is too much track, too much bush, for Richard to search. *I'm safe.* He'll give up in an hour, two at most. He'll get tired, sleepy, and call off the search until the morning. Then my dad will be here for real. My dad and *the whole army*.

I can stay awake until then. Richard won't catch *me* sleeping. He doesn't know how long I can stay awake. Actually, that's one more positive in this extremely bad situation: I am *an expert* at staying awake.

54

Aidan

There's video coverage showing Richard's car – the classic Mercedes – going through the toll booths on the M4, and then, forty-five minutes later, driving through the main street at Glenbrook. Apparently nothing showed up on the CCTV cameras on the flyover at Leura, which implies they're here, on the mountains. Somewhere between Glenbrook and Leura.

It was too late to call off Panther. The operation was well under way by the time I got the radio message from the police.

'Your daughter has been kidnapped. We are concerned about the mental health of Richard McCarthy, and for your daughter's safety.'

Richard! How could I have so drastically underestimated him? Been so oblivious to the signs, the threat he posed? The police seem to think this kidnapping of Jasmin is a way of 'getting even' with me. Trying to hurt me as much as I've hurt him. Or is it more about hurting Jasmin in place of Sophie? Is this about us fathers, or our daughters? Richard: overprotective, obsessed, silently seething. Is this revenge? Desperation? Or is it, as the police suggested on the radio, a genuine mental-health issue?

My men are scattered around the mountainside, climbing cliff faces in the dark, advancing through the forest in the dark, canoeing and firing shots in the dark. I'm meant to be guiding them by radio, from 'headquarters' (a tent erected on a rocky plateau twenty kilometres from Katoomba). It's inconceivable that my daughter is out there too, in the same dark, somewhere on these mountains. And I'm to blame. Richard wants to 'get even' with me.

Chloe was distraught when she came on the satellite phone. She was at the barracks. 'I need to be there, with you, to be helping in some way . . .'

'Chloe, I don't want you driving up here. It's dark, the road is unfamiliar, and you're very upset. There's little that can be done until the morning . . .'

'Jack can drive me . . . I can't just sit here and wait. I can't, Aidan, I just can't . . .'

I was relieved to hear she was with Jack. The chaplain would take good care of her.

But she was so upset she was hardly making sense.

'Sophie pushed this girl . . .'

'What? What girl?'

'A girl at school. Down a ravine. She's dangerous, Aidan. And it's obvious that her father's just as dangerous and vindictive.'

'Hang on, Chloe. Slow down. Tell me what the schoolgirl has to do with Jasmin?'

Chloe struggled to deliver a coherent explanation, and I struggled to get my head around it. Did Sophie really push a girl down a ravine? And the police already knew about this? Yes, Chloe insisted. She'd told the story to the attending police officers when they asked if anyone had a motive to harm Jasmin. But it quickly became clear to the police that Sophie knew nothing about Jasmin's whereabouts. After discovering that her father was also missing, it was in fact Sophie who put two and two together. At least, that's what I construed from Chloe's somewhat garbled account of what had happened throughout the course of the late afternoon and evening, until she'd been able to get hold of me . . . which hadn't been easy, given Panther's limited communications and extensive security protocols. It's good that she went to the barracks. It had stopped her driving straight up here and delivered her into the safe hands of Jack.

Chloe broke down completely towards the end of our call. 'Our girl, our little girl . . .'

The line crackled as the phone changed hands, and then a male voice: Jack. 'I'll stay with Chloe. We'll be on the end of the line if you need to talk to her, or she needs to talk to you. I'll drive her up there as soon as we have confirmation that it's still the right place to go. Don't want to head there and find out we've got it wrong, or they've moved on. Would be too distressing.'

The popular picnic and tourist sites and the local hideouts have already been scoured.

The police are limited in what else they can do until first light (other than send out as many patrol cars as possible, in the hope of spotting Richard's distinctive car on the road somewhere).

'Thanks, Jack. I'm grateful.'

'I'll pray for you all.'

'Please do.'

First light. We can't do anything until first light. It would be different if we were in the city: the street lights assist the technology in the night-vision goggles and can literally turn night into day for the search-and-rescue choppers. But not here, in the mountains, with no lighting and everything more or less monochromatic, in various shades of green.

The colonel has promised me our own chopper as soon as its role in Panther is complete. 'We'll coordinate with the police superintendent . . . You can have the men too.'

'They'll be tired after being up all night.'

'They'll want to help . . . we'll bus them to wherever's needed.'

Somewhere between Glenbrook and Leura. Forty-odd kilometres of dense, impenetrable bush. Where has he taken her? Where is my daughter? Has she eaten? Is she warm? She's scared, that much I know for sure. Jasmin's too damned clever not to be scared.

I phoned Sophie immediately after hanging up from Chloe.

'Where has he taken her?' Desperation caused me to shout.

'I don't know, Aidan. I'm sorry, I really don't know.'

'What did you say to him? What did you say to make him do this?'

'Nothing, I swear. He took this upon himself . . . You must believe me, I'm as horrified as you are . . . He's gone crazy.'

Has Richard harmed Jasmin? Touched her? Already killed her? I could barely bring myself to vocalize the question. 'Would he hurt her? . . . Is he capable of doing something to Jasmin?'

'No, no,' Sophie sobbed. 'I don't think so.'

God, I hope not, I pray not. It's unbearable, even at the milder end of the scale. My daughter being at Richard's mercy. My beautiful daughter, defenceless, scared, not knowing what – or why – this is happening to her.

My job and the safety of my men demand at least some of my attention for the next few hours. I try my best to be there for them, to fulfil my role. But I can't shake off the increasing dread of Jasmin's life being at risk, and the thought physically hurts me. There's a stabbing pain in my gut, a piercing right through the centre of my heart, the sense of being crushed. In the middle of a radio exchange with the head canoeist, I have to abandon my post, rushing out of the tent, leaving the colonel to pick up the reins. Out in the cold night, stars smashed across the sky, a wail erupts from deep within me.

Where are you, Jasmin? Where the damned hell are you?

The pain is excruciating now. It has me doubling over, clenching my fists, howling.

Richard knew what he was doing. This is exactly what he wanted. This horrendous pain and helplessness is precisely what he wanted me to feel.

Richard

I've lost her. *I've lost Jasmin.* She is out in the night, in the cold, in the dark, in the bush. She is cold, hungry, thirsty, petrified. *I have lost her.* My anger has gone. It dissipated with every call of her name, every echo that reverberated back to me: Jasmin, Jasmin, Jasmin, Jasmin. It's part of the cold mountain air, and it's hard to believe that it was ever inside me, that only a few hours ago I was so full of rage I contemplated hurting a child, a little girl, *Jasmin*. In its place there's grief, grief for damage I've already done, and shame . . . a deep, mortifying shame that I've caused this catastrophe. She was running from me. She weighed it all up – I know she did, because she is a smart little thing – and decided that I presented the biggest threat, the worse evil, and that she was prepared to take her chances in the bush, in the cold, with the wildlife. The shame of it. The sorrow.

My phone is dead. Bloody typical. The screen is unresponsive, lifeless, unable to help me or Jasmin. If only I could call triple zero. *If I could just speak to Dee, that would be enough.* She'd know what to do. Whether to stay here and keep searching, or drive off, temporarily abandoning Jasmin but with the aim of getting help. Would the police station in Hazelbrook be open at this hour of night? Does Hazelbrook even have a police station? Would it be better if I went to a house, woke up the occupants, begged to use their phone?

Stay or go? Stay or go?

Dee would know what to do. Beneath her casual exterior, there's a surprising pragmatism.

Oh, Dee, I am sorry. Jasmin too. I'm sorrier than you can imagine.

'Jasmin, Jasmin . . . Can you hear me? I'm sorry. You've nothing to be afraid of.'

How has this happened? How, I ask, did things come to this? It's preposterous. Unfathomable. Was I out of my bloody mind?

'Jasmin, you've got to answer me . . . Jasmin!'

Stay or go? Stay or go? Stay or go?

Aidan

At two in the morning a call comes through from the police. Apparently Richard has turned up at a house outside Hazelbrook, startling the residents by banging on their front door and demanding to use their phone. The residents called triple zero at his request.

The superintendent is there, at the house, with Richard.

'He's very distressed and seems confused. But he's being cooperative.'

Cooperative? This is the man who kidnapped my daughter. I can think of many words, but 'cooperative' isn't one of them. Good thing it's the superintendent there with him, not me, because I'd probably strangle him before he got the chance to say where Jasmin is. From what they can determine, she ran off on him, into the bush. This makes me feel equal parts terrified and proud. All available patrol cars are heading there now, to search the specific area as best they can in the dark.

Chloe is hysterical when I call the barracks to relay the news. 'Our baby girl is alone in the bush. Anything could happen to her. *Anything.*'

Yes, true, but the worst thing – Richard harming

359

her – hasn't happened (if he is to be believed), so the current situation is a sickly relief.

'I'm coming up there. I'm getting in the car right now. I don't care what you say.'

'Just hold on, Chloe. It's easier for me to contact you if you stay put. I know it's hard . . .'

Three thirty in the morning. Another call, but not with the news we wanted to hear. Jasmin hasn't been found. Richard is muddled about which track he took and the police have just wasted an hour searching the wrong damned one. Once again I use the satellite phone to update Chloe and I have to brace myself for her distress.

'No. No. My baby. *Our* baby. Will she be all right, Aidan? Please tell me she'll be all right.'

It's eight degrees outside, relatively mild for the mountains at this time of year, but cold enough to cause hypothermia if one is outdoors for long enough without adequate clothing. *Does* she have adequate clothing? A jacket? Thank God it isn't raining . . . If she was wet, her chances of getting hypothermia would sky-rocket. The only other risk is the wildlife: the brown snake, the red-bellied black snake and the diamond python are all common to the area. We concluded that snakes presented next to no risk for Panther (they should feel the vibrations of us coming and shy away). I hope it'll be the same for Jasmin.

'She should be fine,' I say to Chloe, reassuring myself as much as her. 'It's a mild night up here and it's not raining.'

Five in the morning. The chopper – a Black Hawk – has finished its role in Panther, and the police superintendent has approved its use for the search-and-rescue operation under his command. It lands on the plateau, the noise shredding the pre-dawn calmness, the tent flapping with the downdraught. I sprint towards it, holding my beret down firmly. The pilot, Lieutenant Michael Hurst, is one of our best.

He hands me a helmet. 'Where to, sir?'

'Hazelbrook.'

The stars are beginning to fade, the sky now a murky mix of black and grey. We should be there by first light.

55

Jasmin

I'm cold. Really, really, really cold. Especially my legs, which feel a bit numb, even though I stand up every fifteen minutes to get my blood moving again. And I feel sleepy, which is ironic because I'm freezing and very uncomfortable, and it's just weird that I want to close my eyes leaning against this scratchy tree when I lie awake most nights in my soft, cosy bed. I rub my arms and legs constantly, to try to keep them warm, and I think of all the extension words I've learned at school to keep myself awake, rolling them through my head like a movie. *Sceptical. Infamous. Reluctant. Irritable. Exhilarating. Fantasize.*

I try not to focus on all the sounds around me. Grunting, screeching, howling, and – the most terrifying – the sound of twigs cracking under animal feet. The only sound that isn't terrifying is an intermittent hooting.

Hello, Mr Owl. I can't see you. Can you see me?

It's reassuring to imagine an owl close by, wise, watchful, like a friend. Thinking about the owl makes me cry. Thinking about Mum and Dad makes me cry. Not for long, though, only a minute or two. I don't seem to have many tears left in my eyes.

The other thing I try not to do is look at my watch too

often, because time seems to go *even slower* when I do. I play guessing games. What time is it now? How many minutes and seconds since I last looked? Richard stopped calling out hours ago, but I'm still too scared to move, to return to the track – the only way out of here – in case he's waiting for me.

3.05 a.m.: I relive last week's soccer match, every single tackle and run, imagining another ending . . . where we actually *win* for once. 3.33 a.m.: I'm in Amelia's house, playing Teachers in her bedroom, and here's my mum and dad at the door, coming to collect me. 4 a.m.: Now I'm in Matthew's office, the weighted cape pressing down on my shoulders, realigning my senses. 4.27 a.m.: I'm doing laps for Davy, the grass bouncy under my feet, my breath heavy. *Hurry up, lass.* 5 a.m.: Mrs Stanley is giving me a brand-new list of extension words: *Alertness. Vigilance. Equipped. Expertise.*

Finally, light is seeping into the sky and now there are friendlier sounds: chirping, trilling, cackling . . . birds. I pull myself up from the tree, putting weight on my stiff, heavy legs. Is it safe? Has Richard gone? As I stand there, trying to pluck up the courage to leave my hiding spot, I hear it: a new sound, a clacking, coming from above, getting louder and louder. I only catch a glimpse of it, because of all the trees, but the brown-green colour tells me it's an army chopper, and *I just know* my dad is in it – with the pilot, of course, because Daddy can't fly – looking for me.

'Dad, Daddy . . .'

I hurl myself through the brambles and branches and cobwebs, not caring this time about the scrapes and cuts and spiders.

'Daddy, *Daddy* . . .'

He won't be able to see me here, not with all the trees. But out on the track he will. If I can just get there quickly enough.

Aidan

The forest is especially dense in this part of the mountains, a thick carpet of blue-green as far as the eye can see. Our first pass is a high-level visual sweep of the optimal area, about fifteen square kilometres, concentrating our energy on the network of tracks, fire trails, gullies and clearings (where it should be easier to spot something untoward . . . such as a nine-year-old girl, lost, alone, terrified).

We see nothing, nothing but white patrol cars dotted around, advancing slowly down various paths and trails. From up here the cars look small, insufficient. We've been told that an official search-and-rescue chopper is on the way. When it gets here, we'll divide the optimal area between us.

On our second pass Michael reduces speed and brings the Black Hawk lower. This stage is more thorough, more time-consuming and technology reliant (mainly using the TV camera of the multi-sensor system). The scenery is stunning — rolls of multilayered green, thin strips of orange-brown dirt, sandstone tables and crags, silvery waterfalls and creeks — but I'm oblivious. There's only one thing I'm interested in seeing. A small, surprisingly strong nine-year-old girl. With hair and eyes the same colour as my own. A girl who loves soccer and big words. An hour has somehow disappeared. Michael is talking about needing to refuel at some point. The other chopper has long since arrived and, like us, has nothing to report. There's no sign of my daughter, none at all.

Has she fallen asleep? Hurt herself and fallen unconscious? Then, the most horrible image: her body in a shallow grave of twigs and dried-out leaves. Damn it, stop thinking like that. But the image persists, and the nagging question: *What if Richard is lying?* We were all so quick to believe him – the superintendent, Chloe, me – because he'd virtually turned himself in. We were all convinced by his distress and supposed confusion, desperately seeking assurance that Jasmin was essentially safe and hadn't been harmed. But what if it was all an act? A huge revenge-ridden lie? What if we're not looking for a scared, cold, hungry nine-year-old, but a buried, lifeless one? The faces start to reel in my head. The dead people. The ones I didn't keep safe. They stare right through me. Some of them perfect, just very white and unblinking. Others bloated, discoloured. Or a grotesque mangle of skin, tissue and bone. Not Jasmin. I would die. *Not Jasmin.*

'Aidan.' Michael's voice juts into the macabre reel of images. 'South-west. About thirty degrees.'

It's not the first time he's seen something and asked me to zoom in further. Last time, it was a wallaby – so startled by the noise, it was frozen to the spot – that caught his eye. I adjust the camera accordingly. Yes, there *is* something down there. Something multicoloured.

Michael is already turning the chopper around, going as low as he can, as close as he can.

And there she is. My daughter. And she is moving. Running. Waving her jacket above her head, her mouth open, calling to us, beseeching us to notice her.

'Jasmin!' I hear myself yelling, even though I know she can't hear me. 'Jasmin! Jasmin! I'm coming. I'm coming to get you.'

The trail is particularly narrow. There isn't enough room to land.

'You all right using the winch?' Michael enquires quietly.

'Yeah.'

He puts the Black Hawk into hover while I climb into the back. My hands are shaking as I attach myself to the winch. It's been a while since I've done this: Afghanistan, jumping into a raid, with the real threat of gunfire and/or hand grenades ending my descent. Yet I don't remember feeling as terrified then as I do now.

'Steady,' Michael instructs me, only too aware of the perils of my current emotional state. 'Don't forget the backpack. You might need something from it.'

The backpack has medical supplies, water, food and blankets, none of which – other than the water – are immediately needed, but I slip it over my shoulders anyway.

Turning backwards, I drop down from the open door, swaying through the air. In a matter of seconds I've landed, bouncing gently off the hard, dusty ground.

She is on top of me before I can get out of the harness. A sorry sight: tangled hair, torn clothes and skin. A beautiful, precious sight.

'Hey . . . Hey . . . It's all right now.' I kiss her face, the top of her head, every part of her, over and over again. 'You're safe, Jazzie. I have you. I'm here.'

'I knew it,' she sobs. 'I knew you'd rescue me. I just had to wait.'

Her faith takes my breath away.

Much later, after Jasmin has been given the medical all-clear and has supplied a mature-beyond-her-age statement to the police, when she is back home and safely in her own bed (asleep!), I relay all the small details to Chloe, and when I get to this part – Jasmin's absolute, unshake-able faith in me – I completely break down.

56

Sophie

He has ruined my life. My father has completely and irrevocably ruined my life. He kidnapped Jasmin, scared her so much she got lost in the bush, instigated a major search-and-rescue operation involving the police and the army. What's even more outrageous is that my mother is actually making excuses for him.

'He snapped, Sophie. He just snapped. The doctor thinks he might have some form of post-traumatic stress. From your accident, you know. His reaction to it was never normal.'

Unbelievable! Aidan used the *exact same* excuse: fucking post-traumatic stress. A build-up of tension from spending so much of his life in war zones, then the accident, and *bam!* He said that his guilt got completely out of proportion, made him behave oddly, out of character. Leaving Chloe and Jasmin. Thinking he was in love with me. Fuck him. Fuck him *and* Dad. I was the one who was injured, not them. They have no right, no right at all, to use the accident – *my accident* – as a reason for their crazy behaviour.

A pause stretches down the line. Mum's obviously waiting for a response from me. I scream at her.

'Can you stop making excuses for him? He kidnapped a nine-year-old girl. What the fuck was that going to solve?'

'I know,' she says, her tone placating. 'I know it was a terrible thing to do. The poor child . . . when I think how terrified she must have been. I desperately want to call Aidan and apologize on your father's behalf, but I think I must be the last person on earth he wants to speak to right now . . . But your father, he's *our* problem, we're his family, we *must* support him. The irony is that he was doing it for you, Sophie. At least, that's how he justified it in his head. Which in itself tells you how mentally unbalanced he was . . .'

'For me? He was doing it *for me?* Are you as crazy as he is? Supporting him is the last thing on my mind. *I could kill him.* He's ruined everything. Aidan and I are over, thanks to him. Is he fucking happy now?'

Aidan and I were having some problems, but we'd have got through them, I know we would have. Aidan *owed me.* Despite his feelings for Chloe and Jasmin, he'd have stayed with me for that reason alone. That's how men like him operate. Now, because of Dad's escapade in the mountains, I owe Aidan back. In insurance, we call it 'negating factors'. The end impact is none, nothing, no obligation by anyone.

'Of course he's not happy!' Mum exclaims, her tone becoming indignant. 'He's ashamed, extremely remorseful and out of his mind with worry. You should see all the charges that have been laid against him. And he's been in a psychiatric ward for the last three weeks, Sophie. There are some seriously ill people in there. He misses home. He misses *you.*'

'Well, he can keep on missing me. Because I am *never* going to speak to him again.'

I hang up then, because if she keeps on nagging me to visit him, keeps on defending him and using *my accident* as an excuse, I could end up not speaking to *her* ever again either.

The truth is, this isn't the first time Dad fucked up my life. He was complicit in the Kristina Owens thing too. He had stoked the rivalry between us for as long as I could remember and couldn't bear it whenever she did better than me.

'*You're as good as her, Sophie. Every bit as good.*'

'*But it doesn't matter how hard I try, Dad, or how much I study, she always seems to pip me . . .*'

'*Figure out a way to solve her . . . Use your intelligence, Sophie.*'

Dad must have been complicit because the first thing that came into my head, after the push, before I realized the enormity of what I had done, was 'There! Solved!'

We never spoke of it. Dad threatened to sue the school, forced them to back down, all without asking me outright if I was guilty or innocent. I suppose he couldn't fathom the idea of me being as flawed as that, and he flew into attack mode without pausing to check the facts. I'm not sure the truth would've stopped him, anyway; he'd have gone to any lengths to protect my future.

I've resigned from Real Cover Insurance. The warning crushed me. John Greenland and Alyssa ganging up on me like that, after all I've done, all the effort and long hours and blood and sweat I've poured into my job. I was too humiliated to argue the case any further, to carry on working there. I resigned calmly, with dignity (Jane could have learned a thing or two, had she been watching), said that I was feeling increasingly ill and needed to put my health first – which is depressingly true.

John Greenland didn't even try to talk me round. I've heard since that he's taking great interest in Hannah. It's too much, the thought that *she* could be his new protégée. Hannah, with her plain clothes and blushing face. Hannah, with her pesky twins and her druggie husband. Hannah, who added her bullying claims to Jane's, well aware that the company would feel compelled to act and that she was pretty much wrecking my career.

Hannah and Dad. Between the two of them, they've completely ruined my life, finished off the destruction that was started by the accident.

My pain seems to have gone off the scale, most days an eight point five or nine. I've had to call Dr White and beg him to bring forward my next appointment. In the meantime, it's all I can do to get out of bed in the morning, dress myself, assemble a meal. When will I be well enough again to go for interviews, to hold down another job? Will I be able to find an employer who's flexible, who'll be understanding if I need to take a few days' rest here and there? How will I summon the energy, the drive, the strength to start somewhere new and prove myself all over again?

And I miss Aidan. I miss him so much. It was never just a matter of debt, of him owing me, of me deserving to have him. I loved him from the beginning, as soon as I became aware of his overwhelming remorse, his almost old-fashioned principles, his rigorous approach to life: at last, someone with the same high standards as me. *I miss him so much.* The house feels empty, cold and lonely, lonely, lonely. I miss the meals he cooked, that solid warmth next to me in bed, waking to the sound of him taking his morning shower, and the cup of tea he would present to me before I commenced my struggle with the day ahead.

The loneliness doesn't help the pain. Not at all.

57

Hannah

I told them it was a virus. The counsellor said I should tell the truth, that honesty is always the best policy. I vehemently disagreed. Nine-year-old kids shouldn't have to learn what the word 'suicide' means. It was in my power to spare them that, to salvage their childhood. Of course I'll tell them when they're older. Fourteen or fifteen, I think.

We moved suburbs not only for financial reasons, but also to make it easier to maintain the lie. We left all our old friends behind, cut contact with anybody who might have carelessly let the truth slip out.

Your father killed himself. He did it in the garden shed, while you were doing your homework and your mum was cooking dinner. Your mum found him when she went to call him in to eat. She called an ambulance, even though she knew it was too late to save him. She took you both next door, so you wouldn't see the rope or the ambulance or the truth of how he died. He left a note, his last words saying how he couldn't take the pain any longer, the pain of living, the pain of being alive, and that he knew everyone would understand and forgive him. She hid the note from you too. There was no virus.

Harry's parents understood the need to protect the boys, even though moving house meant a four-hour drive from their farm. They've been to see us twice. The apartment is too small, too intimate, and it's so much harder to hide from the truth when they come. We're all still playing the blame game. How have we found ourselves in this terrible, terrible place? How did this happen on our watch? We'd been dealing with Harry's suicidal tendencies for years (including one other attempt at taking his own life) and although we were worn out on occasion and perhaps a little desensitized, most of the time we were supportive and positive about the future. Now we all feel responsible. Especially me. I tiptoed around Harry. Deferred to his moods. I was so understanding. *Everyone* was understanding. And I felt that had somehow contributed to his decision, made it more palatable, made it easier for him to rationalize leaving us.

Rest in peace, Harry.

Love you, Harry. Hope you are happy now.

Forever young, forever in our hearts.

Our love and understanding always.

I know you're in a happy place now, Harry. At last.

At the time, it seemed like Harry's Facebook friends were giving him their blessing. It was almost as if they were saying, *It's OK. You did what you needed to do*, and this made me fear that we'd inadvertently ratified his decision to take his own life. In our efforts to be as supportive as possible, had we lost sight of the need to be tough about suicide not, and never, being an option? He even said it in his note: *I know you all understand.*

For months and months, I couldn't bear the thought of those tributes and the permission that seemed implicit in them. Now I've read them again, I can see that they're just words. Words from people who don't know what to say. Words from people who are incredibly sad and utterly at a loss. There's no underlying ratification. Harry didn't do what he did because he thought we would ultimately understand. He did what he did because he was in mental agony, and on that particular day the pain became too much to bear.

Harry's depression was considered a pre-existing medical condition when he changed life-insurance policies (as a result of changing jobs) the year before he died, and somewhere in the fine print of the new policy there was a two-year waiting period for pre-existing conditions. Do the people who write these clauses ever stop to think about the practicalities of what they're writing? Do they expect people on the brink of suicide to notice fine print and, even if they do, to be able to hang in there for the requisite time so that their families won't be left destitute?

Last week, John Greenland mentioned that his background is in life insurance. When I know him a little better, I'm going to pluck up the courage to ask him if he would look into Harry's case. John seems a nice man. I think he would help, if he could, if only to tell me to give up on a lost cause. He's been very encouraging these last few weeks.

'You know you could do Part 1 actuarial examinations,' he said the other day. 'You should consider it.'

And I will consider it. I was very good at maths, once upon a time. Good enough to go on that camp, which was for students with 'exceptional mathematical ability'. I will take my career more seriously when my boys are settled and don't need me as much. For now, I'm happy to go to work every day without having to worry about what mood Sophie will be in, how much she will demand of me, and whether I will be able to extract myself on time to get home to my family. I'm happy that I don't need to take work home with me, and that my phone and inbox aren't going off every minute. I'm happy that I've finally found the strength and courage to speak out, to take people to task, even if I am drawing attention to myself in the process.

I've heard that Sophie has regressed and is in an awful lot of pain. We all hurt in some way. We just have to rise above it, keep going. You can't give in to pain. Not even a little bit. Otherwise, before you know it, it will completely take over, destroying your life and the lives of those who love you.

58

Chloe

I have my family back.

That's the first thing I remind myself of when I wake up in the morning, and the last thing I think of at night.

Thank goodness I have my family back.

Even though we will never be the same again.

Aidan is absolutely ravaged by guilt. Guilt about the accident, about moving out from home, about not recognizing the threat posed by Richard, about the long-term impact all this will have on Jasmin. Jack and I have had a few long talks since that fateful night at the barracks. He has since organized some proper counselling for Aidan, in addition to his own ongoing support. Apparently post-traumatic stress takes all shapes and forms, and every human being, even the strongest, most resilient ones, has a limit to what they can take, how much tragedy and destruction and distress they can absorb before becoming damaged, before they start to do things – lash out at a partner or friends, drink themselves to oblivion, self-destruct in various ways – that are out of character, at odds with the real person. Sophie was the tipping point for Aidan. The horror that he had harmed someone, almost taken her life, when his whole existence is about keeping people safe. *And then Jasmin.* Our beautiful Jasmin. Abducted, lost in the bush, horrifyingly far from safe.

It's obvious to me, to Jack, and now to Aidan too, that he's going to need to work through his guilt. To stop blaming himself. To come to terms with all the dead faces he sees when he closes his eyes at night. To come to terms with the accident and the fact that he made a mistake and badly hurt someone. To come to terms with the complicated chain of events that resulted in Jasmin being taken.

Jasmin has been displaying increased clinginess with both Aidan and me, and Mrs Stanley has said that she's slightly subdued in class. Davy thinks she's not as confident on the soccer field, more prone to tears if she gets hurt, but all things considered, she seems to have coped remarkably well. We're seeing Matthew twice a week. In his slow and methodical way Matthew goes over and over what happened that night in the mountains, unpicking every single detail, so that all Jasmin's fears and feelings are out in the open. I'm so grateful that Matthew isn't one to give in to the temptation of a 'quick fix' because it feels vitally important that Jasmin's ordeal is dealt with in a thorough and careful manner. Her sleeping is so-so. Some nights we've one round of push-ups; some nights it's five. But there are two of us again to deal with whatever each night brings. And when I think of what has happened – what *could* have happened – a bad night's sleep is not the worst thing in the world, not by any stretch of the imagination.

Our embryos are still in deep freeze. When we get over this, when we all feel less fragile and in a better headspace, we'll go back to the clinic and try again. It won't be today or tomorrow or even this year. It's going to take time. For now, I am thankful for the family I have. That we are safe and well. That we are all together again, under one roof. That my husband and daughter are seeing the right people, getting all the support and help they need. As for me, I've been looking at online courses to update my degree. Just researching for now, seeing what's out there. Fashion seems so frivolous in the scheme of things, but the researching process has provided a much-needed escape when everything else still feels so raw and precarious. It'll be marvellous once I get started on the course. No more putting everything on hold.

We had no idea who we crashed into that day. No idea that the girl with the dark hair was not a very good person. No idea that her father was as exacting and dangerous as she was. And no idea of the true extent of the damage that was wreaked. At first glance – aside from the cars and our own minor injuries – it seemed the only damage was done to Sophie, her broken body slumped behind the steering wheel. But our family got broken too. Shattered. We just didn't realize it at the time. Now we must do our best to glue it back together.

59

Dee

I went to see her today. Called round to the house. Knocked politely on the door, feeling more like a visitor than her mother. It took her so long to answer, I knocked again, harder, and she was annoyed with me when we were finally face to face.

'I was coming . . . It just takes a while.'

She looked terrible. As pale as I've ever seen her. Her eyes were bloodshot – had she been crying? – and her clothes and hair were nowhere near her usual meticulous standards.

'Sorry,' I heard myself apologizing as I followed her into the house. 'How are you?'

Her answer was terse and delivered without turning her head around. 'I've been better.'

Hunched shoulders, a slight hobble to her gait, she made for the couch, where her laptop, an open packet of crisps and a discarded blanket were awaiting her return.

'Have you been working?' I asked, sitting myself down.

'It's just my spreadsheet.'

The spreadsheet. Hadn't the doctor told her to forget about tracking and rating everything? He didn't like her focusing on her pain, *obsessing*, if I remembered correctly.

Sophie's expression was familiarly mutinous so I decided to let the matter drop until I could check my facts with Richard. Speaking of Richard.

'Your father is feeling a little better. Obviously still devastated and utterly ashamed about what he did, and all the trouble and worry he caused. But he's able to see now how everything got on top of him and he's ready to face all the charges by the police, write a letter of apology to Jasmin, Aidan and Chloe, and start picking up the pieces.'

She tapped some keys on the laptop without providing a reply.

'He would really love to see you. Or hear from you, if you don't feel up to a visit.'

Still no response, no answer, no reaction at all.

'Sophie?'

'I told you!' Each word sounded as though it was coated in venom. 'I told you that I'm *done* with him.'

'He's your father. You can't be *done* with him. It doesn't work like that.'

Nothing. No further response. More typing. In true Sophie fashion, she was digging her heels in. Always such an obstinate, unyielding creature. So difficult to convince, to influence and even to nurture. It's intimidating being her mother. At times.

'Look, I'm to blame too. *I knew* that your father wasn't himself. I thought a holiday would fix things . . . Talk about underestimating the situation! And Jacob also feels responsible.' I ignored her derisive snort at the mention of her brother. 'He regrets not going to the hearing. He thinks he would've noticed that Dad wasn't in his right mind. Jacob only has to think about Milli and Hugo to imagine what Aidan's family has been through, but he's still prepared to step up, to see more of Dad and help him get back on his feet. He said he'd like to see more of you too, help you . . . that's if you want his help. I suppose he's realized that this is make or break for us, for our family. We'll be left with nothing if each one of us doesn't do their bit.'

More silence.

'And Jacob agrees with me that you and Richard are the same. Both of you have such impossibly high standards. And both of you are driven by the notion of perfection, of being the best, and you're unable to bear it when things don't go to plan . . .'

This got a reaction. Sophie's head reared up. Blood flooded into her face.

'*We are not the same!*' she screamed at me. 'We are not . . . the . . . *same.*'

They *are* the same. If the events of the last few weeks have proved anything, it's that. Richard and Sophie are a dangerous mix of passion and coldness, perfectionism and ruthlessness. Capable of greatness but also of bullying, cruelty and downright wickedness. They need people like me and Jacob to moderate them, to remind them that winning and being the best and getting even are not the only worthwhile goals. Grace, compassion and forgiveness are goals too, and I should have done a better job instilling these qualities in my daughter. I stood back, allowed her to attach herself to Richard, allowed him to be her only compass in life. *I failed her.* Allowed too many childhood digressions to go unpunished. All those small cruelties against Jacob. All the praise and primping by Richard, building her up and up until she felt she was soaring above everyone else in terms of ability, talent and entitlement. *That thing with Kristina Owens.* Oh, how it has niggled me all these years. I should have acted long, long before now. I stand guilty of vagueness and inaction. Of allowing myself to be railroaded by Richard. Of not pinning Sophie down and demanding the truth. Of not being switched on enough to tell when she was lying. Of not being proficient at sorting out the big issues from the small, because when a girl gets badly hurt and accuses your daughter, that's a big, big thing.

'You *are* the same,' I repeated quietly, insistently. 'It's important that you acknowledge this, Sophie, and understand what it means. You and your father are capable of the same extreme behaviour. Many times, it has led to success, to wonderful achievements. But it can also lead the other way, drive you to a point where reason goes out the window, where callousness takes over, and then, suddenly, someone is standing in your way and you can't stop yourselves from hurting them . . . You know exactly what I'm talking about, don't you? That time we were called into the school?'

She gasped as it hit her. The realization that I had finally arrived at the truth about Kristina. The realization that what she had done was every bit as awful and obsessive and crazy as what her father had done. The realization that, no matter how hard she denies it, *they are the same*. It's not just the similarity to Richard that's become clear. Jacob, Kristina, that Jane woman from work: I can see where they fit in too. Sophie's like one of those complicated jigsaw puzzles she used to love as a child. I often felt I was missing some crucial pieces. It has taken me thirty-one years to see the full picture.

'Just go,' she said coldly. 'I don't need to hear this.'

Enough, I told myself. *You've got through to her, Dee. That's enough for today. One small step at a time.*

'I'll come back tomorrow,' I said with determined cheeriness, then – with a pointed look at the bag of crisps – added, 'I'll bring some groceries.'

She stayed sitting while I let myself out. At the front door, I hesitated. The door open behind me, I turned back around to face the hall, which had an empty, distinctly desolate air about it, as did the whole house.

The strangest feeling came over me. It was as though I saw my daughter's future in that hallway. Bleak. Painful. Lonely.

60

Sophie

She wrote to me. Kristina Owens. Or Kristina Nolan, as she's now known. She sent me a message through Facebook, and I stupidly opened it without realizing who it was from.

Dear Sophie,

I've tried to put St Brigid's behind me, so when I first heard from Hannah Evans my hand automatically reached for the delete key. I remembered Hannah as a shy, earnest girl in the year below us and so I decided that the polite thing would be to respond, even if only to make it clear I wasn't interested in a reunion. But then I received another message from her, a message that turned my world upside down. She knew that you had been right next to me when I 'fell', not further back down the track, as you'd told the teachers. Hannah didn't see the push, unfortunately, so it's not as if I can take it up with the police, but she has given me something so unexpected, so precious: she has validated my side of the story.

It's thrown me right back to when it happened. All those feelings raging through me while I was trapped in the hospital bed: pain, anger, frustration, helplessness, more pain. My leg was ruined, in pieces, and needed numerous rounds of surgery. I was bedridden for weeks, alienated from my friends, from normal teenage life. The bones eventually mended and I tried to get on with my life. The problem was that, even on the good days, the pain never quite went away. It shadowed me, pulled me back, made it hard to maintain an active lifestyle, or a meaningful relationship (my ex-husband told me I'm bad-tempered), or hold down a permanent job.

A long time ago my specialist told me that I would have to 'live with the pain'. And so I do. I live with it. I've accepted that my career is second-rate. I've accepted that I'm sometimes hard to live with. I've accepted that my body will never be quite right, will never fit back together as it once did. In the last couple of years I've learned how to meditate, and it has changed my life. I've been able to acknowledge and control any negative energy, resentment or anger. But the one thing that has been difficult to accept, to transcend, is the fact that you got away with it. You pushed me, you lied, it was my word against yours, and you've never been held to account. I've accepted what happened to me, but have been less successful with accepting what happened (or rather, didn't happen) to you.

But now this. Not only has Hannah validated my side of the story, she has opened up the possibility that maybe you didn't get away with it after all. Because Hannah said that you were also involved in a serious accident, spent weeks in hospital and have not been able to fully resume your career or your life. On hearing this, I just couldn't help myself: the court records were online, and from the judgement I learned exactly how the accident had happened and the details of your injuries.

And you know what? My first thought was, was it me? Did I make your accident happen? Did I will it upon you? All those

*nights when the old me, the bitter me, used to lie awake, wishing
for revenge, wishing upon you the same misery and suffering that I
was feeling.*

*But no, your accident was not my fault. You were good at
science, Sophie. Remember Newton's third law of motion? For
every action, there's an equal and opposite reaction. That spiteful
push on the side of the ravine slowly gathered momentum and force
over the intervening months and years, and finally culminated with
a car — your car — ploughing into another on Anzac Parade, a
perfectly appropriate reaction to the action you started. You had
this coming, Sophie. It's a matter of physics. It's a matter of
karma. It's a matter of justice in its purest form.*

*Besides, I wished nothing upon you that hadn't already
happened to me: failed relationships; constant, debilitating pain;
and loneliness, because that's the worst thing of all.*

*It's important that you know I'm in a good place now. I have a
new man, a wonderful, caring man who doesn't scare off if I'm
occasionally snappy or having a bad day. I've discovered that
personal happiness is the ultimate salve for pain. It's taken me
many years to get to this place, Sophie. You have a long road
ahead of you. Despite my continuing efforts to be positive and not
be dragged down by bitterness and hatred, I can't find it in me to
wish you luck.*

Kristina

I didn't send a response. What was the point? I had absolutely no intention of compromising myself by either
admitting the truth or apologizing. That doesn't mean I
don't regret what happened. Even though Dad told me to

'solve' Kristina Owens, I didn't actually plan what happened at the ravine. It was a moment of sheer spitefulness rather than something premeditated. She had beaten me by one mark in the maths challenge that morning. One measly mark had made Kristina the Olympiad Champion and relegated me to second place ... again. It was the mark, and it was the fact that she wouldn't allow me to lead the orienteering. She insisted on holding the map, working out all the coordinates. I am one of those people who has to be in charge. With every step along the track, I became more and more infuriated, until I was completely consumed with the need to get even with her. It was like when I used to pinch or hit Jacob, that quick – almost sweet – release to my frustration. Except that I didn't pinch Kristina, I pushed her, and she fell a long way, and broke a lot of bones.

Just because I lied about what happened didn't mean I wasn't sorry. I would never do that again, never lay a hand on anyone, never allow my temper or competitiveness to get the better of me and cause such a bad error of judgement. Witnessing her terrible injuries. Those stressful few days when the school was 'investigating'. Even the glory of being awarded dux wasn't what I thought it would be. It never felt as good as it would have if Kristina had been in the audience, forced to clap and look pleased as I received my plaque. It never felt as good as it would have if I had beaten Kristina fair and square. I learned my lesson. Since then, I've always relied on my intellect, my hard-work ethic and my high standards to get where I want to be.

I'm thrown, though. At the thought of Kristina Owens lying in bed at night, wishing me ill. I'm *rattled*. Her message has penetrated the fugue of pain and sparked something in me. A desire to prove her wrong. A desire *not* to descend into a life of failed relationships, debilitating pain and crippling loneliness. Maybe it's our old rivalry clicking into gear. Or maybe I've spent enough time wallowing and I'm ready to roll up my sleeves, get stuck in again.

Whatever it is, I force myself out of bed early the next morning.

Come on, Sophie. Come on.

I shower, wash my hair for the first time in over a week, and get dressed in smart trousers and a white shirt, as if I'm going to the office. After breakfast, I spend a few hours on my résumé, updating it with my experience and accomplishments at Real Cover. Then I phone some old contacts, and one of the calls proves promising.

By lunchtime I'm both exhausted and invigorated.

I have something to prove. Not only to Kristina but to Hannah too. And Jane. And John Greenland. And Aidan and Chloe. I'm always at my best when I have something to prove. As for Dad, I *will not* be derailed by what he has done and I do not need his kind of help to succeed.

I will come back fighting. It's what I've always done when life deals a blow, and it's the one part of me that can't be broken, or squashed, or questioned.

Acknowledgements

Many thanks to Kimberley Atkins, Eve Hall, Tilda McDonald, Maxine Hitchcock, Sarah Day and everyone at Penguin for your dedication and vision.

Thank you to my merry band of early readers: Erin Downey, Petronella Nicholson, Ann Riordan, Sarah Shrubb, Merran Harte, Conor Carroll and Rob Carroll. Your comments and suggestions were invaluable. (A special mention goes to Ashling Carroll, who wasn't allowed to read the manuscript, but tried very hard to talk me round!)

For technical assistance, I am immensely grateful to Kevin O'Mahony and Seth Gibbard (advance apologies for those instances where I've taken artistic licence, or simply got it wrong!).

Brian Cook, to whom this novel is dedicated, thank you for everything. We've been on a long journey together. We could write a book about it (or maybe we won't).

Thanks to Liane Moriarty and Dianne Blacklock, who helped every step of the way. The bad news is, I'm becoming more and more reliant on your input. The good news is, the Bellinis that magically appear while we talk about everything publishing (and more).

Thank you to my family and friends, who are unfailingly supportive and put up with me constantly pillaging their anecdotes and personal lives.

Finally, a huge thank you to my readers. This book is a little different from the others. I've loved it right from the start. I hope you do too.